D0909762

A Garland Series

# The
# Flowering of the Novel

## Representative Mid-Eighteenth Century Fiction
## 1740-1775

*A Collection of 121 Titles*

# The Reverie

## Charles Johnstone

**Two Volumes
Reprinted in One**

*Garland Publishing, Inc., New York & London*

*1974*

Bibliographical note:

this facsimile has been made from a copy in the
Library of the University of Illinois
(823.J65r)

**Library of Congress Cataloging in Publication Data**

Johnstone, Charles, 1719?-1800?
    The reverie.

    (The Flowering of the novel)
    Reprint of the 1763 ed. printed for T. Becket,
London.
    I. Title.  II.  Series.
PZ3.J6522Re6  [PR3539.J25]    823'.6      74-16307
ISBN 0-8240-1162-7

# THE

# R E V E R I E:

### O R,

# A F L I G H T

### TO THE

# PARADISE of FOOLS.

---

*—All things vain, and all who in vain things
Build their fond hopes of glory, or lasting fame,
Or happiness, in this, or th' other life——*

MILTON.

---

Publifhed by the EDITOR of
The ADVENTURES OF a GUINEA.

---

IN TWO VOLUMES.

## VOL. I.

---

### LONDON,

Printed for T. BECKET, and P. A. DA HONDT,
in the Strand. MDCCLXIII.

# THE

# CONTENTS

## OF THE

## FIRST VOLUME.

---

## BOOK I.

### CHAP. I.

A 2                    CHAP.

# CONTENTS.

CHAP.

# CONTENTS.

A 3 *of*

# CONTENTS.

5

# CONTENTS.

# BOOK II.

## CHAP. I.

## CHAP. II.

## CHAP. III.

## CHAP. IV.

CHAP.

# CONTENTS.

## CHAP. V.

## CHAP. VI.

## CHAP. VII.

## CHAP. VIII.

## CHAP. IX.

CHAP.

# CONTENTS.

CHAP.

# CONTENTS.

## CHAP. XVI.

## CHAP. XVII.

## CHAP. XVIII.

# ADVERTISEMENT.

IN the following work the judicious reader will directly trace the hand of the author of CHRYSAL. The uncommon approbation with which that performance has been received by the Public, determined the editor to spare no pains nor expence, to recover the other remains of so successful a writer. The difficulties attending such an attempt are obvious. From the supposed *Clergyman** alone, into whose hands they first fell, could any account of them be expected : but how to trace him through all the various characters, which such persons usually assume, was the question. At length, after a most fatiguing search, he was indebted to accident for that success which all his diligence had failed of. He was called upon one evening by an acquaintance, to go with him to Bridewell, in search of a servant girl of his, whom the laudable vigilance of the constables had taken up in the street the night before, when she was sent on an errand, and the strict justice of the magistrate had committed to the house of *correction*, as she unluckily had not a penny in her pocket to prove her innocence, or even pay a messenger for going for her master. While they waited in the public room

* See the preface to CHRYSAL, p. 21.—

for the return of a person who was sent for her
discharge, they were struck with the uncommonly droll look and behaviour of the waiter
who served the company with liquor. To divert the melancholy reflections, therefore, with
which such a scene of wretchedness and debauchery must necessarily affect every humane
heart, they called for a pint of wine, and desired him to sit down and drink with them.
The invitation was readily accepted; and the
fellow observing that they expressed some curiosity to know how a man of his apparent
abilities could have sunk into so low a station,
immediately gave them the following outlines
of his history.

"Gentlemen, (said he) there is nothing in
"this life but *ups* and *downs*. Low as you
"see me at present, I have often figured in
"an higher sphere. I have been a player,
"a doctor, an author, and a parson; and
"have acted my part with proper dignity in
"each character till the farce was ended. I
"have also, indeed, amused myself with tak-
"ing a view of life in less exalted stations:
"I have been a broken soldier, a shipwrecked
"sailor, a fool, a madman, and a gypsie; in
"reward for some feats of uncommon clever-
"ness in the last of which characters, I have
"had lodgings assigned me here, rent free,
"for seven years, where, that I should not be
"idle, I have descended to the occupation
"in which you see me. However, I am not
"dispirited. Seven years will not last for
"ever; and I hope to be prime minister yet,
"before I die."——

The

The moment he mentioned his having been a parfon, it occurred to the editor, that this might poffibly be the one whom he had been fo long in fearch of. As foon as he ftopped therefore to drink their healths, " It muft be allow-
" ed (faid he) that you have feen life in va-
" rious lights ; but there is one circumftance
" in your hiftory which I do not underftand.
" You fay you have been a parfon——". " Aye,
" fir, (anfwered the other) one of *your felf-*
" *ordained* ones, who go about the world
" preaching poor people out of their fenfes,
" and then picking their pockets. But my
" confcience was too tender for fuch a vile
" trade, fo I left it and turned gypfie ; though I
" have had reafon enough fince to repent of the
" manner in which I took that ftep, as I loft
" an opportunity of making my fortune by it.
" You muft have heared of the book that has
" made fuch a noife lately, *The Adventures of*
" *a Guinea.* Sir, that book was once mine ;
" but I had not the good fortune to make
" a proper ufe of it. I muft needs attempt al-
" tering, forfooth ; and before I had finifhed,
" fome impertinent fufpicions of my neigh-
" bours obliged me to fhift my quarters fome-
" what fuddenly ; and in my hurry I forgot to
" put up that book along with the reft of my
" papers."——

The editor had fome difficulty to conceal the pleafure which this account gave him, though he was fenfible that the utmoft addrefs was necef-fary, if he hoped to fucceed with fuch a voluble genius. "And pray, fir, (faid he therefore, with
" a carelefs air) were you the author of that
" book ?"——" No, fir, (anfwered the other)

" I was not the author of it, but it was mine
" notwithſtanding. That, and ſome other
" papers of infinitely greater value, were given
" to me by the woman in whoſe hands the au-
" thor left them. If you have read the pre-
" face to that book, you muſt remember ſhe
" ſays, that her old lodger was ſucceeded by
" a *Clergyman*, who left her houſe to go preach-
" ing about the country. I was that *Clergy-*
" *man*, ſir. But it is not the loſs of that book
" which I lament. Well as it has ſucceeded,
" it was not to be compared with another of
" the ſame author's, which I made a ſhift to
" carry off, and which would certainly have
" made my fortune, had I not loſt it in much
" the ſame manner as I did the other. But
" it is in vain to grieve at what cannot be
" remedied ; and ſo, gentlemen, my ſervice
" to you."

" You muſt know, gentlemen, (continued
" he, as ſoon as he had drank off his wine,
" which now began to warm his heart, and ſet
" all his ſecrets abroach) that in the courſe of
" my *miniſtry* I inſinuated myſelf ſo far into
" the good opinion of the wealthy widow of a
" country farmer, that ſhe took me into her
" houſe, to inſtruct her children in the true
" reformed principles of religion, having fallen
" out with her vicar about his dues. If I
" could have contained myſelf, I might have
" lived happily enough with her ; but the fleſh
" was frail ; I was then a young fellow, and
" her daughters were good clever wenches.
" In ſhort, I taught the two eldeſt of them
" other leſſons beſide religion. Such matters
" cannot be long concealed. My kind pu-
" pils

" pils soon began to feel symptoms that shew-
" ed me it was time to decamp; which I did
" accordingly, without taking any leave, to
" avoid the pain of parting: but as I was not
" so well provided for my journey as I could
" have wished, I made bold to break open a
" chest in which the old woman kept her most
" valuable things, and took as many of them
" as I could conveniently carry off. This
" obliged me to leave my own baggage be-
" hind me, which, to say the truth, was of
" no great value, except those papers; and the
" worth of them I was also ignorant of at that
" time; though I am sensible now, that it
" greatly exceeded that of my booty, which
" consisted only of an old silver tankard and
" cawdle-cup, and a parcel of linen; for,
" the beldame kept her cash somewhere
" else."——

This account was far from giving the editor
satisfaction, as he apprehended that it would be
very difficult to prevail on him to make a difcovery that might endanger his life, by telling
where he had performed those exploits. However, he resolved to make the attempt, and,
taking him into another room, told him, if he
would let him know where those papers were
left, he would give him the most sacred assurance that no ill consequence should attend his
confidence, and that he would honestly pay
him the value of them, if he should be so fortunate as to recover them. The other turning
his head on one side, and fixing his eyes in-
tently on him, with a look of inexpressible
archness, for some time, " Why? (said he)
" there is something odd enough, to be sure,

" in

" in afking fuch a queftion; but as you ap-
" pear to be more of a gentleman, than to
" trepan fuch a poor devil as me to the gal-
" lows, I will e'en tell you. As to paying
" me, I fhall leave that to yourfelf, when you
" get them; and fhall only defire a guinea at
" prefent, to buy me fome little neceffaries,
" as you fee I am rather out of repair."—

This demand was immediately complied
with, on which he named a place above two
hundred miles from London. However, without hefitating on the danger of being deceived,
he fet out directly, and found, to his unfpeak-
able joy, that once in his life the other had
acted honeftly. As foon as he had made fome
neceffary enquiries, he went to the old gentlewoman, who was ftill living, and after a little
introductory difcourfe told her, that he had
come, in obedience to the dying requeft of an
unhappy perfon, to make her the only reparation
in his power for the injuries he had done her,
by paying for the things he had taken away.

At the mention of his name fhe burft into a flood of tears; after the firft violence
of which was over, fhe confented to accept of
the fatisfaction he offered, and finding he was
no ftranger to his *friend's* other feats in her family, told him, that matters had not proved
quite fo bad as might have been apprehended,
her eldeft daughter having mifcarried privately,
on his going away; fo that fhe fuffered no injury in her character, and was fince well married to a man-midwife in the next village; as
her fecond was to the fquire's only fon, who,
for reafons beft known to themfelves, made no
objection to her for being with child.—Pleafed
with

with this account, he payed her what she demanded for her things; and then carelessly enquiring whether his *friend* had not left some
books and papers there, had the pleasure to receive them all, tied up as they had been left;
the good woman declaring she had all along
been convinced, that a man who knew so
much of religion as his *friend* the *parson*, would
certainly pay her some time or other; and
therefore she had taken the greatest care of
them.

Flushed with this success, he returned to London, and going to Bridewell to communicate
the good news to his new *friend*, he found that
the guinea he had given him had put an end to
his adventures the very night he got it, one of
his fellow prisoners and he having, for a trial of
their heads, drank such a quantity of gin as
killed them upon the spot. This event gave
him an absolute property in his acquisition, which he now offers to the Public, with
the same scrupulous fidelity he observed in relation to the former works of this author; and
he hopes this honest account, added to what
he said in the Preface to that applauded performance, and the arguments urged in the
Advertisement prefixed to the second edition of
it, will obviate any suspicion of its aiming at
particular characters, or being other than a
mere work of imagination.

POST-

## POSTSCRIPT.

*IT may not, for obvious reasons, be improper to inform the Public, that this concludes the works of our author, of this or any other entertaining kind; the rest of his writings relating solely to his attempts to find the Philosopher's Stone.*

# THE

# R E V E R I E;

## O R, A

## Flight to the Paradife of Fools.

## C H A P.  I.

*Introduction.  A fudden excurfion of an extraordi-
nary nature opens an uncommon view of common
fcenes.*

AS I indulged myfelf one evening in the
pleafure of reading the divine poem
of PARADISE LOST, which I do as
often as health and ferenity of mind
make me capable of enjoying fo fublime an entertainment in a proper manner: when I came
to the paffage * from whence the lines, prefixed to this work are taken, my imagination
caught the facred fire, and I purfued the
thought, 'till, wearied with the inexhauftible

variety which it opened to my view, I funk into that fufpenfion of fenfe, which is called A
R E V E R I E ; when the foul only wakes,
and, breaking through its corporeal incum-
brances, ranges at will over the boundlefs ex-
panfe of creation, and joins in converfe with
congenial fpirits.

The objects about which my mind had been
employed remained fo ftrongly imprinted on it,
that it immediately continued the fcene, but
with that confiftency and connection which dif-
tinguifh the vifions of imagination from the
confufion of common dreams.

I thought I found myfelf (I knew not how
tranfported thither) on the confines of that
world, which MILTON fo beautifully defcribes.
The idea of fuch a fcene raifed my curiofity fo
high, that, in defiance of the dread of venturing alone in a place where I was an utter ftranger, I was going to mix directly with the multitude, that I might take a more diftinct and
particular view of the wonderful things which I
expected to fee there, when a being of moft
tremendous afpect, appeared fuddenly before
me : " Hold prefumptuous mortal ! (faid he,
with a frown that nailed me to the ground) nor
run into a labyrinth, from whence it is impoffible to return, without the affiftance of fome
fuperior being to direct your fteps, and difperfe
the mifts of prejudice and ignorance, which at
prefent obftruct your fight."

Such an interdiction was not ineffectual ; I
ftopped, abafhed and terrified ; but curiofity
again getting the better of my fear, " Pardon,
mighty lord ! (anfwered I, proftrating myfelf
before him) the error of inadvertency, nor im-

pute

pute to thy fervant the fault of his nature. The defcription I have read of this place has inflamed my foul with a curiofity too ftrong to bear. O let thy beneficence indulge it for a moment. To thy direction I refign myfelf. Do thou prefent the neceffary clue to guide my fteps, and open my eyes to the wonders which furround me."

" Arife! (replied he, fmoothing his brow, with a fmile of complacency) I blame not thy curiofity; under the direction of reafon, its impulfe is the ftrongeft and moft extenfive caufe of human knowledge. But the more important duty of my particular ftation permits me not to attend to the gratification of it myfelf. I prefide over thefe regions of folly and confufion, which my ftricteft vigilance is not more than neceffary to keep from falling into utter anarchy. However, thou fhalt not be difappointed. The fpirit who conducts my fubjects hither from the earth will foon arrive. Him will I order to go with you, and give you the gratification you defire, which the nature of his office, and his converfation in the world, enable him to do more fatisfactorily than I can, who am too much taken up with other matters, to attend to fuch trifles as the actions of mankind. And opportunely here he comes. ARIEL, (continued he, addreffing himfelf to another fpirit who juft then joined us) this mortal is permitted to take a view of our myfterious empire. Do thou conduct him in fafety through it, and inform him of every thing that is proper for him to know, and for thee to reveal."

At

At thefe words, he vanifhed from my fight ; and Ariel advancing to me with an air of affability and kindnefs, " Come, thou moft favoured of mortals, (faid he) and enjoy an indulgence hitherto denied to man. The adventurous bard, whofe bold defcription led you hither, fnatched but a general glimpfe, as he flew by. The whole fhall be difclofed to you, and all its myfteries explained."

Encouraged by the manner in which he fpoke, I raifed my eyes from the ground, where fear and reverence had fixed them, and addreffing myfelf to him, " Accept, (faid I) moft gracious fpirit, the warmeft expreffion of my gratitude for this ineftimable favour. Lead where thou wilt, thy willing fervant follows ; but if it be not too much for me to afk, vouchfafe firft to inform me what is this place called, and who are the inhabitants of it ?"

" The world, which is thus opened to your view, (anfwered he) is T H E  P A R A D I S E O F  F O O L S ; where felf-deluded man, thro' endlefs ages, continues to act over the abfurdities in which he blindly placed the happinefs of his life. 'Till you have completed the appointed probation of mortality, and are purified by death, from the ftains and infirmities of a corruptible body, you are not able to fee their actions in their genuine colours, ftripped of the difguifes which impofe upon themfelves ; for as they are actuated by their former paffions, they ftill labour under all the weaknefles and imperfections of their former fenfes : however, I will remove the veil for a moment, and give you a fight of human nature, in a ftate that never was before revealed to mortal eyes."—Saying this, ᵗhis, he touched my eyes with the end of a wand which he held in his hand, when inftantly a flood of light broke in upon them, that illumined all my foul.

It is impoffible for words to convey an idea of what I felt at this view of human life, divefted of all the fpecious colouring which men mutually put on to deceive each other, and that with fuch eagernefs and induftry, as often to hide the impofition from themfelves alfo in the end, and fo become the dupes of their own deceit. Amazed at fuch a fcene, I could not help exclaiming, " O fapient fpirit, what can this be ? The actions of thefe beings bear the ftrongeft refemblance to thofe of man; but there is a vein of folly runs through them all, which makes them look as abfurd and ridiculous as the tricks of children in their mimic plays. Can this be their eternal employment ? Or is it poffible that they fhould be infenfible of the groffnefs of fuch folly !"

" Such is the life of man, (returned the fpirit with a fignificant fmile) and fo appear the moft important of his actions, to beings unaffected with the weaknefs of his nature. This world is, as it were, A REFLECTION of that which you have lived in. In it, AS IN A MIRROUR, you behold the human heart in all its various fituations. You fhall have a view of the whole ; but to make the gratification of your curiofity the more fatisfactory, I will lead you firft to yon fantaftic fcene, where your knowledge of fome of the actors will make the farce more interefting to you ; for you muft obferve, that as this world of ours is but a fhadow of that of man, it neceffarily is divided like it into

B 3        different

different countries, which bear the same names, and are in every respect under the same circumstances as these. But I see your sight is dazzled with this extraordinary degree of light; I will therefore draw the veil over it again, and restore things to that appearance which is suited to your present state."

"Whenever occasion requires, I will remove the obstacles which obstruct human sense, and enable you to perceive the particular objects which I point to, at the greatest distance; free from the confusion that an unlimited view of such a complicated scene must unavoidably throw you into. The walls of the closet shall be transparent to your eye; and the secret whisper sound distinctly in your ear."—With these words, he waved his wand before my eyes; and immediately the scene sunk into its original obscurity.

The spirit then took my hand, and rising with a bound, we glided through the air, with a velocity that distanced thought, though without any apparent motion of our own, till we arrived at the place which he fixed on as a proper station for our purpose.

As soon as we stopped, "We are now (said he) in the midst of the busy scene; but I have made your form imperceptible to those purblind beings, so that you may indulge your curiosity, without interruption or discovery."

CHAP.

## CHAP. II.

*Fruitless reflections. The history of Mr.* SUGAR-CANE *is introduced by that of his illustrious father.*

THE first thing that caught my attention, when I had recovered from the astonishment with which my method of travelling had struck me, was a mixed multitude of all ages and degrees of mankind, clapping their hands, and shouting round a person, who was addressing them in the most insinuating manner, while people, employed by him served them with wine, in quantities sufficient to drown every glimmering of reason, and deprive them of all power of attending to what he said.

My guide saw my surprize, and without waiting for my desiring an explanation of the cause of it, resumed his discourse in these words, which he uttered in a voice, that, to the gross senses of the beings round us, seemed the soft whisper of the passing breeze.

" I see you are amazed at the unaccountable extravagance of the scene before you. This one instance, even were there not ten thousand others equally flagrant, would be sufficient to shew how absolutely folly rules the heart of man.

" Of all the transactions of human life, there is scarce one of more real importance to it than this in which these people are at present en-

gaged.

gaged. They are chusing a person to represent them in the legislature ; to protect their properties, to promote their interests, and provide laws for the preservation and increase of their happiness and glory ; and consequently into the hands of this representative do they commit the care of every thing justly dear to them in the world. (You are to take notice, that in conformity to the illusion under which these infatuated beings act, I speak of them and their actions, as if they still were in the world they have left ; and this caution I give you, once for all, to prevent mistake and confusion.)

" But what are the qualifications required for this sacred trust ? and by what arts does the candidate for it insinuate himself into the confidence of the people, to obtain such an unlimited power over them ? Examine the scene before you, and there you see the whole mystery. The ambitious are plied with promises, the covetous with bribes, and all with liquor, till they are heated to a degree of intoxication sufficient to make them give credit to whatever he says, it matters not how contradictory to common sense, and the conduct of his past life : for who could be expected to sacrifice his fortune, and prostitute his reason in the manner this person does, to a romantic desire of doing service to those who are so wretchedly improvident that they will not serve themselves ? What has he who sells himself a right to expect, but to be sold again ?

" Thus far the electors seem to be the only fools, and to leave a name of still a blacker import to their elected representative. But to a nearer view the imaginary difference vanishes, and

and all appear equally entitled to admiffion into this place.

" For who, that gave the leaft attention to the voice of reafon, would diffipate his own wealth, and facrifice the folid happinefs of independence, to acquire a power of committing a breach of truft, as abfurd as it is perfidious? Or what are the mighty advantages even propofed by the moft fanguine purfuer of fuch a fcheme? Nothing but a deceitful fmile of court-favour, an ignominious preference in the execution of fome iniquitous job, for which he receives the paultry reward of a precarious penfion or employment, the value of which is inconfiderable, in comparifon of what he has lavifhed in the infamous purfuit; not to mention the proftitution of his confcience and honour.

" Nor does the folly of his electors, in fuffering themfelves to be feduced by fuch bafe motives, in the leaft acquit him of perfidy. The moft venal elector who ever took a bribe would refufe the candidate with deteftation, who fhould openly avow the iniquity of his intentions, and tell him, he bought his power on purpofe to fell it again. Profeffions of honefty, however improbable, are always expected; and though partiality palliates to himfelf his own venality and corruption, he looks for promifes of the oppofite virtues from the candidate; which he implicitly believes, becaufe it is his intereft that he fhould have them.

" Thus grofs as this prevarication is, it obviates every excufe the candidate can make for his corruption, and convicts him of perfidy even againft his equally corrupt elector. But not to dwell upon the iniquity of this practice,

B 5       there

there is a degree of folly in it, that would exceed belief, did not too frequent experience prove it. It is selling a man's birth-right for even less than a mess of pottage; for what security has the elector of enjoying his bribe, or the representative his pension, when the very act that earns them these wretched wages of prostitution, absolutely enslaves them to the tyranny of that power which they have thus jointly laboured to erect, and which can deprive them of these and every other emolument of life at pleasure?

" I have been insensibly led into these reflections, by the execrable folly of the scene before us; but, obvious and just as they are, the force of them will appear in a still stronger light, when illustrated by a short view of the life of this very candidate, the circumstances of which prove the truth of every remark that I made, beyond a possibility of doubt. General reasoning is too often founded on false principles, and leads the unwary mind into error; but instances from matter of fact can never deceive.

" His name is *Sugarcane*: he was born in *London*, where his father, for some little time, followed one of the meanest mechanic trades; to which, after unexpectedly outliving the neglects and cruelties of a parish nurse, he had been bred at the parish charge.

" The sanguineness of his temper equalled the strength of his constitution, and would not permit him to remain long contented in so low a station, though poverty seemed to preclude every possible hope of rising to an higher, except by the slow steps of honest industry. But

this

this he defpifed as beneath him ; and being freed from every reftraint of honefty and virtue, by the principles which he had imbibed in his education at a charity-fchool, he refolved to ftrike out a fhorter way, or fall in the attempt.

" Accordingly, in a little time after his marriage with my mother, he quitted his trade, and laid out her fortune, which was no more than the favings of a life of fervitude, on the ftock of a public houfe, as the way in which he could exert his abilities to beft advantage.

" In the courfe of his education at the charity-fchool, he had formed acquaintances with feveral of the moft promifing youths of the age, his fchool-fellows, the vivacity of whofe parts had been early difplayed in offering infults to the very hands which reached them bread, patrolling the ftreets at midnight, beating the watch, breaking up brothels, which refufed to fubmit to their pleafure, and ftanding bullies for whores ; and who as they advanced to riper years fhewed equal genius and fpirit, in ftriking out and executing various ways for remedying the partiality of fortune, and wrefting her favours from the lefs worthy hands into which fhe had blindly given them.

" With thefe he immediately improved his former acquaintance into the clofeft intimacy, not only affording them an harbour in his houfe when they were under apprehenfion of the ungenerous feverity of the laws, for few of them ever fell from the hopes of their youth ; or relinquifhed the practices in which they had been fo early trained ; but alfo frequently purchafing the prizes which they had fo gallantly taken at the hazard of their lives, and fo faving them

B 6 from

from the additional danger of offering them to
sale to strangers, In return for which services
they generally gave him such cheap bargains,
that the profit over-weighed his fears, and confirmed his hopes of making an easy fortune in
a short time.

" But this happy prospect was soon overcast.
Some of his most intimate friends having the
bad luck not to come off so cleverly in their en-
terprizes as usual, his zeal for the public good
prompted him to turn evidence against them ; by
which precaution also, he prevented their making discoveries to his disadvantage. But though
he saved his life by this prudence, circumstances
appeared so strong against him, upon the whole,
as the original contriver, and principal manager
of the scheme, that he was ordered to take a
voyage to the *West-Indies*, to assist in civilizing
the savage natives, and improve the interests of
an infant colony, by his superior abilities and
address.

" I have been so particular in this affair,
which happened when the person before us was
about three years old, because it laid the foundation of his present fortune. His father naturally took him with him ; and as his prudence
had made him be always upon his guard, he
was able to make such provision for his voyage,
that it was neither so uncomfortable, nor his
prospect so desperate as is usual with persons in
his circumstances.

" The first thing he did on his arrival, was
to purchase a plantation, which he was able to
stock so well, that in a very few years, between the profits which he reaped from that,
and the advantages his superior knowledge gave
him

him in other dealings, he not only acquired a fortune beyond his moſt ſanguine expectations, but alſo aroſe to the higheſt honours and power, in that part of the world to which the ignominious manner of his going there was no obſtruction, as it had been the general caſe.

## CHAP. III.

*The hero of the tale makes his appearance. The happy fruits of good education.*

" IT may be judged that his worſhip's mind was too intent upon matters of more moment to permit his taking much thought about the education of his ſon. Indeed, the notions he had formed of ſuch affairs, from the education he had received himſelf, made him think any great trouble or expence about ſuch a trifle quite unneceſſary. He therefore had him taught to read and write a little by an attorney, who had unluckily carried the practice of his profeſſion rather too far in his own country, by ſigning a client's name to receipts for money, without his knowledge, for which he had been compelled to travel hither, where he now ſerved his worſhip in the capacity of his clerk; and the politer accompliſhments of dancing, muſick, fencing, &c. &c. he was inſtructed in by a young gentleman from the theatre, whoſe intenſe application to the buſineſs of his profeſſion had ſo entirely wrapped him up in perſonated characters, that he had unfortunately forgot to lay
them

them aside, and re-affume his own in the common affairs of life ; but had gone in many different ones, according to the parts he meant to play, to different tradefmen with whom he had a defire to have dealings, who, upon the difcovery of the miftake, were fuch illiberal difcouragers of merit, as to impute it to a fraudulent defign, and lay him alfo under the neceffity of making the fame voyage.

" As the young fquire's parts were lively, he foon made a happy proficiency under fuch eminent mafters. Before he was quite fifteen, he could dance, fing, and play on the guittar almoft as well as his mafter ; and repeat feveral fpeeches out of plays, which he had learned by rote from him, to the great delight and furprize of all who heard him : and by eighteen, he could make a fhift to read a play himfelf, and write a billet-doux, as well as was neceffary for a gentleman of his rank and fortune.

" Nor was tne care of his tutors confined to the accomplifhments of his perfon only : they alfo formed his mind in proper principles, civil, focial, moral, and religious. Accordingly, to open his way of thinking, and free him from the narrow prejudices of vulgar education, he was taught, that religion was a cheat ; virtue, want of fpirit, and law a bugbear, fit only to reftrain and terrify the ignorant and poor : and thefe opinions, far from being merely fpeculative, ruled the conftant practice of his life. Bred up among a crowd of flaves, who trembled at his nod, he looked upon himfelf as entitled to treat every one with haughtinefs and tyranny. He indulged every paffion with which youth and flattery could inflame his

heart,

heart, laughed at every thing that was called facred, and enquired what was law, only for the pleafure of tranfgreffing it.

" While his pleafures affected only himfelf, he was fafe from interruption or reftraint from his father; but at length, fome confequences happening to attend them, which interfered with his bufinefs, fuch as the difabling and deaths of fome of his flaves, whom the fquire had diverted himfelf with proving his ftrength and dexterity at his weapons upon ; and the flight of others, for rapes committed on their wives and daughters, he refolved to fend him over to *England*, to polifh his manners, and complete his education.

" Nor were thefe, weighty as they were, the only motives for his forming this refolution. An affair of another nature made him alfo think his fon's abfence neceffary, at leaft, for fome time.

## CHAP. IV.

*Love triumphant over nature, but foiled by art. Theatrical morality.*

" THERE lived in the neighbourhood of his worfhip a clergyman, who had been obliged to leave his native country, to avoid being thrown into jail for a debt he had contracted by going to law, to defend a living which had been given him by a nobleman, to whom he had been tutor, and whofe right of prefentapresentation was disputed by the bishop of the diocese.

" His lawyers had encouraged him to carry on the suit by the most confident assurances of success, and his patron promised him to defray the expence of it ; but, on his being cast by the bishop, his lordship denied his having ever given him such a promise ; and his lawyers absolutely refused to make even the least abatement in the bill of costs, which they immediately brought him, and which was so entirely beyond his ability to discharge, that he had no way of preserving his liberty but by flight.

" It must be thought, that the conversation of such a person could not be much in the taste of his new neighbours ; but the inoffensiveness of his conduct, and the convenience of the influence which his virtues soon obtained him over the ignorant savages, insensibly reconciled them to him, and even gained him some degree of their esteem and respect.

" *Euphranor* (that was the clergyman's name) had a daughter much about the age of our young squire, who was blessed with every beauty of mind and body. Neighbourhood naturally introduced an acquaintance between their families, which was soon improved into a tenderer connection between the young pair.

" Nor was this to be wondered at ! Her it was impossible for man to behold unmoved ; and in the gifts of fortune, and the external advantages of form, he had a confessed superiority over all the young men in that part of the world. As to the defects of his mind, they seemed to proceed rather from want of proper education than from any natural propensity to vice ; and there-

fore,

fore, as he was ſtill ſo young, might eaſily be removed.

" From the time he became acquainted with *Maria*, (ſo *Euphranor*'s daughter was called) his heart felt ſenſations which it had ever been a ſtranger to before. He was unhappy every moment he was from her, yet when in her ſight, there was a majeſtic delicacy in her whole behaviour, that humbled him in his own eyes, and held him in a ſtate of diſtant awe and almoſt adoration.

" This neceſſarily had an immediate effect upon his whole conduct. He grew thoughtful, diſcontented, and reſerved; complained of the deficiencies of his education, which her accompliſhments of every kind ſhewed him in the moſt mortifying light, and avoided the company, and expreſſed an abhorrence of the pleaſures he had always been ſo fond of before.

" Such a change ſoon alarmed his theatrical tutor, (the other had been long diſmiſſed from his care of him) as he ſaw that it threatened the ſubverſion of his aſcendency over him. To obviate ſuch a misfortune required his immediate care; in which he was ſo far from doubting of ſucceſs, that he even hoped to turn it to his advantage, by his experience and addreſs, and make it a foundation for a firmer power than he yet enjoyed.

" Accordingly he threw himſelf one evening in his way, as he was returning from *Euphranor*'s; and obſerving him more than uſually thoughtful, " What is the matter, (ſaid he) clapping him familiarly on the ſhoulder; Has *Dulcinea* frowned upon her love-ſick ſwain? Hah! hah! hah! Come chear up! we will
find

find some way to appease her wrath! What, sigh for a woman? for shame, let no such thing be said: it is beneath you, quite beneath you.

*Who'd be that sordid foolish thing call'd man.---*
*The lordly bull ranges thro' all the field,*
*And from the herd singling his female out,*
*Enjoys her, and abandons her at will.——*

"There's an example for you to imitate; follow the dictates of nature, unsophisticated by priestcraft, and be happy. What mischief have priests done in the world? If it were not for the writings of poets, and the practice of players, to open the eyes of mankind, there would be no such thing as happiness or pleasure. Before men were made fools of by religion, the sexes conversed without restraint, and variety gave a relish to enjoyment: and so it does still in my country. Dear *London!* thou paradise of pleasure! there is opportunity for indulging every passion: opportunity, that is not neglected. There the wise world laughs at every foolish notion which inte feres with delight. Beauty is not kept only to be looked at; it meets desire half way, and courts the use it was designed for ; and so it would here, if men would manage right, and not raise obstacles to their own happiness."

"This elaborate speech had the desired effect. The awe in which the squire had been kept by his mistress, had already begun to sit very uneasy upon him, and his own inclinations confirmed his tutor's arguments. Accordingly he resolved to follow his directions for
**the**

the attainment of a pleasure, which he saw no other prospect of enjoying.

"He no sooner signified this resolution, than it filled his tutor with the highest joy. He embraced him in rapture; and, in the fullness of his heart, disclosed a variety of schemes for accomplishing their design; all objections to the justice of which he easily removed; proving by the unerring morality of modern comedy, that *woman is but a creature made for man's pleasure, and therefore that every method for making her subservient to this original end of her creation, is lawful for him to use.*

"This doctrine he confirmed both by the practice of the finest gentlemen, and by the implicit confession of the finest ladies of the age, who would never go to see the plays, in which those principles are openly inculcated, with such eagerness, nor encourage the players, whose greatest merit consists in giving them all the force and graces of expression and action, and whose own lives are invariably formed upon them, with such distinguished marks of their favour, if they could dispute the truth, or disapproved the practice of them.

"This reasoning appeared so conclusive, that it removed every shadow of scruple; and they directly entered into consultation upon the means for putting their schemes in execution; which they settled without any foolish restraint from the mistaken prejudices of honour, virtue, or religion.

CHAP.

❊❊❊❊❊❊❊❊❊❊❊❊❊❊❊❊❊❊❊❊

# CHAP. V.

*A well-laid scheme disappointed. The great advantage of being well-read in the drama. The scene of action is changed.*

" PURSUANT to their plot the squire went next morning to visit *Maria*, as usual; when he declared his passion with the most solemn assurances of sincerity; as an incontestible proof of which, he proposed an immediate marriage, but to be kept secret from both their fathers, till they should find some happy opportunity of gaining their approbation of it.

" At the former part of this proposal, a modest blush overspread *Maria*'s face; and shewed that her heart had no objection to it; but the first mention of secrecy restored her to herself. She thanked him politely for the favourable opinion he professed to have of her, but assured him, at the same time, that she never indulged even a thought which she imagined improper for her father's immediate knowledge, much less would venture upon the most important action of life, without his advice and approbation.

" The determined manner in which she said this, convinced her lover, that it was in vain to press her farther. He, therefore, returned to his tutor, greatly dejected at the disappointment: for had she consented, the tutor was to have

have difguifed himfelf, and perfonated the
chaplain of a man of war that happened to lie
upon the coaft at that time, to marry them;
which his theatrical talents enabled him to do,
without danger of detection, and then, when
his pupil's paffion was gratified, it was only
confeffing the ftratagem, (and all ftratagems are
lawful in love and war) and parting with her at
once; or, if fhe fhould prove refractory, and
difcover the whole, his worfhip's power, which
would not fail to be exerted on fuch an occafion, was fufficient to bear them through triumphant.

"But unexpected as this difappointment was,
the tutor foon found refources in the fertility of
his own genius to remedy it. After a paufe of
a few moments,

"*Califta!* (faid he, fpeaking to himfelf as if
in deep confideration) *Califta!* and then prove
a criminal correfpondence, both before and after
her marriage, with fome faft friend who would
not deny the charge! Yes! that might do; but
ftay!---*Monimia!* Aye! *Monimia* is the thing.---
Then fpeaking to the fquire, as if he did not
know that he had over-heard him:

"Well then (faid he) if fhe will preclude
herfelf from the poor confolation of pity, let her
blame herfelf. My bow is not trufting to one
ftring. Yes! you fhall have her, my friend; you
fhall have her as long as you pleafe; and when
your defires are fatiated, you fhall get rid of her
without reproach. My plot, it is true, is deeply
laid; but I have precedents enough in dramatic
writ to juftify it. You fhall marry her publicly,
(leave me to reconcile your father to it!) and
then what is eafier at any time than to catch fome

faithful

faithful friend in bed with her, which may be brought about by your stealing from her in her sleep, and letting me, for instance, take your place; after which a divorce will be obtained without difficulty.

" Then pluming himself in his sagacity, and strutting a step or two back and forward with an air of importance, " I have not studied the drama so long (said he) to be at a loss now for a scheme to supplant the virtue of a girl, or elude the vigilance of a bookish doating father ; let her therefore tell him her story, as soon as she pleases, I am prepared for both. As for his worship, I know that he will readily join in any thing to pull down the pride of that parson, in revenge for his having the assurance to arraign his conduct by preaching up to others, and practising himself, a course of life, in all respects, so opposite to his own."

" But deeply as this design was laid, it met with the same fate, and from the same motive, with the former. The moment her lover left her, *Maria* informed her father of his proposal, who in the uprightness of his heart went directly, and disclosed it to his worship. It is impossible to describe the rage into which such a story threw him. He immediately sent off his son to *England*, to prevent the disgrace of his making so unworthy a match : and, far from being obliged to *Euphranor* for making the discovery, bore him ever after the most implacable hatred, for being father to the object of his son's passion.

" As for the tutor, the time appointed for his travels not being yet expired, he was obliged to stay behind, and trust his pupil to his own management."

C H A P.

## CHAP. VI.

*Squire* SUGARCANE *arrives in England. An odd medley of high and low life. Prejudice of education involves him in many disagreeable circumstances, and at length brings him into imminent danger.*

" OUR hero arrived in *England* without any accident. His father, it may be judged, did not burthen him with much advice. Two things only he cautioned him against, which were extravagance, for his pride had prompted him to give him unlimited credit, and matrimony without his express approbation. In every thing else, he left him to his own government, or indeed, more properly speaking, to chance.

" But he might have spared himself the trouble even of this much. The moment his son was out of his sight, he scorned all restraint, however easy and just ; and if his father's advice had any influence upon him, it was only to raise a desire of opposition to it.

" Accordingly, as soon as he got to *London*, he ran into every fashionable expence, with an eagerness that seemed to court ruin. He had houses sumptuously furnished at all places of pleasurable resort; he set up equipages which vied in magnificence with those of a sovereign prince, kept running horses, hounds, and whores ; and, to complete his character, played
deeply

deeply at every game, in which art and experience could give his antagonists an advantage over his ignorance.

" All this he did, from an absurd vanity of following the fashion; to indulge his own taste, which the manner of his education had fixed upon the most vulgar pleasures, and grossest sensualities, he ran into the opposite extreme of low life. Thus he oftener slept in some filthy brothel, than in any of his own elegant houses; while his equipage waited whole mornings at his door, he was in a dirty disguise driving an hackney coach; he got drunk with his grooms, and rode his own races; and the conversation of his dog-boys was the greatest pleasure he reaped from his hounds. The mistresses whom he kept at the most profuse expence, he seldom even saw; his amours rarely soaring higher than the humble patrollers of the streets; and while he was throwing away thousands among gamblers of fashion, his heart languished for a game of put, or all-fours, for a pint of beer, or a dram of gin; and he often stole away, from the most elegant entertainments which luxury could devise, to carouse and riot among chairmen and porters in a night cellar.

" Such a course of life necessarily involved him in numberless scrapes and troubles. Accustomed to converse with none but dependants, and lord it over slaves, who dared not even murmur at his cruelty and abuses, he could not bear to be treated as an equal by persons whose more moderate expences made him think them of inferior fortunes; and on the slightest contradiction to his will, in his servants, or any others of the lower stations of life, would fly

out

out into his usual outrages, beating and wounding them in the most cruel manner.

"The consequences of this conduct were always disagreeable. The former returned the insolence of his behaviour with the most mortifying contempt; or with personal affronts, which pride and cowardice equally prevented his resenting in the only manner that could put an end to them; and the harpies of the law extorted ample satisfaction from his purse for the injuries to the latter, and that often after he had suffered sufficiently before from the superior strength of those who complained of him.

"Such an hurricane of riot and debauchery was too violent to last long. An accident that happened in one of his nocturnal exploits lowered his spirits for a time, and gave his pleasure a less tumultuous turn.

"A party, among whom he was, having sallied out one night from the tavern in the madness of inebriation, to scour the streets, and signalize their bravery on all who should be so unfortunate as to fall in their way, stumbled upon a watchman asleep upon his stand. The figure of the wretch would have bespoke compassion from any human creatures under the direction of reason. He was worn out with age, and appeared an object much more proper to receive, than give protection. But the misery of his appearance only raised their mirth; and one of them of uncommon wit and humour saying what a surprize it would be to the old fellow to awake in the other world, our hero, who was the most drunk in the company, and perhaps most accustomed to such feats, directly drew his sword, and plunged it into his body."

Vol. I.            C            "Such

"Such an action struck them all with horror. They instantly took to flight, in which he attempted to follow them; but conscious affright deprived him of the little strength which liquor had left, and he fell at his length in the street, where he lay unable to rise, though not insensible of the danger that hung over his head, his apprehensions of which were far from being lessened by hearing the wretch cry out murder; as he thought it impossible for him to outlive such a wound, though the joke he had designed was disappointed, and it happened not to put him to immediate death.

"The first cry of murder brought a number of the neighbouring watchmen to the place, who found the squire with his drawn sword lying on the ground by him, and every circumstance of his appearance confirming his guilt. But if this had not been sufficient, there wanted not direct proof of it; for some of his companions considering the consequences of having been known to have been in his company, and aware of the danger that might attend his impeaching them, returned immediately to the place, and charged him directly with the fact.

"On this he was dragged away to the round-house; where his fright soon recovered him from his drunkenness, and shewed him all the horrers of his situation. In vain did he offer immense sums for liberty to make his escape; the affair was now public, and the watchman's wound was declared mortal, by a surgeon who had been called up to dress him.

"Accordingly, after suffering the insults of the watch; and the revilings of his companions, who strove to shew their own innocence by
aggravating

aggravating his guilt, for the remainder of the night, he was taken before a magiſtrate next morning, where the circumſtances of his crime were examined into with the moſt excruciating minuteneſs, and the conſequences of it blazoned in ſuch terrifying colours as were ſufficient to ſtrike the boldeſt heart with deſpair; and when thus properly prepared, he was committed to the common priſon, to wait the ſentence of the law, among the vileſt malefactors who diſgrace the human name.

## CHAP. VII.

*An hair-breadth eſcape. The happineſs of being abſolutely diſengaged in life. An unexpected piece of news ſhews the perverſeneſs of the human heart.*

" THE news of the ſquire's misfortune was immediately ſpread over the whole town, and of courſe ſoon came to the ears of his father's correſpondent; who, though he was highly diſſatisfied with his manner of life, thought it his duty not to deſert him in ſuch a dreadful condition. He therefore went directly to the magiſtrate, and learning the circumſtances of the affair from him, found reaſon to ſuſpect that it was not ſo bad as was repreſented; but was aggravated with a deſign of extorting money from the terrified criminal.

" In conſequence of this ſuſpicion, he ſent for a ſurgeon of character, and going to the

place

place where the watchman lay (an attorney's house) infifted on feeing his wound opened ; when it appeared fo far from being mortal, that the furgeon declared it was not even dangerous, with the leaft care, the fword having happily hit upon a rib, and fo only glanced between that and the fkin.

" On this difcovery, the merchant demanded his friend's being admitted to bail ; and on the magiftrate's confenting, becaufe he did not dare to refufe, went himfelf to the prifon, with the joyful tidings : where he found the defponding wretch furrounded by a gang of follicitors, and knights of the poft, who were planning fchemes for his efcape by perjury and chicane, and at the fame time exaggerating his danger to enhance the price of their owndamnation ; in earneft of which, and to quicken their inventior, they had already received all the money in his pocket, which amounted to a confiderable fum.

" At the firft fight of the merchant, thefe harpies vanifhed like owls at the appearance of the fun. The good man faw the fquire's diftrefs, and judging that it might be a proper time to work upon him, foftened thus by fear, he fat down, and entered into a friendly expoftulation with him on the folly, vice, and danger of fuch a life as he had led ; and concluded by wifhing, that his prefent almoft miraculous efcape might make a proper impreffion upon him, for the remainder of his life.

" The fquire heard the former part of his difcourfe with liftlefs inattention ; but at the mention of his efcape, he fell upon his knees, and, eagerly kiffing his friend's hand, conjured him to confirm the happy word.

" It

" It is impoffible to defcribe his fituation on being fatisfied that his danger was over. His fpirits, ever in extream, were raifed as high as they had been dejected before ; fo fudden a tranfition from defpair to happinefs (for fo his joy for that moment might juftly be called) almoft depriving him of his fenfes. He broke out into fuch inconfiftent extravagancies of exultation, that he made his friend for fome time fear he fhould utterly lofe his reafon. But his ftrength foon failing under fuch accumulated fatigue, his fpirits funk into a fettled calm ; and he left the prifon in the moft rational ftate of mind he had been in fince he came to *Eng : land*.

" The horrors he had endured in this affair made an impreffion on his mind, which influenced the remainder of his life. His danger determined him for ever againft fuch exploits as that which drew him into it ; and the behaviour of his companions gave him fo ftrong an averfion to fuch fociety, that he refufed their vifits of congratulation on his return to his own houfe, and never would mix with them more.

" He was now in fuch a ftate of fufpence, for the choice of his future life, that had any principles of virtue been inculcated in his mind by education, he might moft probably have followed their direction. But when the voice of pleafure, the tumults of diffipation, and vice, were filenced, all was a wretched void within him, and he was really obliged to give into the firft fcheme of active idlenefs which chance fuggefted for want of knowing what elfe to do.

" Juft in this critical time, he happened to receive a packet of letters from home. That of his father he threw carelefsly by, fcarce half read through : but the fight of his tutor's hand raifing an expectation of fome news concerning *Maria*, his paffion for whom he had never been able entirely to fubdue, he opened it with eagernefs, though he had no reafon to expect any account particularly interefting to him.

"His tutor informed him, that his father looking upon her as the caufe of his being obliged to fend his fon to *England*, the moment he was gone fhewed the moft rancorous hatred to her and *Euphranor*, which his power gave him fo many opportunities of wreaking, that he made their lives quite miferable : they refolved, therefore, to leave that country, and feek fome happier retreat elfewhere ; but as they were juft ready to go, *Euphranor* received a letter from the brother of the lord to whom he had been tutor, to inform him of his lordfhip's death, and defire that he would return to *England* as foon as poffible, to take poffeffion of a very confiderable living juft then become vacant in his gift, and which he kept for him ; adding, that he had difcharged the debt, which had been the occafion of his going abroad ; and that on receipt of this news they left the place directly, not more to their own fatisfaction, than to the mortification of his father, at their good fortune and efcape from his power.

"This account threw him into a violent conflict : his heart felt the ftrongeft emotions at the thought of her being in the fame country with him. He at firft refolved to find her out, and pleafed himfelf to think how agreeably

ably

ably she must be surprised at the great improvements she would see in his appearance and address, which he did not doubt would make such an impression on her in his favour, as should greatly facilitate his desires.

" But a moment's reflection overthrew all these flattering hopes; and shewed him the utter improbability of her ever listening to the addresses, or even receiving the visits of a man by whom she had been treated in so base a manner; for to mitigate the severity of his father's rage, and wipe off the disgrace of having proposed marriage to one so much beneath him, he had openly declared the designs he had formed for her ruin.

" But this was not what gave him the greatest pain. The advantageous change in her father's affairs removing the only objection which he thought could be made to her, it immediately occurred to him, that some person of distinction would most probably be captivated by her charms, at her return to *England*, and marry her; and it was death to him to think that she should make any other man happy, though he had lost all hopes of ever obtaining her himself.

" But these disagreeable reflections soon gave place to thoughts of another nature. His mind had been in such a continued agitation ever since his coming to *London*, that he had not once remembered the many fine things his tutor had so often told him of the theatres; nor the luscious descriptions he had drawn of the pleasures to be found in the company of the players of both sexes. But a repetition of

C 4       them

them in this letter had an immediate effect upon him, in his present undetermined state ; and
he resolved to look there for that happiness
which he had missed of hitherto."

✿✿✿✿✿✿✿✿✿✿✿✿✿✿✿✿✿✿

## C H A P.  VIII.

*The pleasures of theatrical society.  The squire com-
mences critic and patron.  He acts the part of
Ixion, and embraces a cloud instead of a goddess.*

" IN pursuance of this resolution he directly
became almost an inhabitant of the play-
house.  He made acquaintances with all the
players; he attended rehearsals, drank tea in the
green-room; and in a very little time had all
the terms of theatrical criticism at his fingers
ends.

" He now thought himself an happy man.
The mirth and wit of the actors, the freedom
and ease of the actresses, and the obsequiousness and flattery of both quite charmed him.
His table was constantly filled with them ;
while they in return for his hospitality convinced him, that he had overlooked his own
abilities, and was really endowed with the
most refined taste, and exquisite judgement of
the age.

" As soon as he had made this discovery, he
assumed all the consequence of this new character.  He retailed the phrases of criticism,
which he had lately picked up, on all occasions
with the most decisive air ; spoke with contempt

tempt of authors whose names he scarcely
knew, and praised those of established reputation ; but all in general terms, and merely as
an echo to the town.

" It may be thought that this course of life,
idle and insignificant as it was, must be more
harmless at least than that which he had led
before ; but still it was not free from its incon-
veniencies also.

" Such a set of company necessarily precluded
him from that of all persons whose conversation might have been either an advantage or
an honour to him ; besides, to support the dignity of his character, he was obliged to set
up for a patron of the polite arts, which laid him
open to the impositions of every ignorant pre-
tender to them ; as he was utterly destitute of
the least degree of judgment to direct him in
the distribution of the rewards which their
flattery and importunities extorted from his ignorance and vanity ; so that, though he had re-
trenched most of his former expences, on his
entering into his present way of life, he found
but very little advantage from his œconomy ;
the cravings of his new dependents proving as
effectual a drain to his money as all his more
shewy extravagancies had been before.

" But this was only a trifle, in comparison
of other consequences which attended this connection. Such a fortune as he possessed was a
lure to every scheming genius, to try their abilities upon him ; the actresses, in particular,
spread open all their nets, to take him in for a
settlement ; at least, if not even entrap him in
the marriage noose, as he was a batchelor.
This was the secret reason of that officiousness

to pleafe him, which has been obferved before; but his attention was too much taken up with the addreffes paid to his underftanding, to admit his minding thofe offered to his perfon.

"At length, however, one of the female adventurers of the ftage hit upon a plan, in which her experience promifed her fuccefs. She faw that vanity glitered through his fhallow heart, and was the ruling principle of all his actions: to catch this, therefore, a gilded bait was all that was neceffary. For this purpofe, fhe contrived to convey him a letter, glowing with the warmeft profeffions of love, but lamenting the reftraint which a fuperior ftation laid her under from making herfelf known, or gratifying the paffion that preyed upon her heart.

"The receipt of this letter threw him into the higheft perplexity; he ran over every fcene of his life, to try if he could, from any circumftance, find out who this enamoured fair could be; but all in vain. However, his ignorance by no means eafed him of his anxiety; he had too good an opinion of himfelf to doubt the truth of what fhe faid; and his darling vanity was too ftrongly flattered by the thought, to admit his flighting fuch an honour, could he poffibly difcover by whom it was done him.

"The fair one, who faw him every day, foon had an opportunity of obferving his diftrefs, which was the fignal fhe wanted to convince her that the lure fhe threw had taken. Accordingly, in a day or two after fhe wrote him another letter, in which fhe appointed him a place of meeting, but under the moft folemn adjurations of fecrecy and honour, when fhe availed herfelf fo well of her theatrical art of varying
**her**

her appearance, and perfonating a fictitious character, that, with the affiftance of the play-houfe cloaths, and a good quantity of paint, fhe paffed upon him for a beautiful young lady of the firft quality, who had accidentally been fmitten with the charms of his perfon.

" The delicacy and modeft referve with which fhe revealed her own paffion, and received his addreffes, gained fo complete a conqueft over his intoxicated heart, that he outwent her moft fanguine expectations, and made diftant propofals of marriage, at the very firft interview ; but thefe the character fhe acted would not permit her to underftand too readily ; and his refpect prevented his fpeaking plainer, on fo fhort an acquaintance.

" But an accident foon removed this difficulty, which was equally diftreffing to them both, though from fo different motives. Going to the play the next evening as ufual, he was furprifed to fee *Maria* glittering in all the pride of drefs in one of the ftage boxes ; the fight of her put him fo much off his guard, that, happening to catch her eye, he bowed to her directly in the moft familiar manner : but what was his confufion, to find, that inftead of acknowledging his falute, fhe turned from him with a look of ineffable contempt.

" Such an affront, in fo public a place, could not efcape notice. The eyes of every one were immediately fixed upon him, in fo fignificant a manner, that he could not ftand it ; but was forced to retire, burfting with refentment, behind the fcenes, where he had the additional mortification to learn, that fhe was above every attack he could make upon her, being lately

married

married to the young nobleman who was fitting with her, and was the same who had recalled her father and her from the place of their banishment.

" It is impossible to describe the malignant passions which tore his heart at this news : his love was instantly turned to the most rancorous hatred ; and envy prompted him to ruin an happiness which he had not been able to prevent.

" While he was revolving various schemes for this purpose, his unlucky genius blundered upon one, which drew that mortification ten thousand fold upon his own head which he designed for her. He thought that the safest way he could take to humble her pride (for his courage was cooled from any attempts which might possibly endanger his dear person) was to shew her, that he had been as great a gainer as she by not being married to her, and to return her contempt in kind.

" Accordingly, at the very next meeting his enamoured fair one indulged him with, he proposed an immediate marriage, which he pressed with such unfeigned ardor, that, after some few struggles between her love for him, and her regard to the dignity of her rank, she consented, her fear of being prevented by her noble friends and family palliating the precipitancy of such a step.

" The exultations of two persons, happy thus in the success of their designs, well supplied the place of pomp and ceremony at the wedding ; but what was the bridegroom's astonishment next morning, to find a faded veteran of the stage in his arms, instead of a dutchess in all the pride of beauty, rank, and fortune ; for the

warmth

warmth of the night had melted the painted
bloom upon her cheeks, and reſtored her to her
natural appearance, which day-light diſplayed
in no very favourable light.

"He ſtarted from her in horror; and as ſoon
as he had recovered the uſe of ſpeech, which
ſuch a ſight for ſome time deprived him of, flew
into the moſt outrageous fury, and ſwore he
would be revenged, in the dreadfulleſt manner,
for ſuch an infamous piece of deceit.

"But his bride was too well acquainted with
the world to be terrified at his threats. She aroſe
with all the expedition, that her delicate regard
to decency would permit, and throwing herſelf
at his feet, alledged the violence of her paſſion
as an excuſe for her ſtratagem; (and all ſtratagems, ſhe ſaid, were lawful in love) beſought
his forgiveneſs in the tendereſt terms, and
vowed the moſt exemplary duty, love, and virtue for the reſt of her life, promiſing to make
ample amends for the imaginary diſparity of
rank; (for his own fortune placed him above
regard to mercenary conſiderations) by her in-
ceſſant attention to his pleaſure.

"Well as ſhe acted her part, the abuſed huſband remained inflexible, vowing to purſue her
with the utmoſt ſeverity; a reſolution which
the remembrance of his own treatment of
*Maria*, now retorted in ſuch a ſignal manner
on himſelf, enforced with every motive of hatred
and revenge.

"But his wrath had as little effect upon her
as her entreaties poſſibly could have upon him.
She aroſe from his feet with an air of diſdain;
and telling him, that if he did not know what
was due to the character of his wife, ſhe would

ſoon

foon inform him, dreffed herfelf with the greateft compofure, and wifhing him a good morning, left him to go to breakfaft with what appetite he could.

" Nor were her threats in vain; fhe went directly to a lawyer, by whofe advice fhe took fuch meafures as obliged her hufband to compound matters with her, and give her fuch a fettlement (as he did not chufe cohabitation) as enabled her to pay the debt of gratitude, and keep thofe now who had kept her in former days.

" This affair broke off all his theatrical connections, and left him as much at a lofs what to do with himfelf as he had been when he firft entered into them. But the death of his father, of which he received the account juft as he had concluded this tranfaction, freed him from this uncertainty, and engaged him in purfuits of a quite different nature from thofe he had hitherto followed.

## C H A P.  IX.

*Mr.* SUGARCANE *commences ftatefman. Signal inftances of minifterial confidence and favour. A common change. The conduct of a patriot.*

" THE death of his father put Mr. *Sugar-cane* (for he muft no longer be called by the familiar title of fquire) in poffeffion of fuch an immenfe fortune, that he immediately confidered himfelf as one of the pillars of the ftate; and looking on every thing elfe as beneath

neath his dignity and importance, devoted himself entirely to the care of nations..

" In purſuance of this reſolution, he waited directly on the miniſter,. and diſplaying his own conſequence in the ſtrongeſt colours, informed him of his deſire to become a member of the ſenate, and offered him his ſervice in the moſt unlimited terms.

" The miniſter, whom long experience had taught to read the human heart, immediately ſaw what uſe he might make of ſuch an offer, from ſo ſanguine a volunteer.. Accordingly he thanked him for the honour of his friendſhip in the moſt polite manner, encouraged him in ſo laudable a deſign, and treated him with ſuch a reſpectful intimacy, as quite won his ſhallow heart.

" As ſoon therefore as he was ſatisfied that he had him ſecure, he told him one day,. with an air of the higheſt ſatisfaction, that he now had an opportunity of ſhewing him the confidence he had in him, and at the ſame time procuring him that rank in the ſtate which he deſerved, by getting him returned for one of his boroughs.

" Mr. *Sugarcane*'s joy at this news may eaſily be conceived ; he thanked him in the warmeſt terms of gratitude for ſo great a favour ; and on the miniſter's expreſſing ſome concern for the expence which might poſſibly attend an oppoſition that was deſigned againſt his intereſt, declared the ſtrongeſt contempt for ſuch paultry conſiderations, and inſiſted on the honour of defraying the whole himſelf.

" Accordingly he went directly down to the borough, where he entered on the complicated
buſineſs

buſineſs of electioneering with ſuch ſpirit, and carried it on at ſo profuſe an expence, that his opponents were glad to ſubmit to the miniſter's terms, which they had abſolutely rejected before, to avoid the vexation and diſgrace of being foiled by a ſtratagem.

" It may be thought that his being made a property of in ſo notorious a manner, would have made him ſee his folly ; but it was no ſuch thing. Far from being offended, he took it as an inſtance of the higheſt confidence in his friendſhip, on the miniſter's repreſenting to him, that the buſineſs of the ſtate could not have been carried on without giving him up for that time, and promiſing to make him ample amends on a more favourable occaſion.

" Groſs as this impoſition was he blindly ſubmitted to it ſeveral times ſucceſſively, cajoled by aſſurances of friendſhip and artful hints of having his ſervices rewarded in the end by a peerage.

" He lived thus upon air for ſeveral years, ſquandering more in purſuit of a ſhadow than the acquiſition of the ſubſtance could ever poſſibly refund him. At length, however, his eyes were opened ; and he ſaw the abuſe he had ſuffered in the moſt mortifying light : but inſtead of being cured of his madneſs, it only gave it another turn. He directly commenced patriot, in the preſent ſenſe of the word, declaiming againſt the miniſter and his meaſures, with as much vehemence and heat as he had declaimed for them before ; and laviſhing his fortune as profuſely, in oppoſition to his intereſt, as he had formerly done to ſupport it.

" Evident as the motives of this change were, the giddy multitude ſuffered themſelves to be

deceived,

deceived by it; or rather indeed, they received it as a colour to palliate the abfurdity of their confiding in him, and juftify their taking the bribes with which he buys them.

"On this fyftem he proceeds now, undifcouraged by the many difappointments he has met with, and the difficulties into which fuch complicated diffipation of his fortune, immenfely great as it was, has thrown his affairs. In his prefent attempt, it is true, he has a profpeft of fuccefs; but how far this will anfwer his expeftation of making him happy, or what ufe even he will make of it, the leaft experience of human life fufficiently fhews.—But I fee an uneafinefs in your looks. If I have faid any thing that you do not comprehend, fpeak your doubt with freedom, and I will refolve it with pleafure".

"This condefcenfion (anfwered I) O moft benevolent fpirit! is agreeable to the excellence of thy nature; and I were unworthy of the favour you offer, if I let a falfe modefty, a proud reluftance to fhew my ignorance, prevent my accepting it. It is moft true, that you have faid fome things which I cannot underftand the meaning of. You fay he commenced a patriot, in the prefent fenfe of the word. Can any word be plainer? Or what fenfe but the obvious natural one can it be taken in?"

"Your inexperience, in the ways of the world, (replied he with a fmile) leads you into this difficulty. Your notions are all merely fpeculative, formed on reflection and not on obfervation. You confider things as they ought to be, fuppofing man to aft upon the principles of reafon, not as they are, under fo contrary a direction; and this miftake of the merely-learned, is is the caufe of the very little fervice which their works do in the world.

" A patriot, in the original and proper meaning of the word, is the nobleft title which can be given to man ; and includes every virtue, moral, focial, and civil. But fo entirely is the ufe of words changed with the courfe of things, that ftripped of every idea which can deferve refpect, it implies only a factious oppofer of the meafures of the court, who pretends a regard to the public welfare, to gain the confidence of the people, and make himfelf of fufficient confequence to be admitted to a fhare of the fpoil which he declaims againft. (You are to obferve that I fpeak in the general. That there are fometimes men who really deferve the title in its moft exalted fenfe, and poffefs every virtue which they make profeffion of, I will not deny ; but they are too few to place in oppofition to the multitude ; and the exception only proves the rule.) You heard with what vehemence Mr. *Sugarcane* harangued againft the minifter, accufing him of betraying the interefts, and over-turning the conftitution of his country, and founding his own pretenfions to merit with the public on the effectual means he defigned to make ufe of, to defeat fuch pernicious defigns. Thefe profeffions you fee have been fuccefsful ; how far they were fincere, there is a fcene juft opening which will inform you."

The crowd by this time was difperfed, fatisfied with what they had got, or expecting no more then ; and the candidate was retired to enjoy his fuccefs with a few felect friends. But fcarce was he feated, when he received word, that

that a ftrange gentleman wanted to fpeak with him in private that moment.

Mr. *Sugarcane* imagined that it was one of his opponents, who was coming over to him, and wanted to make terms ; and therefore gave directions to have him fhewn into his clofet, whither he foon followed him ; but what was his furprize to fee that it was a friend of the minifter's, whom he well knew to be in the greateft confidence with him.

As foon as the common compliments of civility were paid, " You wonder probably, Sir, (faid the ftranger) at this vifit from me, but the motive of it will excufe the abruptnefs. I come to propofe an accommodation between you and the minifter. The neceffity of affairs obliged him to treat you with an appearance of unkindnefs ; but that is now over, and he is willing to make you amends."

" Amends, Sir ! (anfwered Mr. *Sugarcane*, with an haughty air) I do not underftand you. I have difcovered the iniquity, the danger of the minifter's defigns, and am determined to defeat them. I fcorn any accommodation with the enemy of my country."

" This way of talking, Sir, (interrupted the other) may do very well amongft a crowd of drunken voters, but to me it is nonfenfe. If you will deferve the minifter's friendfhip, it is offered to you ; if not, he is not afraid of you. He is fufficiently acquainted with the practices by which you have carried your point here ; and you know what an appearance they will have before the committee upon a petition."

The mention of a petition threw Mr. *Sugarcane* into evident confufion, as he was confcious.

of

of the illegality of his proceedings. This the
gentleman inftantly obferved, and refolving to
take the advantage of it, " My meffage, Sir,
(faid he in a peremptory tone) requires not a
moment's confideration. In a word, will you,
or will you not, be the minifter's friend? This
is the laft time you will be afked."

" On what terms? (anfwered Mr. *Sugarcane* faultering, and even blufhing at his own
bafenefs)" " On the terms you have fo often
propofed, (replied the ftranger)" " How Sir!
I propofe terms to the minifter!" (interrupted
*Sugarcane* with an air of furprize and difdain) I
do not underftand you, Sir. I would have you
to know, Sir"——" Look you, Sir, (faid the
ftranger dryly) this way of talking fignifies nothing, as I obferved to you before; nor have I
much time to ftay. You have folicited, frequently and earneftly folicited for a particular
place: pray, Sir, what was this, but implicitly
offering your fervice to the minifter, if he
would give you that place? Now, Sir, that
very place is vacant, and at your fervice, provided you will write the minifter word, exprefsly and pofitively, to prevent miftakes, that
you will fupport his intereft, in every thing required of you, without referve: and I would
recommend it to you to confider, whether you
are like to get fo much by oppofing him. In
the mean time, to fecure your intereft with
your electors, he confents that you fhall abufe
him as much and as grofsly as you pleafe."

Mr. *Sugarcane* feemed to hefitate for a few
moments, and then reaching his hand to the
gentleman, " Give my compliments to our
friend, (faid he) and tell him he may depend
upon

upon me. I never was his enemy, farther than my intereſt required, and now he has gained that to his ſide, he has gained me alſo."

He then ſat down to write the letter required of him, to prevent his forgetting that he had made terms ; as ſoon as he had finiſhed which the ſtranger departed, to avoid ſuſpicion, and Mr. *Sugarcane* returned to his company, where he profeſſed patriotiſm, and railed at the miniſter with greater rage and vehemence than ever.

## CHAP. X.

*The hiſtory of a cobler, who would correct the times. The beſt way to win the hearts of the mob. He over-acts his part, and is turned out as a wrangler.*

SO glaring a repreſentation of human folly overwhelmed me with confuſion. I was aſhamed of participating, in a common nature, with ſuch monſters of abſurdity, and turned away diſguſted from the odiouſly ridiculous ſcene.

The Spirit read the ſentiments of my heart, and ſmiling with ineffable contempt, reſumed his diſcourſe in theſe words :

" Your vanity is offended at this ſtory, as if it reflected any diſgrace upon yourſelf. This is another inſtance of the folly of man, to think his conſequence ſo extenſive, as to be affected by any thing not immediately levelled at him. Careleſs of deſerving praiſe himſelf, his pride is piqued at the reproof offered to others ;
but

but in this he only betrays his own infirmities. No man was ever hurted at hearing a fault reproved of which he was not guilty himself. The conscious heart is easily alarmed. His too ready sensibility takes the imputation that was never meant, and turns general satire into particular reproach.

As for me, think not that I take pleasure in painting things worse than they really are. If the picture is disagreeable, the fault is in the original; I copy nature, and am equally above flattery and abuse. You must therefore drop this review, if you are dissatisfied with truth in its genuine colours."

" Have compassion, gracious Spirit, (answered I, with a most respectful obeisance) on the weakness of my nature, nor impute to pride the effect of shame. I felt the force of that ridicule, to which you held up such egregious follies, and hope to receive this advantage from it, that I shall never fall into the like myself. Continue therefore the instructive picture, and your servant shall join in the honest laugh you raise, even though it be against himself."

The humility and candour of this declaration removed the Spirit's displeasure, and he proceeded. " Nothing shews folly in a more contemptible light, (said he) than its being repeatedly duped by the same deceit. Of all the pretences which have imposed upon the credulity of mankind, this of patriotism has been oftenest used. The reason is evident ; the whole system of human politics is such a medley of folly and corruption, even under the wisest administrations, that if a superior power

*did*

did not conftantly interpofe, to difappoint the deepeft defigns of man, and obviate the effects of his wifdom, the very face of nature would be changed, and all her works overwhelmed in confufion and ruin.

" Obfervation of this uninterrupted feries of errors and misfortunes, without attention to the fource of them, gives weight to the clamours of every felf-elected reformer, againft thofe in power, and makes the giddy multitude liften to his fpecious promifes of redrefs, as a drowning perfon catches even at a ftraw; their conftant difappointments not in the leaft abating their credulity.

" Nor is affectation of reforming confined to the higher ranks of life, where affluence may feem to give a title to idlenefs, and flatter ambition with a profpect of fuccefs. The meaneft mechanic will undertake to mend the ftate; and if he can but harangue with noife and virulence, will find fools of all denominations to liften to what he fays.

" An inftance of this may be worth attending to ; and yonder little village, at this very time, affords one of a moft ftriking nature. Obferve that man, fitting in all the mimic pomp of ftate, and haranguing to the gaping croud around him, with all the affected agitation and vehemence of voice and gefture of a ranting player, tearing a paffion to pieces on the ftage. Liften to him but a moment, and you will find him utterrly ignorant of every rule of fpeech, as well as every principle of reafoning, continually committing blunders in each beneath a man of fenfe to utter, and which none but perfons under the ftrongeft degree of intoxication
could

could hearken to, without difguft and contempt. Yet by thefe very harangues, frothy, extravagant, and blundering as they are, has he arifen to the ftate of confequence in which you now behold him.

" He was bred a cobler, and worked at his trade for fome years in that very village with tolerable credit : but nature having unluckily given him fome vivacity of parts, without any prudence to direct them, he foon grew weary of working, and fpent all his time in railing at the parifh-officers, and accufing them of numberlefs abufes in the performance of their feveral duties.

" This naturally drew a crowd every market-day about his ftall, to whom he fet forth the public grievances in fo pathetic a manner, and with fuch ftrong intimations of his own integrity and ability to redrefs them, if they would put the power in his hands, that they promifed to chufe him churchwarden at the next veftry.

" Intoxicated with this fuccefs, he immediately enlarged his plan, and ventured to attack the fteward of the manor, for having (as he alledged) encroached upon the common, and extorted exorbitant fees in the courfe of his office. Nor did he fhew greater refpect to the lord himfelf, but had the affurance to charge him directly with countenancing his fteward's opprefflions, and defigning to deftroy the court-rolls and turn all the tenants out of their farms ; and for fear thefe charges fhould be refuted, he involved in them every one in the parifh who had any opportunity of knowing the truth ; and to invalidate their teftimony,

and

and deprive them of all respect, branded them and their families with the most atrocious crimes, publishing every private calumny that malice had ever invented, and raking up the ashes of the dead for scandal and defamation.

"Such a conduct soon won the hearts of the mob, as it pulled down those above them to their own level. Accordingly he became their idol to such a degree, that they implicitly believed every word he said, and resolved unanimously to support him at the approaching vestry.

"But he had over-acted his part, and in the warmth of his passion provoked the better part of the parishioners so much, by his personal reflections and abuse, that before he could be elected, he was presented in the court-leet as a common disturber, and condemned to be set in the stocks for a public example.

"Though in the heat of his patriotism he had often braved danger, and boasted that he would bear any persecution, rather than desert his friends, in such a glorious cause; when it came to the test, his resolution failed him, and he manfully ran away to the county-town, where, as he was out of the power of his persecutors, whose subordinate jurisdiction was confined to their own parish, and could not reach him there, he gallantly bade them defiance, and renewed his abuse, railing at them with all the rancour of impotent resentment.

## CHAP. XI.

*He rises in life, but cannot leave off his old tricks.*
*A repulse overturns his patriotism, which is again*
*renewed by another. The great advantage of a*
*certain quality, generally decried, but as generally*
*practised.*

" AS he had nothing to support him but
what he earned by his trade, which he
had also greatly neglected ever since he had
turned reformer, to the no small embarrassment
of his private affairs, he had reason to apprehend all the miseries of want, on his removal into a strange place.

" But his friends relieved him from his fears,
and generously subscribed their shillings a-piece
to buy him a new suit of cloaths, and set him
up in a shoe-maker's shop ; for he was above
cobling any longer, and had been made free of
the *gentle craft* for a pot of beer, and a fine
speech or two, in one of the little corporation-
towns he passed through in his travels.

" The racket that had been made about him
drew so many customers to his shop, that he
was in a fair way of earning honest bread, if
he could have kept himself quiet, and applied
diligently to his work ; but the itch of reforming had taken such fast hold of him, that he
could not help meddling with other people's
concerns, every where he went.

" Accordingly

" Accordingly in some little time after he was settled in the county-town, he took an opportunity one day, when the principal inhabitants were met together at a charity-feaft, to prefent them with a full account of all the great things he had promifed and propofed doing in his own parifh, had he not unluckily been driven out of it, which he had got an attorney's clerk to write out fair for him, in a fair hand, and on gilt paper, and kindly offered his fervice in the fame manner to them.

" But they had heard his character before, and judging that they could get nothing but trouble by admitting fuch a wrangler among them, prudently declined his offer, and returned him his paper.

" It muft be imagined that fuch an indignity provoked his wrath to the higheft degree ; but he thought proper to fupprefs it, in a great meafure, for fear of difobliging fome of his cuftomers ; and fo only expoftulated mildly with them, inftead of flying out into fcurrility and abufe, as he had done on the former occafion.

" This rebuff damped the ardour of his public fpirit fo far, that there happening to be a law-fuit at that time between that town and the next, about the bounds of their feveral commons on a barren heath, and all the inhabitants not agreeing in their opinions of the town-clerk's manner of carrying it on, and applying the revenu s of the corporation, as is always the cafe, in fuch affairs, he-refolved to change fides, as all great men have done, and offer him that affiitance which the others had before refufed to take, againft him.

' To

" To this purpose he drew up a pompous epistle, which he got the schoolmaster of the town to write out fair, and correct the spelling of; and putting on his Sunday coat, went to deliver it himself, as the surest messenger: but the town-clerk not being at home, he was forced to leave it with his maid, saying he would call next morning for an answer.

" He went accordingly in the highest expectation; but you may judge what was his disappointment, when he was told, that it was impossible for him to see his worship, his shoes being just then carried to the cobler's to be mended, so that he could not come down stairs to him.

" A wise man is never dejected at a disappointment, and often turns a misfortune to his advantage in the end. Our hero thought this an excellent opportunity for getting his worship's custom in the way of his trade; from which he promised himself more solid advantage, than any he could expect from his first scheme. As soon as he received this account therefore, he went directly home, and prepared another epistle, in which he informed his worship, that hearing he had had the misfortune the day before to have one of his shoes rip, he thought it his duty to inform him, that he had discovered a method of mending shoes, that effectually secured them from such accidents ever after, which he was ready to practise upon his worship's, or even to communicate to his cobler, whenever he pleased to consult with him upon the affair. And as a proof of the excellence of this invention, he farther told him, that he had tried it with great success upon his own shoes, which had been

made

made of such bad stuff originally, that they were bursting out every moment; so that he was generally confined two days in the week, patching them up, before he had the good fortune to make this discovery; since which they stood so well, that he did not fear but they would last out their time with satisfaction: and lastly, to enhance the value of this offer, he added in a postscript, that he was the cobler who had been driven out of such a village, by the malice of a parcel of scoundrels, and now kept a shoemaker's shop in that town, where he did not doubt but his talent of speaking would be as serviceable to his worship, by bringing over the mob to his side, as it had been terrible to the others.

" This letter also he carried himself, as he had done the former; and to encourage the maid to deliver it carefully to her master, gave her a pinch of snuff out of his own box, telling her, as before, that he would call again for an answer.

" But cunningly as this scheme was laid, the success fell quite short of his expectation; for the next time he called, the maid returned him both his letters, telling him that her master thanked him for his kind offers, but had no occasion for them at that time; and was beside so very busy just then, that he could not have the pleasure of taking a cup of ale with him, but should be glad of his company some other day.

" It is impossible to express the rage into which this affronting repulse threw him. He returned directly to his former principles of patriotism, and railed at the town-clerk with as much virulence as the most interested of his enemies.                          " Though

" Though modesty is a virtue praised by every body, the quality directly opposite to it is much oftener successful in the world. This was exactly the case with this person. There was nothing, however desperate, in the way of his trade, that he would not undertake, and promise to perform with the greatest confidence, not in the least discouraged or abashed by the many miscarriages he met with. It must be acknowledged, at the same time, that by thus indiscriminately undertaking every thing, he sometimes happened to cobble up a breach, which much abler hands would never have attempted.

" But this was far from proving his having any real merit, any superior skill in his trade, or recommending him to the custom of persons of prudence and consideration ; as among such a number of attempts, it was next to impossible but some should succeed. However, he plumed himself upon every accidental instance of success, as if he was the only one who understood any thing of his business ; and though he was no better than an interloper, as one may say, himself, and had never served a regular apprenticeship to the trade, he treated all his brethren with the utmost contempt and abuse, calling them ignorant pretenders, and blundering fools, who knew nothing of the business they professed.

" Though this conduct naturally disgusted every person of sense, the unthinking shallow crowd was pleased with it ; and taking his abuse of the rest of the craft, for a proof of his own superior skill, so many of them brought their shoes to his shop to be mended, that he

made

made a shift to live tolerably well; which was more than he could have expected, had he modestly waited to be recommended by his merit, and not proclaimed his own praises in this manner."

## CHAP. XII.

*Luck is all. He returns home, and triumphs over his enemies. Great discoveries in philosophy. His story concluded, and himself left in a fog.*

" IT is an old observation, that one lucky hit, no matter how accidental or improbable, oftener makes a man's fortune, than the best concerted scheme or greatest merit. Of this the hero of our tale had the happiness to be a most signal instance.

" One of the principal gentlemen of his own village happening to tear his shoe quite across one day when he was a great way from home, sent for several of the most eminent coblers and shoe-makers of the place to try to have it mended, but after many unsuccessful attempts, they all pronounced it beyond the reach of their art, to make it ever do again.

" As it was quite a new shoe, this gave the gentleman a good deal of vexation, and coming to the town where this person lived in his way home, he was prevailed upon to apply to him. Though his former knowledge of him gave him but a mean opinion of his skill, as the case was desperate he thought is no great matter to try what he could do; accordingly he sent for him,

D 4 who

who no sooner saw the shoe, and heard in what manner the others had attempted to mend it, than he at once pronounced them botchers in his usual stile, and, without the least hesitation, undertook to set it to rights; which he had the good luck to do so effectually, that the gentleman not only gave him half a crown for his trouble (which by the by, many thought to be more than the shoe was worth the first day) but also recommended him to all his acquaintances, so that he had as much business as he could possibly do.

"Could he have been contented, he was now in a fair way of doing very well; but the old lord of the manor where he had formerly lived happening to die, he prevailed upon this gentleman to use his interest with the heir to have the presentment of the court-leet withdrawn, and on obtaining his request left the business of his shop, and went back to his old trade of harranguing the mob, which he did so successfully, that at the next vestry they bore down the gentry by their numbers, and chose him churchwarden, in spight of all opposition.

"In this situation you behold him at present, boasting to his infatuated followers what great things he designs to do, for the good of the parish. But all this ease and confidence in his words and looks are nothing but affectation and grimace. He is sensible, now his having obtained the immediate object of his ambition has given him time to think, that he has climbed to the highest pinnacle of his popularity, from whence he must inevitably soon fall; as it is absolutely out of his power to perform the least part of his fine promises to his deluded party,
who

who will therefore hate and defpife him as ve-
hemently as they admired him before, the moment they find their difappointment.

" Much as a confcious apprehenfion of this
allays the pleafure of his prefent fuccefs, there is
another reflection which comes nearer to his
heart, and fills him with fears of a ftill feverer
nature.

" Though the bufinefs of his fhop, after
that lucky accident of fetting the gentleman's
fhoe to rights, was much more profitable to him
than he had any reafon to have expected, the
natural reftleffnefs, and vanity of his temper
prevented his making the proper advantage of
his good fortune, and providing for a reverfe,
by prudent œconomy : fo that all the horrors
of want already began to ftare him in the face,
as he can never expect the fame fuccefs where
he is at prefent, the better fort of people having,
moft of them taking juft offence at the infolence
of his prefent behaviour, as well as his former
abufe, and having befide no opinion of his fkill
in his trade, and his own party being too poor
to afford him any profit by their cuftom.

" Nor is this all. Provoked at the felf-fuffi-
ciency and arrogance with which he affects to
look down upon all his brethren of the craft,
the worfhipful company in the village where he
now lives have unanimoufly entered into a refolution never to confult with him, on any of
the affairs of their bufinefs, fuch as fixing the
price of leather and hog's briftles, and many
other things of equal importance, without he
will fubmit to be examined in the terms of their
myftery, which would not be likely to prove
much to his credit, as he never ferved an ap-

D 5 prenticefhip

prenticefhip to the bufinefs to learn them as they did; fo that he will be left to trade entirely upon his own judgment, which, befide the hazard and difcredit of it, will alfo lofe him many a good job, as there are feveral people fo fond of acting with due deliberation, that they will not have a crack in an old fhoe cobled without fummoning half a dozen of the moft eminent of the craft, to confult upon the matter.

" His freedom of the trade in general they do not deny, but, by a bye law of their own corporation, they have this power of refufing to confer with him, which they are determined to exert.

" It may be thought that their acting in this manner betrays a prejudice beneath fuch a grave and reputable fociety; but the truth is, they have abundant reafon to juftify their proceedings.

" To gain a reputation on his firft fetting up the fhoe-making trade, he had ventured hap-hazard to affert many things which were contrary to the common practice of his brethren, and reflected great difhonour on them, for having followed fuch abfurd opinions fo long.

" The principal of thofe, and that which he laid the greateft ftrefs upon, was a new difcovery he pretended to have made of *the cause of some particular water's tanning asses-hides better than others.* The fact had long been known to the whole craft, who managed their bufinefs accordingly, and fent their wares to thofe places, fatisfied with the effect, without giving themfelves the trouble of enquiring into the caufe.

" But

" But he looked upon this as beneath his fa-
gacity. He wrote a book, in which he demon-
ſtrated by many learned arguments and curiouˢ
experiments, that *water was water and not fire*;
and to give the greater weight to this important
diſcovery, he made a parade of going to all the
tanners yards about the country, where he
raked in the mud and filth of the common
ſhores, till he was almoſt ſuffocated by the
ſtench; and then proved to the entire ſatisfaction of the ignorant croud that ſtood gaping at
him, *that the ſcum which ſtuck to the ſides of the
ſhores was no longer floating in the water*, and
branded all his brethren of the craft with his
familiar titles of *fools* and *blockheads*, for not
having found out this important ſecret before.

" Such an opinion was beneath an anſwer.
But though his brethren did not think it
worth their while to enter into a diſpute
about nothing with one who gave poſitive
aſſertions for proofs, and anſwered rational
arguments with perſonal reflections, they reſolved to take the firſt fair opportunity of hum-
bling his pride, and ſhewing the world their
contempt of him, which they have now done
in a manner that he will not eaſily get over.

" You now ſee what a poor proſpect he has
of buſineſs in his trade, ſufficient to ſupport him
in the ſtate he aſſumes; but this is not his only
diſtreſs. *The common motive of patriotiſm is
the price for which a man can ſell himſelf and
his party*, to the lord, or ſteward of the manor,
whom he was raiſed on purpoſe to oppoſe.
This price is always in proportion to the oppoſition, which it is in the patriot's power to
give.

" But

" But unluckily for this perfon, his whole confequence depends upon the actual exertion of that oppofition, and muft inevitably ceafe the moment he attempts to drop it. This the fteward knows as well as himfelf; fo that his hopes from that quarter are effectually cut off, fhould his poverty prompt him to make the bafe attempt."

## C H A P. XIII.

*An odd way of expreffing favour or diflike. The hiftory of* THE COBLER *matched by that of* A CRIER.

" I SHOULD imagine (faid I, perceiving that my guide had finifhed his account of the cobler) that he has fomething to fear more immediately than want, which in a great meafure obviates the danger of that.

" You fay his deluded party will defpife him, Will they not do more? Will they not be provoked by fuch egregious abufe, to take perfonal revenge? To pull down his houfe over his head, and bury him in the ruins? or tear him limb from limb, the firft time they catch him in the ftreets? the mob is capable of any outrage, and here they have an appearance of reafon to juftify whatever they do.

" I think his cafe is really defperate, and that the only hope he can have of efcaping is to fly once more to the county town, and follow his trade. His ambition muft be pretty well cooled by this time, and therefore he will be able to

apply

apply diligently to his work, and may poſſibly earn an honeſt and comfortable livelihood."

" To unexperienced reaſon (anſwered the ſpirit) your remark appears juſt. But better knowledge of the ways of man ſhews that ſuch fear is quite unneceſſary. Did the people expreſs their reſentment in the manner you mention, it is moſt certain that they would not be ſo often abuſed as they are by pretended patriots. An example or two of the kind would effectually put a ſtop to that trade, how lucrative ſoever it is, which would be a real advantage to the community in general. But the remedy might be attended with conſequences more dangerous than the diſeaſe. Would the mob, if once permitted to take the power thus into their own hands, never riſe but on ſuch occaſions? would they lay it down when their end is anſwered, and go no farther? would not the beſt members of the ſtate be involved in the ſame danger, on every miſcarriage in their meaſures, though impoſſible to have been prevented by human means. The mob is a many headed monſter, that muſt be kept in ſubjection, or it will become the moſt inſupportable of all tyrants. It knows no mean, and therefore muſt not be truſted with power.

" But as to theſe people, they have been ſo often impoſed upon in this manner before, that the abuſe is become familiar to them, and they will not even feel it after the firſt moment, and then too their reſentment will ſpend itſelf in ſcurrility and invectives, levelled oftener againſt faults in the perſon's private character, than his abuſe of them.

" Indeed

" Indeed nothing can be more ridiculous than the manner in which they exprefs their fentiments on fuch occafions. *While a man is their favourite, they are continually getting drunk with drinking his health, when he is out of favour with them they get drunk with drinking his confufion*; a bumper toaft in either cafe being the higheft, and often the only mark of their approbation or diflike.

" Nay fo far are they from harbouring a dangerous refentment, even for the groffeft ill-ufage of this kind, that, if the party has procured money enough to give them plenty of drink by the very fale of themfelves, they forget all that has happened, and flock to him, with as much pleafure as if he were their greateft benefactor.

" Strange as this conduct may appear, every day's experience furnifhes inftances of it ; but of the many which mark the character of the prefent age, the moft glaring is that of the perfon whom you fee in yonder clofet, fpurning the enfigns of grandeur from him, with an air of diffatisfaction, that fhews their infufficiency to procure their owner happinefs. His whole life is fo ftrong a fatire on this particular folly of patriotifm, that a fhort view of it can not be improper.

" He was born in this manor, where his anceftors, who were but peafants, acquired fo confiderable a property by their honeft induftry, as enabled them to make a better appearance than many of the gentry.

" When he came into poffeffion of his fortune, he lived in fo hofpitable and genteel a manner, that he was greatly liked by his neighbours

bours of all ranks, who never fufpected that his
generofity was ultimately fubfervient to the moft
enterprizing ambition; but a lucky event fecured
his hopes before they difcovered, and could
take any meafures to defeat them.

" There happened to be at that time a vaga-
bond-fellow in the next county, who pretended
a claim to the lord of this manor's whole eftate,
which he talked of going to law to recover, as
foon as he could raife money to fupport the fuit,
for he was himfelf very poor, and lived upon
the charity of one or two great folks, who
maintained him rather to plague the lord, than
from any perfonal regard to himfelf, or opinion
of the juftice of his claim.

" The lord was convinced of his own right,
and very well able to fupport it. However, to
prevent trouble, he gave notice to all his tenants not to give his adverfary any affiftance on
pain of forfeiting their leafes, in which there
was a claufe exprefly to that purpofe.

" But this did not hinder fome defperate fellows, who had ran out their fortunes in whoring
and gaming, or were upon their keeping for
deer-ftealing, and fuch illegal practices, from
joining with him underhand, in hopes that if
he fhould recover the eftate, he might be eafily
prevailed upon, in return for their fervices, not
only to forgive their offences, but alfo to rein-
ftate them in their farms, or grant them leafes
of thofe which belonged to the friends of his
opponent.

" Such a combination naturally alarmed all
thofe who were in the intereft of the prefent
lord, efpecially as it was headed by a very bold-
fpirited turbulent fellow, one of the principal
gentry

gentry of the parish, who had just before ran
away with the wife of one of his neighbours ;
and therefore, though he bullied the husband into compliance, could not expect to live in quiet under a landlord who was remarkably strict
in the execution of the laws.

" This was a fair opportunity for one of such
an enterprizing spirit as this person before us, to
ingratiate himself effectually with the lord of
the manor. Nor did he fail to improve it ; for
putting himself at the head of his family, and
all those whom his hospitality had attached to
him, he drove that gentleman, great a bully as
he was, quite out of the parish.

" So signal a piece of service did not remain
long unrewarded. The CRIER *of the court-leet*
happening to die just then, he was unanimously
chosen into his place the next court-day ; and
the lord thought him so firm in his interest, that
he not only approved of his tenant's choice,
but also made him CLERK *of his own kitchen* the
very next vacancy.

" In this situation of crier he conducted himself
with such address, that he was able to put only those
he pleased on the grand-jury, and by that means
frequently to oppose the steward himself in
things which he knew to be disagreeable to the
parish : at the same time managing matters so
artfully, that he never absolutely broke with him,
nor gave him reason sufficient to justify his
turning him out of his clerkship ; having always some plausible excuse to palliate what he
did, and professing the highest fidelity and attachment to the lord's service, which he took
every occasion of promoting, that he thought
would not injure him, in the opinion of the
people.    5                    " The

" The popularity and power which he acquired by this conduct was far from being agreeable to many of his neighbours, particularly of the better sort, who did not like to see a man whom they looked upon as their inferior rise over their heads in such a manner, that they were become no better than mere cyphers in the parish, not being able to make a petty constable, or get a presentment for mending a road, or even making a stile, without being first obliged to cringe to him for his consent.

## CHAP. XIV.

*Set one knave to catch another. An instance of moderation as much out of course as in character. The parson swallows a sugar-plumb, and does what he is bid like a good child.*

" AT length one of the gentry, a cunning old fellow, who knew the world and all its ways well, resolved to try if he could not supplant him in the favour of the people, by making him appear a favourite of the lord's; after which he knew it would not be difficult to do his business with him also, who was already far from being well pleased with his conduct.

" Accordingly he employed emissaries to insinuate to the parishioners, when their heads were hot with liquor at fares and wakes, that it was imprudent in them, to put themselves so much in the power of a person who held so profitable a place under the lord of the manor

as clerk of the kitchen, as he would not fail
to give up their interest, on any great occasion, for fear of being turned out of his employment.

"These infinuations soon came to the crier's
ears, who, without waiting to let the people
ruminate upon the matter, went among them
directly, as if he knew nothing of what had
passed ; and took occasion to tell them, in the
course of his conversation, that he had accepted
of the clerkship, only that he might be able to
serve them more effectually, by taking care that
the provisions, which they were obliged by their
tenures, to supply for the support of the lord's
house, were not embezzled privately by the fervants, and they put to the expence of more ;
and, as a proof of the advantage of this care, he
assured them, that many a time, when the lord
had given some of his hungry followers a letter
to him, to get a basket of broken victuals, he
had returned for answer, that there was scarce
enough for the family, and so sent the beggars
away with empty bellies.

"This artful turn gave the affair quite another look. They implicitly believed every word
he said ; so that he foiled his enemy, cunning
as he was, at his own weapons, and made the
attack, designed to have over-turned him, serve
to establish his interest more firmly.

"But this disappointment did not discourage
the other, who now had new motives for striving
to get him out of favour ; for having married
two of his sons to the steward's daughters, he
judged that if he could contrive to have the
crier turned out, it would not be difficult for
him to get the younger, who was a fine pro-
                                        mising

mifing lad, and fond of living at home among his friends, chofen in his ftead; by which means the management of the whole manor would come into the hands of his family, feveral of his relations, who all depended upon him, having good employments under the fteward already.

" But how to effect this was the queftion; for the crier's popularity feemed fo firmly eftablifhed, that it appeared dangerous even to attempt any thing againft him. After much deliberation, he refolved, as the method moft likely to fucceed, to fet up a rival againft him for the people's favour; and then he did not doubt, but their own ficklenefs would foon make them quit their old engagements and readily enter into new.

" Nor was he long at a lofs whom to fix upon as moft proper for his defign. The old parfon of the parifh dying fuddenly one day juft after eating an hearty dinner of pork and peafepudding, the lord gave the living to a young man who had lately come into the parifh with the fteward.

" A particular circumftance made this choice very difagreeable to many of the principal parifhioners. The greateft part of the income of the living confifted in the rents of a large quantity of glebe land, which was let out in parcels to feveral people for a certain number of years.

" The leafes, by which thefe farms were held, were never fuffered to run out; for as the parfons were only tenants for life, they had no great regard to their fucceffors; and had therefore come into a method of renewing the leafes

at

at particular times, in confideration of a ftated
fum of money, which was clear gain to them.
By thefe means the tenants looked upon the
lands as their own inheritance ; and had built
houfes, and fettled themfelves upon them accordingly.

" But the late parfon, thinking they had too
great bargains, refufed to renew their leafes at
the ufual time, unlefs they would give him
much higher fines than they had ever given to
any of his predeceffors ; which they refolved
not to do, imagining that as he was very old as
well as very avaritious, the fear of dying without getting any thing would make him abate of
his demand.

" In this manner things ftood for fome years,
neither party chufing to comply, when the
death of the old parfon, and his being fucceeded
by one whofe youth gave him a reafonable expectation of feeing their leafes determined,
when it would be in his power either to turn
them out, or raife their rents to the full value,
alarmed them all in the higheft degree.

" To prevent fuch a misfortune therefore,
they directly agreed to offer their new parfon
the fum which had been demanded by his pre-
deceffor, and which they had always fo pofitively refufed to give him. But what was their
aftonifhment when, inftead of accepting their
offer, he cooly told them, he thought the income of the living, as fettled by the incumbent
immediately before the laft, was fufficient,
wherefore he defired no more ; and prayed to
God to enable him to make as good ufe of that
as he had done.

" Such

" Such an act of true generosity, not only won the hearts of those who reaped the benefit of it, but also gained him the general esteem of the whole parish ; especially as he lived entirely amongst them, and spent his income in the most unbounded hospitality ; not hoarding it up, or laying it out in other places, as most of his predecessors had been accustomed to do.

" On him the crier's enemy pitched, as a proper person to rival him in the favour of the people ; accordingly, having gained his good opinion by going constantly to church, and behaving there with a great appearance of devotion, he took an opportunity one day to insinuate to him, that he ought to exert himself more than he did in the affairs of the parish, and not tamely submit to the usurpations of the crier, who was for engrossing all the power into his own hands, without ever regarding whose right he invaded.

" These insinuations were not without effect. The parson's heart, though above avarice, was not insensible to ambition. He readily took the bait ; and, as he was quite unexperienced in such affairs, submitted himself implicitly to the government of his adviser, who, while he pretended to have nothing but to restore him to the consequence due to his station and virtues, in view, really made a property of him to promote his own schemes.

CHAP.

❀❀❀❀❀❀❀❀❀❀❀❀❀❀❀❀❀❀❀

## CHAP. XV.

*A game of football. A false step gives the crier the better of the match. He kicks the ball in his master's face, but makes all up, and comes off with flying colours.*

" T H E regard with which the parson began to be spoken of by the whole parish soon gave the crier the alarm; which was confirmed by his opposing him in two or three trifling things in the vestry ; in which his opinion was received with such deference, that it was probable he would have risen fairly above him in a little time, had not fortune, the crier's constant friend, stood by·him effectually on this occasion.

" A friend of the parson's had been appointed by the steward, to repair and set up a parcel of scarecrows, to frighten their neighbours cattle from trespassing on their common ; for which purpose, the court-leet had ordered him a sum of money out of the parish stock.

" Such commissions had usually been given as a plausible colour for bestowing so much money, without any design of their being executed. In this sense, did this person understand his ; and accordingly gave himself no trouble about the performance of it.

" The crier, who had connived at many things of the kind before, immediately took fire at this, and resolved to prosecute the man for embezzling the money of the parish.

" For

" For this he had many reasons: he knew that an action, which had such an appearance of public spirit and justice, would greatly repair his credit with the people, which he could not but be sensible was on the decline; and then, as the parson's intimacy with the delinquent would probably make him take his part, he thought that would be a favourable opportunity for giving a check to his growing popularity.

" Nor was he mistaken in his conjectures. The parson, in the warmth of his heart, not only espoused his friend himself, but also engaged all his party to support him, without ever considering that appearances were so strongly against him, that every one, who was not in the secret of such affairs, must harbour a disadvantageous opinion of himself for abetting such an action.

" Accordingly, the next court-day the crier made his attack, and displayed the heinousness of such a flagrant act of injustice to the public in so strong a light, that the mob, who never examine more than one side of a story, were all of his party; so that the parson was not only foiled in his attempt to save his friend, but also entirely lost his credit with the people, who, in the phrenzy of their resentment, loaded him with every scandal and execration, which the most envenomed malice could invent.

" This affair effectually restored the crier's credit; but though he had succeeded in this first object of his design, it was attended with consequences he had not foreseen, and which were far from being agreeable to him.

" The steward, who had appointed the parson's friend to the employment which had in-

volved

volved him in this difgrace, thought it incum-, bent upon him to fupport him in conjunction with the parfon ; and when the crier had carried his point againft them both, reprefented the affair to the lord of the manor, as an infult upon his authority, and a certain mark of difaffection to his intereft. ।

" The crier, who meant nothing lefs than to have embroiled himfelf with the lord, or even with the fteward, was furprifed at this charge. However, he had gone too far to think of retreating now ; and therefore refolved to oppofe their meafures in good earneft the firft time they feemed to clafh with the rights or intereft of the people, which he knew to be the certain way to fecure his party to him, as it would make them all as defperate as himfelf.

" This he did not long want an opportunity of doing. There had been a fum of money raifed by the court-leet fome time before, to defray the charge of repairing the manorhoufe, of which there remained a good part unexpended, there having been more levied than was neceffary for the occafion.

" As it had been the cuftom of this manor to give money to the lord himfelf on thefe occafions to lay out as he thought proper, he had always appropriated any furplus that remained to his own ufe, without thinking himfelf accountable to the court-leet for it : but now the crier, who, by his place of clerk of the kitchen, had an opportunity of looking into all the lord's accounts, finding that the fum was pretty confiderable, propofed to the court-leet to lay it out, in difcharging the bills of fome poor tradefmen which had been left unpaid on a former occafion,

cafion, and to whom the whole manor had
paffed their words; and to this effect he drew
up an addrefs to the lord.

"Though this was a direct attack upon the
lord, and in a moft tender point, there was
fomething fo plaufible in the propofal, that he
did not chufe abfolutely to reject it. However,
not to give up too much, or eftablifh a precedent for fuch attempts for the future, he gave
general orders to the court-leet, to pay off thofe
tradefmen with that money as of his own free
motion, and without taking any notice of the
application, which it had made to him to that
purpofe.

"But the crier, perceiving the defign of this
proceeding, refufed to accept thofe orders, and
infifted abfolutely on having the authority of
the court-leet to difpofe of the money allowed,
in which his old fupport the mob followed his
opinion fo firmly, that the orders were rejected
in fpight of all the parfon and fteward both
could do to prevent it.

"Such a triumph filled the mob with the
moft extravagant joy. They extolled the crier
to the fkies for his public fpirit and fidelity to
their intereft; and were drunk for a whole
week with drinking bumpers to his health,
while they offered every kind of infult to his opponents, particularly the parfon, and branded
them with the moft infamous and improbable
crimes.

"But though the lord had not been able to
make them receive his orders with due refpect,
he refolved to fhew them, that he would have
them obeyed without regard to their oppofition.

"Ac-

" Accordingly, he ordered his receiver to pay the money in difpute to thofe people, and take their receipts for it of his own mere authority, without defigning to confult the courtleet any more about the matter; and, to fhew his refentment to the crier, turned him directly out of his clerkfhip, as he did all his friends out of the feveral employments they had in the manor under his fteward, giving them to the friends of the parfon, and of the gentleman who firft ftirred him up againft the crier.

" The latter was now at the higheft pinnacle of popular glory; the idol of the mob, and the apparent victim of the perfidy and oppreffion of his enemies.

' " But he knew the world too well to be content with fuch an unfubftantial phantom as the favour of a mob. He had laboured all his life, it was true, with indefatigable affiduity to arrive at this point; but he foon fhewed he had other views than thofe he pretended; and that all his profeffions of regard and attachment to the good of the parifh, were only lures to draw in the giddy multitude to truft themfelves fo implicitly in his power, that he might be able to get the price he defired for betraying them when he faw a proper time.

" Accordingly, upon fome hints of his intentions, the lord fent a new fteward to take care of the eftate, the former one having been made difagreeable to the tenants, by the violence and over-bearing of fome of his fervants, who had not fpirit to fupport what they faid, when they were called to account for it, though he was himfelf a good-natured eafy kind of man

5                                                    in

in the main, and had formerly been very well liked by them.

" The new steward and the crier soon came to a proper understanding over an hearty bottle, of which they were both remarkably fond; and the latter bargained to sell his friends, and resign his criers place, in consideration of being made an esquire, and getting a salary to support him suitably to his new dignity.

" It is impossible to express the rage of the mob, at seeing that they had been so long the dupes of his designs. They got drunk for a week together with drinking to his confusion, made scurrilous ballads against him and his family, and loaded him, in his turn, with execrations and abuse.

" But a new patriot standing forth to engage their attention, they forgot the crier, and went on in their old way with as much eagerness and credulity, as if they had never been deceived.

" As for the parson, his polite friend served him nearly in the same manner as the crier did the mob. As soon as his turn was served, and his son chosen into the crier's place, chiefly by the assistance of the parson's friends, he not only dropped his acquaintance, but even gave him up to the crier's resentment; who had privately made it a part of his bargain that he should be struck out of the *quorum*, in revenge for the trouble and expence he had put him to in the course of this affair.

" As the old crier has been so successful in all his schemes, I see you wonder how he came into this place; but if you consider that vanity and an absurd ambition of being made a gentleman, were the original, the leading motives of

• all

all his labours, you will acknowledge that the egregious folly of the end, takes off all merit from the means, and makes his succefs ridiculous.

" Nor is he infenfible of this himfelf now that it is too late. Though the unthinking mean fpirited mob have forgot his abufe of them, and croud to his table to eat his meat and drink his wine, with as much readinefs and pleafure as if their own and their family's intereft had not been fold by him to purchafe them; the reproaches of his own heart embitter his enjoyment of their company, and make their proteffions of refpect naufeous. He pines for his former popularity; and, unhappy in the accomplifhment of his hopes, finds too late, that the end of all his labours is vanity."

## C H A P. XVI.

*Muzzle a bear, or he'll bite you. Three remarkable characters. Boys that play tricks fhould beware of tell-tales.*

I WAS, by this time, fo fick of patriotifm and public fpirit, that, as foon as my guide ftopped, I refolved to beg that he would change the fubject, to fomething more deferving of the obfervation of a rational being.

" Enough, moft judicious fpirit! (faid I) enough haft thou faid to prove the juftice of thy remark. In every rank of life, I fee the fame caufes produce the fame effects. *Coblers* and *criers* differ but in name: but furely it muft be otherwife in higher fcenes, where the great
affairs

affairs of nations are tranfacted. The mind muft be extended in proportion to the greatnefs of the fubjects upon which it is employed, and can never look down to the trifles which engrofs the attention of paultry villagers. Let us therefore turn away fron this fcene of drunkennefs and folly, and feek for matter more worthy of our obfervation elfewhere.

" I will indulge you; (anfwered my guid.) but you will find little advantage in the change of place. Folly reigns every where alike, and more exalted ftations only make it more ridiculous : and luckily a fcene prefents itfelf to our view, which fhews this in the moft ftriking light.

" Turn your eye this way.---You fee thofe three perfons yonder. They are juft entering into a conference upon one of the moft extraordinary fubjects that ever fhewed the inconfiftency of human actions. We will hear it from themfelves ; but firft, while they make the common preface of empty compliments, and unmeaning queftions, which are made the introduction to converfation even on the moft important fubjects, I will give you a fhort fketch of their lives as far as is neceffary to make you underftand what they fay.

" They were born in different manors belonging to the lord who owns that in which the crier made fuch a figure ; but their being educated together at the fame free-fchool gave rife to an intimacy which has grown up with them through life.

" When they were taken from fchool they were put to different profeffions, as intereft or nclination directed. He on the right chofe

E 3            the

the law, in which the acuteneſs of his genius
enabled him to make ſuch a proficiency, that in
time he was entruſted to ſearch for informations
againſt ſuch perſons as treſpaſſed on the lord's
demeſne, or killed his game, and to ſue them
and the tenants who did not pay their rents
punctually.

" This employment was not only very profitable in itſelf, but alſo gave him an appearance
of ſo great conſequence in the court-leet, that
he was generally on one ſide or the other in
every private diſpute that aroſe in the manor.

" The next, as you ſee by his habit, was
bred to the church, in which he laboured ſo
ſucceſsfully, that he got a good vicarage before
he was very old, and, having the character of
being a great ſcholar, was alſo prefered to the
honourable employment of teaching the lord of
the manor's ſon and heir his letters.

" As for the third, he was too idle to take
to any particular profeſſion : but, by the intereſt
of his friends he got into the ſteward's office,
where he had ſeveral petty employments, which
brought him in a good penny in the whole.

" But this was not all. Having always
ſhewn a remarkable turn for making bawbles
and nick-nacks, and being a perfect maſter of
the punctilios of dreſs and addreſs, and all
the other accompliſhments of a ſmall genius,
he was choſen as a proper perſon to provide rat-
tles and paper-kites for his young maſter, and to
teach him to cock his hat, and ride his hobby
horſe with a good grace.

" As they were all known to be very well
qualifed for theſe important places, there was
no objection made to their being honoured with
them,

them; and they executed their several charges with proper dignity and care. But an unlucky affair soon happened, that threatened not only the loss of their present employments, but also to prevent their being ever entrusted with any other.

" You may remember I told you there was a fellow who pretended a right to all the estates of this lord. His family came originally from the manor in which the lawyer was born, and where most of the inhabitants had a strong attachment to him, both as they were naturally very proud, and thought it would be a great honour to them to have their townsman made lord of the manor, and also that they flattered themselves with the hopes of getting good farms from him, in some of his other manors, in case he could make good his pretensions; for they were all as poor as they were proud.

" Beside, there was another reason for their desiring to change their land-lord. Before the estate came into the possession of the present lord, they had been accustomed to have their landlord live among them, and hold his courts and receive suit and service in this manor. But this lord, having many better houses to live in, had removed his habitation; and of course discontinued those ceremonies, so that they lost all that parade of grandeur in which their pride had taken such pleasure.

" Now, as this fellow founded his pretensions on being descended from the family of their old lords they expected that he would come and live among them, as they had done; or at least restore them their court-leets, and all their ceremonies and perquisites again, never considering that the employments and places of honour and

E 4                profit,

profit, which they held in the other eſtates of the preſent lord yielded them more than the en-tire income of their manor.

" It is not ſtrange therefore that the lawyer ſhould have received an early biaſs in his fa-vour; which was alſo confirmed by his being educated at that free-ſchool, the maſter and uſhers of which were all notorious for the ſame principles, and took all poſſible pains to inſtil them into their pupils, in which they were not unſucceſsful, with the lawyer's two friends as well as with many others,

" It happened in ſome little time after they were preferred to thoſe employments above-men-tioned, that a perſon who had formerly been very intimate with them all three, having been educated at the ſame ſchool along with them, ſaid, among a mixt company in the unguarded openneſs of converſation, when wine removes all reſerve, that he had once little thought of their being ever put into places of ſuch confi-dence under the lord of the manor, as he had often ſeen them, on their bare knees, drink con-fuſion to him and all his friends, and ſucceſs to the hopes of his enemy.

" There was ſomething ſo ſingular in this ſpeech, that it ſtruck all the company with ſur-prize; but one gentleman in particular, who was warmly attached to the lord's intereſt, de-ſired all preſent to take notice of what this per-ſon had ſaid, as he was reſolved to put him to the proof of it, it being as baſe in him to throw thoſe aſperſions on the characters of perſons of ſuch note, if they were innocent, as it would be criminal in all who heard him to conceal an affair of ſuch conſequence, in caſe they were guilty.                    " Thunder-

" Thunder-ſtruck at this, the other who had no intention of turning informer againſt his friends, and had only ſaid it in the courſe o fgeneral chat, ſtrove to evade the ſubject, and give the diſcourſe ſome other turn, hoping that the gentleman would think no more of it ; but finding that he would not be put off ſo, but perſiſted in his reſolution, he appealed to the ſanction of private converſation, where all that was ſaid had ever been held ſacred, and the diſcloſing of a ſyllable accounted a breach of the laws of ſociety, and that mutual confidence which alone makes it a bleſſing.

" To this the gentleman anſwered that he was neither ignorant of, nor deſigned to infringe upon theſe laws ; but that here a ſuperior duty intervened and ſuperſeded them ; nothing private being to be put in competition with the welfare of the public which he thought to be concerned in this affair.

## C H A P. XVII.

*A bad excuſe is better than none. The advantage*
*of a friend in court. A maxim in law ſolves*
*all.*

" ACcordingly he went the very next morning and informed the lord of the whole matter, who called all his principal ſervants together, to conſult what was proper to be done in this caſe ; for as it concerned his own family particularly, he would not act without advice, that he should not be suspected of partiality, who all agreed that it ought to be enquired into with the greatest strictness.

" On this the person who had undesignedly given the information was brought before them, when he gave such a vague account of the affair, that the lawyer, who was appointed by the other two, to speak for them all, as best qualified by his profession to defend a bad cause, thought it the best way not to deny the charge directly, but to strive to turn it off, by saying it was not impossible but they might have played such foolish tricks, when they were boys at school, but that the conduct of his whole life ever since he came to man's estate was a sufficient proof of the sincerity of his attachment to his lord ; and, to confirm this, he instanced his having prosecuted with the greatest vigour, several of the parish in which he was born, and even some of his own family, for this very offence with which he was now so absurdly charged, since he came into his present employment.

" Plausible as this defence was, the gentleman judged from the manner in which the story had been originally told, that there must be more in it ; he therefore insisted that the person who had told it should declare positively, and without prevarication or reserve, whether he had ever known them drink those toasts since they left school ? where ? and on what occasions ?

" These questions were too close to be evaded. He was therefore obliged, in defence of his own character, which was now at stake, to declare the whole ; accordingly he said that he

had

had heard them drink them several times, at the
house of an haberdasher of small wares, who
kept a shop in the county-town, where for
many years they used to meet constantly twice
or thrice a week, and indulge themselves in the
most sanguine professions of those principles
over their wine; who was so strongly attached
to that person himself, and so well persuaded of
their attachment to him also, that when he came
to die, he bequeathed his real estate, which was
very considerable, to the lawyer, with handsome
legacies to the other two, leaving him (the informer) but a meer trifle, as he doubted his
being staunch to the cause; and, as a confirma-
tion of what he said, added that the settlement
which the lawyer had since made upon his wife
at his marriage was of that very estate which
the haberdasher had left him.

"This gave a different face to the whole affair. The lawyer in particular gave himself
up for ruined, and would gladly have com-
pounded for the loss, not only of his present
employment, but also of all farther hopes.

"But he had better luck. The majority
of the servants, who had been called into consultation upon the affair, did not think it prudent to establish a precedent for looking so far
back, and one of them particularly, who had
been bred to the law himself, said "that this es-
"tate should be considered as a fee, given by the
"haberdasher to his lawyer, and that it was an
"established rule that a lawyer should say any
"thing that his client desired for his *fee*, without
"being called in question for it; for if it were
"otherwise, and lawyers made answerable for
"what they said, there would be an end to the

business

" bufinefs at once, as the great art and myftery,
" of it confifted in faying any thing that might
" any way conduce to carrying the point, with-
" out regard to decency, truth, or any fuch
" immaterial confiderations : whereas if gentle-
" men of the law were to be called to account
" for what they faid in the way of their bufinefs,
" and for their fee, no one would ever undertake
" a weak caufe, and fo the profeffion would fall
" to the ground. Befide, it was a point agreed
" upon, in all the books, that what a lawyer fays
" for his fee, is never to be confidered as his pri-
" vate fentiment or opinion ; elfe how could law-
" yers rail at, and abufe their moft intimate
" friends, in the mannerthey do every-day, for
" a ftrangerthey know nothing of, and in a caufe
" they are convinced to be wrong, without
" breaking with them, or giving them the leaft
" offence ; as an inftance of which, he added that
" he had himfelf often gone directly from court
" to dine with the man whom he had fpent the
" whole morning in abufing ; therefore no man
" was to be called to account for what he faid
" for his fee : and this opinion he fupported by
" a ftring of quotations from all the grave and
" learned fages of the law ; and by the con-
" ftant and uniform practice of the profeffion
" from time immemorial, to this very day."

" So learned a defence faved the delinquents,
for it would have been unjuft to have made a
diftinction between them. The majority of
the fervants (as I faid) therefore gave it as their
opinion, that the accufation, *though not falfe*,
was malicious, frivolous, and unworthy of farther notice.

" Thus blew over a ftorm, in which their
very friends expected they would have funk.

On

On the contrary, the lawyer was soon after made a juſtice of the peace and deputy to the ſeneſchal of the principal manor, the parſon got a better living, and the hobby-horſe-man on his pupil's growing too big for his care, was prefered by his beſt friend the ſteward to be his head clerk, which places they all enjoy at preſent; while the poor informer drew upon himſelf ſuch univerſal conrempt for his indiſcretion, that he was never able to ſhew his face after."

## CHAP. XVIII.

*Modern modeſty and gratitude. Companions are odious. A good memory often makes a bad companion. It is prudent to make hay while the ſun ſhines.*

" IT might be imagined that after ſuch an affair their preſent preferment ſhould ſatisfy their ambition. But far from it, emboldened by that eſcape, they think there is nothing which they may not do, and the favour that has been ſhewn them ſince, inſtead of making them contented and grateful, has given them ſuch an high opinion of their own merit, which they modeſtly judge to have been the reaſon for it, that they reckon all they have got as nothing while there is any thing elſe for them to deſire, and look upon themſelves as ill-treated, if they are refuſed whatever they pleaſe to aſk.———— But ſoft!————Their conference at length begins.————Let us attend.————

2 " I ſay

" I say, sir (said the lawyer, fire sparkling in
his eyes) that I am ill-used. Had there been
any objection to my abilities to fill such an
employment, or could it have been even pretended that the person who is put over my
head, was superior to me in any respect, it
would have been another case; but, to be continued a deputy, where I had so good a right to
be made principal, is not to be borne. Nor
will I bear it. No man provokes me with impunity.——"

" Really, sir (answered the parson) I cannot but own you have some reason to complain. But what would you say, if you were
in my place? To be taken no notice of where
there were so many opportunities! so many
better livings vacant! it is enough to provoke
the patience of *Job*. After all the pains I have
taken to teach him to read, and my care in
chusing out such lessons as were proper for him,
that he might not receive wrong notions of
things, to be slighted in this manner; it is too
much! He could not have served his former
tutor worse, who was turned off for teaching
him to spell in that profane ballad. But there
is no such thing as gratitude, no regard to past
services, to be found in this world!"

" Indeed, gentlemen (added the third, while
his reverence stopped to take a pinch of snuff,
and the lawyer was walking about the room in
a violent chafe) we are all extremely ill-used.
But you must both allow, that I have much
the greatest reason to complain. You have got
places which afford you a comfortable subsistence,
and if they are not quite so good as you could
wish, you have this satisfaction that they cannot be taken from you.                          " But

" But that is not my cafe. I may be turned
out of the poor pittance I have got, without a
moment's warning, as it is moſt probable I ſhall
ſoon find to my ſorrow, whenever the old ſteward dies. And this is all the reward I have received for the many weary hours I have ſpent
at chuck and puſh-pin with the young heir,
and teaching him to buckle his ſhoes right, and
put on his hat with an air. We have all reaſon to complain, but my cafe is certainly the
hardeſt."

" Your cafe, (replied the lawyer, with a
ſmile of indignant contempt) pray what is your
cafe, good ſir? The paultry menial ſervices you
did about his perſon have been ſufficiently rewarded. Common ſervants ſhould not aſſume
ſuch airs, nor pretend to put themſelves on a
level with their ſuperiors."—

" Paultry menial ſervices! (interrupted the
other, kindling into a rage) I'd have you to
know, ſir, that my ſervices were not paultry ;
and perhaps they give me a better right to expect
favour than any which ſome others can boaſt of,
highly as they may think of themſelves. But
I ſhould be glad to know in what your great
merit has conſiſted, that you are ſo ready to call
that of another in queſtion."

" My merit, ſir, (anſwered the lawyer, taking
fire) my merit, ſir, has conſiſted and does conſiſt,
in my ability in my profeſſion, which has enabled me to do the moſt eſſential ſervice."——
" Service!——To whom? (interrupted the o-
ther dryly) to yourſelf only. Your abilities,
were they ten times greater than they are, have
been amply rewarded by the place you enjoy,
and the large ſums of money they have brought
you

you in from your deluded clients. But pray, ſage ſir, what important ſervice have your great abilities been of to his lordſhip, that he ſhould be under ſuch obligations to you ? I ſhould be glad to know that." -.

" What ſervice ! (replied the lawyer haſtily, being almoſt put off his guard, by ſuch a croſs queſtion) what ſervice do you aſk, ſir ! Sir, I think it beneath me to anſwer a queſtion that betrays ſuch ignorance. But, if you do not know, they did who gave me the employments I hold ; and they knew beſide that my promotion ſecured my whole family. My countrymen always ſtick faſt by one another."

" Hah ! hah ! hah ! great ſervices ! very great ſervices, truly (ſaid the other) I am really aſhamed to hear a man who ſhould know better, mention ſuch things. I am indeed. But you muſt be blinded, quite blinded by your opinion of yourſelf, or you would never attempt to put them in competition with the ſervices I have done his lordſhip, in the inſtruction of his ſon's tender youth."——

" How, ſir ! (interrupted the parſon, who had hitherto liſtened to their diſpute as unmoved as if it had been a viſitation-ſermon, where ſome country curate pretends to teach his betters their duty) you inſtruct his tender youth ! Pray, ſir, have more regard to truth in what you ſay. The inſtruction of his youth was committed to other kind of hands than yours. It is well known"——

" That I got you the little ſhare you had in his education (ſaid the other, catching the word out of his mouth) by informing of your predeceſſor's putting that ballad into his hands ;

and

and that you pofitively agreed to be guided by me, in every thing you fhould attempt to teach him, before you were admitted to come near him. So that if you have any merit in what you did, you owe it all to me. But fome people have very bad memories in things done to ferve them.

"But do you think that teaching him to read was fuch a mighty matter? The clerk of the parifh, though he was good for nothing elfe, could have done that much well enough. That is the leaft part of a young gentleman's education, the very leaft part, and what many a one makes a very good figure without. It is fufficient for people who have their fortunes to make to mind fuch things, gentlemen are above them. They can keep fervants to read and write too for them, without their taking fuch a trouble; and let me tell you, fir, the world thinks the living you got a fufficient reward for all you were able to teach him.

"But, gentlemen, I muft remind you both of fomething which you feem to have forgot. There are other material reafons which not only prevent your getting the preferments you look for at prefent, but will alfo moft probably prevent your ever getting them, and indeed make what you have already gotten be looked upon with furprize and difcontent.

"You muft have forgot the affair of drinking thofe *difaffeated toafts* certainly, or you would never give yourfelves fuch airs as thefe. How can you, fir, expect that the real friends of his lordfhip, if they think at all about the matter, can like to fee the court-rolls intrufted in fuch hands as yours? Or the parifh-regifters in

yours,

yours, fir?---No! no! gentlemen! you may
both reft fatisfied where you are. You will
never rife higher, take my word for it. I know
what defence you made, and how you came
to efcape fo eafily. But your bufinefs is done,
take my word for it; your bufinefs is done."

The mention of the *toafts* was fo unexpected, that it ftruck them both dumb. They
hung down their heads, and heard him out as
convicted criminals do their fentence. But the
lawyer, foon recovering his natural prefence of
mind, " The toafts, fir! (faid he) I wonder
how you can mention that affair to us, in fuch
a manner! Were not you as deeply concerned
in it as we?"———

" I wifh I had, (replied the other) and then
I fhould have been as well rewarded; for to be
fure you got a good *fee*, and *lawyers may fay
any thing for their fee* Well, it is an old faying, that it is good to have a friend in court.
Your brother brought you off with flying colours; and we too had good luck to be in fuch
good company, or I know not how we fhould
have efcaped. You brought us off, as well as
you drew us into the danger.

" However, that efcape has not made me fo
vain as to think I was not in fault. I have not
the affurance to raife my expectations fo high as
you do, and am humbly content with what
they pleafe to give me, confcious that any
thing is an extraordinary favour, and more than
I fhould have received in any other lord's family in the kingdom; for which reafon I fhall
ftrive to make hay while the fun fhines; and as
foon as a fhower comes, retire into a fnug corner, and enjoy my good fortune with thanks.

" As

" As for you, gentlemen, who afpire to higher honours, you will find, perhaps, when it is too late, that you had better have followed my example. And fo, moft worfhipful Mr. Senefchal, and moft reverend Mr. Rector, I wifh you both a good morning. —— Paultry, menial fervices ! '"

With thefe words, he flung out of the room, leaving his two friends ftaring at each other in a fituation whimfical enough.

**\*\*\*\*\*\*\*\*\*\*\*\*\*\*\*\*\*\*\*\*\*\*\*\*\*\*\*\*\*\*\*\*\*\***

## C H A P. XIX.

*Signal inftances of greatnefs of fpirit. Confiftency of character maintained. A fcene of uncommon tendernefs.*

THE parfon was the firft who broke filence. " Indeed, my friend, (faid he, fnuffing up his pinch, and fhaking his head in a melancholy manner) I fear there is too much truth in what he fays, and that we fhall never be able entirely to get over the confequences of that unlucky difcovery; for which reafon I will e'en ftrive to make myfelf eafy, and not lofe the enjoyment of what I have, by fruitlefs attempts for more."

" You are to do as you pleafe, Sir, (anfwered the lawyer peevifhly) but I fhall not ftoop to be guided by the advice of fuch a mean fpirited fellow. We fhould never have been forgiven, had they dared to fhew refentment againft us; and the fame motive will make
them

them not chufe to provoke us too far by their refufals. I know how to deal with them. I will fpeak to all my friends. They are not bafhful in afking, nor eafy to be repulfed; and if their intereft fhould be unfuccefsful, I will take another courfe, which feldom fails. I fhall not fubmit tamely, I promife them."

" And pray, my dear friend, (replied the parfon) may I afk what courfe that is?"

" I will oppofe all the meafures of the lord's fervants in the court-leet, (returned the lawyer) and that in fuch a manner, that they fhall not be able to make any objections to my conduct, but what will add to my confequence in the opinion of the people. I have a whimfical thought juft come into my head. What would you fay, if I fhould turn *patriot* upon the occafion? I have precedents enough to juftify me. And then the variety of fuch a fcheme will be highly entertaining. I like the humour of the thing much.

" As for the Senefchal, I'll foon make him fick of his fuperiority. I'll contradict every fyllable he fays in the court-leet. My word there is as good as his, and my friends will ftand by me, right or wrong; fo that I'll make them forry for what they have done for me, if they will not do more; and that will gratify my refentment at leaft, if my ambition is difappointed. No one ever provokes me with impunity."

" Nay, for that matter, (replied the parfon, fetting his hands a kimbo, and putting on a look of importance) I do not mean to be quite paffive neither, I affure you. I feek peace, it is true, but then it muft be on my own terms, or I fhall not enfue it, I promife them.

" Nor

" Nor fhall I long want an opportunity of letting them know my mind. The veftry will foon meet on fome extraordinary affairs, when I will object to every thing the rector propofes; and that will vex them all not a little, for to my knowledge they have fome things in view, which they will not like to be oppofed in; fuch as *making fome alterations in the old furplice and caffocks, and enlarging the church, and widening the approaches to the communiontable*; but I will not confent to the ftirring a ftick or ftone, or clipping off the moft ragged fhred; all things fhall remain as they are, merely to difappoint them; and then how filly will they look in the eyes of the crowds, whom they have promifed to make room for?

" They fhould not have let me know their fecrets, if they defigned to break with me in this manner. No! no! I do not mean to be quite paffive neither, I affure you. Our cloth has never been noted for tamenefs and fubmiffion. I will feek peace, but it fhall be on my own terms, I can tell them."

The two friends then fhook hands, and applauding each other's fpirit, parted for that time, to prepare for putting their virtuous refolutions in execution.

" What fay you now, (faid the Spirit with a fmile) to modern modefty and gratitude?——But it is unneceffary to make any reflections on fuch a fcene as this. They occur of themfelves, with force fufficient to make a rational being fick of the world, and all its ways; and I hope you are convinced, that changing the fcene makes no effential change in the profpect. Folly reigns every where alike. The palace is

no

no more exempt from it than the cottage:———
But foft!—I fee fomething yonder, which will
be worth attending to. You have hitherto been
principally engaged in viewing the folly of ambition; I will now fhew you the effects of love,
its potent rival in the human heart."

Saying this, he directed my eye to a chamber, where lay a woman languifhing under a
general decay of nature. Much as fuch a ftate
muft necefsarily weaken the force of beauty,
there was a fymmetry in her whole figure, a
foftnefs and delicacy in her looks, which even
thus in ruin charmed the beholder, and fhewed
how refiftlefs they muft have been when the
warm glow of health infpired their bloom.
But ftill an air of debauchery fullied all thefe
charms; and her whole appearance befpoke a
life worn out in vicious pleafures, which had
taken fuch deep root in her heart, that whenever fhe opened her eyes, a feeble glance of
loofe defire glimmered through all the horrors
of her prefent ftate.

Every thing around her fhewed the higheft
affluence and moft tender care; and the moft
elegant accommodations ftrove to make ficknefs
tolerable, and compenfate, as far as poffible,
for the want of health.

But what particularly ftruck me was the tender, anxious affiduity with which fhe was
waited upon by a perfon, whofe appearance
fhewed him to have been bred to a profeffion,
and on an element, neither of them very remarkable for foftening the manners, and giving
the mind fuch a compaffionate humane turn.

He was kneeling at the foot of her bed,
chafing her clay-cold feet with his hands, to
**try**

try if they could communicate any warmth to them. She seemed not infensible of such an act of tenderness, and raising her head from the pillow, " How shall I reward my hero, (said she, with a feebly-wanton leer) for all his care? Will this poor person of mine ever be in a condition to repay his pains and trouble with pleasure?"

" Let me but once more see my dearest girl well, (answered he, with a look of fondness and pity) and I shall think myself amply overpaid for all. Is there any thing that I can do, to give you ease or satisfaction? Command my fortune; command my life; myself, and all in my possession, are solely yours."

" I want nothing, (replied she) while I have you. Stay but always with me, and I have no other wish. But why should I defire this! What pleasure can you find in the company of a poor sick creature, who is incapable of feeling any herself? I blame you not for feeking that satisfaction elsewhere, which it is no longer in my power to give you."

" Why will my dearest life (returned he, with an air of concern) think so meanly of me, as that I can have pleasure in any other company but hers. I never leave you a moment, but when my duty indispensibly calls me; and as soon as that is over, I fly back to you again with all the impatience of a youthful bridegroom."

" And when will that hateful duty call you again? (added she) How long may I promise myself your company now, without such painful interruption?"

" My

"My love, (returned he) I am this very moment under a necessity of waiting on the admiral. I have had notice that my ship is ready for sea; but I will forego all my hopes of honour and advantage rather than leave my dearest love, till I see you better. I have framed an excuse to evade my going this voyage; and by that time my ship returns, I promise myself that you will be able to take a trip with me in her to Lisbon, where the warmth of the climate will effectually restore your health."

"And how long will it be (said she) before you return from the admiral? I insist upon knowing to a minute, that I may not be tortured by any unexpected delay."

"I fear, my love, (answered he) that it will be impossible for me to leave him before dinner. He has so often asked me, that it will look like disrespect to refuse him always. Besides, as I go to sue for a favour, it would be ill-judged to give him offence. But you may be assured I will not stay a moment that I can avoid. By seven at farthest."——

"By seven! (exclaimed she) and must I! Can I live so long without you!—Well! since it must be so, go; but do not be surprized to find me dead, when you come back."

"My dearest love! (replied he, embracing her most tenderly) this is the last time I shall leave you. I design to tell the admiral that I am going out of town; so that nothing shall interfere with my care of you. Adieu! my love: let me find you in better spirits at my return.

CHAP.

❋❋❋❋❋❋❋❋❋❋❋❋❋❋❋❋❋❋❋❋❋❋❋❋❋❋❋❋❋

## C H A P. XX.

*The opening of a new scene gives occasion for some reflections, which will probably be least agreeable to those who have most occasion for them.*

DISTRESSED as the disconsolate fair one seemed at his departure, the moment he left the room opened a new scene. " Now is the time ! (said she, raising herself up with a spirit that could not have been expected from her looks) now is the time to put my design in execution ! If I miss this opportunity, I don't deserve to find another." Then turning to an elderly woman who waited upon her, " Fly, nurse, (continued she) bid my sister come to me instantly, and observe the last directions I gave her."

The woman obeyed without delay ; and the lady being left to her meditations, " Now shall I be happy ! (resumed she in a transport) Now shall I be in some measure revenged on that object of my soul's aversion, man ! O ! that I could treat the whole perfidious sex in the same manner, exposing them equally to the ridicule of the world, and the reproaches of their own conscious hearts ! But, as that is impossible, let this mean spirited, doating fool, bear the weight for all. If I fall a victim to the vice of man thus in the prime of life, it is some consolation, that I can wreak my resentment upon him, who seems alone to merit

better from me. The world will attribute what
I do to other motives; but I difclaim them
all, and act only from the principle of revenge."—Saying this, fhe funk back upon her
pillow, waiting with the utmoft impatience for
the return of her meffenger.

There was fomething fo fuperlatively bafe
and wicked in thefe fentiments, and the hy-
pocrify which preceded them, that I could not
avoid expreffing the pain, they gave me to my
guide. As foon as fhe had finifhed her meditations therefore, " O gracious fpirit! (faid I)
what life muft this vile woman have led, to
harden her thus againft every fenfe of virtue and
humanity? and what uncommon injuries can
fhe have fuffered, to fire her foul with fuch an
implacable paffion for revenge ?"

" Her life (anfwered he) has been that of a
common proftitute; a life that neceffarily ef-
faces every tendernefs of nature, as well as
every principle of virtue: and the injuries
which ftimulate her to thefe more than favage
fentiments have been no other than the ufual
unavoidable occurrences of her wretched profeffion."

" How! (exclaimed I) does proftitution work
fuch a total change in woman's nature? bad,
too bad I am fenfible its effects are; but I
have always thought, that fome, and thefe not
the leaft amiable of the virtues, were not quite
inconfiftent with it; I thought I had feen inftances of benevolencee, charity, and filial
duty, exerted by fome of thofe unhappy creatures, which would have been an honour to
the chafteft of the fex. But I find I have been
in an error."

" Chaftity

" Chaftity (replied he) is not the only virtue of woman ; but ftill, it is fo eſſentially neceſſary to the perfection of her nature, that the
want of it, if it does not abfolutely incapaci-
tate her from every other, debafes any feeble
inſtances ſhe happens to exert of them."

" Nor can it be otherwife.   The moment a
woman is known to violate this virtue, ſhe is
looked upon as a diſgrace to her fex, and given
up to infamy, even by the very perfons who
fiıⁱⁱ feduced her to, and ftill participate in, the
crime they perfecute."

" Debarred thus from the benefits of fociety,
where virtue is confirmed and enforced to
imitation by example, ſhe is obliged to con-
fort with her fifters in vice, who to filence the
voice of confcience, and keep up their fpirits to
purfue their miferable trade, vie with each
other in wickedneſs; and, glorying in their
ſhame, profeſs to deny the truth, and ridicule
the practice of thofe principles from which
they have departed, till they harden each other
in their iniquity, and become incapable of reformation."

" In fuch an abandoned ftate of reproba-
tion, what merit can there be in a fingle act of
virtue, that contradicts the conftant tenour of
their lives, and owes its rife perhaps to accident, vanity, or caprice? how light will it be
found in the balance, when placed oppofite to the
innumerable vices among which it ftands, and
which always contaminate it in fome circumftance or other?

" But this even is not all.   The moft profligate of them fees the neceffity of putting
on the appearance of fome virtues, to palliate

the

the horror of her profeffion. This is the reafon of the error in which you may have been. Man requires but weak proof to convince him of what he wifhes to be true; and therefore readily believes the reality of this appearance, and receives it as a fufficient atonement for the vice which gives him pleafure."

" Think me not too fevere in what I fay. There may perhaps be fome inftances to the contrary; but they are too few, in comparifon with the others, to draw a more favourable conclufion from : and the danger which would attend fuch a conclufion is fufficiently great to juftify fo prudential and falutary a feverity."

" The only fafe rule to direct the judgment by, in all fuch cafes, is this, *that a perfon who perfifts in the wilful breach of any one moral virtue, cannot be fincere in the profeffion of any other*; as a proper conviction of the duty of any muft neceffarily and invariably enforce the practice of all; that is, with allowance for the unpremeditated lapfes of human infirmity.

" Nor is there a more dangerous error than this, of thinking that vice and virtue can be fo far reconciled as to inhabit the fame breaft; or, *that it is poffible to compound for the obftinate, habitual tranfgreffion of one duty, by the occafional performance of another*; the mean mercenary motive to fuch a performance taking away every fhadow of merit from it, and contradicting the unalterable effence of virtue, which is pure obedience."

The fpirit's reflections were interrupted here by the return of the nurfe, with the perfons for whom fhe had been fent. The moment they entered the room, the fick lady
forgot

forgot her ailments, and raising herself up, "Well, sister (said she, looking at them with eagerness and delight) I suppose these gentlemen have been informed on what occasion they have been brought here. The moments are precious. Let us therefore do our business without delay; and then we may enjoy ourselves."

As soon as she said this, one of the gentlemen drew out pen, ink, and paper, and sat down directly to write her will, which she dictated with a readiness, that shewed she had long studied it. When he had finished, she read it over carefully, and signed it, in the due form of law, before the other gentlemen, who were brought on purpose to attest this extraordinary transaction.

The moment this important affair was ended, the lawyer received his hire, and then he and the witnesses departed, to prevent surprize; when she immediately sunk into a state of weakness, that shewed her end was approaching very fast, the extraordinary effort she had made on this ocasion having quite exhausted her strength and spirits.

Dreadful as such an alarm must naturally be, it shook not her resolution. On notice of her friend's return, she dismissed her sister, without the least mark of tenderness or regret, though the only relation she had in the world, and prepared to go through with her design with a constancy worthy of a better cause.

CHAP.

## CHAP. XXI.

*A life concluded in character. An uncommon legacy of love and gratitude. A particular circumstance, necessary to be attended to through the course of this curious work, is explained.*

AS soon as he entered the room, he ran to her bedside with the utmost impatience, where he found her languishing in the arms of death.

Such a sight awoke his tenderness. He fell upon her neck, and wept over her in bitterness of heart. So genuine an expression of love operated as it were mechanically upon her, who had long been accustomed to return the caresses she received, however insipid or loathsome to her. She opened her eyes; and, forcing a faint smile of fondness, "How could you think *(*said she*)* that I could live so many tedious hours without you? It is well, that you are come at length, to bless my eyes with one view more of all that they delight in. Take care of this poor body; see that it is laid with decency in the grave; and sometimes bestow a thought on one whose heart's last wish was to give you pleasure. I have a sister who would perform that melancholy duty; but I have long broke all connection with her for your sake. You are the world to me; and every tender tie of nature is summed up in your love."—With these words, she fainted in
his

his arms : nor ever recovered ſtrength to utter another.

As ſoon as her diſconſolate lover recovered from the firſt tranſports of his grief, he gave orders for her burial, with a magnificence that far exceeded the preſent ſtate of his own affairs ; but this he thought himſelf under an obligation to do, in return for her whole fortune, which ſhe had bequeathed to him, by a will made in the beginning of her illneſs; and which amounted to a very conſiderable ſum, though all earned by vice and infamy.

The next morning, after this laſt token of his regard was paid, he was ſurpriſed at receiving a viſit from a perſon to whom he was an utter ſtranger. After the common compliments of meeting, the gentleman told him, that he was come from the ſiſter of the deceaſed lady, to take poſſeſſion of ſuch effects of her's as might be in his hands.

" I am ſorry, ſir, (anſwered the widowed lover, with a ſmile) that ſhe ſhould have given you this unneceſſary trouble. My deareſt girl's effects and fortune are all in my poſſeſſion ; nor ſhall I part with them to any one."

" How, ſir ! (replied the ſtranger) Not part with them to the heir at law ! Pray by what right do you claim to keep them ?"

"And pray, ſir, (returned the captain, ſomewhat offended at the manner in which the other ſpoke) by what right do you aſk me that queſtion ? "

" Sir, (ſaid the ſtranger) I am employed by her ſiſter, to make a legal demand of her undoubted right ; and if you do not chuſe to comply with it in this amicable manner, I know

how

how to apply in another, that may be more effectual, though perhaps not quite so agreeable."

"That is to say, (retorted the captain) you
are the lady's lawyer. Well then, good Mr.
lawyer, as I desire to have as little conversation
as possible with you, and all the worthy gentlemen of your profession, I will shew you my
right."——Saying this, he unlocked a bureau,
and taking out a paper, "Here, sir, (said he)
is the lady's will, by which she has bequeathed
to me every thing in her possession. If you
please, I will read it to you."

"Very possible, sir, (answered the lawyer,
with a significant smile) I do not doubt but it
may be a will of her's; and therefore shall not
give you that trouble. But, pray sir, will you
give me leave only just to look at the date of
that will?"

"The date! Yes, sir, (replied the captain)
here it is. It bears date about a year ago, just
in the beginning of her illness."

"I see, sir; (added the lawyer) and in return for your readiness to shew me that, will
now shew you my client's title for making her
demand. Here, sir, is a will made the very day
before the lady died, by which she cancels that,
and every other will she may have made, and leaves
her whole fortune, real and personal, to her sister,
charged only with a few legacies to her particular friends : and though you may not be much
conversant with such affairs, you must certainly know, sir, that the last will takes place. As
you are one of the principal legatees, I will
read it over to you, if you please ; at least that
part in which your legacy is mentioned."

The

The captain's furprize at this piece of news was fo great, that he had not power immediately to make any reply; accordingly the lawyer, taking his filence for an affent to his propofal, opened the will with great deliberation, and clearing his voice, with an hem or two, proceeded to read: "*Item*, in return for the great
" expence and trouble which my dearly be-
" loved friend captain *Lovejade* has been at, in
" taking care of me, during this painful and
" tedious illnefs, I give and bequeath to him
" a lock of my hair, which I defire he will have
" put-into a locket, and wear next his heart,
" for my fake."

" Hold, fir! (interrupted the captain, rouzed by fuch a cutting infult) let me fee that will. Why, villain, this is not her hand! I knew it was not poffible. This is a bafe and impudent forgery, for which you fhall all be punifhed with the utmoft feverity."

" Pray, fir, (anfwered the lawyer coolly) fufpend fuch an injurious opinion for a moment. Look at the paper again, and you will fee that it is not an original will, but an attefted copy of one, regularly proved this very morning in the Commons, where you may fee the original any time you pleafe. As you may think proper to take advice in a matter of this confequence, I fhall wait for your anfwer to my client's demand till to-morrow morning, when I will call upon you for it; if you do not chufe to fave us both that trouble, by fending all the lady's effects to her fifter's houfe this evening; to prevent any miftake in which, here is a copy of a fchedule of them, which we have figned by the deceafed, and bearing equal date

F 5 with

with her will : and so, sir, I wish you a good morning."

"Pray stay a moment, sir, (said the captain, a good deal cooled by such an unexpected stroke) and give me leave to ask you a few questions. Though she has played me such a base trick, I presume I have a right to demand a reimbursement of the very great expences which her long illness and burial have cost me; and for which, you must be sensible I have received no consideration. You appear to be a person of character, and as such I expect a direct and candid answer from you."

"I am glad, sir, (answered the lawyer) that you see reason to entertain a better opinion of me, than you were pleased to express a little while ago ; but I cannot give you such an answer as will be very pleasing to you. You say you have received no consideration ; pray, sir, did not the lady cohabit with you, both before and during her illness ? Now, sir, light as you may make of such a matter, the law admits of such cohabitation as a valuable consideration, not only for whatever expences a man may be at while it continues, but also for the recovery of a promised maintenance, after it ceases : and therefore you can have no right to expect payment, especially as you buried her of your own free will, and without consulting her heir. If you have any farther commands, I will wait upon you when you please ; but at present I am in haste. A gentleman waits for me at the coffee-house. Sir, your servant."

It is impossible to describe the captain's situation at the discovery of such a base deceit. He railed at the whole sex in the grossest terms, and cursed his own credulity for
being

being made a dupe to one of the moſt infamous of them.

When he had vented the firſt tranſports of his rage in this manner, it occurred to him, that the whole might poſſibly be a contrivance of the ſiſter's and her lawyer, who having ſome way learned that he was out that day, fixed upon it as a proper time to date their pretended will.

But this conjecture was ſoon overturned, upon examining his ſervants, who all informed him of the nurſe's having gone out immediately after him, and brought their miſtreſs's ſiſter, with that very perſon, and three more whom they did not know, who were ſhut up in her room a conſiderable time, and went away but juſt before he returned.

Diſappointed in this hope, he went directly to an attorney of his acquaintance, in whoſe judgment he had a confidence, to try if there was not ſome redreſs in the law for ſo groſs an abuſe as he had ſuffered ; but he had the mortification to find, that he muſt ſubmit to the whole, and be ſatisfied with *the lock of his beloved's hair*, though he wanted not that legacy to keep her eternally in his remembrance.

" Well, (ſaid my guide, as ſoon as this extraordinary ſcene was ended) what is your opinion now of the virtues of a proſtitute ? Their profeſſion is, to pretend regards they never feel ; and you ſee ſhe has preſerved a perfect uniformity of character to the end of her life ; and yet ſhe was one of the moſt remarkable of them all for the virtues you mentioned. As to her lover, baſe as her treatment of him was, he drew it upon himſelf, by his infatuated dotage,

and

and deferved to be deceived for placing confidence in a woman whofe whole life he knew to have been a feries of deceit.——What is the matter? You feem furprifed at fomething."——

"O gracious fpirit, (anfwered I) what can this mean? We have attended the progrefs of this laft fcene through a feries of many days; and yet I fee all the other objects round me exactly in the fame fituation as when it began. How can this be? Have their actions been fufpended, till we fhould be at leifure to attend to them?"

"Your furprize (replied he) is natural. You judge according to the mode of man's conception, whofe limited faculties are incapable of comprehending things at once; and therefore are obliged to receive them in a flow fucceffion, which you call time. But beings of a fuperior nature are not under that difadvantage. Our powers are more extenfive; and the fhorteft glance fhews us the whole progrefs of the moft complicated tranfaction, bringing all its parts together in one view before us. This power I have for the prefent communicated to you, as I could not otherwife attend to give you the information you defire in the tedious courfe of human comprehenfion. But you will underftand this better, when I tell you, that what feemed to you a feries of many days, in reality was not a minute, according to your manner of fpeaking. Attention to this will prevent a like furprize on future occafions."

CHAP.

✿✿✿✿✿✿✿✿✿✿✿✿✿✿✿✿✿✿✿✿

## CHAP. XXII.

*An account of an univerſal genius. Some curious
ſecrets in the trade of an author; with a new
way of replying to impertinent remarks.*

WHILE I was reflecting on what my
guide had juſt ſaid, "Turn your eye
this way, (contined he) and obſerve that perſon
yonder. He is one of the ſtrongeſt inſtances of
the danger of indulging an indiſcriminate deſire
of praiſe; and being ſeduced by the firſt ſmiles of
ſucceſs to form ſchemes for acquiring even
the moſt imaginary pre-eminence over the reſt
of mankind.

"To underſtand the nature of the diſtreſs,
which, as you ſee, corrodes his heart, and
makes him incapable of enjoying the favours
fortune has heaped upon him, it will be neceſſary to take a ſhort view of his life.

"He was born in one of the lower ranks of
the people, where neceſſity ſilences the voice
of ambition, and obliges men to have recourſe
to the more immediately uſeful arts, of induſtry
and labour, to ſupply their own wants, and miniſter to the convenience of thoſe above them.
But though the poverty of his parents prevented their extending their views beyond their
own ſphere, in the way of life they propoſed for
him, a dawn of genius, which marked the
opening of his youth, prompted them to exert
the utmoſt of their abilities in giving him the
firſt rudiments of a good education.

"Such

" Such care, when dictated by prudence, and not the fond refult of injudicious partial vanity, is feldom unfuccefsful ; though for a while it feemed to counter-act their principal defign, by leading him into purfuits of a different nature from thofe marked out for him, and making him defpife and neglect the low illiberal profeffion he was bred to.

" But one of thofe lucky accidents which govern life, and fhew the infignificancy of human forecaft and wifdom, effected what their moft fanguine fondnefs could never have fuggefted the remoteft hope of.

" After he had languifhed for fome years in obfcurity and indignant difcontent at the feverity of his fate, he happened one day, in a mixed company, which had met upon fome public occafion, to fit next to one of the moft ingenious perfons of the age.

" The converfation in fuch places generally turns on fubjects the leaft agreeable to men of reafon ; and is carried on with fuch noife and confufion, that, in their own defence, they are obliged to enter into private chat with thofe next them, to avoid being applied to, if they appeared difengaged.

" Accordingly, the gentleman afked him fome of the common queftions which lead into difcourfe, defigned only to confume time ; but he, ambitious of appearing to advantage in the eyes of a perfon of his character, foon took an opportunity to divert the converfation to thofe fubjects which he knew would be moft pleafing to him; in which he difplayed fuch extenfive reading, fuch delicacy of tafte, and depth of judgment, with fo modeft a diffidence

in

in his own, and submissive deference for the opinion of the other, that he politely invited him to his house, for the pleasure of improving their acquaintance.

" From that day, his prospects began to brighten. The gentleman, pleased with the thought of having rescued a man of such abilities from obscurity, not only received him into the closest intimacy, but also introduced him to the knowledge of such of the great as were most eminent for patronizing literary merit, whose favours in a manner prevented his very wishes.

" The first advantage he took of this happy change was to quit the mean profession he had been educated in, and enter into the most reputable in which the abilities of the human mind can be exerted ; where the interest of his new friends soon crowned his fame with the solid reward of an honourable and affluent establishment.

" During the life of his friend he preserved his esteem by the most artful and delicate address. Sensible of the implacability of literary rivalship, he carefully avoided the particular paths the other had advanced in to that envied eminence he now enjoyed, and to which he asserted a kind of exclusive right, directing his studies so different a way, that far from being jealous of an emulation, his friend gave the sanction of his own most sanguine approbation, to establish his fame ; and at his death gave the strongest proof of his confidence in his abilities and integrity, by entrusting him with the care of some of his works, which were not yet published.

" So

" So honourable a testimony established his reputation in the highest esteem; but a vain ambition of appearing in the absurd character of *an universal genius* soon precipitated him from this envied height.

" For the reason of the reserve which had hitherto kept him within his proper bounds being now removed, he resolved to give his parts their full scope; and to shew that his taste for the works of imagination was equal to his judgment in the abstruser pursuits of science, he published a collection of *old ballads, with notes and emendations, critical and explanatory*; in the course of which he discovered such a contempt for the opinions of all other writers, and obtruded his own with such an air of authority, without deigning even to give any reasons in their support, that he provoked the universal indignation of that irritable race; one of whom, in particular, levelled the canons of ridicule against his work, in such a spirited, poignant manner, that, in despite of his confidence in his own opinion, and contempt for that of others, he was obliged to suppress it, at a very considerable expence.

" The least slip on the summit of a precipice is dangerous. The first disgrace he met in this affair gave his reputation a deep wound; and another work, published soon after, in which he advanced opinions contrary to the general sense of mankind, and undertook to support them, by arguments either trifling, or evidently subversive of them, entirely ruined it for ever; and he became of no more consequence in the literary world than if he was actually dead.

" How-

"However, that very opinionated confidence which drew him into this difgrace, prevented his finking under the weight of it; and enables him to look down with difdain upon all who prefume to differ with him, without even vouchfafing to take the leaft notice of their objections.

"But under this appearance of unconcern, his heart is a conftant prey to the pangs of difappointed ambition, and the moft rancorous envy; and he fecretly defcends to the meaneft artifices, to reftore his loft credit, and deftroy that of his hated rivals."

Juft as my guide had concluded his account of this extraordinary perfonage, a man entered to him, whom he feemed to have expected for fome time. "I fuppofe, fir, (faid he, without deigning to take the leaft notice of the profound refpect with which the other approached him) you miftook the time when I let you know I fhould be at leifure to fee you; or you would not have made me wait this half hour."

"I moft humbly beg your pardon, fir, (anfwered the other) but I was delayed by an unexpected affair. A particular friend of mine called at my fhop, juft as I was coming to wait upon you, to inform me, that there was a very fmart pamphlet to come out in a day or two againft your laft book. As I happen to have connections with the printer, I went to him directly, and by much intreaty prevailed upon him to let me have one of them in fheets, which I have here brought with me, in order that you may have an anfwer to it ready, before it can have done us much mifchief.

Here

Here it is!— Will you pleafe to look into it?"

" No, fir! not I! (replied he) I am not at leifure to read *fmart* pamphlets at this time"

"But, fir, (returned the other) confider what a prejudice it may do your book."—

" A prejudice!—No, fir, that is impoffible; (interrupted he peevifhly) quite impoffible, that a thoufand pamphlets, though never fo *fmart*, in your expreffive phrafe, fhould do any prejudice to that book. Nothing can do a prejudice to that book in the opinion of the learned and judicious."

" If they cannot do the book a prejudice, fir (faid the bookfeller, as he now appeared to be) I know to my coft, that they can prejudice the fale of it; which is fo heavy already, that I am like to be at a confiderable lofs, if fomething cannot be done to pufh it on. And for this purpofe, I have here brought you all the books and pamphlets which have been written againft it; and fhall take it as a favour, if you will write a general anfwer to them all together; in which it will not be amifs, to throw in fome perfonal reflections againft the authors, that may provoke them to reply; by which means a controverfy may be fet on foot, that may raife a curiofity to read the book.

" Many a book is helped off this way, that elfe would have lain long enough upon hands. Nay, I know an author of eminence who always anfwers his own books, and then replies to the anfwers again, and both with fuch animofity, fuch ripping and tearing, that one would fwear they were written by the bittereft enemies; by which management, he not only

fells

fells his book, but alfo makes a good penny of the controverfy too."

" Well, and pray good fir (anfwered the author, who had liftened to him all this while with the greateft appearance of indifference) what do you tell me this fine ftory for? do you want me to imitate the practice of your eminent authors?"

" Pardon me, fir! (replied the bookfeller) I would by no means give you that trouble. I am fenfible your time is too valuable to be fpent that way. But I hope you will think proper to anfwer the objections which have been made by others. Your own reputation, as well as my intereft are concerned. You knew I paid you an high price for the copy, and have printed the book in the moft elegant and expenfive manner, and it would be hard to let me lofe by it now."

" I have told you often, (returned the author haughtily) there can be no danger of your lofing. Such a book muft neceffarily fell; and the attacks of thofe infignificant fcribblers only prove its merit. Envy is always the fhadow of excellence. However, as you feem to be alarmed at thefe anfwers, or whatever they are called, to fatisfy you I will reply to them."

" Sir, I am much obliged to you (faid the bookfeller, putting a parcel of books and pamphlets out of his bofom and pockets) here they are. You fee there have been a good many nibbling at you."

" Pray, fir, (faid the author, with an air of difguft) do not give yourfelf the trouble of taking them out. I have no manner of occafion for them.                                          " I

"I beg pardon, fir, (anfwered the bookfeller) I did not know you had them. Then I will only leave this laft, which you have not feen."

"Sir, I have not feen any of them (replied the author) nor do I defire to fee them. Pray be fo good as to take them all away together."—"How, fir! I thought you faid you would anfwer them."—"True, fir. But I did not fay alfo that I would read them, I hope."—"Sir,—I do not underftand you, fir. How can you an-fwer books, without reading them?"

"Sir, you afk a great many queftions. Why, fir, I know that any thing written againft that book muft be nonfenfe, which I will fay in the preface to another book I am now writing: and this will be a fufficient anfwer."—"And in the mean time, before that book comes out, they will have damned the other eternally. Sir,—Sir,—I beg pardon; but I cannot help fpeak-ing. I am much afraid that. fuch an anfwer will not be fufficient. That—that—that is, only giving your opinion of your own book."—"And pray, fir, whofe opinion is better? who is a better judge?"—"I do not fay any one is a better judge, fir. But, fir, the public may require a—a—a more particular anfwer. If that would do, any author would fay fo much in defence of the worft book that ever was written."

"Well, fir, (faid the author, putting on a look of offended dignity) as I do not think that book the worft that ever was written, I fhall not fay any more in defence of it, let the public expect what they will. I am pofi-tive it muft work its way, in fpite of a thoufand

1and such ignorant cavillers. But, to make you easy, if it should not sell, I will make good the loss to you. You shall not suffer by it."

"I am much obliged to you, sir (answered the bookseller, making a most profound reverence) That is sufficient, full sufficient. I hope you are not offended at my anxiety. I would by no means."——

"Pray, sir, (replied the author) let me hear no more of it. If you are satisfied, I hope that is enough." -

## C H A P. XXIII.

*Extraordinary instances of one author's regard for the reputation of another; with a short method of silencing competitors for literary fame.*

THE adjusting of this delicate affair dispelled the cloud that hung upon their brows, and restored their mutual complaisancy and good humour.

"I imagined, sir (said the author, reaching the bookseller his snuff-box, as a pledge of perfect amity) you must have had some particular business with me, by the earnestness with which you desired to see me."

"Sir (answered he) I wanted to beg your opinion of that manuscript which I took the liberty to send you last week. The author called upon me yesterday; and insists upon having my definitive answer this afternoon."
——"And pray what does he ask for that fine affair?"——"Sir, he says he will not abate of

the

the price I wrote you word; which, high as it is, I think I had better give him, as his name will not fail to sell the book."

"Sir, you know your own business best; but I am satisfied it can never sell, and will certainly ruin the gentleman's reputation: to prevent which, as I have a great regard for him, if I thought my interfering in it could never come to his knowledge, I would even buy it myself, and burn it; by which means his necessities would be supplied, and his character saved."

"You are very good, sir. There are few who would be at such an expence, to serve a friend now a-days. As to his knowing any thing of the matter, I hope you are sensible you can depend upon me."

"Then, sir, here is the money to give him."
—"The money, sir! yes, sir, that is just the author's money. But pray what do you design to let me have, for my profit on it. You cannot expect that I should buy and sell, without some profit?"

"Profit, sir! I did not imagine you could desire profit in such an affair as this, where you have no trouble, nor run any risk of loss."

"No trouble, sir! Dear sir, you little think what trouble I shall have with this gentleman about the publication of this book; nor how many evasions and lying excuses I must invent, to put him off. The generality of authors, it is true, give themselves no farther trouble about a book the moment they receive their copy-money. It is equal to them, whether it is burned or published. But this is a different case. This gentleman expects to establish a character by his works."                                "Well,

" Well, fir, and what profit do you expect ? "

" Why, fir, every thing being confidered, I cannot poffibly let you have it for lefs than as much more as the author gets."

" How, fir! as much more as the author gets! is not that a very unreafonable demand ?"

" Not at all, fir. Not in the leaft. But if you think it is, I am far from preffing you to give it. It is paying very dear, to be fure, for doing a man a piece of fervice; and I fhall lofe confiderably alfo, by obliging you. Why, fir, there is fuch an expectation of this book, that the common number of a firft edition is befpoke by the trade already. In fhort, I do not know what I may lofe by parting with it. As to its being double what the author gets, that is no rule. What authors get is but a trifle, in comparifon of the profits of a good book. The gentleman had but an hundred for that atheiftical book you anfwered ; but the bookfeller made a good thoufand of it. I was very unlucky in miffing that book."

" I hope, fir, the anfwer made you amends. You paid no fuch price for that ; and chriftian charity will not let me doubt its felling better than fuch a vile book. The age, bad as it is, cannot be fo depraved as to prefer that book to the anfwer."

" Alack a day, my dear fir. The anfwer was quite another fort of thing. It never fold at all. No body had the leaft defire to read the anfwer."

" That is very odd! very odd indeed ! Well, fir, I fhall not difpute with you. Here is the money." " Sir,

" Sir, I thank you. But that is right! Have you heard, sir, that the gentleman who wrote that other book, the first edition of which I bought up for you, along with the right of copy, from the publisher, and sold again for your account, to the pastry-cooks and chandlers shops as waste paper, has written another on one of the most interesting subjects that can be conceived, which he designs to publish himself; as the trade, prejudiced by the supposed miscarriage of the former, have refused to give him his price for it."

" Obstinate, shameless wretch! To write again, after suffering such a disgrace! But is there no way to prevent his exposing himself in this manner?"

" No, sir, but by buying his books from him, which, as I said before, is a very dear way of doing him service; especially as his pride makes him hold it at a very high price, to shew that he is not conscious of any demerit to have deserved the former disgrace."

" Opiniated coxcomb! However, I will disappoint his vanity, at least for this time; so even buy it for me as cheap as you can: and I hope you will not desire any profit in this affair."

" Only the allowed profit of the trade. Ten per cent, no more; though you must be sensible, that as the failure of the former book proceeded not from any want of merit in it, I might reasonably expect to make much more by publishing this myself. There is another affair, that gives me a great deal of uneasiness. The author of that book in which you made the alterations called at my shop yesterday, and
abused

abufed me in the groffeft manner, charging the mifcarriage of the book entirely on them, and threatening to take perfonal revenge of me, if I did not difcover who had ferved him in fo bafe a manner. I put him off for that time as well as I could, by declaring that I knew nothing of the matter, and would make the ftricteft enquiry about it; but what to fay to him when he calls next I know not, as I imagine you would not have your name mentioned."

" Ignorant blockhead! The only merit in the book is in thofe alterations. No! my name muft not be mentioned by any means; and your beft way is to infift that you know nothing of the matter; and if he gives you any abufe, or offers to threaten you, put him into the hands of a lawyer, and he will foon make him quiet."

" Indeed, I believe that is the only method of getting rid of him. Sir, I wifh you a good morning. I fhall obferve every thing you have faid to me."

As foon as he was gone, the other began to reflect upon the tranfactions of the morning. " Well, (faid he, after mufing for fome moments) if I do pay fomething dear for thofe books, I remove two formidable rivals without any more trouble; and not that only, I can alfo take what I like out of them, and infert it in my own works; in doing which there is nothing unfair, as my buying them has made them abfolutely my own property. As to anfwering thofe pamphlets, it is by no means worth my while. I will not immortalize fuch paultry fcriblers, by taking any notice of them. Had *Virgil* treated *Bævius* and *Mævius* with proper contempt, their names had perished with themselves, and not been handed down to latest posterity, in his works."

## CHAP. XXIV.

*A rare example of modesty and respect, on a most trying occasion. A sure way of getting a good character; with some short reflections on literary ambition, and other more serious matters.*

AS he was in the midst of this modest meditation, a servant came to let him know that a particular gentleman was come to wait upon him. "Shew him into the parlour (said he) I am engaged at present. When I am at leisure to see him, I will ring."

"He is come (continued he, as soon as he was alone) to insult me with the success of his insignificant, trifling book. But, I will mortify his pride; he shall see that I am not in the number of his foolish admirers."

Saying this, he fell into a silent contemplation of his own consequence, which he indulged so long, that his visitor shewed the height of complaisance, in waiting for him.

At length, however, the important bell rung, and he was admitted; when advancing with a profound reverence, "I have made bold to wait upon you, sir, (said he) to impart an affair that I hope will not be unpleasing."

"Pray, sir, what may that be?" (answered the other, without descending from his dignity, by making any return to his salute.)

"Sir,

" Sir, (replied he, rubbing his hands, and looking at them, as if to admire their whiteneſs) I have a very advantageous offer made me, to write a ſecond part to my laſt book ; I ſhould be glad to know in what particular manner you would have me mention you in it."
—" Mention me, Sir! I do not underſtand you."

" I mean, Sir, what you would have me ſay of your works, as I deſign to take notice of all the eminent writers of the times."

" Sir, I am obliged to you for your intention to pay me a compliment ; but I had much rather you would let it alone. I have no ambition to be claſſed among your *eminent* writers, nor even mentioned in their works. I would gladly have excuſed it before."

" I hope you do not think it a diſcredit, ſir, to be ſpoken of in a work that has ran through fifteen editions ?"

" The number of editions is moſt certainly an excellent proof of the merit of a book ; witneſs *Onania*, and the *Pilgrim*'s *Progreſs*. Indeed, my friend, I muſt be candid with you. I had much rather that book had never been publiſhed, for your own ſake. I know the breath of preſent approbation is apt to intoxicate; but if you will make *an eſtimate of the manners and principles of the times*, you will own that it implies a diſcredit to pleaſe ſuch an *effeminate* debauched taſte as reigns at preſent ; and that no work which ſucceeds now can poſſibly meet the approbation of poſterity. And who would be at the pains of writing, if it were not for the hope of making his name immortal ?"

" All, ſir, have not the ſame ſublime way of thinking, nor the abilities to execute it,

which

which you are bleſſed with ; but that muſt not make us neglect to improve the talent given us. Preſent fame in ſuch matters as theſe is preſent profit; and that is the firſt object to be deſired in my humble ſtate.  For the opinion of poſterity, I muſt rely upon the manner in which you ſhall pleaſe to mention me in your works : but there is one thing in which I muſt have expreſſed myſelf imperfectly, as you ſeem to have miſtaken my meaning.  When I mentioned eminent writers, I was far from deſigning to rank you in a claſs with any other.  There are degrees in eminence ; the firſt of which, I am ſenſible, you poſſeſs alone, and that in ſo diſtinguiſhed a manner, that your writings only are ſufficient to vindicate the age from the reproach of ignorance and barbariſm.  The eminence of other writers is only in compariſon to the common herd of mankind, and raiſes them not to a level with you, "there ſitting where they dare not ſoar."

"Well, ſir, if you think my name will be of ſervice to your book, I am ſatisfied that you ſhould inſert it ; and, to ſave you, trouble will write that part myſelf, as I did on the former occaſion.  But, pray ſir, do you not think it neceſſary to anſwer the objections made to your laſt book before you write another on the ſame ſubject ?"

"No, ſir, not in the leaſt ; I intend to follow your example, and take no notice of them."

"But—ſir—your caſe and mine are quite different.  My works are deſigned for future ages, and therefore cannot be affected by ſuch feeble attacks.  But yours, which are but the bloſſoms of a day, are liable to be blaſted by

by

every breath of wind. The deep-rooted oak feels not the breeze that overturns the gawdy tulip."

"Pardon me, fir, I prefume not to make any comparifon. I am juftly fenfible of the difference. However, as I do not find that they have been able to do me any prejudice, I fhall take no trouble about them. You will pleafe to let me have your account of your own works as foon as you can, as I fhall fend the book to prefs directly. Sir, your moft humble fervant."

There was fomething fo defpicably mean and difingenuous in thefe laft fcenes, that I was really glad when they were ended.

"You fee (faid my guide fmiling) how low ambition can ftoop. Of all the paffions which actuate the human heart, the ftrongeft and moft univerfal is the love of fame, next to thofe of felf-prefervation and continuing the fpecies; both of which even it often furmounts.

"To this in fome, however miftaken fenfe, may every purfuit of man be traced. The felon who fired the temple had the fame defire of an immortal name with him whofe better genius prompted him to build it; and moft of the atrocious crimes which difgrace the hiftory of mankind, may in fome meafure be deduced from the fame principle.

"But of all the inftances of the tyranny of this paffion, the moft violent and at the fame time the moft abfurd in its effects, is literary ambition.

"The obvious motive of a perfon's undertaking the laborious tafk of writing to the publick, is a benevolent defire to promote their happinefs, either by informing the underftand-

ing,

ing, or alleviating the cares and anxiety of life by rational entertainment.—I mention not those whom necessity drives to this method of supplying their wants.

" But there are very few who write from this motive alone ; and even of those who may have originally set out with it, scarce one perseveres without yielding to biasses of a nature directly contrary, and sacrificing the most sacred principles of strict and moral virtue to a vain lust of popular admiration, and a jealous envy of his competitors ; the virulence of which not only poisons the enjoyment of that fame which he has already acquired, but also precipitates him into schemes for engrossing more, which disappoint his design, and deprive him of what he really deserves."

" Of the justice of these observations (said I) this person is a sufficient proof ; but there is one thing the reason of which I cannot comprehend, and that is the servile complaisance with which the other author bore his haughtiness, and the fulsome adulation he paid him in return of his insults and contempt."

" You may remember (answered he) I told you he was advanced to an honourable establishment in his profession. In virtue of that establishment he has many opportunities of preferring others to very lucrative employments under him. This is the secret motive of that behaviour in them both, which gave you such just offence.

" Of all the professions of men, there is not one whose principles are so pure from every reproach of this kind as this ; yet such is the force of human perversion, that there is none in
which

which those vices of servility and pride are so universally practised; and that with so little disguise, that, as if the very institution was inverted, the former is become the general means of rising in it, while the latter is looked upon as the first prerogative of power, and borne with patience, from an hope of exerting it on that exaltation which all aspire to; for, however strange it may sound in speculation, experience invariably shews that meanness and pride spring from the same base principle, and always succeed each other on a change of circumstances."

## C H A P.  XXV.

*The pleasures of being a great man. Mysteries in politicks. One drawn-battle leaves room for another. Children and fools fall out at play.*

' TURN your eye now (continued my guide) to yonder little village, and behold a shadow of human grandeur, that may enable you to form a just estimate of the substance. That person whom you see embarrassed with the ensigns of state, and sinking under the weight of his imaginary importance, was one of the principal servants in his master's house.

" So near a view of power fired him with an ambition to exert it himself, though in the most limited delegation. Accordingly, he prevailed with his master to make him steward of that manor where he now is; some particular circumstances in the tenure of which oblige him to indulge the tenants with all the pageantry of

power,

power, all the formalities of liberty, though without any of the real advantages of either.

" Nor is the power entrusted to their temporary governors more solid. The servant of the superior servants of his master, he goes with his hands tied up; and acts a part prescribed for him, in which the least departure from his orders is immediately over-ruled, and his presumption checked with a severe reprimand.

" Such a mockery of command is the most painful aggravation of servitude. It is an insult that makes even wretchedness more wretched. Yet so strong is the vanity of the human heart, that the inestimable advantages of independence are daily sacrificed to this worthless, empty shew.

" How this mimic state is supported by those monarchs of a day, and what pleasure it affords to balance the pain of such a tantalizing situation, you will soon see. But that you may more distinctly understand the scene, which is just ready to open, it is necessary to give you a general sketch of the principal things upon which it turns.

" I observed to you, that there are some particular circumstances in the tenure of this manor. The chief of these, and that on which all the rest depend is, that " *though* " *subordinate to, and dependent on the principal* " *manor, in which the lord resides, it is still a di-* " *stinct manor in itself, with a right to hold* " *courts, and make laws, for its own government ;* " *but that these laws are not to be of force, till* " *they are approved of by the courts of the prin-*
" cipal

" *cipal manor*, *which courts have also a right to*
" *make laws to bind this*."

" The perplexity and contradictions in this
complicated affairare too evident to require being
pointed out ; yet, far from ftriving to remove
them, in the proper management of this very
perplexity confifts the whole myftery of the politicks of this manor.

" For the ftewards, and thofe whom they
can attach to their party by lucrative employments, always make a pretext of the articles of
*fubordination* and *dependence*, to oppofe every attempt made in the court-leet by the apparent
friends of the manor, to promote its feparate
intereft ; as, on the other hand, thofe friends
eagerly catch at and infift on the oppofite ones,
of *its being a diftinct manor*, *and having a right
of making its own laws*, to embarrafs the ordinary courfe of the government, and embroil the
ftewards with the people, by propofing laws in
their confequences deftructive of that dependence; 'till, wearied out by finding that their
labour is in vain, or *(as is much oftener the
cafe)* obtaining fome place or penfion, the real
objects which they had in view, they at length
drop their oppofition, juft in the critical moment when it might have been expected to produce fome important confequences.

" Thus all things remain in their former
ftate of uncertainty and confufion ; each party
thinking they have done enough in baffling the
attempts of the other, and not abfolutely giving
up the caufe of contention, but leaving the field
open for future difputants, to try their fortunes
on a more favourable occafion."

" It

"It muſt appear ſtrange to you, that the ſteward ſhould be ordered to obſtruct the intereſt of a manor belonging to his lord. The whole ſyſtem of human politicks is incomprehenſible. The reaſon for this conduct is this: The ſituation of that manor is ſo convenient for commerce, and the other natural advantages of it ſo many, that they apprehend if it was not kept under by every diſcouragement and reſtriction poſſibly reconcilable with the fainteſt ſhadow of liberty, it would ſoon rival, if not run away with the trade of the principal manor, in which its wealth almoſt wholly conſiſts; and conſequently, as wealth is the foundation of power, in time ariſe above its ſubordination, and perhaps ſhake off its dependence."

"One thing, by the way, I muſt obſerve to you, which makes this conteſt ſtill more exoradinary; this is, that it ſubſiſts entirely between the manors themſelves, the inhabitants being all connected by every tie of nature, thoſe of this manor, or their anceſtors, having all removed from the principal one thither.

"Such diſcouragements and reſtrictions are not ſubmitted to without great reluctance by the inhabitants, who cannot ſee themſelves cut off from making the proper advantages of the bleſſings of nature, and languiſhing in unneceſſary poverty without repining, and indignation at a treatment which appears to them equally ingrateful and unjuſt; as they have always preſerved their filial duty to their mother-country untainted, and on all occaſions diſplayed the ſteadieſt attachment to its general intereſt, and to the family of the preſent lord."

"Theſe

" Thefe natural fentiments of the people are on every occafion inflamed to a degree of madnefs, by a fet of men for that time called *patriots*, (I have told you the import of this word as it is ufed at prefent) who, by pathetick harangues on fo favourite a fubject and promifes of redreffing thofe grievances, gain their confidence fo far as to be put at the head of a plaufible oppofition to the meafures of the fteward, which they perfift in 'till their zeal is cured by a *proper* application, and they obtain the objects which they had all along in view.

" Thus, you fee, the whole fecret of thefe difputes confifts in pelting each other with a fet of words which have no determinate meaning, and are therefore ufed in different fenfes by the oppofite parties, as occafion requires; and that the controverfy may not be improperly be compared to *a game of draughts*, where a number of men are facrificed to raife one to power ; and when the game is ended all are promifcuoufly thrown by, and the antagonifts part as good friends as ever.

" But there is nothing in thefe difputes more unaccountable to inexperienced reafon, than the manner in which they are carried on. As the event of the game is always forefeen, it fhould be imagined that they might play their cards coolly, and without wrangling about tricks which can make no alteration in the fuccefs. But the conrrary is always the cafe ; and no fooner are they engaged, than, forgetting that they are only *playing booty* on both fides, they fall together by the ears with the moft virulent animofity ; and dropping the matter originally in difpute, break out into the

groffeft.

grosseſt outrages of perſonal reflection and abuſe, as if the ſole point to be gained was only who ſhould make their antagoniſts appear in the blackeſt light.

" Horrid as this more than brutal ferocity appears, it ariſes from that ſource of all evils, intereſted deſign. The worthy *patriots* are ſenſible that every ſtroke they give the ſuppoſed oppreſſors, affords the malignant pleaſure of revenge to thoſe who think themſelves oppreſſed; with whom it alſo confirms their intereſt, by leſſening their fears of a reconciliation, which they know by ſad experience is always made at their expence; as the oppoſite party retort the abuſe thrown upon them with equal eagerneſs, to obviate the deſign of the others, and gratify a natural deſire of revenge, and all without the leaſt regard to truth or juſtice.

" Thus are the moſt ſacred bands of ſociety broken, to ſerve a deteſtable purpoſe; and wounds given often to the pureſt characters impoſſible ever to be healed.

" You now ſee what a deſirable object this ſhadow of power is. Indeed the diſagreeable circumſtances which attend it are ſo many, and ſo ſoon diſſipate the intoxication of vanity, that very few would groan under them for the appointed time, if their reſolution was not ſupported by a proſpect of gain, of which, though none ever ſtood in leſs need, not one ever was more greedy than this perſon before us, whoſe own private conduct has alſo aggravated all the unavoidable inconveniences of his ſituation, and made it many times more diſagreeable than it need to be.

3

" For

" For as the nature of his office neceſſarily
embroiled him with the greater part of the tenants, ſo the haughtineſs of his behaviour has
given ſuch offence even to thoſe whoſe intereſt
it is to be upon good terms with him, that moſt
of them have dropt all friendly intercourſe.
Nay, ſome have gone ſtill farther, and, in the
warmth of their reſentment, threatened to call
him to a ſevere account for ſome ſlights, they
apprehend he has offered to their privileges,
of the honour of which they are jealous to a
degree of madneſs, as ſoon as he ſhall be di-
veſted of his aſſumed character, and deſcend into his own : a threat equally diſagreeable to
the delicacy of his honour and his conſtitution."

* * * * * * * * * * * * * * * * * * * * * *

## C H A P. XXVI.

*A good way to make up for a bad market. Myſte-
ries of ſtate-preferment. Servants muſt not ad-
viſe their maſters. The comfortable effects of modern honour. An heavy cloud gathering.*

AS ſoon as my guide had concluded this account, I turned my eyes to the perſon
who had given occaſion to it. He was ſitting
in a ſumptuous apartment, and by the anxiety
in his looks ſeemed to be waiting for ſome body
on buſineſs of importance.

I had not obſerved him long when the one
he expected entered, and advancing to him
with an air of familiarity, which ſeemed to
agree

agree but badly with the difference in their appearances, " Well, sir, (said he) I have seen those people, but do not find that any of them care to deal with us, though I offered them lumping penny-worths; for I never liked to stand higgling for a trifle one way or the other."

" What can be the meaning of this? (answered the steward) I thought those things were always ready money; none of my predecessors ever missed selling them."

" Very true, sir; (replied the other) but they had better times; better times to make their markets in. At present every one is so taken up with the disputes in the court-leet, that they can mind nothing else. I wish all those *patriots*, and all the patriots that ever were, or ever will be, were at the devil. They do nothing but make disturbances wherever they are. The brokers, who used to find out customers for your predecessors, imagine that those fellows will carry every thing before them this time; and therefore do not care to meddle with the affair, for fear of being brought into a scrape with such a spiteful crew; and even the mob is so strongly seized with this same spirit of *patriotism*, that the very toll-gatherers have refused to buy a clerk-ship of the market; nor has one of the militia men bid a single penny for that vacant halbert; so that if it were not for what we got by the sale of those vicarages, we should have made a damned bad hand of it indeed."

" This is bad luck; (returned the steward, shrugging up his shoulders) damned bad luck; but we must try to bring it up some other way.
My

My wife was speaking to me this morning about a scheme she has got in her head, of inviting all her female acquaintances to make a party at *Loo* every sunday evening, when she does not fear stripping them of every penny in their pockets, by her dexterity at packing the cards, and slipping *Pam*. Now, I think it would be no bad addition to her scheme for me to get the men together at the same time at dice, when your old trick of cogging might be of rare use; especially as I should be ready to witness for you upon all occasions, and even bear you through by my authority, should you be so unlucky as to be caught. Eh! what do you think of this?"

"Why, faith, (said the other) very well. It may do very well. As to my being catched, let me take care of that. I have not practis'd so long among the expertest hands in the county-town, to be catched now by a parcel of country-bumpkins. Or, even if any of them should suspect me, I know how to bring myself off. It is but pretending to be affronted, stripping directly, challenging him to fight, and before he can be on his guard, hitting him a plump in the bread-basket, that shall make him throw up his accounts; and I'll engage he will have but very little stomach to accuse me after. Many a scrape of the kind have I bustled through in this manner, where a faint-hearted fellow would have confessed the fact, and been dipped in an horse-pond. No! No! Let me deal with them. Nay, for that matter, you know I can bring others off too, besides myself. You would not have escaped with a little dry *drubbing* that day,

if

2

if I had not played a good ſtick in your defence.  Never fear me; I can fight."

"Well, (interrupted the ſteward, who did
not ſeem much pleaſed with the latter part of
his ſpeech) but muſt we let thoſe fellows, thoſe
*patriots*, go on thus, without oppoſition?  Is
there nothing to be done to ſtop them?"

"Why, aye! (ſaid the other) that is juſt
what I was going to mention.  I think the beſt
way is for me to go down directly to the court-
leet, which is now ſitting, and try what a little
bullying will do, ſince fair words have failed.
I have known a kick and a cuff prevail more
than an hundred fine ſpeeches before now.  If
they ſhould run reſtive, I am not afraid to take
a bout with the beſt man among them.  I have
not forgot my old knack at a croſs-buttock yet;
that I have not.——But, that's right!  What
do you deſign to do about that place of keeper
of the court-rolls?  I have a thought juſt come
into my head, that may perhaps be better than
giving it to any of thoſe fellows.  What do you
think of giving it to me, and I will return you
half the profits; or, if I can ſell it, half the
purchaſe-money?".

"Give it to you! (anſwered the ſteward)
How can that be?  You are no lawyer; and
you know that place has always been in the
hands of one of that profeſſion.  The laſt was
reckoned the ableſt attorney in the whole
country."

"If the laſt was an able attorney, (replied
the other) his predeceſſor knew no more of the
matter than myſelf; ſo that we can eaſily get
over that objection."

"But

" But then, your offer is quite too low ; (added the fteward) half the profit, or half the purchafe-money ! No! no ! That will never do. But if you have a mind to take it at one fourth of the profit, or purchafe, you fhall even have it ; and you fhould confider that this is juft fo much for nothing ; all clear gains."

" With all my heart, (faid the other) be that as you pleafe. I mentioned it folely for your advantage, as you are not likely to make any thing of it, as matters go. I had no view to myfelf at all in propofing it.——Well ; now if you have nothing elfe to fay to me, I will go and fee what I can do at the court-leet."

" Nothing (anfwered the fteward) but to wifh you fuccefs : and, do you hear ! let me fee you as foon as you return. I fhall be impatient to know what paffes."

As foon as this neceffary perfon was gone, the fteward began to prepare for the reception of a vifitor, who was to be treated with a little more ceremony.

This was one of the principal gentlemen in the manor, in whom age had cooled every paffion but that of attachment to his intereft, in which he was now fo clofely connected with the fteward for the time, though he had long been one of their warmeft oppofers, that, without the leaft attention to their perfons or private characters he affifted to carry on the bufinefs of his office with all his power.

The pains which the fteward took upon this important occafion were fufficient to have made laughter burft his fides. He placed himfelf before a large glafs, where he adjufted his drefs, moulded his vifage into due dignity, and prac-
                                              tifed

tifed the nod of ftate with a proper mixture of condefcenfion and pride.

Juft as he had finifhed conning over his leffon, the gentleman entered, and paying his compliments to him in a polite and refpectful manner, which the other returned with more than Spanifh gravity and pride, "I am come, fir, (faid he) to talk to you about thofe people who have given you fo much trouble ever fince you have been in your prefent office. I am afraid you have not taken the proper method of treating them. I am well acquainted with their tempers, and know what way they are to be managed. It is better to comply a little with a fet of wrong-headed men, than be continually involved in broils, which at beft can bring nothing but vexation."

"Comply with them, fir! (anfwered the fteward, putting on an air of importance) No, fir; that I fhall not. I know the dignity of my ftation, and fhall never debafe it by making compliances with a beggarly mob."

"Sir! fir! (replied the other) this way of fpeaking may do you much harm. In this fame beggarly mob are many perfons upon a level with any man in his private capacity, and who are fo far from begging from others, that all they defire is to keep their own. I have feen too much of thefe difputes, and know by experience that nothing is to be done with thefe people but by fair means. You may buy, but can never bully them into any thing. In a word, fir, you are fent to do your lord's bufinefs; which you muft be content to do in the beft manner you can."

"L

" I believe, fir (returned the fteward, fwelling his nofe like an angry turkey-cock) you forget whom you fpeak to, or you would not prefume to talk in fuch a manner. The bufinefs muft be done by thofe who are hired to do it, who muft work for their wages as they are ordered, whether they like it or not. Now, fir, as you are one of thofe, I tell you that I want your obedience and not your advice ; and that if any thing mifcarries, I fhall impute the fault to you, and *ftrike you off the lift.* I fuppofe you have a private underftanding with thofe fellows, that makes you fo fanguine in their behalf ; but you muft remember that you are not at the head of your mob now ; and therefore muft not think to parly with your mafters, and make conditions as you did then. *The moment you capitulated you loft your confequence ;* and now are no more than any common hireling."

It is impoffible to defcribe the condition into which this fpeech threw the perfon to whom it was addreffed. Confcious of the juftice of what he faid, the bafe and defpicable ftate to which he was fallen ftruck him with the fevereft remorfe and anguifh of foul. He ftood for fome moments in a conflict of paffions, which deprived him of the power of making an anfwer ; till impatience at the imputation of guilt, however juft, by the falfe pride of man, called *honour,* rifing fuperior to all the reft, and taking poffeffion of his whole foul, he refolved to do himfelf immediate *juftice,* for fo grofs an affront.

CHAP.

❁❁❁❁❁❁❁❁❁❁❁❁❁❁❁❁❁❁❁❁

## CHAP. XXVII.

*A strange apparition disperses the cloud. A new me-*
*thod of making a good steward. The perilous ad-*
*ventures of the knight of the halter, with other*
*savoury matters.*

JUST as he was going to execute this resolution, open flew the door, and in rushed a person with an halter about his neck, and
every sign of the most violent fear in his whole
appearance. His lengthened visage was as pale
as death. His eyes rolled wildly round the
room, and his knees knocked together, as he
ran and threw himself at the steward's feet, unable to speak a word.

The steward, whose delicate nerves were
instantly susceptible of the least affright, started
back in horror from so terrible an object; and
would certainly have fallen to the ground, had
not the gentleman who was with him, forgetting his resentment, or thinking him beneath it,
ran to his support; at whose repeated desire he
ventured to lift up his eyes, when he made
a shift to recognize his valiant friend, who had
left him not long before to go and bully the
court-leet.

While he was gazing in astonishment at so
strange a sight, the terrified trembling wretch,
though still under the illusion of his fears, recovered strength enough to cry out, "O save
me! save me! They are coming! they are
coming."

" Such

Such an exclamation awoke the steward from his stupefaction. He took the alarm, and throwing his haggard eyes around the room, returned at the same instant, in a feeble faultering voice, " Wh— wh— who are coming?"

There was something so extraordinary in this scene, that the other gentleman, who was ready to burst with laughter at the droll figure which the steward and his friend cut, staring and stammering at each other, could not tell what to make of it.

When he had enjoyed the sight for some time, he spoke to *the Knight of the Halter*, who was still upon his knees with his hands joined together, and lifted up in a suppliant posture, and telling him his danger was over, be it what it would, he stooped to take off that apparent cause of his fear.

But no sooner did he touch it, than the other, whose imagination was still full of the scene he had just gone through, mistaking him for one of his pursuers, fell at length upon the floor, for he was unable to rise, and roared out with all his might, " O spare me! murder! mercy! spare me! spare me! I never will attempt the like again! never say or do any thing offensive to the people, or prejudicial to the interest of this manor, while I live! O spare me! spare me!"—

This exclamation, while it seemed to direct the gentleman's conjectures to the cause of the wretch's fright, made him still more earnestly curious to learn the particulars of it. For this purpose he raised him from the ground, and by many soothing and encouraging expressions, at length restored him to his senses.

As

As soon as he had recovered himself so as to be able to speak, " O, sir, (said he to the steward, who had stood all this while staring at him without power to utter a word) what have I undergone since I saw you? never will I enter that court-leet again, while I live. I hope the doors of this house are shut, and that there is no danger of their pursuing me, even here."

" Who should pursue you, sir? (answered the gentleman, for the steward had not yet opened his mouth, and this speech was far from restoring his spirits) or what have you undergone to put you in such a fright? you see you are safe here : no one dares to enter this place in pursuit of you. Compose yourself then, dear sir, and tell us what has happened to you."

The knight of the halter at this went to the door, and clapping his ear to the key-hole, to listen whether there was any noise, bolted it fast, and then returned to the steward, who had by this time recovered himself so far, as to make a shift to repeat the desire of the other gentleman, that he should tell what had happened.

" As soon as I left you, sir (said he, throwing his eye every moment towards the door) I went directly to the court-leet, where I took the first opportunity to do as I had said; for one of the jury-men happening just then to drop some expressions of dislike at your manner of doing business, I took him up short; and said, that he deserved to be well drubbed for his insolence, in presuming to find fault with his master; and that if they did not do their duty they should be made to do it; or their courts should be taken away from them, and their

manor

manor governed by the laws of the principal manor, without all this fuſs and trouble.

" At theſe words the whole court took fire, every one calling out to me at the ſame inſtant for ſatisfaction. But I was prepared for this, and therefore, to go through with my ſcheme, I roared out as loud as they, that I was ready to fight the beſt man among them, in ſupport of what I had ſaid, and for a guinea by, if they pleaſed, and inſtantly began to ſtrip.

" But they ſoon let me know that this was not the way of fighting they choſe; for, like a parcel of blood-thirſty villains, they inſtantly clapped their hands to their ſwords, ſaying, they ſcorned that vulgar manner, and expected the ſatisfaction due to a gentleman, which I might take my choice of ſword or piſtol, to give, as I liked.

" But I begged their excuſe there. I liked neither: for, though I could give and take as hard knocks as the beſt of them, I knew nothing of their damned ſwords and piſtols; I had never been uſed to them; and did not chuſe to run the hazard of loſing my life to learn now. I therefore thought it beſt to try if I could not ſatisfy them ſome other way; and accordingly as ſoon as I could be heard, begged their pardon if I had ſaid any thing to give them offence, and promiſed to take better care for the future.

" The reaſon of this ſudden change in my manner of ſpeaking was too evident. They inſtantly turned from me with a contempt worſe than any thing but their anger; and I began to hope that I ſhould come off with a

ſpit

ſpit in the face, or a kick on the breech at
worſt.

" But unfortunately the affair had taken
wind, and juſt as I was going to ſteal away, in
broke the mob in the moſt violent fury ; and
while ſome of them laid hold of me, the reſt
behaved in the moſt outrageous manner, railing
at you and all your friends, and breaking open
every room in the houſe in ſearch of you.

" As they were at this work, ſome of them
happening to find your ſteward's gown and cap,
one unlucky dog ran out, and in an inſtant returning with the great *wooden-man* that you
have ſeen ſtanding as a ſign at the ale-houſe
door in the next ſtreet, they directly clapped
your gown and cap upon it, and placing it in
your chair at the upper end of the hall, called
it by your name and ſaid, it was juſt as good a
ſteward as your honour.

" There was ſomething ſo droll and ridiculous in the figure you cut (I mean the wooden-
man in your gown and cap) that provoked and
terrified as I was, I could ſcarce refrain from
laughing along with the reſt; eſpecially when
one of them ſtooping behind the chair, made
a ſpeech for you, that ſeemed to come from
the wooden-man, and took off your voice and
manner to the life.

" But this was all a joke to what followed.
For no ſooner were they tired with ridiculing
and abuſing you in this manner, than turning
all their rage upon me, they threw that halter
about my neck, and led me away to hang me on
that great high ſign-poſt before your door, where
ſome of them had even the aſſurance to talk of
                                            hanging

hanging you alfo, if ever they fhould lay hands upon you."

"But, luckily, juft as we came to the fatal poft, one of the jurymen, more moderate than the reft, and a great favourite of the mob, happened to meet us, and, laying before them the confequence of fuch an action, by much a-do procured me an opportunity to make my efcape in hither; which I did in the manner you faw, without even ftopping to take off the halter from about my neck, as I imagined they were all at my heels. And I heartily wifh, that we were well out of this damn'd riotous place; for I am very much afraid that now the mob is rifen, they will break into the houfe, and hang us all up."

It is impoffible to defcribe the different expreffions of fear which fucceffively appeared in the fteward's face, while the other was telling this ftory : juft at the terrible conclufion of which, a cat happening to dart a-crofs the room after a moufe, his apprehenfions immediately took the alarm, and imagining the mob was breaking in, he gave a loud fhriek, and fell down in a fwoon.

The gentleman inftantly ran to his affiftance ; but the moment he ftooped over him, he received fuch a favour from the effects of the poor man's fright, that he ftarted back, and clapping his handkerchief to his nofe, ran to the other fide of the room.

The knight of the halter, who was now pretty well recovered, perceived what had happened, and calling the fervants, gave their mafter into their care.

✿✿✿✿✿✿✿✿✿✿✿✿✿✿✿✿✿✿

## CHAP. XXVIII.

*An appearance of danger the most convincing ar-
gument. A strange character of a strange sort
of people. The best foundation for popularity.
The mystery of patriotism, with some low prejudices of education.*

THE first thing the steward did, as soon
- as he came a little to himself, and had
got over some of the various effects of his fright,
was, to send for the gentleman, and tell him,
that his confidence in his friendship was so
great, he was resolved to be guided entirely by his advice for the future ; and accordingly he gave him power to make what
terms he thought proper, with those whom he
had held in such contempt but a few hours before.

The gentleman had now an opportunity of
returning the haughtiness with which the
steward had treated him in the morning ; but
thinking that such a manifold humiliation as
he had undergone sunk him beneath his resentment, he scorned to take any farther advantage of
it, than just to give him some advice, how to
carry on the business of his office with less
disgrace to himself, and less trouble to those
concerned with him, than he had hitherto
done.

2

Ac-

Accordingly, "How, fir, (faid he) can you condefcend to take advice from me?——and make compliances with a beggarly mob?"

"Dear Sir, (interrupted the fteward, alarmed at his mentioning things which tended only to make matters worfe) do not think of any thing that is paft! I am forry, very forry!—and beg your pardon moft fincerely."

"You defire me, fir, (replied the gentleman, without deigning to take any notice of his apology) to bring about a reconciliation between you and thofe gentlemen, on whatever terms I think proper. Before any terms are offered, it will be neceffary to alter fome things at which they have taken juft offence. Till this is done, it is in vain to attempt a reconciliation; or even fhould a kind of one be patched up for the prefent, it is impoffible it fhould be fincere, or lafting; and then, the fecond difagreement will be worfe than the firft.

"Now, fir, if you are willing that I fhould point out thefe things with freedom and candour, and will promife to alter them, in cafe I fhew juft reafon for it, I fhall moft readily undertake to reftore harmony between you and them yet; and am not in any doubt, but I fhall be able to accomplifh it."

"My dear friend, (returned the fteward, overjoyed at thefe words) I fhall hear any thing you fay with the greateft pleafure, and will punctually follow your advice in every particular."

"I muft inform you then, fir, (faid the gentleman) that you fet out upon a wrong principle in your behaviour to the tenants of

this

this manor, on your firſt coming among them; and this laid the foundation of all the uneaſineſſes which have ariſen · between you ſince.

" The characteriſticks of theſe people are *pride*, *hoſpitality*, and *courage*; all which a natural impetuoſity of temper makes them apt to carry into extreams."

" As moſt of them are deſcended from, or allied to the beſt families in the whole country, and as they enjoy, in appearance at leaſt, the ſame honours and privileges here as the tenants of the principal manor do, though they are ſenſible that they want the eſſential part of them, which is power, they look upon themſelves as on a level with any of their lord's tenants, and are ready to take fire at the leaſt ſlight which they apprehend to be offered, either to themſelves or their darling privileges.

" As to their hoſpitality, it is acknowledged in terms of the higheſt reſpect, by all who have ever happened to come among them; and though they have not equal fortunes with you of the principal manor, the cheapneſs of their country, or their wanting opportunity to gratify many of the moſt expenſive artificial wants, which diſſipate the wealth of the others, enables them to indulge the generoſity of their tempers in a manner which very few other people have any notion of; and for their courage, it is too well known all over the country, to require any proof.

" Do not think, ſir, that I am labouring an unmerited panegyrick on people, becauſe we happen to be of the ſame country. I am above ſuch a vain, weak prejudice, and ſpeak my
opinion

opinion as difpaffionately as I fhould on any point of meer fpeculation.

" Far from being inclined to flatter them, I am fenfible that thefe qualities are too often carried, as I have faid before, into an extream, which makes them ceafe to be virtues. Their pride hurries them into violations of the moft amiable of the focial virtues ; their hofpitality fwells into profufion, and ends in intemperance ; and their courage, by being made fubfervient to miftaken notions of honour, on every trifling occafion degenerates into a favage fiercenefs that is a difgrace to humanity.

" Now, fir, inftead of paying attention to thefe foibles, (to call them no better) and attaching them to you by a proper addrefs, as a moment's cool reflection would have fuggefted, by an unlucky miftake you either overlooked them quite, or thought them not worth fhewing any regard.

" Thus you treated themfelves with haughtinefs, and fhewed an open contempt for their idolized privileges. You expreffed a difapprobation of the hofpitality with which they entertained you, and ran into the oppofite extream yourfelf to a fhameful degree ; and you affected to inveigh againft the vicious excefs of courage, with an indifcriminate afperity that feemed to betray a general want of it.

" Confider a moment, and you will confefs that the confequences of this conduct could not avoid being difagreeable. They returned your haughtinefs with hatred. Your avowed contempt of their privileges alarmed their apprehenfions of an invafion of them, and poifoned the weapons they prepared for their defence; and the leaft fufpicion of want of fpirit finks a man into the loweft degree of contempt.

" I am fenfible, fir, that it muft be very difagreeable to you, to hear thefe things. Be affured it is not lefs fo to me to repeat them; but before a wound can be healed, it muft be probed to the bottom. A falfe tendernefs only prevents the cure.

" What I would advife therefore is, that you fhould immediately treat the gentlemen of the manor with politenefs and refpect, and as your equals, except in the office which you have the honour to fill:——that you fhould partake of their hofpitality with an appearance of fatisfaction, and return it with grace and magnificence;——and that you fhould take all opportunities of rewarding true courage, to fhew that your diflike is only to the vicious extream.

" If you obferve thefe few fhort hints, I will engage that you recover the refpect of the tenants; and then every thing you defire follows. I fpeak from experience. I have known great things done, folely by this conduct. This was the fecret that won one of your predeceffors the hearts of the whole mob, and kept them fo quiet all the time of the riots in the next manor, by which he gained fuch honour: and no one who has obferved this rule has ever failed to do his bufinefs without trouble; as it obviates every attempt to make him perfonally difliked, the firft ftep to embarraffing his meafures.

" Nor is there any difficulty to difcourage the attempt. Affability amply rewards itfelf in the

pleafures

pleasures of friendly intercourse, aud a proper politeness is the most certain way of preserving respect.

"As for hospitality, it in some measure includes every social virtue, and yields such happiness in the exertion, as often over-balances prudence, and leads into profusion.

"It is inconceivable what extraordinary things have been and may be done, by this virtue only. It gains the most solid and extensive influence. No resolution is proof against the pleasures of a genial hour. Among these people in particular, the very excess of hospitality is of more weight than every other virtue, and even compensates for the want of all the rest. *Give them but drink enough, and do with them what you please.* They can see no fault in the man who makes them drunk; they will see no virtue in him who will not.

"It was this, and this only, that enabled me to maintain such an absolute power over them, as I did for many years. My house was always open, and my table flowed with wine; but, when I had any point to carry, I broke through all bounds. I pressed them to drink; I set them an example myself; and in the height of their spirits never was refused any thing I asked, however contrary to the dictates of reason, or interest.

"In these unguarded moments, the charms of hospitality are irresistible; nor will pride permit them to revoke in a cooler hour what they have then promised. The *harangues* of *orators*, the *promises* of *patriots*, make no impression, unless the head is warmed with wine, to receive them with proper force.

"As

" As for thofe *patriots*, there is one unerring way of dealing with them. Treat them with complaifance, and an appearance of regard, and you take off half their confequence. The mob will immediately imagine, that there is a fecret underftanding between you and them, and defert them with indignation; by which they will be obliged to fubmit to your own terms, without even the trouble of a formal capitulation.

" For, to capitulate they always intend, be their profeffions never fo fanguine and high, as foon as they have fatisfied their paffion for popularity, and their price is offered; being convinced that their oppofition in reality fignifies nothing when combated thus with addrefs; and that their confequence confifts merely in the want of judgment in their opponents, though they are permitted to play out their farce, to keep up an illufion fo pleafing to the people, and fave appearances.

" Thefe are the principal things neceffary, indeed indifpenfibly neceffary, to carry you through your office with eafe and reputation; though there are alfo fome others which will be found very conducive to that defirable end, and which I fhall therefore take the liberty juft to touch upon flightly.

" This manor, though it has made large advances of late, is yet a century behind the principal one, in the refinements of luxury and liberties of pleafure. Many things therefore, which are conftantly practifed there, cannot be done among us, without hazard of giving offence to prejudiced weak minds.

" One

" One inftance will be fufficient to prove this, and ferve for a rule to judge by in other cafes.

" The belief of a revealed religion is yet pretty general here, and the forms of it therefore neceffary to be obferved with an appearance of refpect, as the vulgar and ignorant are apt to entertain a difadvantageous opinion of perfons who flight them.

" For this reafon the polite cuftom of *playing at cards, on the days appointed for religious duties,,* which prevails fo univerfally among people of fafhion with you, is looked upon here with a kind of horror, as a manifeft violation of laws human and divine. I therefore think the public practice thereof improper, in your houfe efpecially, to which all are apt to raife their eyes for example ; not that I am infenfible of the convenience of fuch an agreeable way of paffing a tedious evening, which fuperftition has devoted to idlenefs.

" But, befide this reafon, there is another alfo, which makes *gaming,* not only on thefe days, but at any time, highly improper in your family. It is a maxim with gamefters always to deny their winnings, always to magnify their lofs. Now, when it is known that there is deep gaming carried on at your houfe, when all who go there are heard to complain of their loffes, and none to own their gains, the conclufion formed by the generality of the world will be very unfavourable. They will imagine that you do not play fair ; or, at leaft, that your expertnefs gives you an advantage, which it is ungenerous to take : and there is no character which thefe low-bred people hold in greater de-

H. 5. teftation

teſtation than that of a *gambler*, or *cheat at play*, though in never ſo genteel life or high ſtation; with which their prejudice is ſo ſtrong, that they cannot aſſociate any one virtue, or good quality.

" I ſhall not trouble you with any farther particulars. I have now given you my advice, with freedom and ſincerity; and, if you approve of it, ſhall be proud of aſſiſting you to put it in practice."

" Sir, (anſwered the ſteward, who was now ſufficiently humbled to hear any thing, and had ſtood all this time, like a ſchool-boy that had been caught robbing an orchard, while his maſter reads him a lecture on the eighth commandment, without any other thought but getting out of his preſent ſcrape at any rate) I am much obliged to you for your friendſhip; and ſhall obſerve every thing that you have ſaid with the greateſt care. But, in the mean time, if you think it proper, I ſhould be very glad that you would take ſome method of letting thoſe people know my reſolution, and ſettling matters with them upon ſome amicable footing; for I cannot bear to live any longer in this horrid way. As I ſaid before, I ſubmit the terms intirely to you, and ſhall confirm whatever you pleaſe to do.

" Such an unlimited commiſſion flattered the gentleman's vanity, as it proved his conſequence with both ſides. Accordingly he undertook it with pleaſure, and acquitted himſelf with ſuch addreſs, that in a ſhort time all parties appeared ſatisfied, and the ſteward had a proſpect of a little peace to enjoy his grandeur, after ſo much trouble and affright."

CHAP.

## CHAP. XXIX.

*A famous war-scene. The modern art of general-ship. A new method of reformation, with the lamentable history of a penitential procession.*

" *He that's convinc'd against his will*
" *Is of his own opinion still.*"——

THOUGH the steward, to extricate him-self from the difficulties in which he was entangled, had assented to every thing the gen-tleman proposed, there was something so con-trary to his natural disposition in the scheme of life laid down for him, that he very soon grew weary of it, and performed his part with such a bad grace, as in a great measure destroyed the merit even of what he did.

While he was plodding on thus, through thick and thin, an affair happened that shewed his character in a new light.

*A gang of outlawed smugglers* had landed in a remote part of the manor that lay upon the sea-side, to look for some provisions and other necessaries, of which they were in great want.

The inhabitants not caring to have any dealings with them, hunger forced them to pil-lage two or three cottages near the place of their poultry ; and to send a threatning mes-sage to the next village, that if they were not immediately supplied with some bread and cheese and a barrel of beer, they would go and plunder that also.

Suc-

Such a piece of insolence provoked the young fellows of the village so highly, that they brandished their cudgels, and were for marching off directly to attack them. But there happening to live two or three warm pedlars in the place, who did not chuse to run the hazard of having their packs rumaged by such customers, in case the young fellows should be over-matched, they prevailed upon the parish-officers to comply with the demand; and in the mean time sent an account of the affair to the steward, that he might take proper methods for driving those fellows away.

Bad news encreases faster in its progress than a snow-ball. The account, by the time it reached the steward, was exaggerated in the most formidable manner. The smugglers, who were only a few shabby half-starved wretches, were multiplied into an army, provided with every military appointment; and the courage and conduct of their captain raised to an equality with the greatest generals of the age.

Such a representation was far from being agreeable to the steward. He immediately summoned all the principal gentlemen of the manor, to consult what was proper to be done in such an emergency; and after hearing all their opinions; that the affair was of so little consequence, it would be sufficient to send the petty constable, with his attendants, he gallantly declared his resolution to raise the *Posse* of the manor; and march against them himself.

" Gentlemen (said he, setting the button of his hat before, and looking fiercely) I know more of this matter than you imagine, perhaps. . .ave been a serjeant of militia for some years,
**and**

and know how to give the word of command. *Prefent your firelock !—To the right about !— Shoulder your mufket !— Fire !—Aye ! aye !* Let me alone, I know what to do, I will teach them what it is to have a foldier to deal with."

Accordingly he gave orders to have the *Poſſe* raifed directly ; and as he knew that fighting was only one part of the duty of a commander, he refolved to fhew the extent of his abilities, by making proper preparations for his important expedition.

The buftle and hurry on fuch an occafion kept up his fpirits for that day pretty well ; but upon confulting his pillow, he found that of all the occupations of ambition, war was leaft agreeable to his conftitution. He confidered, that be the enemy never fo few, a fingle fhot would do his bufinefs ; that his own piftol might burft, or his men fire aukwardly, or in fhort a thoufand accidents happen which he had no defire to be in the way of.

Nor was his refolution raifed any higher by the advices he received the next morning ; and which were continually coming in one upon the heels of another, each ftill more terrible than the laft.

In this diftrefs he bethought himfelf, that as it was impoffible for him to draw back now, without expofing himfelf to contempt for ever, his only refource was to wafte time in making preparations, till the fmugglers, either terrified at the report, or content with their booty, fhould think proper to go off.

Accordingly he fet all hands to work to put the old guns, piftols, fwords, and bayonets, that were ftuck up as trophies in the manor-

hall, in order; and particularly to ſcour *a ruſty
ſuit of armour* that had hung there for ages,
which he deſigned to wear himſelf, for fear of
accidents, conſidering prudently that *the ſafety of
an army often depends upon that of their leader.*

While all this was doing no body ſeemed ſo
buſy as he, running here and there, urging the
workmen to make haſte, and giving them new
orders every moment, which countermanded
the laſt.

But all theſe great preparations might have
been ſpared; for the ſmugglers had been ſo
roughly handled by ſome of the country-fel-
lows, whom they had attempted to rob of their
butter and eggs; and who, if they had any arms,
would have let but few of them go home to
tell the ſtory, that ſeeing the reſt of the neighbourhood preparing to attack them, they prudently took to their boat, and made off while
they could.

For the people not having military ſkill enough
to ſee the neceſſity for ſuch great preparations,
againſt a few poor deſpicable wretches, had reſolved not to wait for the ſteward's arrival, but
to drive them away themſelves.

It is eaſy to conceive his joy at this account,
the merit of which he modeſtly took intirely to
himſelf, writing the lord of the manor word,
that *frighted at the fame of his preparations,
they had ran away, without daring to await his
approach.*

The airs he gave himſelf on this occaſion
are impoſſible to be deſcribed with proper force.
He borrowed a book of military diſcipline from
an old ſoldier in the neighbourhood, and getting ſome of the terms by heart, talked of
noth-

nothing but *armies*, and *battles*, and *marches*, and *sieges*, shewing how he would have attacked them if they staid; how he would have cut off their retreat; besieged their entrenchments; in short, done every thing that ever had been done by the greatest general on the greatest occasion.

The very appearance of a military passion, though thus in burlesque, began to reconcile the mob to him; especially as they had not an opportunity of seeing into the ridicule of it. But an accident soon happened that effectually turned his heart against them for ever, and made him resolve to get from among such a turbulent crew, as soon as he could.

As he was busied one Sunday afternoon in his usual employment, of repeating his oft-repeated lesson in military matters, to some company who had dined with him, his wife enters in a violent hurry and disorder, with a piece of paper in her hand, and reaching it to him, "There (said she) read that, and see what we are to do! it is a fine thing truly, to live in a place where the mob is to direct their masters. For my part, let me but get safe home once more; and I will give them leave to treat me as they please, if ever they catch me here again."

The steward, on looking into the paper, found it to be a kind of a letter, directed to his wife, and signed *The Mob of the Manor*, to let her know that, " understanding she had made an appointment to *play at cards* that evening, at one of her neighbours, they took the liberty to inform her, they would do themselves the honour to be of her party."

The insolence of such a message suprized all present; especially the gentleman who had

made

made up matters between the mob and the
steward before, and happened to be one of the
company; "What can this mean, madam?'
(said he, thinking that his former mediation
gave him a right to interfere) I hope there was
no foundation for such a report."

"What report, sir? (answered she) I do not
understand you"

"Why, madam, (replied he) the scandalous
report of your designing to play at cards this
evening."

"I do not know what you call a scandalous
report (returned she, with a look of disdain)
my neighbour, Mrs. *Tosspot*, came yesterday to
tell me that she had got a keg of choice old
rum, and as she knows I am very fond of a
glass of good punch, invited my husband and
me, to meet half a dozen other neighbours at
her house to play a game at cards, and spend
the evening. This is all I know of the matter."

"And really madam (said the gentleman)
this is a great deal more than I am glad to
hear; as I was in hopes I had convinced Mr.
Steward of the impropriety of this before."

"Well, my dear (said she, turning to her
husband, without deigning to make any reply
to the gentleman) what do you design to do?
it is almost time. Will you go?

"Not I indeed (answered he, shrugging up
his shoulders) I have no desire to meet such
company, I assure you."

"And so we shall miss our share of the
punch (returned she, whispering him) this is
hard! very hard! and after I have set my mind
upon it so, too."

"I

" I cannot help it (replied he) I will not run the hazard."

" Then get rid of thefe people as foon as you can (whifpered fhe again, after a little paufe) I have a thought in my head that will do as well as going." And then fpeaking aloud, " Well my dear, I fubmit to you; but as we do not go there, I think it would not be amifs if we went to church, the bell rings."

" And pray, madam (added the gentleman) give me leave to advife you not only to deny your having had any fuch appointment upon your hands, if the affair fhould take wind; but alfo never to attempt a thing of the kind again while you are here; for I can tell you, this new correfpondent of your's, *the mob* of this manor, is particularly whimfical fometimes, and may unluckily do fomething that would make you cut a very ridiculous figure."

To this, the gentlewoman did not think it worth her while to make any anfwer, but turning up her nofe with an air of contempt, went out of the room.

As foon as fhe was gone the gentleman began to read the fteward a lecture on his breach of promife, to which I gave no more heed than himfelf, my attention being diverted to a more entertaining object.

" You heard the gentleman fay (faid my guide) that the mob of this manor is fometimes whimfical: look yonder, and you will fee a proof of it.

On his faying this, I turned my eye to the next ftreet, where I faw half a dozen fhabby fellows following a gentlewoman's chair carelefly, and as if they were ftrolling without any
parti-

Particular defign, till it ftopped at the door of
an houfe which I found to be Mrs. *Tofspot*'s,
when in an inftant two or three hundred of
them rufhed out of the bye lanes, and alleys,
where they had been lurking for the purpofe,
and furrounding the chair juft as the chairmen
were going to carry it into the houfe, one of
them ftopped it, and lifting up the head,
defired the gentlewoman very civilly to walk
out.

"What is the matter? (faid fhe, with an air
of authority, as if fhe thought to intimidate
them) what do the fellows mean?"

"Only to give you a little good advice, madam (anfwered he that fpoke before.) And
therefore I hope you will pleafe to come out of
your chair quietly, and not oblige us to be fo
rude as to pull you out! never fear, madam!
we do not defign to do you any hurt."

As it might be dangerous to difobey fo abfolute an authority, the gentlewoman complied
directly, amazed and terrified as fhe was; and
ftanding in the midft of them, the fame fellow
who appeared to be the orator of the mob, proceeded: "We underftand, madam (faid he,
making her a low bow, and holding his hat in
his hand, which he had very politely pulled off,
when he firft fpoke to her) that you are coming here *to fpend the evening at cards* : now,
as we know that to be a very profane, wicked,
and pernicious cuftom, and what has brought
many an one of our companions to the gal-
lows, we think it our duty not only to prevent
you this time; but alfo to take care that you
fhall never be guilty of the like again. We
therefore humbly infift, that you give us your
*oath*

*oath* here, in the fight of all thefe good people, that, from this bleffed moment, you will never play at cards, dice, or any other game, on the *fabbath-day*, while you live. Here is the book; obferve, it is *the Bible*! You muft fwear without any equivocation, or mental refervation whatfoever. Come! it is for the good of your foul."

The gentlewoman was by this time fo terrified, that fhe would have fworn to impoffibilities, to get out of fuch hands. She therefore obeyed them without hefitation; upon which the whole mob gave three huzza's, that made the ftreet ring; and then the orator, addreffing himfelf to her again, "We are glad, madam, (faid he) that you complied fo readily with our requeft, as we fhould have been very forry to ufe any violence; and we hope your example will be followed by the reft of your party, for we defign to make a general reformation; but, firft, we will do ourfelves the honour to fee you fafe home, as you can have no bufinefs in that houfe now."

With thefe words, the whole mob began to move; and the gentlewoman judging rightly, that it would be in vain to make any words with them, was obliged to turn about, walk home with them, and liften with an appearance of attention to the pious exhortations of the orator, who walked clofe by her fide all the way, with his hat under his arm, and handed her every now and then over the kennel, with as many fantaftic airs as a firft-rate fop.

It is impoffible to conceive a droller figure than fhe made on this occafion, walking fo far through the dirty ftreets, (for they took care to

lead

lead her the longeſt way about) in the midſt of ſuch a ſhabby crew, in all the frippery fullneſs of dreſs, powdered, frizzed, and furbelowed to the very tip of the mode; and conſequently without any thing on her head to hide her ſhame, and ſave her from the rain, which fell plentifully all the time.

As ſoon as the proceſſion arrived at her door, the orator made her another ſpeech; and then the mob, giving her three chears more, left her to her meditations, and retired to finiſh their pious work.

But they were too late now; the birds were flown. For, as the *ſwearing* part of the ſcene had paſſed under Mrs. *Toſſport*'s window, ſhe, and ſuch of her company as were come, had a full view of it, and none of them being piouſly enough inclined to perform ſuch a penitential ceremony, as ſoon as ever the mob moved off with the gentlewoman, they all ſlipped out at the back-door, and made the beſt of their way home; and Mrs. *Toſſpot* herſelf, juſt then receiving a card from the ſteward's wife, to let her know, " that ſhe " had been taken ſo very ill of the *cholick*, that " ſhe could not poſſibly wait upon her that " evening, but ſhould be glad of a glaſs of her " rum, as ſhe imagined it might do her good," took a couple of bottles in her lap, and hurried away to her, to tell her the news, and congratulate her on having eſcaped ſuch a ridiculous diſgrace as had befallen their friend, at the circumſtances of which they had many an hearty laugh over their punch.

" You ſee, (reſumed my guide) *the vulgar ſometimes ſees right*, though their method of proceeding is rather irregular. But this example,
no-

notorious and ftriking as it is, will have no effect. The practice againft which it was levelled is become a fafhion, and, like every
other fafhion, muft have its run, 'till fomething elfe, perhaps equally improper, fuper-
fedes it."

From that day the fteward never enjoyed a
moment's happinefs, being continually appre-
henfive of fome fuch infult from the mob, as
he could not refolve to defift from the practices
which gave them offence; accordingly, when
the time of his departure arrived foon after, he
hugged himfelf on his efcape, and laid down
his grandeur with ten times greater pleafure
than he had felt on taking poffeffion of it; and
in return for the uneafinefs he had drawn upon
himfelf, carried away an heart invenomed with
the moft rancorous hatred againft the whole
manor, the effects of which he refolved never
to mifs any opportunity of making them feel.

## The END of the FIRST BOOK.

# BOOK II.

## CHAP. I.

*The happiness of having more money than a man knows what to do with. The extensive knowledge of the lovers of* Virtu, *accounted for. Poets not judges of painting.*

BEFORE I had time to make any reflections on the ridiculous inconsistency in the conduct and characters of all the actors in this last scene, a person caught my eye, who seemed to promise more pleasing entertainment than I had hitherto met with. He was just entering into the prime of life, and appeared to be in possession of every advantage that could enhance the enjoyment of that season of delight.

So bright a prospect filled my heart with joy. " At length, O gracious spirit! (exclaimed I in an extasy) at length I have found a man whose life affords another view beside wretchedness and folly, and reconciles me to humanity. Let us observe him for a moment, and share in a bliss that seems to be so pure."

" The joy you express (answered my guide) is the genuine emanation of exalted virtue, which, rising above the malignity of envy, finds its own happiness in that of others. I shall there-

therefore comply with your requeſt with pleaſure, and leave you to form your own judgment
on ſo intereſting a ſubject."

Proud of this permiſſion, I directly fixed my
attention on the object of it.

Though the day appeared to be far advanced,
he was juſt out of bed, and ſitting at breakfaſt,
in all the luxury and ſtate of royalty. When
he had ſwallowed a diſh or two of tea, with
evident diſreliſh, " What ſhall I do with myſelf to-day? (ſaid he to himſelf, rubbing his
head, and ſtretching in liſtleſs laſſitude) I am
quite ſick of this inſipid kind of life, ſtill plodding, plodding on, in the ſame dull, taſte-
leſs round, without any variety, any thing to
expect, or even wiſh for. It is not to be
borne."——

Then muſing for ſome moments, " What
muſt they do whoſe ſtinted fortunes deny them
the gratification even of the few deſires they
have, when the higheſt affluence cannot procure me any ſatisfaction?—and yet, they evidently enjoy an happineſs which I am a ſtranger to. There is ſomething in this, more than
I can comprehend. I will think of it ſome
other time."

Turning then to his man, " What day of
the week is this, Thomas?"

" Sunday, my lord."

" Sunday! Order the horſes. I will take
a ride this fine morning.—And what ſhall I do
with myſelf the reſt of the day?— Let me conſider! Did not I promiſe to dine with her
Grace, and go with her to Mrs. *Squeakum*'s concert, and afterwards to lady *Modiſh*'s rout, and
then return and ſpend the evening with the
Duke!——

Duke!——Pfha, I am furfeited with mufick;
the very thought of it makes my head ake.—
And for routs, they are ftill worfe.  To be
fqueezed and crouded among a parcel of people
of all forts and conditions, who come together
meerly to make malicious remarks, and pick
each other's pockets!  It is intolerable.— I am
tired, quite tired of them all; of myfelf, and
every thing in the world.——That is right.
Now I think of picking pockets, let me fee
how I came off laft night, at the club!"

Then pulling a card out of his pocket,
" Aye! here it is.  What a black lift!  *Lord
Palmwell* 1000——*his Grace* 500—— *Sir John*
200—— *Mr. Shuffler* 1500—— *Capt. Gamble*
2000—— befide all the money I had about me.
Death! This is too much.  There muft be
fome management in it, that I fhould always
lofe!  I pofitively will not go among them any
more."

He was interrupted in thefe agreeable meditations by the entrance of a fervant.  " My
lord, (faid he) the groom has fent an exprefs,
to know if your lordfhip has made any bets on
your new horfe, and what particular directions
you pleafe to give about his running to-morrow,
if your lordfhip does not defign to fee him ftart
yourfelf; and to let your lordfhip know, that the
mare, which he told your lordfhip he was under fome apprehenfions of, is to be fold; fo that
if your lordfhip pleafes to buy her, you may be
fure of the horfe's winning."

" To-morrow!  Aye.  Send him word, that
I will be there.  And, do you hear! order the
poft-coach, and fend to *Mr. Shuffler*, *Capt. Gamble*, and *Sir John*, and let them know I go directly,

rectly, and shall be glad of their company. And tell *Rackum* I want him.——I have never seen that horse run yet, though he cost me so high a price : and this is the last king's plate of this year. I must not miss seeing him now, by any means."

" My lord, (continued the servant) here is a messenger from his Grace's gentleman of the horse, to acquaint your lordship that the sale of the stud is fixed for to-morrow, and cannot be put off as was intended. He says, they are all to go without reserve."

" All, does he say ? then I must be there. There are several *tip top* things among them, which I would not miss of on any account. You need not order the coach ; and send the groom word, that he may do as he sees proper about the mare. I can't be there myself." .

" My lord, (said another servant, who entered just then) Mr. *Connoisseur* is below ; he says, your lordship ordered him to send up his name. And Mr. *Stanza*——I would have denied him, but he says he has business of importance."

" Aye ! of importance to him, I doubt not.—Let them come up. As I have nothing else to do, their nonsense may divert me."——Then stretching again, and giving a long yawn, he arose from the table, which was directly removed, and walked a turn or two about the room.

As soon as the gentlemen entered, " Your servant, Mr. *Connoisseur* ! (said his lordship) Mr. *Stanza*, what news from *Parnassus ?* With what new inspiration have the Muses indulged their votary ?"

" My

" My lord, (returned the former, with a mysterious air, before the poet had time to scan his syllables for a reply) when you can spare me a moment's private audience, I have something to communicate to your lordship, that you will find worthy of your attention."

" Mr. *Stanza*, (said his lordship) if you'll take that new play that lies in the window, and look it over in the next room, I shall be glad to hear your opinion of it."

The poet made a bow of assent; and taking up the book with a contemptuous smile, retired, not a little offended at his being obliged to give place to a mechanic.

" Well, Mr. *Connoisseur !* and what is this important secret?"

" My lord, it is an important secret, I assure you. Your lordship may remember I have told you that a gentleman of judgment, who had spent several years in visiting the cabinets of the curious in every part of *Europe*, out of which he had found means, at a very great expence, to procure many of the most admired pieces, was daily expected home with his valuable collection. Now, my lord, this gentleman is just arrived; and as I have had a constant correspondence with him all the time he has been abroad, for it was chiefly by me he was directed in the choice of what he bought—
" How! were you abroad too along with him? I did not know that."——

" No, no, my lord! I was not with him; but that did not prevent my being able to direct him. For your lordship must know, that there is a regular correspondence established between all the lovers of *virtu* in Europe, by which means we are as in-

intimately acquainted with every thing in each other's country as in our own; so that I could give him my opinion what was proper for him to purchase in every place where he went, as well as if I was upon the spot with him.———— As I was saying, This gentleman no sooner landed, than he sent me immediate notice, upon which I went directly to him; and as I am well acquainted with your lordship's fine taste, I have by much entreaty prevailed upon him to let you have several of the most capital pieces in his collection, before he exhibits them to the public for sale; for which purpose your lordship may have a sight of them privately to-morrow, if you please, when I will wait upon you, to point out the proper ones to compleat your noble collection, and prevent your being imposed upon in the price; not that any price can in reality be too high for such master-pieces of art."

" To-morrow, do you say? Can it not be put off for a day or two? I am engaged to-morrow."

" My lord, that is impossible. All the *Virtuosi* in England will know of his arrival in twenty-four hours, and then it will be out of his power to oblige your lordship; and you will lose an opportunity never to be retrieved."

" Well then, I think I will go. Here, *Thomas*, bid *William* go to his Grace's to-morrow, and buy whatever he likes; I cannot go myself."

" I hope your lordship approved of the bargains I made for you at the last sale; (continued *Connoisseur*) some of the landscapes came high; but they are very fine, very fine indeed,

and

and will make a noble appearance in your lord-ship's gallery. Are they put up yet, my lord?"

"Eh! Egad, I never once thought of them. Do you know any thing of those pictures, *Thomas*?

"My Lord, the upholsterer nailed them up on the garret-stair-case; he said, they were not fit for the gallery by any means."

"He is an ignorant puppy, and deserves to be turned off for presuming to disobey my directions. How should he know any thing of paintings!— My lord,—— your lordship may depend on my judgment. They are capital pieces. The garret-stair-case! ignorant, impudent blockhead!"

"Hah! hah! hah! This is exalting into degradation, I think. But I will look at them myself when I am at leisure, and see that justice is done them."

"At what hour shall I call upon your lordship in the morning?"

"About twelve. Suppose we take *Stanza* with us. A poet should be a judge of painting. Call him in."

"A judge of painting! hah! hah! hah! a most excellent one, truly! How should such low-lived creatures have judgment in things they have not even an opportunity of seeing. They never travel to improve their taste, and enrich their minds by studying the excellencies of the foreign schools. They have no notion of any thing beyond an English daub. I must beg your lordship not to take notice of this affair to any one, as it would entirely ruin the sale of the whole collection; and especially to such a

fellow

fellow as that, whofe vanity at fuch an unde-
ferved honour would make him blab it directly. A poet never kept a fecret yet. Their
very profeffion is to prate. I beg your lordfhip will not mention a fyllable of it to him."

Saying this, the lover of *virtu* took his leave ;
and meeting Mr. *Stanza*, as he was coming in,
they faluted each other in the moft polite and
friendly manner.

## CHAP. II.

*Succefs no proof of merit. The impropriety of
being pleafed againft rule. A curious account
of the great advantages of the ancient drama.
Painters not judges of poetry.—— A capital
defect in the defigns of two famous architects,
with the wonderful effect of a bow window.*

"WELL, Mr. Stanza, (faid his lordfhip)
what is your opinion of that play ? do
not you think it has a great deal of merit?"

"My lord, (anfwered the poet with a fmile)
I fhould be very cautious of differing in opinion
with one of your lordfhip's judgment and tafte ;
but I imagine you cannot be ferious in your
approbation of this——this——this play, if you
pleafe to call it fo ; for, indeed, it might as juftly be called any thing elfe."

"How, fir! and do not you approve of it?
I fhould be glad to hear your reafons for
difliking a piece that has had fuch uncommon
fuccefs."

"Suc-

" Succefs, my lord !——Succefs, at prefent, is a very poor proof of merit. The tafte of thefe times is too low and grofs for works of true excellence. As to this, it is a meer *farrago* of imperfections and faults. It is defective in the three great unities, and wants the moral majefty of a chorus to give it dignity and importance."

" I do not know what it wants ; but this I am fure of, that it affects my paffions ftrongly, and gives me pleafure which I am not able to defcribe ; and where this is done, I do not fee any neceffity for thefe unities, or any thing elfe. That is all I defire."

" I am forry to hear it, my lord ; very forry to hear that you fhould have fubmitted your own better judgment to a corrupted tafte, fo far as to be pleafed againft rule. If your lordfhip will do me the honour to perufe this play, which I have written exactly on the plan of the ancients, and made bold to dedicate to your lordfhip's patronage, you will foon fee the impropriety of being pleafed by thefe modern monfters, and the advantage of adhering to thofe rules which you feem to make fo light of.

The unities fave the poet the fatigue of inventing, and the reader of attending to unforefeen incidents and furprizes ; and for the chorus ! it is the beft *fuccedaneum* that ever was thought of to fupply the place of imagination ; for, when the writer, at any time, can fay no more in the characters of the drama, what is eafier than to make the chorus throw in a ftring of moral fentiments, which can be picked out of any book ? and fo the whole goes on without trouble. I have thus explained to your lordfhip

the

the neceſſity of obſerving the laws of the drama, which you will farther find illuſtrated in this piece."

" I am ſorry *Connoiſſeur* is gone; ſhe would have been a proper perſon to decide this matter. Poetry and painting are ſiſter-arts."

" Some people, my lord, have thought proper to call them ſo; but with what juſtice any one who conſiders the difference between ſenſe and imagination can judge. Every poet, indeed, is moſt certainly a painter; that is, his deſcriptions ſtrike the imagination as ſtrongly as if the objects were actually preſent to the ſenſes. But no painter, I believe, can claim an equal ſhare of the poet's praiſe, as the utmoſt excellence of his art is confined to one narrow ſcene, and diſplayed on materials not only ſubject to accident, but alſo to neceſſary decay; whereas the labours of the poet laugh at time, and look up to eternity, and are capable of being multiplied in ſuch a manner as to be enjoyed by millions in the ſame moment. Where do the works of *Apelles* and all the famous painters of antiquity, live now, but in the poet's lays? They confer that immortality which makes the others ſo proud; though, puffed up by preſent praiſe, they pretend to put themſelves on a level with their benefactors. In a word, my lord, as much, indeed ten thouſand times as much, as the eye can ſee farther than the hand can reach, is poetry above painting."

Juſt as the poet had concluded this laboured panegyrick upon his art, a ſervant informed his lordſhip that Mr. *Architrave* waited below. " Bid him come up, (ſaid his lordſhip, and then turning to *Stanza*) You aſſert the honour of

the

the Mufes with fuch fpirit, that you deferve to be their peculiar favourite."

" Your lordfhip is pleafed to compliment. Will your lordfhip give me leave to lay this humble imitation of the ancients at your feet? Your patronizing it will not be a difhonour to your tafte, in the opinion of the learned. If your lordfhip will pleafe to look at it——."

" Some other time, when I am at leifure; at prefent I am engaged."

" My lord! the dedication only;—it will not take up a moment, if you will give me leave."

" Sir, I really am engaged; but any other time——."

The poet faw it was in vain to prefs any farther, and was going away with a look of the higheft difappointment and dejection; which his lordfhip obferving, " Stay, Mr. *Stanza*; (faid he) though I cannot read your dedication at this time, it is but juft that I fhould make the mufe fome return for her compliment. A few pieces perhaps may not be unacceptable."——

." My lord, (anfwered the poet in evident tranfport) your lordfhip's moft noble munificence merits all the mufe can do; nor fhall her grateful voice be filent."

With thefe words he made his lordfhip a moft refpectful obeifance, and retired with an happy heart.

Before he could make any reflections on the fudden change which the money fo manifeftly made in the poet's looks, a perfon entered with a roll of papers under his arm. Mr. *Architrave*, (faid his lordfhip) where have you been this age? I thought you were dead."

" My

" My lord, (anſwered the other, unfolding his roll) I have been employed in obeying your lordſhip's commands, which it was impoſſible to finiſh ſooner. Here is the plan you ordered me to draw; which, if properly executed, will do credit not only to your lordſhip's taſte and magnificence, but alſo be an honour to your country, where the true beauties of architecture have hitherto been moſt unhappily neglected. We have never had any eminent maſters in that moſt noble art among us here. Never one."

" How, ſir! Never any eminent architects in England? I have heard *Jones* and *Wren* ſpoken of in a very different manner in *Rome*."

" *Jones* and *Wren*, my lord, were well enough for their times, and in ſome things; but their taſte is quite exploded now. Why, my lord, there is not one *bow-window* in all their deſigns. Do but look over this plan, and conſider the various beauties in all its parts; they will give you a proper notion of *Jones* and *Wren*. No! no! they are not the thing! *Jones* and *Wren* would not do now a-days. You ſee, my lord, the boldneſs of this deſign. It is quite new. I ſcorn to borrow from any one. To the ſimplicity of the ancient ſtyle I have added the ornaments of the modern, and ſo blended the better parts of both. Obſerve the uniformity, and yet the variety in this noble front; the ſtrength and beauty of the compoſition; and then the bow-window at the end! No building can be complete without a bow-window. Does not your lordſhip think it has a very fine effect?"

" I think it has a very reverend effect if you will, (anſwered his lordſhip, who had been

hum-

humming a tune, and never caſt his eye upon the paper 'till that moment) and makes the houſe look juſt like a church. And what will the execution of this plan come to?"

" My lord, I have not yet made the eſtimate, but I know it will be nothing to your lordſhip's fortune. Not above thirty or forty thouſand pounds, or ſome ſuch matter. But will not your lordſhip pleaſe to examine it a little? I am confident you will like it; it is exactly in the preſent taſte, in every part."

" I do not doubt it, ſir. The nobleman who recommended you to me, aſſured me of your abilities; and I can depend upon his judgment. At preſent I am not at leiſure."

" Your lordſhip has had a proof of my abilities; that magnificent houſe which I have built for you."——

" Very true! I had quite forgot that. Not indeed that I can form any opinion from that houſe, as I have never yet had time to ſee it ſince it was finiſhed."

The ſteward, whom his lordſhip had ſent for, coming in juſt then, " *Rackum*, (continued he) Mr. *Architrave* will give you an eſtimate of the expence of a new houſe which I deſign to build yonder on the green; and do you ſet the people about it as ſoon as you can."

The ſteward made a bow; and *Architrave*, imagining his lordſhip might be upon buſineſs, took his leave.

CHAP.

❋❂❀❂❀❂❀❂ ❀❂❀❂❀❂❀❂❀❂❀❂

## CHAP. III.

*No bag without a bottom. The advantage of keep-*
*ing a good resolution, an evening spent in taste ;*
*and a jaunt to BATH. The misfortune of want-*
*ing something to wish for ; with some uncommon*
*reflections in praise of what no one desires to pos-*
*sess.*

" MY lord, (said the steward) I was told
your lordship wanted me."

" Aye!—But I have forgot for what,—Yes!
here, take this card, and let me have draughts
to discharge the several sums marked upon it ;
and as much more for my own use."

" My lord, I most humbly beg your lordship's pardon for the liberty I am going to take.
It is impossible for any fortune to support the expence at which your lordship lives at present ;
absolutely impossible ! All the money which was
saved during your lordship's minority is gone ;
and though your income is so very great, I must
beg leave to tell you money does not come in
fast enough to defray the ordinary expences of
your immense houshold, without the addition
of these other demands. I really do not think
there is so much as this in your banker's hands ;
and if your lordship draws it out thus, I shall
be at a loss to find a supply for your necessary
occasions."

" Not money enough !——That is impossible ; absolutely impossible ! I have never spent

half that money. Do not tell me any such thing."

" My lord, here is the account. I do not defire to have my word taken for it. I have vouchers for every fhilling. I only wifh that too many of them were not of this kind. Will your lordfhip pleafe to look at them?"

" No, I cannot at prefent; I am not at leifure. Some other time, perhaps, I may. Let me have this money directly; and if matters really are as you fay, you muft confider of fome method of putting them on a better footing; for I fhall leave it all to you."

" Your lordfhip mentioned fomething about building an house before that gentleman; I prefume you were not ferious!"

" Serious!—Yes. I defign to have it begun upon directly."

" My lord, I am afraid I take too great liberty; but I cannot help it. I have long wanted an opportunity of fpeaking to your lordfhip, but you were never at leifure. The other house that your lordfhip begun fo long ago has been at a ftand for a confiderable time for want of money to carry it on; and to begin another now, would look like madnefs. I beg your lordfhip's pardon; but I think it my duty to inform you of thefe things."

" Well! well! I will think on them fome other time. Make hafte with that money againft I am dreffed; it is time for me to go out."

His lordfhip then, as great hafte as he was in, found leifure to refign his perfon into the hands of his valet de chambre for an hour; and *Sir John* and *the Captain* calling upon him juft as the important bufinefs of dreffing was ended,

he

he paid them their demands; and forgetting all
his refolutions to the contrary, as well as his
engagements elfewhere, went directly with them
to the club.

The manner in which he fpent the reft of
the evening and the night there, where luxury
had exhaufted all her invention to provoke fated
appetite, and force nature into the groffeft exceffes, is beyond defcription. I fhall only fay,
that his ufual luck attended him, and he loft all
his money to the fame fet; his vexation at
which aggravated the effects of his debauch,
and made him a little fickifh when he awoke
next afternoon.

The firft thought that came into his head as
foon as he got up, was to go to a celebrated
water-drinking place, at a confiderable diftance,
where the fick and idle refort with equal eagernefs for health and pleafure.

Accordingly he fent for a particular gentleman whofe company he was fond of, and fet
off directly, attended by a retinue equal to that
of a fovereign prince, without ever thinking of
his other appointments.

On his arrival there, he plunged at once into all the fafhionable follies of the place; but
he had ran through them fo often before, that
they had loft the charms of novelty, and could
afford him no pleafure. He therefore returned
home as precipitately as he went, though without any determined fcheme, any thing even in
hope or expectation that could promife him fatisfaction.

The confequence was natural. He fell directly into his former courfe of life, driven
about, like a feather in the wind, by every puff
of

of vanity, without any impulse or power of his
own to direct him.

There was something so dreadfully wretched
in such a life, that I turned from him in horror. " What is your opinion now? (said my
guide, with a mortifying smile) Do you imagine that riches alone are sufficient to confer
happiness?"

" I am convinced, and ashamed of my er-
ror; (said I) but yet the very confutation of it has
opened a most valuable secret to me. I see that
poverty is in reality the greatest blessing of life,
or rather, indeed, the only one that can make it
at all tolerable. It engages the attention in
pursuits which take it off from the inevitable
miseries of nature. By delaying the gratification of the appetites it makes them keen, and
makes that gratification a pleasure. By preventing surfeit, it preserves the power of enjoyment. In a word, it keeps the soul awake with
expectation, and enlivens it with hope, without which life is a burden too heavy to be
borne; the highest enjoyment soon palling upon the sense, and making the anxiety of new
pursuits necessary to dissipate the pain of disappointment. Thus the reputed wretch, who
begs from door to door, is really happier than
he whose riches put every gratification in his
power; the hope of getting a morsel of bread
to appease the cravings of hunger keeping the
attention of the former fixed upon one point,
while, for want of any particular object to wish
for, the other sinks into listless indifference, and
loses his relish for all.

" But though I have been disappointed of
the pleasure I proposed in this last view, it has
opened

opened another to me, which I hope will be more fuccefsful.

" The gentleman whom his lordfhip took with him in his fantaftic expedition to the water-drinking place, feemed to enjoy every thing with fuch pleafure, as afforded the ftrongeft contraft to the taftelefs apathy of the other. With your permiffion, I will obferve him a little longer. I imagine I fhall not be difappointed as I was before."

My guide fmiled; and, giving a nod of affent, I directly turned my eyes to the perfon of whom I had been fpeaking.

## CHAP. IV.

*Hiftory of Mr.* CHAMÆLION. *The pleafure and advantages of the friendfhip of the Great. Epifode of Monfieur* FRIPPEAU *and his lady opens fome fecrets not very pleafing to the hero of the tale.*

THERE was fomething fo prepoffeffing in his looks, fo irrefiftibly engaging in his manner, together with the great advantage of a ftriking figure, that it was impoffible to behold him without regard; but, upon a nearer view, that eafe and happinefs of heart which had particularly attracted my notice, did not feem fo genuine and fincere as I had at firft imagined.

He was dreffed in the moft elegant and becoming tafte, juft ready to go out, and waited

only for the return of a servant, whom he had
sent with a letter. "It is impossible (said he
to himself, as he walked back and forward in
his room) that I should be disappointed. His
Grace has often assured me of his friendship,
and wished for such an opportunity as this of
doing me service. It is impossible that I should
be disappointed."

While he was pleasing himself with these
reflections the servant returned with an answer
to his letter. His eyes sparkled with joy, and
he opened it with an eagerness that shewed the
height of his hopes; but they were soon depres-
sed. He had scarce cast his eye on the contents, when a gloomy cloud overcast his whole
countenance. The letter fell out of his hand;
and sinking back into a chair, "What an unfortunate wretch am I, (said he, shrugging up
his shoulders, and lifting up his hands and eyes
to heaven) to let a false delicacy thus destroy
my fairest hopes? Why did I not go to him
the moment the place was vacant? Persons in his exalted station have their minds
taken up with so many cares of greater consequence, it is no wonder they should forget the
connections of private friendship."

Then taking up the letter, "*Extreamly glad*
—(said he, repeating some parts of it aloud, as
he read it over) *too late*——*but yesterday*——*any
other occasion*——*sincere friend*——."

Just as he concluded, a thundering at the
door announced the arrival of a visitor; and
instantly rushed in a young nobleman of the
first rank, who running up to the gentleman,
"Dear *Frank*, (said he) I am glad I have found
you at home. You must come with me directly.

ly. A party of us have this minute taken a frolick to go and beat up his lordſhip's quarters in the country for a few days; and you will juſt make up our ſet. Come along with me; your ſervants will overtake us where we dine."

"My dear lord, (anſwered the other, as ſoon as he was permitted to ſpeak) I am afraid I cannot poſſibly have the honour of attending you. Some buſineſs—"

"Pſha! damn buſineſs. What have we to do with buſineſs? I ſay, you ſhall come. We ſhould have no pleaſure without you. If you want money, I can ſupply you till you return. Come along."

"I am much obliged to your lordſhip; that is not the thing. Unluckily, I am engaged."

"Never mind that. Say I forced you away. Lay the blame on me. For you muſt, and ſhall come."—Saying which, he dragged him away, ſcarce giving him time to tell his ſervants where to follow him.

The whole expedition was of a piece with the manner of their ſetting out; a continuance of rambling, riot, and noiſe; till ſick of the fatigue, and ſome new whim coming into their heads, they returned home in as great a hurry as they went.

I could eaſily ſee that the perſon whom I particularly attended to, was far from enjoying ſuch a ſcene, and gave into it merely in compliance with his company, againſt his own better taſte and judgment. This made me expect that I ſhould ſee him to more advantage on his return home, when he ſhould be at liberty to purſue his own inclinations; but I ſoon found,

to

to my great difappointment, that I had been too hafty in forming my opinion of him; his whole life being one continued round of dangling after thofe whom fortune had placed in a fuperior rank.

Such a proftitution was fo grofs, that I was foon fick of it; which my guide perceiving, " You find the confequence (faid he) of judging from appearances. You thought this perfon happy becaufe of the ferenity of his countenance, and the relifh with which he feemed to enjoy every thing that had the name of pleafure; but this was all grimace, affected only to make him agreeable to the company whom he has devoted himfelf to, in the manner you have feen.

" It may not be improper to give you fome account of his motives for a conduct which feems fo ftrange.

" His name is *Chamælion*. He was born to a moderate fortune, and entered into the notice of the public with the advantage of every accomplifhment, both natural and acquired, which could attract efteem; but it is the proper ufe which makes the bleffing. Thefe advantages, which in a much lower degree have laid the foundation of many a fplendid fortune, by an unhappy mifapplication have been the caufe of his ruin; for, inftead of improving fo favourable an introduction by prudence and care, and applying himfelf to any of the various purfuits in which the good opinion they gained him might have been of real fervice, he became intoxicated with the flattering reception he met in the gayer world, and, neglecting every thing elfe, gave himfelf up abfolutely to idlenefs and diffipation.                    " The

" The expences of such a life far exceeded his fortune ; but he difregarded this, believing the profeffions of friendfhip which were made him by his companions, and flattering himfelf that they would make him ample amends for the facrifice of his time and fortune, by procuring him fome lucrative employment, that fhould enable him to live always among them. How juft this expectation was, you will foon have an opportunity of feeing."

On this I turned again to *Chamælion*, the crifis of whofe fate I now perceived to draw on apace. The next morning after his return, he went to pay a vifit to one of his noble friends, who had not been upon the party in the country.

After fome common chat, " I am going this morning ( faid the lord ) to thank my good friend, his Grace, for a very unexpected favour. You remember the parfon's daughter, whom you admired fo much when you were in the country with me laft fummer. After you left me, want of fomething elfe to do made me e'en take it in my head to make love to her, which the tender turtle received fo kindly, that fhe foon made me a return of all the happinefs in her power.

" There is nothing fo furfeiting as intriguing with your loving ones. I was foon tired of my fond *Phyllis*, and glad to fly from her to town. But that gave me only a fhort relief; I had not been in town a week, before fhe ftowed herfelf in a ftage-coach and followed me. This threw me into the greateft diftrefs. Her old father had been my tutor ; and though I cannot fay I am a fhilling the better for all the

the pains he pretended to take with me, he acquitted himself so much to the satisfaction of my wife father, that, when he came to die, he made him a trustee to his will, and left him such a power over me, that I cannot raise one shilling on my estate beyond my annual income, without his express consent. You may judge by this what a fine situation her elopement threw me into; especially as I was just then solliciting her father to let me raise a sum of money, to discharge my debts of honour, which you know are pretty considerable.

" It was in vain to argue with the foolish baggage. She fell into fits, pretended love; and at last stopped my mouth entirely by declaring herself with child.

" While I was in the height of this perplexity, his Grace happened to call upon me; and enquiring what was the matter, for I could not conceal my uneasiness, I e'en told him the whole affair; upon which he said, in the most friendly manner, that he knew but one way to extricate me; which was, if I could prevail upon her to marry any person whom it might be thought she had run away to, he luckily had a place, then in his gift, which would be an handsome provision for them. You may be sure, I thanked him most sincerely for so great a piece of friendship, and, the moment he was gone, summoned *Frippeau*, my valet de chambre, and made him the proposal, who readily embraced it, and soon prevailed upon her to agree to it also; on which they were directly married, and we concerted matters so, that I not only appeared innocent to her father, but also have the merit of providing for her by
-my

my intereſt with his Grace, which I took care
to place to the account of my regard for him;
ſo that I think he cannot refuſe me any thing I
aſk of him; and this very morning the bridegroom has been with me, to let me know he
has taken poſſeſſion of his place."

It is impoſſible to deſcribe the ſituation of
*Chamælion* during the latter part of this ſtory.
Reſentment, ſhame, and rage ſwelled in his
heart, and tortured every feature of his face.
Suppreſſing them, however, as well as he could,
" What place, my lord, (ſaid he) has the hap-
py man got ?"

"Why! that there place which I have ſo often
heared you ſay you ſhould like. Egad! I think
I ſhould have articled for a ſhare. The raſcal
could never have raiſed his expectations quarter
ſo high otherwiſe. At leaſt I ſhall claim a right
to renew my acquaintance with his lady, if ever
I ſhould have a mind. Hah! hah! hah!"

" And pray, my lord, (continued *Chamælion*)
When did his Grace confer this obligation on
your lordſhip?".

" One day laſt week,—while you were in
the country. But do not you think, *Frank*,
that I have well got over this affair?"

" I could have told you ſomething, my lord,
(ſaid the other, with a ſpiteful ſneer which all
his art was not ſufficient to ſuppreſs) that
would have leſſened your anxiety about that
fair lady."

" Aye! What was that? What do you know
of her?"

" Only, my lord, that her love muſt certainly have been very violent for your lordſhip,
when

5

when your fervant could fo readily prevail upon
her to marry him. Hah! hah! hah!"

"Why? Aye! that is very true.——But—
but—but confider——confider——What elfe
could fhe do?"

"And your lordfhip may add, that monfieur
*Frippeau* is a man of parts, and mafter of prevailing arguments. I fee he has conducted his
fcheme cleverly."

"Eh! I do not underftand you. His fcheme!
No. It was my propofal, not his."

"Yes, my lord, I perceive the propofal was
your's; but the plan I have good reafon to
think was his."

"His! No, no; not at all. It was his
Grace's. *Frippeau* knew nothing of the matter, till I informed him of it."

"Not directly of this I grant you, my lord;
but that he had formed fome plan of the kind I
am very clear?

"How could that be? What fhould make
you think fo?"

"Becaufe, my lord, he and this lady, to my
certain knowledge, had a very good underftanding long before the time you fay you firft
made your addreffes to her."

"A good underftanding! What do you
mean? Prithee fpeak plainer."

"I mean, my lord, that monfieur and madam had had an amour; and that, inftead of his
marrying your lordfhip's whore, and fathering
your baftard, by a prudent participation of what
he could well fpare he has had the addrefs to
take in your lordfhip to provide for him and
his hopeful family. That is all I mean, my
lord."

"An

" An amour with her! Impossible! I am sure
it could be no such thing. What can have put
this nonsense into your head!"

" My lord, it was put into my head by my
happening to catch the fond pair clasped in the
folds of love one evening, in the arbour at the
bottom of the gardem."

" 'Sdeath! when was this?" ———

" The very evening after we went into the
country. It would have done you good to see
how lovingly the turtles billed. The joy they
expressed at meeting shewed that they had been
well acquainted before."

" Damn their joy! But how the devil came
you not to tell me of this?"

" Because, my lord, she bribed me to secrecy
by the same favour. Besides, I could never
suspect that your lordship would have been
made such a dupe of by a country-girl."

" Infamous bitch! And to pretend so much
love for me all the while! But I will be revenged. I will have the scoundrel turned out
directly, and let the whore's father know of all
her tricks."

" And he will give you all the vexation he
can in your affairs, in return for the share
you have had in them. Nor is it in your power
to turn out *Frippeau* now. He has a patent for
his place, and defies you."

" Confusion! What must I do?

" Why, my lord, you must even go and return your thanks to his Grace for his great favour so worthily bestowed, and submit patiently to the abuse you have received, because it is
not in your power to redress it."

Saying

Saying this he took his leave, somewhat con-
soled for the ill treatment he had met with from
his Grace, by thinking that his lordship, who
thought he had received the benefit of it, was
still more abused than he.

## CHAP. V.

*Misfortunes multiply.  A new method of engaging
the assistance of the great.  Common occurrences.
CHAMÆLION breaks with his great friends
rather unpolitely.  His history concluded with
some odd reflections.*

SEVERELY as he felt this stroke, it was
but a trifle to the misfortunes which began
now to pour in upon him.  From his lordship's
he went on his usual errand, to the person
who had hitherto supplied him with money on
a mortgage of his estate; but, to his unspeak-
able surprize, instead of complying with his demand, the scrivener told him very gravely, that
he could not advance any more upon that security; and desired he would take measures for
paying him off without delay, or he must fore-
close the mortgage.

It is impossible to express the astonishment
into which this speech threw him.  As soon as
he recovered himself a little, " Surely, sir,
(said he) that estate must be worth considerably
more than my debt to you.  The clear rent is
eight hundred pounds a year; and the last time
we settled I owed you but fourteen thousand
pounds,

pounds, interest and principle, since which I have not had any more from you; so that you must certainly be mistaken. The estate is worth several thousands more."

"Look you, sir, (answered the scrivener) as you have always dealt with me like a gentleman, I will strain a point so far as to give one thousand pounds more; but that is on condition, that you execute a sale of that estate to me directly; and that is by five hundred more than I would give any other man I deal with."

"I am much obliged to you for your friendship, sir; but think that fifteen thousand pounds is rather too little for eight hundred a year."

"Why, there it is now. You gentlemen who have estates in land think there is nothing like them; but we know the contrary. Money, money, sir, is the thing. Sir, I can honestly make ten per cent, or perhaps more, of my money, every day I live now; and this without being plagued with tenants breaking, and repairs, and taxes, and I do not know how many vexations which attend landed estates. No! No! Money, Money is the thing."

"Ten per cent! Aye, that you can, and more to my certain knowledge, or my debt could never have amounted so high by some thousands. But this kind of talking signifies nothing. Tell me directly, what is the most that you will give me?"

"Sir, I cannot give any more than I have said; and out of that you must pay all the costs of making the conveyance too."

"Then, sir, you never shall have my estate, you may be assured. I am not reduced to submit to such iniquitous extortions yet."— With which words he turned about and left the room, sensible that it was to no purpose to attempt using any arguments with one of his profession.

He was well enough acquainted with the world, to know that the scrivener would never have made such a declaration till he had every thing prepared to put it in execution, and consequently that his own situation admitted not of a moment's delay.

Accordingly he went directly to a gentleman who had often hinted a desire to purchase his estate, if ever it should be to be sold, as he plainly foresaw it must in the end; with whom, in the present agitation of his spirits, he concluded a bargain in a very few words, that left him without a foot of property upon earth.

The forming a resolution, be it what it will, is real relief to a mind in distress, by taking off the attention from that distress, and fixing it on the means of executing the resolution.

From the moment he determined to sell his estate he enjoyed a tranquility which amid all his pleasures he had long been a stranger to; and though he was sensible that he should have but a very poor pittance remaining to found his future hopes upon, when all his debts were paid, the thought of disappointing the scrivener's base design gave him such pleasure that he scarce attended to his own ruin; or, if he had any sense of it, the illusion that had drawn it upon him, and under which he still continued, took off half its horrors.

" When my friends see (said he) that I stand in need of their assiance, they will give it without even putting me to the pain of making applicaplication: and I have money enough due to me among them, to support me as usual, till some such opportunity offers: all cannot be so basely insincere as his grace."

Supported by this hope, he went to spend the next evening among them with his wonted spirits: but a consciousness of his desperate circumstances made his apprehensions so delicate, that he construed the common pleasantries of his companions into personal insults, and left them abruptly, as much surprised at his behaviour as he was offended at theirs.

But they were not long at a loss to account for it. One of the club, who had been on the same errand himself that day with the lawyer who drew the conveyances of the other's estate, and learned the affair from him, coming in just after he had gone away in that odd manner, directly told them the whole affair, heightened with the additional embellishments of his own good-nature, such as the purchase of his estates not having paid half his debts, and his being reduced now to a condition worse than beggary.

This opened a field for curious speculations. Instead of regretting a ruin, which they had themselves been the occasion of, they all ran out into the grossest ridicule, and severest invectives, against his foolish vanity, for pretending to live upon an equality with persons of superior rank and fortune; the most extravagant of the whole set, and those especially whose circumstances were reduced nearest to a level with his, declaiming loudest in the praise of prudence and œconomy, and railing most against him for the opposite vices.

The conclusion of all was, that it would no

longer

longer be proper for them to admit him into their company : but, as forbidding him directly might too probably be attended with consequences they did not chuse, they unanimously resolved to take the safer method of treating him with a coldness, that to one of his delicacy could not fail 'to answer the same end, without exposing them to such danger.

As for him, the manner in which he passed the remaining part of the night is too horrid for description. After cursing his own folly and their baseness, till his spirits were quite exhausted, he at length bethought himself, that the particular expressions which had given him such pain were in the common stile of their conversation, and in all probability without any personal application to him, as it was scarce possible, that they could have received any account of so recent a transaction.

The consolation which this thought gave him, enabled him to take some rest ; so that when he arose, he repaired to the usual place, in pretty good spirits : but this was only like a gleam of sun-shine between two storms; the behaviour of his companions, in consequence of the generous resolution of the night before, soon removing every doubt of their meaning and design.

Stung to the soul at this, he started up, and looking at them with the fierceness of desperation ; " I plainly see, said he, in an haughty tone, that my ruin is no secret ; nor am I at a loss to account for the prudential motives of this behaviour: but you are mistaken, my worthy friends, if judging of me by yourselves, you think I am mean enough to sollicit, or re-

ceive

ceive any favour from you. Moft of this company are in my debt, both for money won and lent. The payment of that is all I require, and what I will infift on. If I owe any of you any thing, let it be demanded now, as this is the laft time I fhall ever come among you."

The firft word he fpoke caufed an univerfal filence, nor were any of them very ready to break it when he had ended, but fat looking at each other as at a lofs what to fay, and expecting who fhould fpeak firft.

This behaviour almoft difarmed his rage, and turned it into contempt; cafting his eye therefore round him with ineffable difdain, " I give you time, faid he, to confider of my demand till to-morrow, when, if I have not a fatisfactory anfwer, I fhall apply perfonally to each in another manner"— Saying which, he flung out of the room.

The threat implied in thefe laft words influenced fome of them whofe debts were but fmall to pay him: but the greater part, fheltering themfelves in the privileges of their rank, gallantly thought proper to take no notice of his demand.

But this was not their beft protection : provoked as he was at the bafenefs of their behaviour, his pride would not permit him to repeat a demand, which, from his prefent circumftances might be imputed to necefiity. Accordingly, tired of a place where every object he faw upbraided him with his folly, he purchafed a commiffion in the army with the poor remains of his fortune, and fought to filence the reproaches of his own mind, by the tumults and horrors of war.

Of

Of all the instances of human folly which I had yet seen, this affected me most. "O gracious spirit! (said I with an heavy sigh) how wretched is the state of man, that the finest endowments of mind are not sufficient to secure him from falling into this inexplicable labyrinth! Is there no land-mark to warn him from the danger? No clue to guide his steps in safety through the giddy maze?"

"The brightest endowments (answered he) serve only to make folly more conspicuous, and aggravate the pain of ruin by reproach, except they will submit to the direction of prudence.

"But the contrary is too often the case. The vivacity which results from great parts is above stooping to any restraint, especially from a virtue that appears to be meerly negative.

"Hence it is that you see the greatest follies are generally committed by men of the greatest genius; as, on the other hand, the most solid advantages are obtained by moderate abilities, when directed by that unerring guide. Of the former you have seen a striking instance in this person, and every view of life makes it unnecessary to give any of the latter.

"As to him, there is no species of folly more extensively fatal than that which proved his ruin. Every one, who, listening to the allurements of idleness, neglects to improve the present moment, and depends on chance to bring on another day that which application might procure him now, is guilty of it. All have the means of rational success within their power when they first set out in life, and the many who miscarry owe their misfortune mostly to the want of applying those means properly.

C H A P.

## CHAP. VI.

*A rare character. Description of a lady's closet. Pleasing meditations; with one side of a remarkable conversation. The history of Cælia and Strephon. Masqued batteries most dangerous in love as well as war.*

WHILE the spirit was making these reflections, I happened to cast my eye upon a female whose appearance raised my curiosity to take more particular notice of her.

Though she was descending fast into the vale of years, and time's inexorable hand had robbed her charms of all their bloom, there was a sweetness and sensibility in her looks, an elegance and grace in her whole form, which made the very ruins of beauty look lovely, and were impossible to be beheld without the tenderest emotions.

She was sitting in a favourite closet, the first view of which suggested an idea of the owner's character. It looked into a spacious garden that hung over the banks of a silver stream. At the lower end a variety of evergreens and flowering shrubs formed a number of little arbours, and spread a fragrance through the air, that disposed the heart to softness, and filled it with delight. Beyond them a row of venerable oaks bounded the view, among which the stream, stealing insensibly from the sight, made the whole prospect most romantick and grand. The windows were set out with flower-pots of the finest china. On

the

the ceiling was painted the ſtory of *Apollo* and *Daphne*, by a maſter-hand. A large book-caſe, carved in the *Chineſe* taſte, and highly gilt, covered each end of the cloſet, and diſplayed a complete collection of all the plays, poems, and romances in the modern languages, which treat of love as a ſcience, and heighten its pleaſures by the powers of imagination. A glaſs that reached from the floor to the ceiling was placed againſt the pier between the windows, and, correſponding with one of equal ſize on the oppoſite ſide of the cloſet, ſerved to ſhew the whole perſon at one view ; and a variety of maſquerade-habits, for the characters of nymphs, nuns, ſhepherdeſſes and queens, with all their different inſignia, hung up in regular order on each ſide of the door, and made the whole of a piece.

She ſat at a table placed before one of the windows, with a huge folio open before her, on which ſhe leaned her elbow as ſhe meditated on what ſhe had been reading, with her head reclined upon her hand, and her eyes fixed upon the ceiling ; her ſpectacles lay upon the book, to mark the place where ſhe had ſtopped, and her ſnuff-box and handkerchief beſide it.

After ſhe had been muſing thus for ſome minutes, " Happy days ( ſaid ſhe, with a ſigh) when love and honour governed the world ! when ceremony gave place to ſincerity, and inclination went hand in hand with virtue ! Why did I not live then ? Why was my lot reſerved for theſe dull iron times ? I might have been a gentle ſhepherdeſs, and ſpent my bliſsful life with ſome ſelected faithful ſwain in ſweet *Arcadian* vales, awaking with our tuneful pipes the ſlow-paced morn, when we aroſe to tend our
fleecy

fleecy care ; and, flumbering away the fultry noon, clafped in each other's arms, in cool fequeftered fragrant bowers, befide fome purling ftream, whofe murmurs lulled each wearied fenfe to reft."

Then, taking a pinch of fnuff, and rifing from her chair, " Or elfe I might have been fome beauteous princefs (continued fhe, as fhe walked with a majeftick air acrofs the floor) whofe fame had filled the world, and brought adoring princes to my feet."——

She was interrupted in thefe pleafing meditations by the entrance of a fervant with a letter. Difmiffing him with a nod, the moment fhe faw the well-known hand, and then kiffing the direction, fhe opened the letter, and read it over in a perfect rapture.

" O *Strephon !* (faid fhe, as foon fhe had ended) who can refift thy fweet perfuafive tongue ? Such eloquence fure never fued in vain ! Yes, I will meet you. *Cælia* will meet her *Strephon* with all the ardour of unfated love."

When fhe had thus given vent to her tranfport, fhe fat down again very compofedly to her beloved ftudy ; at which fhe continued till fummoned unwillingly to dinner.

A lover's repafts are never long. As foon as fhe had made an hafty meal, fhe fet out with all the eagernefs of expectation for the fhady walk at the bottom of the garden. The throbbing of her heart, as fhe approached this fcene moft opportune for love, made me imagine fhe was waited for by fome favourite fwain, whom I expected to fee clafp her immediately in his arms

But

But, though no such lover appeared, she seemed neither disappointed nor displeased. The moment she entered the walk, "I come, my dearest *Strephon!* (said she, spreading her arms to embrace the empty air, and talking as if to some one present) your *Cælia*, punctual to your appointment, comes to spend a rapturous hour in conversation with her soul's beloved. Here will I lean upon your arm, and hearken to the music of your voice, as we walk along the flowery margin of this limpid stream. These conscious shades, the nymphs, and naiads of the stream and grove, shall witness for the purity of our passion".

And then again, as if replying to something he had said, "I own the force of what you urge. Persuasion hangs upon your tongue; and yielding nature pleads so strongly in your behalf, that virtue hardly can resist: but spare the panting suppliant, nor seek to triumph farther over a prostrate foe."——

—"How can you wrong me so? Fantastick honour! No! I despise the thought. Leave me the sacred substance, virtue, and I will chearfully give up the fading shadow, though censure pour forth all her invenomed rage against me."——

—— "Exalted generosity! Then I am safe. Had you pressed farther I had been undone. My rebel hear was ready to revolt."——

In this rapturous flighty strain, she continued her imaginary conversation for just an hour, pausing at every period, as if for a reply, using all the gestures, and shewing the attention of one engaged in deep discourse: then taking leave, with the most passionate expressions of regard, she returned to her company, with whom she spent the rest of the evening in the highest spirits;

rits; and that she might preserve the loved idea
full upon her mind, as soon as her maid left the
room, sat up in her bed in all the flannels of the
night, and putting on her spectacles once more
read over his dear letter before she could think
of going to rest, and then put it carefully under
her pillow to tempt delightful dreams.

There was something so unaccountable in the
conduct of this lady, that, strongly as curiosity
attached my attention to such an extraordinary
scene, I could scarce contain myself to the conclusion of it; but was several times going to ask
my guide what it could possibly mean.

He read my astonishment in my looks; and
as soon as the drawing of her curtain closed the
farce, " I see, said he, that you are at a loss
what to make of this woman's fantastick behaviour. It is a species of folly so little known
in common life, that it has not yet been distin-
gished by any particular title; and will, therefore, be best understood by a short account of
her life.

" She was born, as you see, with every advantage of beauty, rank, and fortune, which all
received a higher lustre still from the uncommon
endowments of her mind. So fair a morn pre-
saged a cloudless day; and hope looked forward
with assurance for a life of happiness and honour.
But she soon fell from this envied height; and
her misfortune was wrought by such unlikely
means, that it seemed to have been designed on
purpose as a punishment and check on human
confidence and vanity."

" A gentleman, of whom it was hard to
say, whether nature was more liberal to his
mind, or cruel to his person, unfortunately

hap-

happened to fix his eyes upon her; and either from inclination, or to fhew the power of his wit, by infpiring her with love, in defpite of his deformity, directly marked her out for his addreffes.

"Flattery is the incenfe always offered to female beauty, and love the only language which it hears : but neither did he think the proper weapons for beginning his attack. He was fenfible that the former would only reflect reproach on his own unpleafing appearance, and obviate the fuccefs of the latter, if offered before art had palliated the defects of nature.

"He refolved therefore to proceed upon another plan; and accordingly, wherever he met her, inftead of entertaining her with hackneyed, fulfome compliments, and unmeaning addreffes, he affected to difcover new beauties in her mind, which raifed his attention above every thing elfe; and difplayed the charms of his own underftanding fo delicately in the praife of hers, that fhe infenfibly became enamoured of his converfation, to fuch a degree as to be indifferent to all other.

"One favourable circumftance is often fufficient to remove the moft difadvantageous opinion. The difguft which his deformity raifed foon fubfided, and her attention was fo fixed upon the perfections of his mind, that fhe quite overlooked the defects of his form: this was a great advance; but difficulties ftill as great remained, and which required the moft confummate art to conquer. Virtue was the rule by which fhe guided all her fteps, and Fame the darling paffion of her foul.

"But

" But he was not at a lofs how to proceed. As he had before avoided flattering her beauty, for fear of drawing contempt upon himfelf, fo he now refrained from mentioning the very name of love, left her virtue fhould take the alarm, and defeat his defign. His converfation was entirely fentimental: and he never even glanced at fenfual pleafure, but to fhew his difapprobation of it.

" Such a conduct foon won the confidence of her unexperienced, unfufpecting heart; and there was fomething fo flattering in the thought of being the felected friend of fuch a perfon, that fhe could not refift it, but gladly met his advances half way, and returned his profeffions wit the moft folid and boundlefs efteem.

" The tranfition from friendfhip to love is imperceptible, and feldom fails between the different fexes: but here the very means which had procured the former at the fame time feemed to preclude all hopes of the latter for ever.

" But if this difappointed his defires, it facilitated the gratification of his vanity; to which his heart was no lefs a flave. Secure in the purity of her own heart, fhe was eafily led into breaches of thofe uneffential forms which cuftom has arbitraily eftablifhed as the infeparable fhadows of virtue, and too many fubftitute in the place of the fubftance.

" Envy inftantly founded the alarm, blazoning the imaginary fall in the blackeft colours, before the innocent victim of her rage was fenfible that fhe made the leaft flip."

CHAP.

✠✠✠✠✠✠✠✠✠✠✠✠✠✠✠✠✠✠

## CHAP. VII.

*The history of* CÆLIA *and* STREPHON, *continued.—An extraordinary method of holding conversation at a distance. People often pay for peeping. Love is a riddle.*

"THE effects of innocence and guilt often bear so near a resemblance as to be mistaken for each other. Provoked at such injustice, she thought it beneath her to pay any farther regard to the caprices of public opinion; and, conscious of her own innocence, piqued herself on persisting in what had been so basely misrepresented: but this imprudent pride was imputed to another cause; and she was said to be hardened by guilt into a defiance of shame.

"Her *friend*, who had designedly led her by the hand into this labyrinth, thought he now had a proper opportunity to unmask his whole design. Accordingly he began to change the the tenour of his discourse, and try to pervert her principles, or tempt her passions to rebel against them. He drew pleasure in the most alluring colours, and softened the horrors of vice by every specious artifice: arguing against the excellence of virtue from the general opposition of nature to its dictates; and, by a daring perversion of divine truth, attempting to prove the very necessities of guilt as the proper means to merit the rewards of Innocence." But

"Though his tongue
"Drop'd manna, and could make the worse
appear
"The better reason; for his thoughts were low."
She

She saw that " *all was falſe and hollow,*" and refuting his arguments with an indignant aſperity, convinced him that all attempts of the kind muſt ever prove in vain: nor was this diſappointment ſo ſevere as may be imagined. Vanity had at leaſt an equal ſhare with deſire in his original deſign againſt her; and age and infirmities had now ſo far cooled the latter, that he was eaſily contented with the gratification of the former.

" For this reaſon he readily agreed to a propoſal of hers to hold an intercourſe of ſoul, into which ſenſe ſhould never be admitted; and as it might not be in their power to meet ſo often as they muſt deſire each other's converſation, they ſettled rules for a correſpondence by letter, which nothing ſhould ever interrupt.

" From this time, to enable her to ſupport the heavy weight of public cenſure and neglect, of which ſhe now began to be ſenſible, ſhe was obliged to have recourſe to books; and the turn of her thoughts naturally ſuggeſted the choice you ſaw.

" Nothing is more dangerous than flying for relief from any diſtreſs to folly. The natural propenſity of the mind to it is ſo ſtrong, that the fainteſt ſhadow of encouragement from reaſon links them inſeparably for ever. The pleaſure ſhe took in theſe books grew upon her inſenſibly, till ſhe loſt all taſte for every other enjoyment; and the ſtudy of them wrought ſuch a change in her mind, that ſhe ſoon relaxed the rules of her correſpondence, and deſcended to write like other mortals.

" How

**3**

" How far this humour might have been improved, it is not fair to conjecture: perhaps, what was her friend's confolation before was her protection now. However, he keeps up his correfpondence with all the ardour of defire; but as this change in the ftile might feem to lead to a more material one in their conduct, fhould they meet frequently as before, he luckily thought of the fantaftic expedient which you faw her put in practice of retiring each of them alone at an appointed time, to converfe in the power of imagination as if together; and to give a confiftency to their thoughts, the fame letter which makes the affignation appoints the fcene of it and the fubject of the converfation.

" There is nothing fo extravagant or abfurd but habit will reconcile; efpecially when it flatters any favourite paffion. Ridiculous as this thought of holding an imaginary converfation muft appear, fhe was fo pleafed with it, that it foon became her greateft entertainment; nor to this day will fhe fuffer the moft ferious concerns of life to interfere with the enjoyment of it.

" Of this fhe has given inftances, which have been attended with circumftances of fo fevere ridicule as muft have cured any mind of fuch a folly, that was not under an abfolute infatuation. I will relate one for the whimfical fingularity of it.

" Soon after this method of converfing was fettled between her and her friend, while her charms were ftill in all their glory, a nobleman of the firft rank was fo fmitten with them, that he refolved to propofe an union with her for life, concluding that the cenfures which had been

levelled

levelled againſt her, and were now almoſt forgot, ſomething more recent having given the
tongue of ſcandal other employment, were only
the effect of envy at her ſuperior excellence.

" The firſt hint of his deſign was received
with pleaſure by all her friends; and he was
even beginning to make ſome advances in her
eſteem, when an unlucky accident at once
overcaſt ſo fair a proſpect.

" As he was walking alone with her one
morning in the garden, and ſtriving to give his
converſation ſuch a turn as ſhould introduce a
declaration of his paſſion, as if by accident and
without the painful formality of a direct addreſs,
a ſervant delivered her a letter, which in the
abſence of impatience, ſhe inſtantly opened,
without ever reflecting who was preſent.

" The pleaſure ſhe diſcovered in her looks
while ſhe was reading it raiſed his curioſity to
know who her happy correſpondent could be,
for he ſaw the direction was in a man's hand;
and an accident ſoon preſented him an opportunity of gratifying it : for ſhe had ſcarce ran the
letter over, when recollecting the impropriety
of what ſhe had done, ſhe haſtily attempted to
put it up, and making him an apology for ſuch
a breach of ceremony, reſumed her former converſation ; but with ſuch an inconſiſtency and
abſence of mind as evidently ſhewed ſhe was
thinking of ſomething elſe.

" But, inſtead of putting the letter in her
pocket, ſhe had in her confuſion dropped it on
the ground, which he directly perceived, and
the nature of his intentions making him think
he had a right to take every method of gaining
information in any thing that might affect his
hap-

happiness in so delicate a point, he resolved if
possible to avail himself of the accident, and get
a sight of it. Accordingly he led her away to
some company who were in another part of the
garden; and as soon as he saw her engaged in
conversation, feigning an excuse of having
dropped his handkerchief, went back in search
of the letter, which he readily found; and
opening it without hesitation, saw to his utter
astonishment and confusion, that it contained
the most rapturous exultations of successful
love; for the further gratification of which, it
appointed a meeting in the shady walk at the
bottom of the garden that very evening.

It is easy to conceive his situation at this discovery. The first impulse of his rage was to
find out the bold invader of his happiness, and
sacrifice him to his just resentment, as he concluded, that he could not be ignorant of his intended alliance with that deceitful wanton : but
the difficulty was to discover who he was, for
the letter was signed only with the fictitious
name of *Strephon*; and he could not expect that
she would inform him, should he charge her
with her baseness, and demand his name.

" But he was not long at a loss. He readily
judged that she would be punctual to an assignation, which evidently gave her such pleasure. He
therefore resolved to take no notice of what he
had discovered ; but to try if he could not by
some means or other gain admittance into the
garden, and conceal himself near the scene of
appointment, so as to be able to detect them in
such a manner as should deprive them of every
colour of defence or extenuation, and justify
the severity of his meditated revenge: and for
fear

fear the loss of the letter should alarm her, he laid it exactly in the place he found it; and turning short into another walk, had not gone many steps, when he saw her running with the utmost anxiety in her looks in quest of it, as he also perceived by the joy that sparkled in her eyes when she returned to the company, that she had found it.

" The next part of his plot succeeded without difficulty: he readily got admittance in disguise at the back-door of the garden, as if to gratify common curiosity; and had not been many minutes in his concealment, when he saw her hasten to the place of assignation with all the eagerness and impatience of love.

" His disappointment then was the same as yours. He heard her hold her imaginary conversation in the same manner; and as it was impossible for him to comprehend what it meant, that very circumstance only doubled his anxiety to develope such a dark and unaccountable scene.

" But though he had not detected her in the flagrant manner he designed, his scheme was not entirely disappointed, as she had made the discovery he wanted, by her frequent repetition of her lover's name in the course of her conversation. As soon therefore as she retired, he resolved to go directly to him, and require an explanation of the whole affair: but what was his surprise to find that he had been confined to his room for many months by the gout, nor had a prospect of quitting it soon ! He therefore thought that he should only make himself ridiculous by mentioning the motive of his visit, and so passed it off under the appearance of common ceremony.

CHAP.

### C H A P. VIII.

*Continued.— Perplexity worse perplexed. A slight prejudice of education opens a new scene of confusion. A curious account of a* JUGGLER. *He foils the Devil at his own weapons; but is surprised himself in the midst of his triumph.*

" THIS naturally encreased his perplexity. He now considered the affair as a master-piece of intrigue ; the mystery of which he was determined, if possible to discover. With this design he directly dispatched a trusty servant to try if he could find out among the servants of the other, whether there was any intercourse between them and that lady ; who immediately returned with an account, that scarce a day passed in which they sent not letters to each other in the most publick manner ; and particularly, which was the principal point of his enquiry, that her footman had received one for her that very morning.

" The astonishment into which this account threw him may be easily conceived. The avowed libertinism of this gentleman's character gave him too just reason to form the worst opinion of any intercourse with him ; at the same time that the manner in which it was carried on seemed to contradict its being of an improper nature : but, as this might also be only a finesse, he resolved to try if he could not make use of it to confirm that very suspicion which it was devised to elude.

" Accordingly

" Accordingly he employed the fame fervant to corrupt the gentleman's porter, by a confiderable bribe, to let him have a fight of the next letter he received to fend to her, which he folemnly promifed to return fo foon, that it fhould not be miffed.

" The porter had had too much connection with the great to be proof to fuch a temptation. He gave the letter, and the nobleman had the farther aftonifhment to find, that it contained not only another affignation, but even fpoke in raptures of the pleafures of the laft.

" This involved him in tenfold darknefs. He fcarce knew how to believe his fenfes; and began to confider whether the whole might not poffibly be a dream. As foon as he recovered a little from his aftonifhment, he returned the letter; and prepared in the fame manner as before to be a witnefs of this moft furprifing fcene, when upon feeing her former incomprehenfible extravagancies, he directly concluded fhe was under the delufion of fome fafcination, and that the gentleman ufed more than natural means to bring her into this ftate, to ferve fome bafe purpofes of his own.

" Full of this notion, which an unhappy prejudice of education, his imagination having been filled in his infancy with fuch terrors of withcraft and incantation, as it was impoffible for reafon ever abfolutely to get the better of, made him more readily give into, he flipped away unperceived by her, and running to the houfe, alarmed the whole family with a dreadful account of her being, at that very inftant, under the dominion of an evil fpirit.

" It

" It is impoffible to defcribe the confterna-
tion into which this ftory threw them all; efpecially the lady's mother, who, in the weaknefs
of extreme age, had refigned herfelf to the illufions of a fet of pretended reformers, whofe
*method* was to fill the minds of their infatuated
followers with imaginary terrors, that they
might the more eafily mould them to their own
iniquitous purpofes. They ftared at each other
for fome time, in all the ghaftlinefs of affright,
unable to fpeak a word : but he knowing that
the time of her *poffeffion* would foon be at an
end, and having obferved before that no traces
of it remained after the expiration of the appointed hour, defired that they would come out
with him directly, and be witneffes of the truth
of what he told them.

" On this, fome of the boldeft ventured
with him, while the reft went pioufly to prayers,
and coming upon her unperceived, over-heard
her in high difcourfe, which they readily believed his lordfhip's opinion to be with an evil
fpirit, whofe voice even fome of them confi-
dently afferted they heard talking to her, though
he did not appear to their fight.

" As foon, therefore, as her taking leave of
her imaginary companion made them think
the fpirit was withdrawn, and that they might
approach her without danger, they all rufhed
upon her, and holding her faft, while her furprize deprived her of power to afk the reafon of
fuch treatment, hurried her directly into the
houfe.

" It had happened, that while they were out upon
this important expedition, her mother's ghoftly
guide had called in as ufual, to enquire into the
state

ftate of her confcience, and to exchange fpiri-
tual for bodily comforts. The fight of him
filled them all with joy. " O Doctor, faid the
good old lady, you are come in a lucky moment."—And then wringing her hands, " my
poor unhappy daughter! O doctor, the enemy
has furprifed her; the foul fiend has taken
poffeffion of her body! O my daughter, my
daughter!"——

" As it was impoffible to conceive what fhe
meant, the doctor turned to another of the
company, whofe grief and affright had not fo
far overpowered her reafon; who in a few
words informed him of the whole affair. Though
upon all occafions, he affumed an appearance
of the higheft refolution which his pretended
fanctity of life could infpire, his foul was fecretly a flave to every terror which confcious
guilt could raife to ftartle the moft bigotted
fuperftition. Such a ftory, therefore, was far
from being agreeable to him: however, as it
bore not the leaft appearance of probability, and
efpecially as it was impoffible for him to retreat
now, without forfeiting his credit for ever, he
refolved to hide his fears, and act his part in
defiance to his confcience, as he had often
done in other cafes, be the confequence what
it would.

" While he was forming this refolution, he
ftood with his hands and half-clofed eyes raifed
to heaven, as if wrapt in mental adoration and
prayer, to invoke the divine affiftance: an attitude which he had practifed fo often, whenever
he wanted time to confider how he fhould extricate himfelf out of any difficulty, or carry
on any glaring impofition, that he now fell
into

into it mechanically. Then turning to the trembling matron, "Fear not madam," said he, in a flow folemn voice, and with an air of importance, "the prayers of the faithful are able to prevail over all the powers of Satan. Thy daughter fhall be reftored: my fpirit hath received aflurance, and longs to undertake the conteft. Now fhall thou behold the prince of darknefs put to flight, and all his ftrength defeated by the word of feeble man: but faith does all."——"Juft as he faid this, he heard them forcing the fuppofed demoniack into the room, and fummoning up all his courage and effrontery, prepared to exorcife her according to a ritual of his own invention: the terror, that in fpite of all his efforts to conceal it glared in his eyes affifting his impofition, and paffing upon all prefent for the emanation of enthufiaftick rapture.

"All defcription falls fhort of fuch a fcene. The aftonifhed patient was obliged to undergo the whole ceremony, without being permitted to afk the meaning of it, every time fhe attempted to fpeak her voice being drowned by a general exclamation of affright and folemn adjuration to filence, which her amazement made her the more eafily comply with.

"As fhe fat therefore in filent wonder, without any appearance of diftraction, during the laft act of the farce, the * *Juggler*, as foon as it was finifhed, addreffing himfelf to her mother, "I told you madam (faid he with an air of

---

* See PICART's *ceremonies and religious cuftoms.* Vol. III. P. 94 &c.—

triumph),

triumph), that my *method* was infallible: it was partly invented by that sage and pious prince *James* I. to whom the policy of Satan's kingdom was as well known as that of his own; the rest is an addition of mine, in which the success testifies that my spirit was not denied divine assistance: scepticks and infidels may scoff and doubt; but to pious faith is given demonstration."——

Then turning to his patient, "And you, my daughter, should repent of all your evil ways, and turn your heart to righteousness, lest the evil one should not only come again and take possession of his former habitation, but also bring others more wicked than himself with him; so that your last estate would be worse than the first. Open your heart therefore to the entrance of faith, and obey the *call* of grace."

This edifying address had an effect very contrary to what was intended. The authoritative air with which he delivered it, and the insinuations of some secret guilt in his exhortation to repentance, provoked her spirit, naturally high, to such a degree, that her anger getting the better of her astonishment, "I desire to know, sir, (said she, with a look of indignation and contempt) by what right you presume to speak to me in this insolent manner? Overpowered by violence, and out of respect to a person whom I am sorry to see join in such an unnatural combination, I have submitted to listen to the incomprehensible nonsense, by which the sacred name of the Deity has been profaned in the ridiculous farce, which you have just been acting: but I am not under the same obligation to bear with you."

The

" The refentment that flashed from her eyes, when she began to speak, had raised the apprehensions of the company, that she had not been sufficiently exorcised, which were too strongly confirmed by what she said : respect, however, if not perhaps fear, prevented their interrupting her, till a tame jack-daw that had got up to the top of the house happening to chatter as he fell down the chimney, just as she said these last words, they all thought the *Juggler*'s prophetick fears fulfilled ; and that a legion of devils was coming to take possession of her, and falling upon their knees at the same instant, the *Juggler* began to run his lore over again in the most violent agitation ; his superstitious imagination taking the general alarm, while the rest hung down their heads, nor dared to raise their eyes for fear of seeing some horrible sight.

## CHAP. IX.

*The History of* CÆLIA *and* STREPHON *concluded.*
*The* JUGGLER *juggled ; and the mystery cleared*
*up at last. Habit too powerful for conviction.*
*The advantage of making the first story good.*

" THIS doubled her distress, and almost communicated the infection to her. The terror glaring in all their ghastly looks convinced her that there was something in their conduct more than she could comprehend, and that they did not act thus meerly to insult and ridicule her as she had imagined. Unable therefore

fore to refift her impatience to be informed in
the meaning of it, fhe ftepped up to her noble
lover, for no one dared to hold her any longer,
and addreffing him with an earneftnefs that fhewed the anxiety and aftonifhment of her foul,
and added not a little to the affright of his,
" To you, my lord, (faid fhe) I apply for relief from an amazement and perplexity which
torture me almoft to madnefs. What means
the violence which has been offered to me ?
What means this incomprehenfible behaviour of
all prefent? You have given me reafon to imagine I held fome place in your efteem; by
that I adjure you not to let me burft in ignorance."

" Though his lordfhip's fright was little inferior to that of the oldeft woman prefent, and
fcarce left him power to comply with her requeft, there was fomething fo affecting in this
application, that he could not refift it. " Madam (faid he, looking earneftly at her as he
arofe from his knees) I hardly know how to
obey your commands, for fear of giving you offence."

" Fear not, my lord, (anfwered fhe, impatiently) I afk for information, and defire to be
told the truth."

" Then, madam, I am forry to tell you that
you were feized in the garden on an opinion of
your being at that inftant under the power of
witchcraft, if not actually poffeffed by fome evil
fpirit; and to deliver you from fo dreadful a
fituation was and is the motive of that behaviour at which you feem to be fo much furprifed."

" Be-

" Bewitched! Poffeffed! Patience. Kind heaven, grant me patience! What can have given occafion to an opinion fo bafely infamous and abfurd?"

" Before he had time to reply, the unlucky jackdaw hopped from the chimney, and, without giving him any warning, perched upon the *Juggler*'s head, who happened to kneel very near with his back toward it, and at the fame inftant repeating the tremendous chatter, caught him by the nofe, which was thrown up in his ufual attitude, as he muttered over his incoherent ejaculations.

" Such an attack was too dreadful to be borne. The affrighted wretch threw himfelf forward on the ground, and in the guilty terrors of his imagination, thinking all the devils of hell had laid hold on him to revenge the infolence of his pretending to an authority over them, roared out with all his might, " O fpare me! Spare your poor fervant, and I will never give you the leaft difturbance more! Never prefume to offend you by mimicking a power which I too well know I am not poffeffed of! Do what you pleafe with all the world befide, but fpare your faithful indefatigable flave! Spare me at leaft for this time, and take me wholly when I die."

" His lordfhip, who by his having rifen to anfwer the adjuration of his miftrefs, had an opportunity of feeing the caufe of the poor *Juggler's* fright, the ridiculoufnefs of which opened his eyes to the abfurdity of the whole fcene, burft out into an immoderate fit of laughter, in which fhe joined him with all her power.

As foon as he was able to fpeak, " Never fear, doctor, (faid he) I'll infure you, for this
time;

time; your master has given you the reprieve you desire, and left this honest jack-daw to witness the bargain."

"It is impossible to express the effect which this speech had upon all present. They instantly raised their heads, and turning their eyes to the prostrate *Juggler*, saw the jack-daw busied in tearing his wig, which had unluckily, tangled about his claws.

"This sight instantly put an end to all their fears: they raised a peal of laughter that shook the room, which sufficiently informed the unfortunate juggler of his disgrace, who, rising from the ground in the utmost confusion, slunk away without daring to shew his face, especially as he had made such a fatal discovery of his ignorance and impostures, as it was impossible for his most inventive assurance and hypocrisy to extenuate.

"But the company was too intent upon other matters to take any farther notice of him. As soon as the tumult of their mirth, in which all strove to hide the remembrance of their past folly by their present loudness, had subsided, they made all possible apologies to the lady for their behaviour, and expressed the highest astonishment at their own weakness, in giving credit to such a ridiculous story, at the same time fixing their eyes upon his lordship as the author of it.

"This threw him into a very disagreeable situation. He saw that it was necessary for him to exculpate himself; but how to begin, or in what manner to do it, he was utterly at a loss.

"The

The lady and he ftood looking at each other thus, for fome time, till at length her impatience made her break filence. " I hope, my lord, (faid fhe) that you are fatisfied with the fuccefs of your exorcifm; and now that I am reftored to myfelf, fhould be glad to know your lordfhip's reafon for entertaining an opinion not only fo injurious to me, but alfo fo ridiculous in itfelf."

"Madam, (anfwered he, in the higheft confufion) I fee the abfurdity of the fcene in the ftrongeft light; and fhould be fincerely glad that the removal of one difficulty convinced me, that the opinion which gave rife to it was as ill-grounded as I am fenfible the confequences of that opinion have been ridiculous."

" For heaven's fake, what can that difficulty be, my lord? Speak! Speak without referve! That delicacy which at other times is necef-fery, is improper in fuch cafes as this, and muft give place to plainnefs and fincerity."

"I mean, madam, thofe myfterious converfations which you hold in the fhady walk, *you beft know by what means,* with an abfent perfon."

" *Means,* my lord !— *By what means!*— I don't underftand you."————

" Such converfations, madam, can be held only by the affiftance of evil fpirits, or under the illufion of fafcination: this is what I mean, madam! And I wifh I was not obliged to add, that your manner of acting, at the fame time, was fo extravagant, that nothing but being under fome fuch unhappy influence can account for it."

It is not eafy to conceive the confufion with which thefe words ftruck her. In the
flightinefs

flightiness of a warm imagination, she had considered this method of holding an ideal conversation, not only as innocent and safe from reprehension, but also as something of a refined and elevated nature, never suspecting its being subject to so ridiculous a construction, nor indeed giving herself time to reflect, that she must certainly be taken notice of one time or other; and some such wrong construction put upon it, as it was impossible that reason ever could suggest the most distant conjecture of the right.

"But her eyes were now opened, and she saw her folly in its most mortifying consequences. At first she was undetermined how to act, whether to attempt passing it off as no more than a meer whim of her own, without any meaning or design, or candidly to confess the whole; for she saw the indispensible necessity she was under to give some account or other of it.

"The difficulty was distressing; the latter must betray a mystery, which, as too sublime for common minds to comprehend, would only expose her to farther ridicule; and the former she thought would shew a levity and childishness which must bring her understanding in question.

"This reflection determined her. When once a woman entertains an opinion of her own understanding, there is nothing which she will not sacrifice to preserve it. "I find myself reduced, my lord, (said she, after some pause) to the disagreeable necessity of disclosing what I will own I had rather conceal. The conversations which have given occasion to all this folly

and

and difturbance, are fo much out of the common way, that, to fet them in a proper light, it
will be neceffary to trace them to their original."

" She then, in a few words, ingenuoufly told
the whole, in the manner I have related ; and,
to confirm the truth of her account, produced
feveral of her *friend's* letters, making appointments for, and fixing the fubjects of their imaginary converfations.

" His lordfhip, who, from the circumftances he knew, though for obvious reafons
he had thought proper to conceal his knowledge of them, was convinced that fhe had
told the truth, afked her pardon in the politeft manner for the part he had unwittingly
acted in the affair, and was fo charmed with
her ingenuity, and the delicacy and fublimity
of her fentiments, that he left her, ten times
more in love than ever."

" But when he came in a cooler moment to
reflect on the character of her *friend,* and the
unhappy confequences of utter lofs of reafon,
which fuch a flightinefs of imagination might
too probably end in, even though his other
apprehenfions could be removed, prudence prevailed upon him, to put a violence upon his
inclinations, and break off, while it was yet in
his power, fo dangerous a connection.

" As to the lady, her mind was fo much
taken up with her darling folly, that inftead of
being cured of it by all this vexation and difgrace, fhe immediately gave her *friend* an account of the whole, and appointed a *meeting*
that very evening in her clofet, to enjoy a
laugh together at fo whimfical an affair.

" From

"From that time she has dreamed away her life in the manner you saw, an absolute blank in the creation, uselefs to herself and all the world; fo unaccountable a story raising such a prejudice against her, that no one ever sought an alliance with her after.

"Nor were the confequences of it much lefs difagreeable to her *friend*. The *Juggler*, who was fenfible that he had totally forfeited his influence in that family by the unfortunate adventure of the jack-daw, was refolved to obviate the effect of their telling the story, and be revenged for the mirth they had indulged at his expence, by making fuch a reprefentation of the whole as fhould throw the burden entirely upon them.

"Accordingly, the very next morning, he entertained his flcck with a moft melancholy tale of a lady of diftinction's being bewitched by a certain gentleman, and holding frequent converfations with him, in his abfence, by the affiftance of an evil fpirit, under whofe dominion he had put her; and how he himfelf had offered to deliver her by the power of his prayers; but that her friends, out of a perverfe pride, had refufed his affiftance, and affected to make a jeft of the affair; and then, with the higheft appearance of piety and compaffion for fo deplorable a cafe, offered up a long and fervent prayer for her deliverance.

"This reprefentation he knew would prepoffefs his followers in his favour, and prevent their giving credit to any thing that might be faid to his difadvantage, however notorious and true: and though he did not directly tell the perfons names, he, as if without defign, gave

fuch

ſuch a deſcription of them, that no one could be at loſs to know whom he meant.

" This ſtory, as he intended, was induſtriouſly propagated, with the advantage of ſuch circumſtances as every relater thought proper to add; in conſeqence of which not only the lady was aſhamed to ſhew her face, but there was alſo ſuch a prejudice raiſed againſt her *friend*, that for a long time he was inſulted and reviled by the mob in the moſt opprobrious manner whenever he ſtirred out, and more than once was in danger of having his innocence put to the teſt of a *dipping*; the deformity of his perſon unhappily agreeing with the idea which the vulgar entertained of witches, and confirming their prejudice againſt him; while by this addreſs of making good the firſt ſtory, the ſecret by which he had ſo long ſupported himſelf againſt the force of numberleſs detections of the blackeſt nature, the *Juggler* had the ſatisfaction to ſee his enemies overwhelmed with a ſtroke which he had ſo dexterouſly ſhifted from his own head."

C H A P.

XXXXXXXXX * XXXXXXXXX

## CHAP. X.

*Different appearances of the fame object feen in different lights. A whimfical reprefentation of the laft efforts of gallantry, with other no lefs curious matters.*

" YOU may perhaps have a curiofity (continued the fpirit) to fee one who has acted a part in every refpect fo extraordinary as this gentleman. Behold him yonder; and acknowlege the power of a wit able to conquer the antipathies of nature, and make fuch a perfon the object of a tender paffion."

The aftonifhment with which the fight of him ftruck me is not to be conceived. Though I was prepared to expect an appearance remarkably difagreeable, my imagination had never framed an idea of fuch abfolute deformity as now met my eyes. The defcription would be too difgufting. Turning from him haftily, " Is it poffible, O my guide, (faid I) that this can have been the object for whom that beauteous creature facrificed her happinefs ? I have feen too many inftances of the frailty and capricioufnefs of the female heart; but never did I think they could rife fo high as this before."

" View him again, (faid he, touching my eyes with his wand) and then let me hear your fentiments."

"O gracious fpirit! (exclaimed I, in a tranf-port) what lovely creature can this be? Such beauty never did my eyes behold before this moment. What grace! what elegance!—— And then the unbounded generous benevo-lence!—— That fpirited fenfibility and fire!— Sure he muft be the mafter-piece of nature! Some favourite work of heaven, to fhew man-kind an inftance of perfection."

"Such is the light! (anfwered he with a fmile, as he touched my eyes again with the wand, and reftored the gentleman to his former appearance) fuch is the light in which his writings reprefent him; and fo does the brilli-ancy of his wit dazzle the delighted imagina-tion, and make his very defects appear perfec-tions. I have given you this view of him, to convince you of the error of judging too haf-tily from the firft appearance. Not that you are to give too implicit credit to this either. To form a proper judgment of a man, his ac-tions muft be confidered; and though the mo-tive may in reality often alter the intrinfick merit even of thefe, the error will be pardon-able. Obferve his prefent employment, and it will give you a juft idea of his character. Such parts of his paft life as may illuftrate this, and afford inftructive entertainment, I will afterwards draw a fhort fketch of."

On turning my eyes then to the gentleman, I faw him in the moft whimfical fituation pof-fible to be conceived. He was fitting up in his bed, wrapped in flannels, and fupported by bolfters, with a writing-table before him, fixed upon a frame that ftood acrofs the bed, to pre-vent its bearing on his feeble knees.

On

On this lay an heap of love-letters, odes, and sonnets, the subjects of which were so ill suited to his condition, that they almost seemed to be a satire on it, at the same time that he perused them with an appearance of pleasure, which made his very infirmities ridiculous, every attempt at laughter being echoed by a groan, every feeble smile followed by a frown of agony.

As soon as he had read them through with attention, he reclined his head upon his shoulder, and, shutting his eyes, fell into a meditation on the manner in which he should answer them.

When he had mused for some moments in this posture, " Sylvia!—— (said he, thinking aloud) Sylvia!— Aye, she begins.——Raptures and fire for her!—Damon must press her home. Youth and luxuriant health require a bold address. The thought will warm me, elevate my fancy!—O my shoulder!—My back too!" Then calling to a servant, " Fetch me another blanket. The cold shoots through me. There! That will do!——So much for Sylvia! (continuing his former soliloquy) Who comes next? —Corinna.— Wanton baggage!—Amoret must wooe in double entendre! Lewdness scarce wrapt in gauze must be his cue.—This cholic—Oh! —Some cordial! Fill the glass. O my bowels! —So. Now I'm better.—— Then for Pamela. I'm tired of Musidorus. I must drop her. That unimpassioned sentimental strain gives me the hip. I'd sooner write a sermon.—Chloe!— Lucinda!—Phillis!——Aye. They'll come of course! I need not study much for them."

Having

Having ran over the lift of his correfpondents in this manner, he directly began to anfwer them, as faft as the frequent interruptions of his various pains and aches would permit.

It is inconceivable with what addrefs and fpirit he affumed all thefe different characters, in fpite of the repugnancy of nature, in his enfeebled tortured ftate to every fenfation of pleafure. Gay, grave, or loofely light, cold, amorous, pious, or profane, he was every thing to every one, according to the part he undertook.

The fatigue of fuch a tafk was too great. As foon as it was finifhed, his fpirits failed him, and he funk back upon the bed, where he lay in more than infant imbecility, while his fervant removed the writing-table, and locked up his works.

" What think you now' (faid my guide) of the volubility of human genius?—Of the power of imagination to create its own happinefs?"

" It is impoffible (anfwered I) not to admire fuch abilities, though the ufe they are put to almoft takes off their merit : for, what can be conceived more ridiculous and difgufting than to fee old age mimicking the levities of youth, and pretending paffions which it can no longer feel ; paffions too powerful of themfelves without fuch irritation, and to which nature that makes their impulfe irrefiftible prefcribes myfterious privacy and reftraint."

" Yet fuch (replied the fpirit) has been the conftant bufinefs of his life, and to this foolifh vicious vanity have abilities been proftituted, which proper application would have made an honour to himfelf, and an advantage to his

4                                              country.

country. Sometimes, it is true, he has broke the chains of this infatuation, and given instances of the most exalted powers and virtues of the human mind; but the force of habit soon sunk him down again to his former folly, and the glory of these short emersions, like lightening flashing through the darkness of the night, seemed only to shew his indolence in a more striking light.

" You have seen the number of sonnets and epistles he has now wrote in varied characters, and to various persons, and justly reprehended the folly of an amusement so inconsistent with his present state, so much beneath his better reason.

" But how much higher still will your indignation rise when you know, that of all those in writing to whom he thus consumes the few remaining moments of his life, two only have any existence out of his own imagination, *Celia* whom you have just now seen, and one more, whose vices have been a disgrace to her *sex*; though, to indulge his absurd vanity, he shews these labours of his folly as the genuine produce of a real correspondence.

" The history of the former you already know; that of the other, though not so much out of common life, is filled with incidents which would afford abundant matter of entertainment, were they not foreign to our present purpose. One only in which this gentleman was concerned I will relate, as it illustrates his character in the strongest light."

**CHAP.**

❀❀❀❀❀❀ ❀❀❀❀!❀❀❀❀❀❀❀❀

## CHAP. XI.

*Anecdotes of a celebrated female. A fencer foiled at his own weapons.| Secret of a correspondence not so uncommon as unaccountable; with a striking instance of vicious vanity. A new scene.*

" THIS celebrated female was one whom her vices of every kind had reduced to the necessity of striving to subsist by stratagem, when debauchery had anticipated old age, and worn off the bloom of those beauties which had been the first cause of her fall, and the price of whose prostitution had since afforded her a wretched support.

" In the promiscuous acquaintance of such a life, she happened to fall into the company of this gentleman, and, readily forming an idea of his character, judged that he was a proper subject for her to try her talents on.

" Accordingly she wrote him a letter, professing a passion, the extraordinariness of which for such an object she palliated by praising the charms of his mind, and turning the imaginary advantages of external beauty into the most delicate and poignant ridicule; and proposing a correspondence, on condition of his giving her an inviolable assurance, that he never would take any methods to find her out, as it was absolutely impossible for them to have any personal intercourse whatsoever, gave him an address, by which she took care it should not be in his power to trace her.

" This

" This was attacking him at his own weapons. The vivacity and wit difplayed in her
letter, for nature had been as liberal to her in
the endowments of mind as in the beauties of
form, and her way of life, which had worn out
the latter, ferved only to polifh and give a
keennefs to the former, furprifed and charmed
him beyond expreffion. Befide, myftery doubles
the pleafure of intrigue, by giving fcope to the
imagination inceffantly to frame new fchemes
of delight, and keeping the attention always
fixed. He therefore readily accepted her offer,
and begun a correfpondence, in the courfe of
which fhe raifed his defires fo high, for he was
not then quite funk into his prefent ftate of de-
crepitude, and played with them fo artfully,
fometimes feeming to difcover an inclination,
and then ftarting difficulties as from virtue, and
giving equivocal hints of dependence in her
circumftances, that fhe led him infenfibly to
make her moft liberal offers, if fhe would only
indulge him with an interview on terms of the
ftricteft honour ; and, to remove every doubt of
the fincerity of his intentions, figned his propofal regularly with his own name, the correfpondence between them having been till then
carried on under the fictitious ones of *Corydon*
and *Phillis.*

" Though this was directly what fhe aimed
at, fhe ftill affected difficulties, and expreffed
doubts to preferve appearances, and draw him
to explain and confirm his propofals beyond a
poffibility of retraction or evafion ; and then at
length complied with his defire of an interview,
with all the diffidence of virgin modefty, *the*

(*y*

*coy, reluctant, amorous delay* of unexperienced young defire.

" Raifed to the higheft pinnacle of expectation by this management, his aftonifhment may be eafily conceived, when he met an old acquaintance at the place of affignation. His difappointment was fo great, that he ftared at her for fome moments before he could believe his fenfes.

" But fhe foon convinced him that he was no longer under a miftake. Throwing herfelf at his feet, fhe conjured him to pardon a deception which neceffity and hopelefs love equally fuggefted; and, wretched as he muft know her circumftances to be, offered to return him all his letters, and depend entirely on his generofity, if he would only allow her to enjoy perfonally that place in his efteem which he had honoured her correfpondence with; and appealed to all her letters, if fhe had been guilty of any other deceit than that tacite one of not revealing herfelf directly; or had given him juft reafon to form any particular expectation from this meeting, in which he could fay he was difappointed.

" She was fufficiently acquainted with him to be convinced of her fafety, in making this offer. His ample fortune raifed him above regard to money; and no human heart ever glowed with a more benevolent readinefs to difpenfe it to the relief of the diftreffed. Befide, fhould he fhew any defign to take an ungenerous advantage of this confidence, there was a material difference between actually giving up his letters, and making fuch an offer, which fhe could eafily retract.

" It

" It was some time before he recovered himself sufficiently to give her an answer. At
length, having weighed every circumstance dif-
passionately, he raised her from the ground,
and smiling, with a beneficence that dissipated
all her doubts, " Make no apology, madam,
(said he) for a device that has afforded me the
highest pleasure I have ever enjoyed. All mankind wears a mask; and happy are they to
whom the pulling it off proves no greater difadvantage. If I have shewn any surprize at
seeing you, it was only at my own inattention,
that had not before discovered the beauties of
your mind in so much conversation as we have
had together."

" He then assured her of his friendship, and
in return for the generous offer she had made
him of restoring his letters, gave her a confiderable sum of money, to settle her affairs;
which she preferred to an annuity, that might
prove precarious."

" Since that time she has been, though privately, his principal correspondent in different
characters, which she assumes with as much
ease as himself, to give variety and afford matter for agreeable surprize, the pleasure of which
he never fails to reward liberally on the discovery: thus she is the *Cynthia*, *Chloe*, *Constan-
tia*, *Phryne*, *Phillis*, &c. of his muse; and indeed sends him all the letters he shews with
such ostentation as from different persons, except those he often does himself the honour of
writing to himself, *Cælia*'s being in general too
particular for publick inspection.

" In one instance only has their correspondence been made public, which was by her addressing

dressing to him a specious apology for the particular vice of her profession, in which she lessens the merit, if not denies the necessity, of the opposite virtue that has ever been esteemed the indispensible test of female honour. His accepting such an address at a time of life when the subject of it was meer matter of speculation to him, is a strong though not uncommon instance of the force of vicious habit, which can thus influence old age to a ridiculous vanity of insinuating a taste for the most reprehensible pleasures of youth, by countenancing them in theory, after the practice is become impossible.

" But the greatest danger of this infatuation is, when it fixes upon a particular object. Its force, which before was weakened by dispersion, is then collected into one point, and the extravagance of its effects encreases in proportion as the abilities for its gratification fail."

" Observe that person walking in deep meditation, by the side of yonder stream. The situation he is in at this very moment is one of the most striking instances nature has ever shewn of the difficulty of shaking off the ascendency which loose, lascivious blandishments and female artifice will insensibly gain over the heart, in spite of the strongest admonitions of reason and virtue.

" While he is forming a resolution, on his steadiness, in which depends the crisis of his fate, I'll give you a few general sketches of his past life, as far as is necessary to explain his present perplexity."

CHAP.

❊❊❊❊❊❊❊❊ ❊❊❊❊ ❊❊❊❊❊❊❊

## C H A P.  XII.

*Account of a remarkable perfon. Common confe-*
*quences of a common connection. The fcene*
*changed. A good partner often helps out a bad*
*game.*

" HIS youth opened with every profpect
of happinefs and glory, which an exalted rank and the moft promifing abilities of
mind could prefent; nor did his rifing years
difappoint the moft fanguine hopes formed of
him, till an unlawful paffion, after his fhadow
had begun to lengthen in the vale of life, poifoned his domeftic peace, and gave his mind a
loofer turn.

" Happening to go to one of the fcenes of
public entertainment with which this place
abounds, he was ftruck with fomething in the
appearance of one of the female performers.
Curiofity to know whether her converfation
was equally agreeable with her looks prompted
him to intimate a defire of fitting half an hour
in her company, after her performance was
ended. His rank raifed him above refufal; fhe
received his invitation as an honour, and exerted her powers of pleafing to fuch advantage,
that, though he had not the leaft intention of
entering into any particular connection with
her when he defired this interview, before they
parted he propofed to her to quit her prefent
precarious occupation, and live with him.

" The beauties of such persons, as well as their talents, are too often venal. She complied with joy; and fashion, if not absolutely justifying such indulgencies, at least making them pass uncensured, he not only received her publickly in the character of his mistress, but also, to remove every obstacle to his pleasure, procured her profligate husband an employment in one of the distant colonies; who readily made the infamous though advantageous exchange of an abandoned wife, for an independent subsistence.

" When a woman of this cast once gets admission into a man's heart, she leaves no artifice untried to gain the absolute dominion of it. Hers were too successful. By her insinuating address she soon improved the influence of her charms to such a degree, as to be an over-match for reason in all his resolves, and in some measure to become the sovereign arbitress of his fate.

" Virtue makes many struggles before it will entirely give up an heart of which it once has had possession; of this the perplexity in which you behold him at present is a signal proof. Surfeited with the tumultuous gratification of loose desire he languishes for the pure tranquil happiness of connubial love. On this important occasion prudence and inclination have gone hand in hand in directing his choice, of the success of which reason sees no room to doubt. The only difficulty is, to break the chains of his present unhappy connection, as the generous delicacy of his heart will not permit him to put on an appearance of dislike, or exert an authority over one absolutely in his power, and who has always been subservient to his pleasure; and she

is too firmly attached to her own intereſt to underſtand the milder hints of rejection which he
has of late given her. The throws of ſuch an
heart in this trying conflict may be worthy of
attention."

Juſt as the ſpirit ſaid this, the perſon of whom
he ſpoke ſtopped ſhort, and knitting his brow,
as if in the act of forming ſome important reſolution, " It ſhall be ſo! (ſaid he, with vehemence, and ſlapping his right hand upon his
heart) It ſhall be ſo; I'll ſhake off this diſgrace-
ful infatuation, and return once more to the
deſerted paths of virtue and of glory."——At
theſe words a bluſh of conſcious indignation
overſpread his face; and his eyes ſparkled
with the ardour of a reſolution which inſtantly
enlivened all his fame.

He was prevented from purſuing his meditations any farther by the approach of a perſon,
the ſight of whom ſeemed to double his emotion.
This was he to whom the education of his
youth had been moſt worthily entruſted, and
who had for ſome time felt the moſt poignant
grief, at ſeeing the fruits of all his anxious care
blaſted by the baleful influence of this paſſion,
though reſpect for his ſuperior ſtation had hitherto kept him ſilent on ſo delicate a ſubject.

But he was no longer able to contain himſelf. A ſenſe of duty over-ballanced all regard
to forms, and he reſolved to acquit himſelf
of the ſacred office of a friend, by ſhewing ſo
deſtructive an error in its proper light, be the
conſequence never ſo diſagreeable to him. With
this reſolution he had followed him hither,
when the gentleman advancing to meet him,
anticipated the painful attempt. " My friend
(ſaid

(said he, embracing him with ardour,) my friend is come in an happy moment to confirm the resolution of my soul: I see at length the fatal error into which I have unwarily fallen, and am determined to avoid its snares for the future. That wretched woman shall no longer lead my heart astray."—

"Hear, gracious heaven! (said the good old man, dropping upon his knees and raising his hands and eyes in extasy), and ratify that resolution."—Then catching his hand, and pressing it eagerly to his lips, "O my friend!—my son!"—sobbed he, while the big tears rolled down his reverend cheeks, and choaked his utterance.

Such eloquence was not to be resisted. "My friend!—my father!" answered the gentleman, falling insensibly on the good man's neck, and mingling tears of piety and joy in the honest over-flowing of his heart.

After some moments spent in this silent rapture, "Infatuated wretch that I was (said the gentleman, raising the other tenderly in his arms) to slight the friendly admonitions which my conscious soul read in thy troubled looks: how could I give that worthy heart such pain!"

"Name it not, my son (answered he, in a voice of extasy) think not of any thing that I have suffered. This blessed account of thy return to virtue has amply overpaid it all. May heaven enable you to keep this sacred resolution so worthy of your truly-noble heart; and I have nothing more to wish for in this life."

"Fear not! (replied the gentleman) your friend shall never act unworthy of himself again! shall never more disgrace your virtuous care.
This

This is not a sudden gust of passion. Reason and virtue, which have inspired the thought, will bear me through the execution. Never will I enter yonder monument of my folly, (pointing to a sumptuous house which he had built for his mistress) till the sorceress is removed. The enchantment under which she held me is at last dissolved, and I am my own master again: nor is this all; I will go this minute, and offer my heart and hand to one who will do honour to my choice: you shall accompany me, plead for your friend, and be surety for the immoveable firmness of my resolution, my truth, and honour. A servant can deliver a mandate of my dismission to that unhappy creature."

"Saying this, he stepped into his chariot, which he had ordered to attend him there; and taking the venerable old man with him, drove to the lady's house, on whom he had in secret fixed to be the partner of his life, where he urged his suit so powerfully, and was so well assisted by his advocate, that as reason could suggest no objection to the fair one, and her heart really felt none from inclination; she shewed her assent to his proposal as far as was consistent with the forms observed on such delicate occasions.

"Flushed with this success, as soon as ever he went to his own house, he sent a peremptory message to his mistress, to quit her present habitation directly, and retire to some other better suited to her condition, promising to make such a provision for her future support as should place her above the temptations of necessity, in which he found her, if her ready obedience to this order,

and regular conduct for the remainder of her
life should merit such a favour. In a cooler
moment, he would have found it difficult to
send so harsh a message; but his spirits were
now up, and he could think of nothing but the
happiness he had in view in his intended marriage.

"This was a stroke for which his mistress
was quite unprepared. Her astonishment therefore at receiving such an order may be easily
conceived. At first she doubted the authenticity
of it, and threatened the servant with his master's severest wrath for such an insolent abuse of
his name: but when his persisting in it convinced her of the fallacy of such an hope, she
resolved to try all possible means to avert the
misfortune; and as she was free from every attachment of personal regard that might have
made grief disturb her mind, her ready genius
soon suggested the most effectual one to her.

"Accordingly, the first thing she did was
to gain the servant to her interest by a considerable bribe, and promises of farther favour,
when this storm should blow over; the
sudden, and groundless violence of which,
shewed, she said, that it could not last;
and then giving him instructions what to say
to his master, prepared to act her own part in
this important scene, according to the success
he met with.

"The gentleman, as soon as the servant returned, naturally enquired how she had received
his message: "Sir, (said the fellow, who had
put on a melancholy look, and now sighed as
from the bottom of his heart) she at first could
scarce believe what I said; but when I had removed

moved her doubt, she lifted up her eyes for
some moments without speaking a word, and
then fell into a fit, from which I thought she
never would recover: however, she came to
herself at last; and when a shower of tears had
given her heart some ease, and she was able to
speak, " Tell your master, said the dear lady,
as she sat upon the floor, that it is my duty
to obey his orders, be they what they will;
though I little thought ever to have received
such as these, and in so scornful and cruel a
manner. Sure he might have spoke to me himself, without exposing me to servants! But I
have no right to complain: God bless him and
prosper him in all his ways; "—and then she
wept again, and wrung her hands in such
agony it would have melted an heart of stone.—
Saying this, the fellow wiped his eyes which
had been well onioned for the purpose, and
hung down his head, as if he was overcome
with grief.

" It is impossile to describe the gentleman's
situation when he received this account. He
was affected by her distress in the severest manner. The generous humanity of his heart
would have shared in the sufferings of his greatest
enemy, what then must he have felt at those of
one whom he had so lately been accustomed to
think of with the tenderest regard! His delicacy also was hurted at having sent such a message
in such a manner, and he disdained the thought
of exerting authority with rigour, where resistance was impossible. In a word, though his
resolution was not absolutely overturned, he
secretly began to wish, that he had not been
so precipitate in putting it in execution,

The

" The servant saw the conflict in his heart; and, faithful to the trust he had basely undertaken, as soon as he was dismissed from his presence, flew to acquaint her with it.

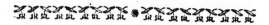

## CHAP. XIII.

*Looking back often dangerous. Female artifice triumphant over reason and virtue. The natural consequences of this. A remarkable instance of the effect of complying with the fashion.*

" THIS account confirmed her wavering hopes; she resolved not to lose a moment, but strive to improve the impression which her associate had thus fortunately made in her favour, before the unknown motive of her disgrace should have time to counteract it. Accordingly she went directly to his house, and as he had not taken the precaution to forbid her admission, rushed into the room where he was, in a well-imitated phrenzy, threw herself at his feet, and embraced his knees, in all the apparent agony of heart which the fondest despair could dictate, before he could possibly prevent her.

" There is nothing more dangerous than looking back to former scenes of pleasure; it softens the mind, and makes it long for a repetition of them. The account of her distress had awakened his compassion, and he was undesignedly running over all the engaging qualities and soft endearments which had given him

such

such delight the very moment she entered the room.

If the description could affect him so strongly, what then must he not feel from the sight? He was not proof to such an attack. All his resolution vanished in an instant; he raised her from the ground, and, embracing her tenderly, restored her to the empire of his heart with tenfold the authority she had possessed before.

"The only difficulty that remained was how to break off his engagements with the lady, whom he had just paid his addresses to in so serious and public a manner: as for his friend, he concluded rightly, that after this relapse he should never see him more.

"He was not long at a loss. Even in so delicately distressing an affair as this, his soul detested disingenuity, and he resolved to make her admire his candour at least, though she might blame his fickleness. Accordingly he wrote her a letter next morning, to tell her, that upon examining his heart more nearly, he found another had taken such strong possession of it, that it was not in his power to give it with his hand; wherefore he thought the latter alone unworthy of her acceptance, nor should presume to press the offer of it any farther.

"The lady's indignation was equal to her surprize, at so despicable an instance of levity: she thought it beneath her to return an answer to such a letter, or take any notice of the writer; to shew her perfect indifference and contempt for whom she soon after listened to the addresses of another.

"As for him, his condition became worse than ever. According to the common though mistaken

taken

taken notion of over-bearing contempt, he gloried in his difgraceful folly, which he carried to ten times more extravagant exceffes than before; while fhe, convinced that he had now faftened his chains too ftrongly ever to be fhaken off, returned his fondnefs with indifference, and at the very time that fhe was making him the dupe of her mercenary defigns, took every occafion of treating him with infolence and tyranny.

"The confequence of this was natural. Deftitute of domeftic peace, robbed of the approbation of his own mind, and confcious of the contempt of every man of fenfe and virtue, he grew carelefs of himfelf, his affairs ran to confufion and ruin, and his name became a by-word among all his acquaintances."———

"O my guide, (faid I, fhocked at fo deplorable a fall) how powerful are the wiles of woman! How dangerous is it for a man to let her get an afcendency over him? If once he refigns the reins which nature wifely put into his hands, I fee that it is impoffible for him ever to refume them again, and affert the juft prerogatives of his fuperior ftation!"

"It may perhaps be too much to fay that it is abfolutely impoffible; (anfwered he) though many circumftances concur to make the attempt moft difficult. Prefuming on his greater ftrength, man thinks it beneath him to be upon his guard againft her, till fhe has taken fuch firm poffeffion of her authority, that it appears lefs painful to fuffer, than ftruggle to fhake off a tyranny whofe chains are riveted fo faft. Or, fhould he venture on the attempt, fhe makes her very weaknefs a defence, and expects

pects to be let conquer, becaufe fhe is unable to refift, throwing herfelf upon a generofity to which her own heart is a ftranger. The event is generally more favourable than fhe deferves; and a falfe tendernefs permits her to retain a power which falfe fecurity firft gave her an opportunity to ufurp.

"But the fevereft cafe is to be governed by a woman who is herfelf a flave to any particular vice, or folly. To break the double chain is a difficulty few have refolution to attempt; and fewer have attempted with fuccefs.

"Of this you may behold a ftriking inftance in yonder houfe, which prefents you with a fcene of fuch confufion. That gentleman whom you fee in all the apparent agitation of the moft determined wrath, gave his heart and hand together to the lovely woman who fits befide him melted into tears. The advantage of the match, according to the mercenary maxim which prevails at prefent, was on her fide; but love overlooked fuch mean confiderations, and he thought his elevated rank received honour from her participation.

"Her heart felt all the ardour of fo generous a paffion; fhe devoted herfelf entirely to his happinefs, and, by her obfequious attention to every motion of his will, gained fuch an influence over him, that he foon forgot he had any will of his own, and refigned himfelf abfolutely and folely to her direction, pleafed with a yoke which fondnefs would not let him feel the weight of.

"From the firft dawn of reafon in her mind, fhe had ever expreffed the ftrongeft diflike to the idle drudgery of play; but now the tyran-

ny of fashion obliged her to give into a practice which was become the cement of society,
the general business of genteel life. Example
can soften prejudice, and habit even reconcile
antipathies. The reluctance with which she
complied with this custom soon wore off, and
she entered into the very spirit of gaming with
an avidity that exceeded her former aversion.

" Her husband, whose heart happily was untainted with this fatal vice, was alarmed at a
madness which he saw in all its dreadful consequences. He knew the rich must always lose;
the numbers who are destitute of any other
means of subsistence, beside their expertness in
the mysteries of play, making a property of their
folly; and experience had shewn him to what
black expedients women will have recourse to
repair their losses, how debts of honour are too
often paid with honour · itself. He resolved
therefore to take the first opportunity to warn
her against indulging a passion, the apprehension of whose consequences gave him so much
pain ; judging that his advice would have more
weight when it should seem to arise from some
immediate cause, than if obtruded abruptly, or
offered only in cool speculation.

" Nor did he long wait for the occasion he
desired. Observing an uncommon uneasiness
in his wife's looks one morning as they sat
alone at breakfast, he enquired what was the
cause of it, with all the tender anxiety of love. A
guilty blush overspread her face; she hung down
her head in the utmost confusion, and could
scarce find spirit to say, on the most earnest
entreaty, that she had lost a sum of money at
play the night before, which she could not pay
with-

without his affiftance, her private ftipend, ample as his love had made it, having all funk in the fame gulph before.

" The pain fhe evidently felt at making this difcovery, flattered him with an hope that fhe would for ever after avoid the occafion of it. He therefore would not aggravate her concern by faying any thing juft then ; but giving her the money fhe had loft, and an additional fupply for her own neceffary occafions, told her, with a look of inexpreffible tendernefs, that fhe fhould never feel any uneafinefs in his power to remove.

" However, not entirely to mifs fo favourable an opportunity, he took occafion next morning, from fome late occurrences of a fimilar kind among his own acquaintances, to exprefs his difapprobation of that pernicious practice in the ftrongeft terms, and drew the confequences of it in fo black a light, that, unable to bear the reproaches of her own confcience, fhe burft into tears, and, falling on her knees, implored his pardon in the moft affecting manner.

" Rejoiced at this behaviour, which he thought a proof of her concern for what fhe had informed him of the day before, and an happy affurance of her never falling into the fame error any more, he raifed her from the ground, and, embracing her tenderly, told her he had not fpoken in allufion to any thing paft, which he had thought no more of fince, and hoped that no future inftance of the kind fhould ever recal it to his remembrance.

" This was more than fhe was able to bear. She funk down upon her knees again, and, as foon as a flood of tears had given her utterance,

M 5        owned

owned in terms of the warmeſt contrition, that, tempted by an hope of recovering her former loſs, ſhe had ventured to play again the night before, but with the ſame ſucceſs, having not only loſt all the money he had given her, but added conſiderably to her debt alſo.

## CHAP. XIV.

*Worſe luck, and more of it. A new method for breaking a bad habit. Travellers often return without their errand.*

" THE huſband's aſtoniſhment and diſtreſs at this unexpected news may be eaſily conceived. He ſtood ſome moments before he had power to ſpeak. At length, raiſing her from the ground, though not with the ſame emotions as before, " I had flattered myſelf, my dear, (ſaid he with a ſerious look, and accent of reproof) that the concern you ſhewed yeſterday ſecured me from any more follies of this kind; but I ſee I was miſtaken. However, I will pay your debts once more; but remember, I tell you, this is the laſt time I ſhall do ſo. My fortune, though ſufficient with prudence and œconomy to ſupport the dignity of my rank, is not equal to ſuch boundleſs diſſipation, by which I may be ruined before I am aware. Nor is this all; other conſequences too often follow this paſſion, the remoteſt apprehenſions of which I cannot bear.

" Diſtant

" Diftant as this infinuation was, it ftruck her to the foul. Though fhe was confident of her own virtue, too many melancholy inftances fhewed that in the general it was not unjuftly founded. She begged that he would have a more favourable opinion of her, implored again his pardon for what was paft, and promifed in the ftrongeft terms never to give him the fame caufe of difpleafure more. This was all he defired; he directly gave her the money; and, throwing his arms around her neck, fealed her forgivenefs with a kifs of rapture.

" It is a juft obfervation, that vices take the deepeft root in weakeft minds. This accounts for the common remark that woman, when once fhe goes aftray, is more profligate and harder to be reclaimed than man. Of all the paffions which mark the character of the prefent age, that which runs into the moft extravagant and incorrigible excefs, even in the ableft minds, is this of gaming; what havock then muft fuch a tyrant make where it fcarce meets any oppofition from reafon? How difficult muft it be to break its chains?

" She had promifed more than fhe was able to perform. The love of play had taken too faft hold of her heart ever to be entirely expelled, and in a very little time drew her into the fame diftrefs again, with this additional aggravation, that fhe knew not how to apply to her hufband for relief, as fhe had formerly done. But fuch an affair could not long remain concealed from his knowledge. Her creditor, on two or three breaches of promife, applied to him directly for it by letter. What he felt on receiving fuch a demand is not to be defcribed. He anfwered

M 6                    coldly

coldly, that he would enquire into the affair, and then went to his wife's father to afk his advice, how he fhould wean her from fo dangerous an habit, telling him the preceding circumftances without exaggeration or excufe.

" The father's wrath arofe almoft to madnefs at fuch an account.   He propofed methods which were not only improper, but even impoffible to be purfued ; and treated her hufband's propofal of removing her from the temptation, as there was no probability of reclaiming her otherwife from the folly, as an inftance of unmanly weaknefs rather than the effect of prudent moderation and tender affection : however, as his paffion cooled, he was obliged to yield to the juftice of his arguments ; and he undertook to enforce her obedience by his authority, fhould fhe attempt to oppofe her hufband, whofe love made him diffident of his own refolution in fo delicate a ftruggle.

" To avoid a conteft that muft be equally difagreeable to them all, they judged it would be the beft way to give her the firft intimation of the defign, in fuch a manner as fhould convince her that it muft be in vain for her to oppofe it.   Accordingly, as her hufband and fhe were fitting at breakfaft next morning, when the news-paper was brought in as ufual, the firft glance fhe caft on it prefented her with an advertifement, (placed in the moft confpicuous part of it for that purpofe) giving notice of a fpeedy fale of all her hufband's coaches, horfes, furniture, &c. who intended to go and refide abroad with his whole family for fome years."

" Starting

" Starting in aftonifhment, " Good God, my dear, (faid fhe ) look here! what can this mean ?——

" To pay this demand," (faid he fternly, pulling her creditor's letter out of his pocket, and reaching it to her.)

" It is impoffible to defcribe her fituation at this fight. Confcious guilt deprived her of power to fpeak or move. She ftood petrified with fhame and horror.".

" I am forry, madam, (continued he) that you have driven me to this extremity; but I will not facrifice my fortune, if not perhaps worfe, by ftaying any longer in this place.". .

" O, forgive me !——Try me !——Try me but once more !—— I promife "—— She was unable to fay any more, a gufh of tears choaked her utterance; which he waited for her to give full vent to before he would purfue his purpofe any farther. In this critical fituation you behold them at prefent, your own obfervation of their conduct in which will be more fatif-factory than any defcription. Take notice only, that his wrath is worked up to this height by art, and that his refolution is fcarcely proof to the fight of her diftrefs; while, on the other hand, vexation gliffens through her tears, and fhews that fhe is lefs grieved for the caufe than alarmed for the confequence of his difpleafure, which fhe is this very moment cafting about how to evade."

When my guide had concluded this account, I fixed my attention on the fcene which had given occafion to it. The firft violence of the lady's grief had begun by this time to fubfide, which her hufband thinking the proper moment to make an impreſſion on her : " Madam, (ſaid he, replying to her laſt words) my reſolution is unalterably fixed ; you know what faith I ought to place in promiſes."

The reproach implied in theſe words ſtung her pride. She had been too long accuſtomed to receive implicit obedience to every thing ſhe ſaid, to bear ſuch an affrontive inſinuation paſſively, and reſolved to ſhew that ſhe would not give up her authority ſo eaſily. Riſing therefore in an inſtant above her ſuppliant mood, " I know too, ſir, (ſaid ſhe, with an indignant air) that I am not your ſlave, nor to be forced to any thing againſt my will. You may keep your reſolution, and go if you pleaſe, mine is to ſtay ; nor ſhall you find it leſs unalterable than your own."———

" Madam ! madam ! this falſe ſpirit ill becomes you ; nor think it will avail. Your tears were far more powerful ; but all are now in vain ; and I will be obeyed." With theſe words he left the room, proud of having ſupported his reſolution ſo manfully, and went to give orders for the immediate execution of his deſign.

But ſhe was far from thinking of obedience yet. Her heart was ſo wedded to the pleaſures of her preſent way of life, that ſhe looked on leaving it as the ſevereſt puniſhment. Beſide, her pride was piqued by the authority with which he ſpoke ; and ſhe reſolved to ſuffer the worſt effects of his anger rather than to ſubmit to a yoke which ſhe thought ſhe had ſo effectually ſhaken off.

When

When she had formed this resolution, the next difficulty was how to execute it. The first thought that occurred to her was, to throw herself upon the fondness of her father, whose indulgence she had ever experienced in the most unlimited degree, and did not doubt but she should find equally on the present occasion. She accordingly flew to him directly, and, pouring out the anguish of her heart before him, implored his protection against her husband's lawless tyranny.

Not to appear prejudiced by any former misrepresentation, he heared her story with the greatest attention; and then, condemning her from her own mouth, flew into a rage a thousand fold severer even than her husband's, upbraiding her with ingratitude to his love, and disobedience to his just authority; and drawing her crime, and the too probable consequences of it in such dreadful lights, that, terrified at the horrid representation, she gave up all farther thoughts of opposition, and only besought her father to mediate a peace, on condition of her absolute obedience in every action of her future life.

Such a reconciliation was easily effected; he desired no more, but paid her debt directly: and all things being prepared for their departure as soon as possible, he set out on his intended exile, taking his whole family with him, in hope that a passion which had given him so much uneasiness would wear off, when the opportunity for gratifying it should be no more.

But, like the wounded hart, she bore the deadly arrow in her side; and, though she complied, because she could not help it, the re-

6　　　　　　　formation

formation intended by this harſh expedient was far from being probable. The poiſon had taken too faſt hold to be cured by any change of climate, and ſhe languiſhed to return to her own country, only that ſhe might return to her beloved pleaſure; while her huſband thus ſacrificed to a vain hope the flower of a life which his exalted rank and abilities might have made an honour to himſelf, and an advantage to his country.

## CHAP. XV.

*Anecdotes of a profeſſed wit. A lucky hit made the moſt of. Too much of one thing won't do A rough retort of a coarſe jeſt; with other curious matters of the ſame kind.*

" YOU ſee (ſaid my guide) the conſequence of indulging a paſſion, till the gratification of it becomes an habit; though there may be but few actually ſo fatal as this of gaming, the exceſs of any other will be attended by effects far from deſirable, and end in ridicule a leaſt, if not in ruin.

" Obſerve that man who ſtands in yonder coffee-houſe, pumping his brain for pleaſantry, and labouring for wit to entertain the ſneering croud around him, whoſe fulſome compliments and ironical applauſe paſs upon his vanity for a tribute juſtly due to his merit. He is one of your profeſſed wits, whoſe good opinion of
them-

themfelves makes them think every one obliged to admire what they fay.

" He was raifed to this eminent ftation by the fuccefs of a ballad he wrote fome time ago, of which it may be difficult to determine whether its merit lay in its oddity, its obfcenity, or its profanenefs. However, the thing took with the public tafte in fo extraordinary a manner, that the happy author not only got the price of a new coat by the fale of it, but was alfo admitted to the tables of all thofe who liked fuch buffoonery, to entertain them, and their company; where, having an eye to bufinefs, he always took the opportunity when they were in high fpirits and could refufe nothing, to follicit fubfcriptions for a collection of *old faws* which he had picked up and tagged fome how together, by which artifice he contrived to make a good penny of them alfo.

" Elevated with this fuccefs, he thought he had nothing more to do but publifh *a fecond part of the fame tune*, to make his fortune at once; but, to his great mortification, he found himfelf miftaken; for, the novelty that recommended the former being now worn off, there was little or no notice taken of it: befide, he had exhaufted the fpirit of obfcenity and profanenefs fo thoroughly in the firft part, that there remained nothing for him now but dregs, too coarfe for the groffeft tafte, though he ftrove to make up for the quality by the quantity, of which he gave moft plentiful meafure.

" Severe as this difappointment was to him in every refpect, he affected not to feel it; but, modeftly imputing it to the badnefs of the public tafte, takes the liberty, by way of reprifal, to

turn

turn every thing that it approves into ridicule,
with a petulance little short of scurrility ; and,
to support the character of a privileged wit, never misses an opportunity of being impertinent
to every person he converses with.

"Such a conduct cannot always escape reproof ; some, and those severe strokes of it, he
frequently meets from those who have not a
taste for his jokes, or do not think that a pretence to wit gives a privilege for ill manners.
An instance or two may not be unentertaining,
and may also give you a notion of the dangers
which attend such a practice.

"Talking away the other evening at his
usual rate, in a mixed company, one of his
random-shots happened to hit the profession of
a gentleman present. As there was nothing in
what he said more than common cant, the
other, who was a man of years and character,
would not have thought it worthy of his notice,
had not our hero at the same instant looked
him full in the face, and burst out into a loud
laugh.

"As this was fixing the stroke rather too
close to be overlooked, the gentleman gravely
asked him what he laughed at, as he really
could not see the wit of what he said.  "Not
see it, sir, (said the other, starting from his seat
and going up close to him) then, sir, you may
smell it, if your nose is not as dull as your apprehension ;"  and letting a great f——t, raised a louder laugh than before.

"This was an insult too grossly personal to
be borne. The gentleman rose up, and, without
saying a word, gave him a kick on the offending
part, that drove him to the other side of the
room,

room, and then, ringing the bell, coolly ordered the waiter to turn that ftinking cur down ftairs. This naturally turned the laugh to the other fide. The unfortunate wit had occafion, for all his affurance, to ftand it; and the poor efforts he made to turn it off with a joke only fhewed his impotent vexation, and made him appear, if poffible, ftill more ridiculous.

" The proper province of wit is, to difcover and point out a relation and refemblance in fome particular circumftances, between ideas obvioufly inconnected and unlike; and by that means fhew them in a light the novelty and oddity of which may give a pleafing furprize. To do this, the mind muft be endowed with a power of viewing a variety of things in all their fhapes and fituations at the fame inftant, and a readinefs at catching thofe fugitive refemblances, and fhewing them in obvious and ftriking colours.

" Thus far reafon can trace the origin and effects of a faculty, equally mifunderftood and mifapplied; or, I might rather fay, indeed, whofe name is ufurped by another of the moft contrary nature : for inftead of this fpeculative manner of exertion, and the inoffenfive and delicate entertainment arifing from it, the employment of what is at prefent called wit, is to difcover and invent perfonal misfortunes and defects, and difplay them in the groffeft lights of ridicule and infult, as the pleafure which it gives arifes from the bafeft and moft malignant motive, that of a man's feeling a fecret fatiffaction on feeing that others are as bad as himfelf, or perhaps fuffer a difgrace which he efcapes.

" But

"But generally as this pleafure is enjoyed, the authors of it always meet a juft return of averfion and contempt for that proftitution of their abilities, by which they afford it. This is not fo ftrange or ingrateful as it may appear. As thofe who can have a tafte for fuch entertainment are confcious that they themfelves are liable to be made the fubjects of it to others, they naturally fear and hate the perfons who may poffibly bring them into fo difagreeable a fituation.

"Thus the moment a man profeffes himfelf a' wit, he, as it were, declares war with all the reft of the world ; as in return every one lies on the watch to pull down and punifh fo invidious a prefumption. Of this he continually meets the moft mortifying inftances, to which the means he is obliged to make ufe of to fupport fuch a character, lay him conftantly and defencelefsly open.

"Befide this kind of wit, which preys upon particulars, there is another more malignant in its effects, becaufe more extenfive ; though motives of the fame ungenerous nature with thofe which recommend the other, make it pafs almoft uncenfured even by the injured objects of it, who are afraid to complain for fear their feeming to feel its force fhould be taken for an acknowledgment of its juftice, and fo make the injury irremediable. This is turning *profeffions* into ridicule ; by which means individuals are precluded from the fruits of their honeft induftry, and the community robbed of their contribution towards the general ftock : for, however abfurd a prejudice raifed in that manner may appear to reafon, experience fhews

too

too many unhappy inftances of its influence to admit its being doubted.

"But though the fufferers do not think proper to complain, they never mifs an opportunity of returning an attack they fo feverely feel; and many *a wit* has paid dearly for his pleafantry, when he has happened to come into the power of thofe whom he has fo irreconcileably offended. Of this the perfon before us lately experienced an inftance, difagreeable enough to furfeit him of this his very favourite practice as long as he lives.

"Of the many profeffions which he has wantonly fallen upon, the medical art has felt the fevereft fallies of his uncommon turn for ridicule. As he was riding one day to pay a vifit to a nobleman, who had defired him to come in that manner, that he might take a view of the extenfive and grand improvements about his feat, the heat of the day, and his being unufed to that method of travelling, expofed him to fome injuries which made his fitting on a faddle very painful to him.

"While he was in this diftrefs, he happened to go by the houfe of an apothecary on whom he had exerted his unlucky talents with the moft injurious fuccefs, having fixed his general ridicule of the profeffion upon him, by a particular defcription of his perfon irrefiftibly ridiculous. Without thinking of this, or dreading any retaliation from a refentment fo juftly provoked, he called upon him, and, making known his complaint, defired his affiftance.

"The apothecary, whofe difpofition was equally fpiteful and droll, refolved not to mifs fuch an opportunity of taking a fignal revenge

for

for all the mortifications which the other had brought upon him. Accordingly he defired him to alight for a moment, with all the placid politenefs of his profeffion, and made him up two plaifters, one of which he himfelf moft officioufly applied to the part affected, directing him to put on the other when that fhould come off; and, refufing to take any return for a piece of fervice which he affured him the pleafure of conferring amply overpaid, wifhed him an agreeable ride.

" The plaifter had the defired effect, and he felt no farther pain during the reft of his journey; at the end of which, finding that the motion of the horfe had rubbed it off, he took an opportunity to ftep afide, juft before he went to dinner, and put on the other, as he had been directed. The firft application of this was attended with fenfations far from pleafing; however, he thought that muft proceed from his being more chafed than before, and concluding that they would foon go off, went directly in to dinner, where, as if fortune combined with his foe, he was placed between two young ladies, equally fprightly and arch.

" He had not been feated long before the plaifter began to operate, in a manner that made him fincerely fick of his honourable fituation  He was in torture impoffible to be fupported; and what added to his diftrefs, he knew not how to get away to remove the caufe of it, confcious that the difcovery of a trick he was now fufficiently fenfible had been played him, would fix a ridicule upon him, which he fhould never be able to fhake off, as he had had too many proofs of the pleafure

sure every body took in every thing that gave him the least vexation or disgrace. This made him resolve to sit it out, intolerable as the pain he suffered was.

" But he had more plagues to encounter than his utmost forecast could provide against. The ladies between whom, he sat soon saw that he was in some uneasiness, and resolved, with the usual good-nature of the sex, to aggravate it, for their own entertainment, by every teazing trick they could devise. Accordingly, winking to each other to act in concert, they drew their chairs closer to him, so as to make it impossible for him to stir, which necessity was now beginning to make him think of, in spite of all his resolutions, and made the most malicious conjectures at his want of his usual mirth and spirit; to awake which they pushed him from side to side with their elbows, though every time he moved upon his chair pierced him to the soul.

" The effects of the plaister were by this time become so violent, that nature was no longer able to support them. He fainted away in the midst of the company, and was removed to another room, to undergo a scene of raillerie and ridicule, if possible more severe than his pain.

CHAP.

## C H A P. XVI.

*Instances of the compassion common on such occa-
sions. The practical joker enjoys a double triumph
over the wit. Other worse consequences of the
prostitution of genius.*

" THE first thing that struck him when
he came to himself was the ridiculous-
ness of his situation. He was laid on his face,
across a bed, in the midst of a number of servants, who, in undressing him, had discovered
his ailment, some of the consequences of which
they were busied in removing with wet cloths,
in the same manner as a nurse cleanses an infant. It was some minutes after he recovered
his senses before he was able to speak, during
which time he had the mortification to hear the
unfeeling wretches round him cracking their
coarse jests at his misfortune. At length too
rough an application to the part affected extorted an involuntary roar, which shewing
them that he was come to his senses, they instantly changed their scoffs for a curiosity equally disagreeable, all opening upon him at once
to enquire what had thrown him into that condition.

" It may be thought he had no great inclination to answer their questions. He thanked
them for their care, and, desiring they would
let the chaplain know he wanted to speak to
him as soon as he had done dinner, begged to
be left alone.

" His

" His meditations in such a situation could not be very pleasing. He was not at a loss to discover the cause of what had happened; and cursing his own foolish confidence for putting himself any way in the power of one whom he might naturally suppose to be his enemy, resolved to take the severest revenge which the law could procure him, for so painful an injury, without making any allowance for the provocation that had prompted it. He comforted himself with these thoughts as well as he could, till the arrival of the chaplain, whose resentment for some lashes of wit made him in no haste to come, had not the curiosity of the rest of the company, which was raised by the representation of the servants, accelerated his motion.

" As soon as he entered the chamber, the poor sufferer, whose pain was far from being entirely removed, exclaimed in the anguish of his heart, " O my friend, I have sent for you to implore your assistance to inflict a proper punishment upon the villain who has brought me to this disgrace and torture."— He then recounted the affair of the plaister, as I have related it to you, and concluded with conjuring the chaplain to use his influence with his lordship, to do him justice for an outrage which, according to the laws of hospitality, affected himself, as it was offered to his guest.

" His reverence sat picking his teeth in the greatest composure while he was telling his tale, at the end of which, " Pray sir, (said he, with an air of the most insulting indifference) what would you have me do?"—"Do sir, (answered the wit, provoked beyond his patience at the other's behaviour) chew the cud of your laft meal till you are fo happy as to get another, that you may not lofe a moment's enjoyment of that pleafure which feems to be the fole end of your exiftence."—

"Stung by the feverity of this reproach, the chaplain directly left him without making any reply, and returning to the company told them, that the violence of the pain had difordered the poor man's head, and made him ftark mad. Such a reprefentation afforded matter for many curious remarks, in which the affinity between wit and madnefs was moft learnedly difcuffed, while they were finifhing their wine, without ever thinking of procuring the fubject of their fpeculation any relief.

"At length curiofity prompted his lordfhip to fee fo ftrange a fight, in hopes of confirming by his behaviour fome nice obfervations he had been making on the nature of madnefs, evident fymptoms of which he declared he had perceived the moment he faw him that morning; but he was difagreeably difappointed to find the chaplain's account without foundation, and the man in his fenfes, fo that he was deprived of the merit of his judicious difcovery, on which he had plumed himfelf not a little, and his theory was left unfupported by the proof he had appealed to. However, he concealed his chagrin, and, enquiring into the particulars of fo extraordinary an affair, for the chaplain's account was far from being fatisfactory, revenged himfelf for his difappointment by laughing in the moft mortifying manner at every ridiculous circumftance; a behaviour that aggravated the other's diftrefs, as he was reftrained, by refpect, from making any reply,　　　　　"When

" When they had fufficiently enjoyed the
fcene, one of the company, more compaffionate
than the reft, bethought himfelf that it might
not be improper to do fomething for the relief
of the poor fufferer, whofe appearance fhewed
that his pain was not much abated. Accordingly, upon confultation, it was agreed to be the beft
way to fend for the apothecary who had made
up the plaifter, as he muft neceffarily know
what was proper to remove its effects, better
than any one elfe. The diftreffed patient would
gladly have avoided fuch an interview, if only
to difappoint his enemy of the pleafure of triumphing in the fuccefs of his trick : but perhaps for that very reafon his lordfhip infifted on
it, and he was fent for directly.

" This exceeded the apothecary's hopes. He
obeyed the fummons with the greateft pleafure;
and on his arrival, having firft prudently expreffed his furprize, and afferted his innocence
of any evil intention in what he had done, was
fhewn up to his patient, who no fooner fixed
his eyes upon him, than burfting into the moft
violent rage, " Villain! (faid he) what bafe
trick is this you have played me ? But be affured that I will have the moft exemplary fatisfaction ! I'll make you know"——

" Sir, (anfwered the apothecary, with a fly
grin) have a little patience, and all will foon
be well. I am forry that an innocent joke
fhould give you fuch offence."——

" A joke, wretch! Do you call putting me
to fuch torture and difgrace a joke?"——

" Nothing more, I affure you, fir; and if
you will give me leave to apply this liniment
to the place where your complaint is, I'll en-

gage to remove it in a few minutes; and as for the difgrace, there is nothing in it; it is only matter for a few days laughter, and it will then be no more thought of."——

"No more thought of! Yes, it will be always thought of; and I fhall never be able to fhew my face again after the ridiculous figure I have made by your curfed means; but if I forgive you, may I be the laughing-ftock of every fool I meet."——

"Surely, fir, a man of your reafon and benevolence cannot harbour fuch an implacable refentment! What would you do if you were in my cafe? Unprovoked by the leaft offence, you wantonly fell on my uncouth figure, on the profeffion by which I earn bread for myfelf and my family, till you have made both fo ridiculous, that children hoot at me as I go along the ftreets, and their equally wife parents flight my fkill, and pafs by my fhop with contempt. The blifter on your pofteriors will foon be healed; nor can the difgrace you feem to take fo heavily to heart, be attended with any confequences worfe than a laugh, which you are well able to fhift from yourfelf to fomebody elfe; but with me the cafe is quite different; my very fubfiftence is attacked, and the happinefs of my family facrificed, merely for a mifchievous jeft, and to fhew your powers of ridicule."——

"Struck with the juftice of this reproof, the Wit had not power to make any reply, but fubmitted in filence to receive the other's affiftance, who, fatisfied with this double triumph, foon put an end to his pain by a proper application. When this relief had reftored him a

little

little to his fpirits, he took the apothecary by the hand, fqueezing it eagerly, "Dear doctor, (faid he) I acknowledge that I have been to blame, much to blame; but I never confidered this matter in a proper light before. All that I can do now, is to make you any reparation in my power, and to promife that I will never be guilty of the like indifcretion again. Never will I indulge wit any more at the expence of giving pain to an honeft heart."—

"This refolution lafted while he was under the apothecary's hands; but no fooner was he recovered than he relapfed into his old humour, which he even indulged with greater latitude and virulence than ever, that he fhould not appear to have been difpirited by what he had fuffered. As to the other, his trick was attended with fuccefs beyond his moft fanguine hopes. Befide the prefent pleafure of revenge, the moment this ftory took wind, the ridicule which had been fo prejudicial to him, recoiled with tenfold force upon his adverfary, and he recovered his former credit and refpect.

"But this perfonal licentioufnefs, though perhaps the moft immediately painful to particulars, is not the worft inftance in which this perfon abufes the talents nature has beftowed upon him with more than common liberality. You fee the levity of his looks and behaviour; the fame folly infects his writings to the moft extravagant excefs. In thefe he is diffipation itfelf. Starting from one fubject to another, he jumbles all together the lighteft and moft ferious, fo as to make them appear equally ridiculous, facrificing every thing to raife a laugh,

N 3
·as

as if that were the sole end of genius, the sole object of erudition.

" Nor is this all ; there are some things over which nature herself commands to throw a veil. To lift this up therefore, and make them the subject of wit and pleasantry, even in the almost boundless liberty of discourse, is a great offence ; but in writing it is absolutely unpardonable, as that perpetuates the evil, and lays the foundation for debauching generations yet unborn. This is the grossest prostitution of powers given for a better purpose, and is always brought to a severe account."

## CHAP. XXII.

*An old observation confirmed by a new character. A remarkable instance of the inconsistency of the human heart. A curious love-scene proves that the pleasure of variety is sometimes attended with danger and inconvenience.*

" BUT, as I have remarked on other occasions, it is the proper application that effectuates the blessing. Without this the best gifts of heaven become a curse, and only aggravate the evils they were bestowed to prevent.

" Observe that person who struts about yonder in a military habit, pleased with the ensigns of his profession, as a child with a new bawble. Every favour, by which fortune could seem to secure human happiness, had she heaped upon

**his**

his head in the moſt unbounded manner ; but
this very profuſion produced the contrary effect : and miſerable in imagination for want of
ſomething to wiſh for, he has renounced ſuch
an inſipid plenty, and plunged himſelf, for variety, into the real miſeries of a way of life,
which is permitted only as a puniſhment on
the follies and vices of mankind.

"It has been obſerved, that from a cloſe attention to the firſt eſſays of the opening mind,
a preſage may be formed of the future life. The
diſtinguiſhing characters of his youth were a
ſated indifference to every thing in his poſſeſſion ; an inconſtancy even more than childiſh in
all his purſuits, he ſeldom perſiſting in any to the
attainment of its object. As the affluence of
his fortune made any particular application not
abſolutely neceſſary to him, this fluctuating im-
becillity of diſpoſition paſſed unnoticed, and his
inattention to every prudential regard in all his
actions, was extolled as generoſity and magnificence of ſpirit. But the event has proved the
error of this judgment, the ſame weakneſs having ruled the conduct of his riper years, and
made him an eaſy prey to every idle paſſion of
his own, to every mean deſign of his more in-
digent companions. To recapitulate every inſtance of this would be to make an hiſtory of
his whole life. It will be ſufficient juſt to
touch upon one or two, to ſupport the character I have here drawn, and as they ſo ſtrongly illuſtrate the inconſiſtency of the human
heart.

"On his arriving at that period of life, when
men are concluded to be capable of conducting
themſelves, the firſt thing which the care of his

N 4                    friends

friends fuggefted to fecure his happinefs, for
their eyes at length began to be opened to the
dangers attending fuch a difpofition, was to
find out a female, whofe prudence might be a
fhield to his levity, and prevent its worft effects; and whom reafon and inclination fhould
go hand in hand, in recommending to his
choice as a partner for his life. In this delicate and important fearch they were not long
undetermined. They fixed upon one to whom
envy herfelf could make no poffible objection.
Born in an exalted rank, and rich in every favourite gift of heaven, fhe feemed defigned to
crown the bleffings of an happy life. The
moment fhe was mentioned to him he received
the hint with rapture. In the intercourfe of a
general acquaintance his heart had not been
infenfible of her charms, and on the nearer attention of fuch a defign, he foon perceived the
more valuable beauties of her mind. By the
affiftance of his friends, he preferved his refolution fo long as to make his addrefies acceptable,
and received, in her hand, a feal of the moft
perfect felicity which this life is capable of enjoying.

"But fcarce was he in poffeffion of this juft
object of every rational defire, when the natural inconftancy of his temper prevailed, and he
flighted an happinefs for which all others fighed,
only becaufe it was in his poffeffion. Accordingly he foon relapfed into all the licentioufnefs
of his former life, and vainly fought in loofe
variety for that pleafure, which his perverfe infenfibility prevented his enjoying at home.'

"Such pleafure is always purchafed with
vexation and pain. As he was prowling about
one

one evening for his ufual game in the galle-
ries of the theatre, he happened to fee a female
whofe appearance had fomething in it more
than commonly pleafing to him. He immediately addreffed her in the familiarity of fuch
places, and was not lefs ftruck with the fpright-
linefs of her converfation than he had been before with her beauty. Encouraged by her freedom, and confiding in the fuperiority of his
rank, at the end of the play he hefitated not to
propofe retiring to one of the nighbouring ta-
verns, to improve fo agreeable an acquaintance.
This fhe pofitively refufed, though in terms
which implied not any refentment at the propofal, nor prevented his preffing her at leaft
to give him another meeting at the play-houfe,
which fhe at length confented to do.

"In two or three interviews of this kind,
which fhe let herfelf be perfuaded to indulge
him with, fhe played her part with fuch addrefs,
that fhe gained an abfolute conqueft over him,
removing by her well-acted modefty every fufpicion of her real character. At length, when
he had brought her blufhingly to confefs a return of his paffion, and filenced every other
fcruple, fhe ftarted the laft difficulty, of the
danger of being detected by her hufband, as fhe
unhappily was a married woman. This difcovery was far from being agreeable to him. He
loved his pleafures; but he was far from defiring to have them enhanced by any appearance of danger. However, he had gone too
far to retreat now; and therefore, putting the
beft face upon the affair, he prevailed upon her
to run the hazard of this difcovery, by promifing to protect her againft her hufband's refentment,

ment, fhould any fuch thing happen, and to make a provifion for her that fhould fave her from any difagreeable confequences of it.

"His ability to perform fuch a promife, which fhe was no ftranger to, and the perfua-five argument of feveral very valuable prefents, in the end prevailed upon her. Accordingly one evening, when her hufband was *engaged abroad,* fhe let him in at the back-door of her houfe, with the greateft appearance of privacy and fear, and conducted him foftly up to her own chamber. He had not been many mi-nutes in poffeffion of his defires, when all on a fudden the door was burft in, and a drawn fword was held to his breaft, by a man who appeared to be in the moft violent agitation of frantic rage.

"Villain! adulterefs! (exclaimed he, foam-ing at the mouth, and rolling his eyes wildly around) have I then caught you at laft?——This inftant fhall your adulterous blood pay the price of my difhonour!—this inftant will I" —

"O mercy! mercy! (cried the trembling female, holding up her hands, and tuning her voice in the moft plaintive tone) Spare us!—fpare us but a moment!——Murder not our wretched fouls as well as our bodies."——

"The hufband ftarted at thefe words, and feemed loft in thought, while his lifted arm hung over them in the air. She faw the critical moment, and jogging her lover, who lay pe-trified with fear, "Speak to him, (faid fhe) perhaps your words may have effect! his heart was ever tender and humane."——

"Rouzed by this addrefs, the poor felf-con-victed culprit attempted to affay him with the beft
argu-

arguments his fear could fuggeft. "Think not of a revenge (faid he) which muft prove as fatal to yourfelf as to us; but name any reparation you pleafe to require, and it fhall be inftantly made. My fortune is fufficient"—

"Reparation?—No.——Nothing but blood can make me reparation, (anfwered the hufband, rifing to tenfold rage after the paufe) my honour, my love for that ungrateful woman will hear of no other reparation.—As to myfelf, my life I value not at a pin's fee; all that is dear to me is now loft."——Then finking, as it were, into foftnefs, "And can I wound that breaft fairer than monumental alabafter? O woman! woman!"——

"At thefe words he held his hand to his eyes, to hide his tears, and fobbed aloud as in the anguifh of his foul. The lovers thought this fit of foftnefs favourable to their fears, and, flipping out of bed, naked as they were, threw themfelves at his feet, and befought his mercy in the moft moving terms. After fuffering a conflict of fome moments, he funk backwards into a chair, and, bidding them put on their cloaths, fat as deliberating how to act in fuch a diftreffing fituation.

"In the mean time the lover, who thought that his life depended on the refult of this deliberation, renewed his offers of reparation with the greateft earneftnefs, while his partner in guilt applied for mercy, with every argument that could move compaffion. His *tender* heart was not proof to fuch a double attack. After paufing for fome little time, "And what reparation can you make (faid he) for robbing me of the love of a woman, to obtain whom I have
facri-

facrificed my whole fortune, and plunged my-felf into debts, which have driven me to the brink of defpair? but I thought nothing too much to fuffer for her, bafe and ungrateful as fhe is."——

"I will not only inftantly enable you to dif-charge thofe debts (anfwered the lover eagerly, catching a glimpfe of hope from that capitulat-ing queftion) but I will alfo fetle fuch an an-nuity on you for life, as fhall raife you above the neceffity of ever contracting any more."——

"What fhall I do? (exclaimed the hufband, as in an agony) fhall I compound my difhonour for a price? fhall I perifh in want and defpair? —What fhall I, can I do?

"The irrefolution implied in thefe words, gave the terrified lovers new hope. They af-failed him again with every argument they could devife, which they purfued with fuch fuccefs, that at length he fubmitted to receive a repara-tion for an injury not to be recalled. When this firft point was gained, the terms were foon fet-tled, the eagernefs of the lover preventing the other's making any demand, by the largenefs of his offers. A lawyer, who was a friend of the hufband, and luckily happened to be in a neigh-bouring coffee-houfe, was directly called in, and foon confirmed the compact beyond a pof-fibility of revocation; one article of which was, that the lover fhould make a feparate provifion for his miftrefs, the hufband's delicate fenfe of honour not permitting him to have any farther intercourfe with her.

CHAP.

## CHAP. XXIII.

*A new motive for turning soldier; with a short
view of the military profession. The scene is
changed, and a more extensive prospect opened.*

" EVERY circumstance of this transaction
bore such glaring marks of imposition,
that any other person would have seen through,
and avoided the deceit; or at least, when that
was too late, have shewn a proper resentment
of it, by dropping all farther commerce with the
base woman who drew him into such a snare,
and was evidently an accomplice in the whole.
But, blind to all conviction, he grew fonder of
her than before, and, seeming to have changed
his very nature, proved constant to her longer
than he had ever been to any other object; tho'
far from striving to retain him by any appearance
of regard, any obsequiousness in her behaviour,
now that her independence, the first object of her,
designs, was established, she affected on all occasions to treat him with the most insolent contempt, and openly bestowed upon others those
favours which had cost him so dear.

" While he indulged every vicious passion in
this profligate manner, the condition of his deserted wife deserved the highest compassion. Sensible of the danger of expostulating on so delicate
a subject, she seemed not to see the slights which
he hourly shewed her, but, drying up her tears
whenever he approached her, always met him
with a smile of tenderness and respect. Smo-
thered grief preys with double violence upon the
heart. Though she did not complain, she could
not avoid feeling the pain of such treatment under

der which she pined insensibly away, like a flower cankered at the root.

"But that which reason could not do, was effected by the natural inconstancy of his temper, and a new whim supplanted his profligate mistress in his thoughts. His country happened to be engaged in war; the noise of drums and trumpets turned his head, and he must needs be a soldier, for want of something else to give him employment. As soon as this caprice took possession of him, he bought a commission in the army directly, and set about learning the military trade with as much eagerness as if he was obliged to follow it for bread; and, to shew his proficiency in tacticks, even went so far as to write an elaborate *treatise* on the mighty advantages of a soldier's *turning out his toes* in his marching.

"When he had with infinite pains got his company trimmed and disciplined to his mind, contrary to the expectation of all who knew him, he pursued the humour so far as to go with them into the field, where they soon had an opportunity of signalizing their valour, at the expence of near half their lives. But an unlucky visit of compliment to the colonel deprived him of the glory of sharing in the danger of that day, though the gallant behaviour of his men reflected sufficient honour on him, for having trained to such excellent discipline, and inspired them with so noble a contempt of death. Encouraged by that success, he persists in his pursuit of fame, the vicissitudes of the military life keeping his mind continually employed, and saving him from the fatigue of a moment's reflection; an evil to avoid which he has ever had recourse to some new scheme of active idleness." "I

" I thought it impoffible, (faid I) O my guide, that the heart of man could be fo abfurdly perverfe! The general motives for embracing the military life are neceffity, an enthufiaſtic paffion for fame, and perhaps, in a very few inſtances, a difintereſted ſpirit of patriotifm. But here none of thefe can be alledged; for the laſt his temper is too indifferent; too liſtlefs and unſteady for the purſuit of fame; and his affluence raiſes him above neceffity, which is the moſt univerfal of all : fo that he literally facrifices the moſt folid advantages of life for nothing, and runs into danger and diſtreſs, becaufe he is incapable of enjoying the oppofite bleffings."

" To the motives which you have affigned (returned the fpirit) you might have added avarice and ambition, from both of which he is alſo conſtitutionally exempt. As to the dangers and diſtreſſes in which you imagine he muſt have involved himfelf, though fufficient to deter any man of reafon from plunging wantonly into them ; in fuch cafes as his, they are far fhort of what inexperienced apprehenfion may reprefent. The private centinel who hourly expofes his life for a morfel of bread to fupport it, and the fubaltern officer who leads that foldier to fight, ſtruggle with difficulties, and encounter dangers, which nature fhudders at the thought of ; but afcend to the higher ranks, and a great part of thofe terrors vaniſh. Their carriages fave them from fatigue, their tables are heaped with delicacies, and luxury reigns in their tents. The day of battle, in which alone they are expofed to danger, is in fome meafure a day of reſt to the others ; the motions and manœuvres, in which the modern art of war moſtly confiſts,

3                                                        har-

harraffing the unhappy foldier with greater hard-
fhips, and expofing him to more dangers than
any general engagement. But of this you will
be a better judge when you have taken a view
of yonder fcene of war. We have dwelt too
long upon the minute concerns of private life,
of individuals, however ftrongly marked out for
obfervation, by titles, wealth, or folly. We will
now enlarge our view, and fee whether the conduct of nations is more rational ; whether the
clouds of folly and vice which overcaft the cottage, and produce domeftic unhappinefs in lower
life, may not, when raifed into the higher regions, burft into ftorms and thunder, and make
an univerfal wreck of all the works of nature.

The END of the FIRST VOLUME.

# THE

# REVERIE:

## O R,

# A FLIGHT

### TO THE

# PARADISE of FOOLS.

---

*—All things vain, and all who in vain things*
*Build their fond hopes of glory, or lasting fame,*
*Or happiness, in this, or th' other life——*

MILTON.

---

Published by the EDITOR of
The ADVENTURES of a GUINEA.

---

## VOL. II.

---

LONDON:
Printed for T. BECKET, and P. A. DA HONDT,
in the Strand. MDCCLXIII.

# THE
# CONTENTS
## OF THE
## SECOND VOLUME.

---

## BOOK I.

### CHAP. I.

A                    CHAP.

# CONTENTS.

## CHAP. IV.

## CHAP. V.

## CHAP. VI.

## CHAP. VII.

## CHAP. VIII.

## CHAP. IX.

# CONTENTS.

## CHAP. X.

## CHAP. XI.

## CHAP. XII.

## CHAP. XIII.

## CHAP. XIV

## CHAP. XV.

## CHAP. XVI.

A 2 CHAP.

# CONTENTS.

BOOK

# B O O K  II.

## C H A P.  I.

## C H A P.  II.

## C H A P.  III.

## C H A P.  IV

## C H A P.  V.

## C H A P.  VI.

C H A P.

# CONTENTS.

## CHAP. VII.

## CHAP. VIII.

## CHAP. IX.

## CHAP. X.

## CHAP. XI.

## CHAP. XII.

## CHAP. XIII.

# CONTENTS.

6                                      C H A P.

# CONTENTS.

## CHAP. XX.

# THE

# R E V E R I E;

## O R, A

## Flight to the Paradise of Fools.

---

### C H A P. I.

*The scheme changes with the scene. A remarkable*
*instance of military equity. The soldier's view*
*in war. Every man for himself, the rule in*
*war as well as peace.*

THE feats of heroifm, and the glory,
which according to the general prejudices of mankind, I had been accuftomed to affociate with the idea of
war, made me promife myfelf much pleafure
from this change. The fpirit read my fentiments in my looks, and fmiling expreffively,
" You are now going to take a view of fcenes,
" (faid he) the nature of which will make your
" utmoft care requifite, to efcape the illufions

" which furround them on every fide, and are
" fo ftrong as to deceive the very actors of them.
" The limitation of the human faculties makes
" it neceffary, that objects fhould be prefented
" to you in a regular fucceffion; as that gene-
" ral view which conveys knowledge intuitive-
" ly to fuperior beings, would only dazzle your
" mind, and involve it in perplexity and con-
" fufion. But this the more important duties
" of my office will not permit my attending to,
" at prefent. I have already devoted as much
" time to your gratification as I can fpare. You
" muft therefore proceed alone, and make your
" own obfervations. For this reafon it will be
" proper to place you immediately in the fcene
" of action. Your attention will there be freed
" from the diftraction of a more diftant and
" complicated view; and you fhall have other
" affiftances, to remedy the inconvenience of
" my abfence."——Saying this, he took my
hand, and tranfported me, inftantaneoufly, in
the fame manner as before, into the country
which was the feat of the war.

High as my expectations had been, this nearer
view of the paths of human glory chilled my
foul. I turned my eyes away in horror; and,
in the inftinctive impulfe of affright, moved
clofe to my guide for protection. " I have
" often cautioned you (refumed he, in an ac-
" cent of reproof) againft forming your judge-
" ment of any thing too precipitately. But
" now you were delighted at the thought of
" this profpect. In a moment, you ficken at
" the fight. Is this confiftent with the charac-
" ter of a rational being? Your prefent fears
" of danger to yourfelf are as idly groundlefs,

" as

" as your hopes of receiving pleasure, from be-
" holding the miseries of others, were then un-
" justifiable. I have told you, that your form
" is imperceptible to human sense. It is also
" impassive to the injuries which affect morta-
" lity, under all the weakness and imperfections
" of which you see the beings before you la-
" bour, as strongly as when in your world.
" You may therefore mix with the multitude
" without apprehension, and make your re-
" marks on every thing that occurs, with deli-
" beration and ease; to enable you to do which,
" I have freed your mind from the prejudices
" that have hitherto obstructed your reason, so
" that you will now behold all things in their
" genuine colours; and as some knowledge of
" the past lives of the persons concerned in the
" scenes you are going to enter into, may oc-
" casionally be necessary to explain their present
" actions, your faculties are enlarged with a
" power of looking back, and reviewing the
" whole series, as readily and distinctly as you
" do the objects recorded in your memory.
" Your motions also, as you are unincumbered
" with matter, depend absolutely on your will,
" by a single act of which you may transport
" yourself whither-soever you please, in an in-
" stant; and so trace the most complicated
" transactions through all their intricate extent,
" from their obscure causes, to their as unex-
" pected conclusions, with precision and per-
" spicuity. A right use of these advantages will
" give your curiosity the most rational satisfac-
" tion. Nor are you confined to any particu-
" lar scene. When your soul is surfeited with
" war, and sickens at the thought of military

" glory,

" glory, you are at liberty to feek new fubjects
" of remark, through all the wide extent of
" human life, which is expanded to your view.
" One thing, though, I muſt caution you
" againſt, Forget not that you are a mcer un-
" concerned fpectator of all the events you be-
" hold; nor prefume on any account to inter-
" pofe, be they ever fo intereſting to you. The
" leaſt attempt of this kind will inſtantaneouf-
" ly deprive you for-ever of the indulgence you
" now enjoy. I am fummoned hence. When
" it is proper to reconduct you to the world of
" man, I will attend. Till then, obferve the cau-
" tion I have given you, and proceed without
" farther limitation or reſtraint."— With thefe
words he vaniſhed from my fight.

The firſt emotions of my furprize at being
left in fuch a condition may be eaſily conceived.
But they laſted not long. I foon felt the advantages of the favours beſtowed fo liberally upon me ; in the confcioufnefs of which I loſt all
fear, and directly prepared to avail myfelf of
them, in the moſt extenſive manner. The
more than martial animoſity with which this
war appeared, by the defolation of the country,
and the miferies of the inhabitants, to be carried on, made me conclude that it muſt have
arifen from fome moſt important caufe. To
learn this I directly entered into the army that
lay heareſt to me, where I imagined I fhould
readily receive the information I wanted ; judging that every individual muſt be acquainted
with the motives for a war in which he hazarded his life, and of courfe they muſt be the
fubject of the general converfation.

The army was compofed of mercenaries of different nations hired by a foreign power, whofe own fubjects made a confiderable part of it, tho' under the fupreme command of one of the former; and was led hither, into the country of an ally and friend, according to the rules of military equity, to defend the fovereign's own dominions from the invafion of an enemy, who with equal juftice marched his forces to the indifcriminate oppreffion of friends and foes, through whofe territories they paffed, to wreak his vengeance on this part of his adverfary's fubjects, for injuries he imagined he had received from another, who were fuperior to his power, and with whom thefe had no connection in nature or intereft, other than (in this cafe) the misfortune of being under the government of the fame fovereign.

This general account I foon learned, and faw abundantly confirmed, both by the appearance of the army, and the manner of its proceeding; but of the real origin of the war, or the end propofed by it, except *plunder* and *pay*, the foldiers appeared utterly ignorant, and indeed unconcerned about them, plodding mechanically to the field to fight, with as much indifference as oxen do to plough.

Shocked at an infenfibility fo difgraceful to beings who boaft of the bleffing of reafon, I advanced to the commander, from whom I hoped to learn fomething fatisfactory, in matters fo immediately conducted by himfelf. He was fitting in his tent, at a table covered with difpatches he had juft received from the court by which he was employed. When he had looked them over, with evident phlegm, and

difregard. "Thefe people (faid he) muft think
" me as great a fool as themfelves, to fend
" me fuch orders; orders which common
" fenfe might inform them I will not obey.
" The people are out of humour, forfooth, at
" the length and expence of the war; and fo
" their wife mafters want me to pufh it with
" more vigour, to bring it to a conclufion. But
" they will find themfelves miftaken, I promife
" them. No! No! I will have no general
" actions; nothing that can poffibly be decifive
" either way. That is not my bufinefs. The
" profits of my command are too confiderable
" to be thrown away in that manner. If I
" fhould be beaten, they will inftantly chufe
" another general, without ever confidering
" that I only obeyed their own orders. And if
" I obtain a compleat victory, the war is at
" an end; and of courfe my profit alfo. No!
" No! I will have no decifive actions. While
" they are mafters of a ducat to pay me, I will
" protract the war. When their money is all
" fpent, they may go to battle as foon as they
" will; and whether they win or lofe, is a mat-
" ter of indifference to me. In the mean time,
" they fhall have marching, and fkirmifhing
" enough, to fatisfy their paffion for fighting,
" and prevent their complaining of idlenefs. I
" am commander in chief; and while I am, I
" will do juft what I pleafe, which is to promote
" my own intereft as much as I poffibly can.
" If I can manage matters fo, as to hold my
" poft for two or three campaigns more, I fhall
" get money enough to fupport the dignity of
" my illuftrious houfe with proper fplendour.
" Nor is it poffible for them to detect my defign.

" fign. The difproportion in numbers between
" my army, and that of the enemy, is fuch as
" fufficiently juftifies my cautious conduct ; at
" the fame time, that the difference in the ap-
" pointments and goodnefs of the men fecures
" me from danger of difgrace, and makes the
" glory I acquire in this defenfive war cheaply
" earned. Indeed the greateft difficulty often
" is to divide their force, and direct their ar-
" dour in fuch a manner, as to prevent their
" defeating their enemies totally, againft all
" difadvantages, and contrary to my inten-
" tions."

## C H A P. II.

*A gilded bait to catch a gudgeon. The beft cure for
a matrimonial furfeit ; with a new motive for
entering into the military life.*

HAVING finifhed his meditations, he went
out to a number of his officers, who attended at the entrance of his tent. His behaviour on this occafion fhewed the mafterly addrefs with which he purfued his private fcheme.
To his own countrymen he fpoke with the utmoft indifference; and giving them fome general orders about the duties of the camp, difmiffed
them flightly, and with an appearance of dif-
efteem. But to the foreigners by whofe fovereign
he was employed, he carried himfelf in quite a
different manner. His eye wore a fmile of familiarity and complaifance, whenever it met
the meaneft fubaltern of the corps; and he fcru-

pled

pled not to compliment them, at the expence of the reft of the army, by propofing their example to general imitation.

So flattering a preference had the defigned effect; the fatigues and dangers by which they acquired it were immediately forgot; and they even appeared eager to undertake more, to fupport fo diftinguifhed an honour.

The general faw with fecret pleafure the ardour with which he had inflamed them; and refolved he would not let it cool, for want of employment. Advancing to their particular commander, who juft then joined him; "My "dear friend, (faid he, with an air of the moft "cordial efteem) I have this moment received "fome intelligence, that enables me to give "your brave countrymen an opportunity of "fignalizing that valour which has eftablifhed "them in the exalted reputation of being the "beft foldiers in the univerfe. You will felect "five thoufand whom you think moft proper, "and let them be ready to march an hour be- "fore night. When you return from doing "that, we will concert our meafures, and fix "on a perfon to carry them into execution. It "is a mafter-ftroke, and will do honour to any "officer; for I cannot doubt of the fuccefs of "an enterprize undertaken by your gallant "countrymen."

The officer, who free from deceit himfelf, fufpected none in any body elfe, heard him with the higheft joy, and glowing with a paffion for glory, which the general thus artfully fann'd, refolved, without even waiting to know the nature of the attempt, to take the command himfelf, and fo reap all the honour. "Your High-
"nefs

" nefs (anfwered he, with evident emotion )
" does them honour by all your commands. I
" fhall not have any occafion for felecting,
" where all are equally good, and equally am-
" bitious of meriting your approbation. As
" for an officer for the command, I believe I
" can find one to whom, I hope, your High-
" nefs will have no objection."

Saying this, he proceeded directly to get every
thing ready, while the reft of the army, inftead
of being offended at having the poft of honour
thus partially given from them, hugged themfelves in the eafe and fafety they enjoyed by the
difgrace.

There was fomething fo ftriking in the readinefs with which the officer catched at the bait
that was laid for him, that I became fome-how
anxious for the event, and refolved to obferve
him particularly through the affair; and therefore followed him, when he went to give the
neceffary orders to his men.

If I had been furprifed at the ardour he
fhewed, I was infinitely more fo, to find that
the fame fpirit ran through all his countrymen;
the very private foldiers, whofe ftation might
have been fuppofed to exempt them from the
enthufiaftic notions of honour which idlenefs
and affluence infpire in the more exalted ranks,
to fuch a degree as to make men break
through the firft law of nature, to run into danger with delight, *turning out* to a man, at the
firft mention of the matter; and vying with
each other who fhould be of the party;
though the appearance of many of them fhewed
that they were already exhaufted by fatigue, and wanted reft and refrefhment, to re-

ftore

ftore their ftrength to any degree of equality
with their fpirit.

Among men actuated by fuch an emulation,
the leaft preference muft have bred envy, and
been attended with difagreeable confequences.
Senfible of this, the officer thanked them all,
in the moft engaging manner for their readinefs; but faid, that, according to the indifpenfible rule of military difcipline, he muft neceffarily take thofe whofe duty came in turn, con-
foling the reft with the thought that they could
not long want an opportunity equally glorious
of proving their fpirit in an army, where they
were honoured by the general, with fo peculiar
a preheminence.

This delicate affair being adjufted, the heroes
whofe happy fortune it was to go prepared
themfelves with the higheft emulation, while
the others drew off in evident dejection at their
difappointment.

As their leader rode along the lines, to take
a particular view of them, I obferved that he
addreffed one of his fubalterns, and was anfwered by him in a ftrain of familiarity, that
feemed inconfiftent with the diftance between
their ftations. " Well *Tom*, (faid the former,
" with a fmile) this is a fudden call. How
" will *Venus* bear to have her *Mars* torn from
" her arms fo foon? She ought to have a little
" longer time to reconcile her to the military
" life, before fhe is left by herfelf in a camp."

—— " In a camp! No! no! I fhall hardly
" leave her in a camp."

—— " No! What then do you defign to do
" with her?"

—— " Why? fend her to indulge her medi-
" tations

" tations with her old friend, *Will Buck's*
" Lady. It will be good entertainment for
" them to compare notes."

—— " But if you did not mean to keep her
" here, why were you at the trouble of bring-
" ing her? I imagined it was becaufe you did
" not know how to part with her."

—— " How to part with her! I thought you
" knew me better than to think fo. Why,
" man! the very contrary was the reafon. If
" I did not defire to part with her, what fhould
" make me bring her here? No! No! It is
" not come to that with me yet. I turned fol-
" dier, at firft, merely to get rid of my wife;
" and I hope I may be allowed to take the fame
" method to get rid of my miftrefs too, when
" I am equally tired of her. Befide, I have a
" better plea now than I had before. My ho-
" nour, man! My honour is engaged. I muft
" not quit my colours upon any account, at
" fuch a time as this. If the fond charmer
" fhould take pet, and go home to her friends,
" with her finger in her eye, to be revenged on
" her fwain for his indifference, fhe has my fin-
" cere confent; nor fhall my beft affiftance be
" wanting to make an honeft woman of her, by
" getting her a good hufband. She has examples
" enough to keep her in countenance. But if
" the conftant dove will not defert her roving
" mate, why, faith, I do not well know how
" to fend her back againft her will; and muft
" in compaffion pay her a vifit now and then;
" though, by the by, it fhall be as feldom as
" poffible, to give her company fomething like
" novelty; which, in my opinion, is the only

" thing

" thing that can make the company of any wo-
" man tolerable."

———" But, won't this be breaking faith with
" her ? I presume you must have made her
" many fine promises of love and constancy,
" before you could bring her to take such a
" step? "

———" Promises! Aye, promises enough for
" the matter of that; but she was a fool if she
" believed them, when she had a proof that
" I should not keep them, before her eyes.
" She could not be so blindly vain, as not to
" know that novelty was the only advantage
" she had over my wife, whom I may proba-
" bly return to by and by, for the same reason,
" when a campaign or two shall have sharpened
" my appetite. A campaign is the best reme-
" dy in nature for a matrimonial surfeit. It
" cures a man's qualms, and sends him home
" as keen as a country-bridegroom."

———" But, are you sure that she will leave
" you so readily? The same spirit that enabled
" her to come to such a place as this, may dif-
" pute your authority to send her back. She
" has paid a dear price for your company, and
" may not chuse to give it up. Women when
" once they love have much more constancy in
" their temper than men."

———" Constancy! Say rather, obstinacy.
" But I have taken care of that matter. I
" have wrote a letter to my wife, in which I
" made professions of the highest esteem, and
" desired the favour of her company, to com-
" pleat my happiness; promising, that *Chloe*
" and I would study her satisfaction and plea-
" sure in every instance."

—" Good

——" Good Heavens! What could you
" propose by that? You could never think she
" would be mean, or mad enough, to ac-
" cept of such an invitation; an invitation,
" that only added insult to the ill-treatment
" you had given her before."

" Accept of it! No, I neither expected nor
" desired that. I had schemes of a very diffe-
" rent kind in view. I know you have never
" suspected me, for forming any deep designs;
" but this will convince you of the contrary.
" This Letter, little as you think of it, will
" serve two very important purposes. It will
" prevent my wife from obtaining a separate
" maintenance out of my estate; for, as it is
" her duty to follow me wherever I please, she
" cannot now pretend that I have abandoned
" her: and, on the other hand, it gives me
" an opportunity, at this and any other time,
" to get rid of my mistress's company, by tell-
" ing her, that my invitation is accepted; for
" she would fly to the extremity of the globe
" rather than meet her. He! What think you
" now? Am not I a good politician? Egad, I
" always mistook my talents; if I had applied
" myself in time, I might have been prime mi-
" nister before now. Ha! ha! ha!"——

——" If you were conscious of this incon-
" stancy in your temper, how came you to
" marry? That should have been the last thing
" I would have done."

—— " That is very true. But Sir *John*
" *Brute*'s reason was mine. I wanted to go to
" bed to her, and she would not consent on
" any other terms: the consequence of which
" was, that when my end was obtained, I grew
" tired

" tired of my bargain, and so turned soldier to
" get quit of it."

――" I am surprised to hear you say this.
" I always understood that you had other mo-
" tives for your military turn; an ambition of
" command, and thirst for glory."

――" Very true. Glory and command are
" pretty things, to be sure; but they are not
" equally the passion of all people. Your good
" luck in losing your wife, made me hope that
" my turtle would have broken her heart, in
" the same manner; but she was not so oblig-
" ing; and therefore I have tried this method
" of preferring another publickly to her. I
" know the force of female vanity; and if this
" scheme should luckily succeed, I'll give up my
" hopes of a truncheon, and retire as *Scipio*
" and other great men have done. If I once
" get my neck out of the yoke, I'll take care
" how I thrust it in again, or even enter into
" any connection that I cannot break when I
" please, without being obliged to have recourse
" to this expedient. No! No! I am not quite
" so fond of glory as you are. I can be con-
" tent at home; that is, when I am master of
" my own house."

" Is it possible that you can be serious? This
" is so contrary to the opinion of all your
" friends, that I must believe you only jest.
" Your birth and fortune give you a title to the
" highest employments in the state, in what-
" ever capacity you chose to apply yourself;
" and we all thought, that preferring the mili-
" tary, as the most honourable, you had come
" hither to qualify yourself for them."

――" Aye!

———" Aye! as you have done! And pray," " what are you the better? In reward of all " your fatigues and dangers, you have the ho- " nour to be put under the command of a fo- " reigner, who would not presume to put him- " self upon a level with you in any other light; " and laughs at you in his sleeve, for your con- " descension. Very fine encouragement, true- " ly! No! No! Let the poor fight for pay, you " and I want it not; and all the real advantages " of honour our anceftors, bleffings on their " memory for their pains, have tranfmitted to us. " Let us then enjoy the happinefs that is in our " poffeffion, and not lofe the fubftance thus, " to grafp at the fhadow."

The other, who had liftened to him before with contempt, was fo ftruck with the latter part of his difcourfe, that he rode away abrupt- ly to avoid hearing any more of it.

❀❀❀❀❀❀❀❀❀❀ ❀❀❀❀❀❀❀❀❀❀

## C H A P. III.

*A toilet fet out in a new tafte. The advantage of knowing how to play one inconvenience againft another; with an interefting inftance of love and honour in the modern ftyle.*

THIS extraordinary converfation raifing my curiofity to fee the fair female who had originally been the fubject of it, I followed her lover, while his leader was preparing for his expedition.

She was fitting alone in his tent, in a fituation

tion not eafy to be defcribed. Educated in the lap of luxury, fhe had multiplied the wants of nature ten-thoufand-fold; and required affift-ance every moment for neceffities created by caprice. Though her lover's fortune placed her above the real diftreffes of fuch a place, and fupplied her with moft of the convenien-cies, as well as all the neceffaries of life, fhe had numberlefs artificial occafions, which habit had made in a manner indifpenfible to her, and which, as it was impoffible to provide for then, in fuch a vague unfettled ftate, fhe exerted as much contrivance to fupply, as had firft enabled human ingenuity to find out the moft important conveniencies of life; though with this effen-tial difference, that as the end was fantaftic here, the means neceffarily appeared ridiculous.

We found her at her toilet, which was a fumpter-trunk, fet upon one end, and covered with a foul fhirt. On this fhe had placed a pocket-mirrour, and on each fide of that a row of phials, and gallipots filled with colours, cofmetic pafte and wafhes which fhe always carried about her. Her combs and brufhes were fet out on the faucers fhe had juft been ufing for breakfaft. Her fhoes and ftockings lay on the bed, which was alfo her feat; and to wafh herfelf, fhe made ufe of an utenfil, which had been placed under it for another occafion. With this apparatus, all fet in form, fhe was as atten-tively bufy at the important work of dreffing, as if fhe was going to make her appearance at a drawing-room. Her lover's entrance inter-rupted her. "Fie, *Damon*, (faid fhe, blufhing "at the ridiculous figure fhe made) how can "you intrude fo rudely into a lady's ruelle? "**You**

" You fee I have fet out my toilet. The bed
" and the trunk ferve for every thing. Dumb
" waiters are fometimes moft convenient; hah!
" hah! hah!"

The moment I faw her, I could perceive that
this gaiety was all affected; that, fick at heart,
fhe flew to levity for relief from the torture of
reflection. Such a ruin was fufficient to raife
compaffion in any mind not utterly loft to every
fenfe of humanity, as well as virtue. She was
juft entered into the prime of life; her form elegant and ftriking; and her features, if not
faultlefsly beautiful, yet glowing with fuch luxuriant health, fuch animated fenfibility, as had
the effect of the moft perfect beauty. But
in her prefent fituation, all thefe charms appeared to difadvantage. A gloom of confcious
guilt overcaft her fmiles; and amidft all her
mirth and endearments, fhe was afhamed to
look up, and meet the eye of the very author
of her fhame.

When fhe had forced out the laugh with
which fhe concluded the above fpeech, her
Damon, fmiling with an air of indifference,
" Neceffity is the mother of invention, my dear
" Chloe; (faid he) and yours feems to have been
" well fet to work. But I come to tell you fome
" news that I fear will interrupt you. I am
" ordered out upon action directly; and as it
" is like to be a warm affair, I think it is bet-
" ter to provide for your fafety before I go,
" for fear of any thing's happening to me.
" You would be horridly at a lofs by your-
" felf, in fuch a place as this, if I fhould be
" killed."

She ftarted at the mention of action; but his
laft

laſt words ſtruck her with terrors too ſtrong for her to bear. For ſome moments ſhe ſtood like the ſtatue of horror, unable to move or ſpeak; but her very fears at length gave her utterance. "Good heaven! (exclaimed ſhe) What "do you mean? What action can you be or- "dered into that ſhould endanger your life? "Did you not promiſe me, that you would "quit this accurſed life directly? Did you not "prevail upon me to come here with you, on- "ly that you might lay down your commiſſion "without diſrepute? You cannot, ſhall not, "think of going into any action! You muſt "come away this moment."

———"That was my deſign, my dear, if it "had not been for this unlucky affair; but "now it is impoſſible for me to ſtir. If I re- "turn, I will that moment lay down; but I "cannot poſſibly do it ſooner. It would be "an eternal blot upon my honour."

———"Honour! (returned ſhe, with a ſigh, "that ſeemed to burſt her heart) How can you "mention that word to me? If you are reſolved "to go, I will wait the event here. Should "you be brought back wounded, my care may "not be unneceſſary! If worſe ſhould happen, "the horrors I ſhall ſuffer till I receive the "account, will compleat my averſion to life, "and make me glad to follow you. I have "now no buſineſs in this world without you."

The agony in which ſhe ſaid this would have melted any other heart; but he felt it not. Finding her proof to this argument, he therefore had recourſe to his laſt expedient. "I am "much obliged to you, my dear, (ſaid he, quite "unmoved) for your kind intentions to take

care

" care of me; but I hope I fhall not want it.
" Befide, there is another thing, which embar-
" raffes me a good deal. I have juft received
" an account, that my wife, out of her exam-
" plary love and duty, has accepted my invi-
" tation, and is coming to us directly."

" To us! (anfwered fhe, alarmed almoft to
" diftraction) Is it poffible? What fhall we do?
" Where fhall I fly! I never can, never will fee
" her. I had rather die ten thoufand deaths,
" than look her in the face."

―――― " To be fure, I allow it muft be rather
" aukward; but the mifchief is, I cannot tell
" how you will avoid it, if you ftay here."

―― " You muft write to her peremptorily, this
" moment, not to come; and when you leave
" this place, take a different route from what
" you intended, for fear fhe fhould not obey
" you."

―― " Aye! but the worft is, I don't know where
" to direct to her. She fet out immediately, on
" receipt of my letter; and as the poft is obliged
" to come fo far about, for fear of being inter-
" cepted by the enemy, and fhe travels with
" paffports the fhorteft way, fhe may be here
" this evening, for aught I know: and then it
" would be fo grofs an abufe not to fee her,
" even after her undergoing the fatigue of fuch
" a journey, at my exprefs defire, that I can-
" not avoid waiting for her. Decency at leaft
" muft be obferved."

―――― " Decency! How can you infult me
" by mentioning fuch a word? I flighted that,
" and every thing elfe, for you. Had I paid
" any regard to decency, I fhould not have been
" here now in this condition."

" Nay,

———" Nay, for the matter of that, my dear,
" I am not much behind you. I fhewed as
" little refpect to thefe things for your fake as
" you could for mine. But let us not enter
" into fruitlefs difputes. What are you re-
" folved to do? for I muft march within this
" hour."

———" Honour! decency! But I am juftly
" ferved. What am I refolved to do! Say ra-
" ther what you intend to do with me, and do
" not torture me any longer in this manner;
" for I fee plainly enough, that my prefence is
" a pain, which you want to get rid of at any
" rate. Honour! juft heaven!"

———" Why child, if you are determined to
" think fo, it is in vain to reafon with you.
" You fhall do juft as you pleafe; either go
" or ftay. What I meant to propofe was this:
" You remember your old friend, who took a
" frolick with *Will Buck* two or three years
" ago. She lives in a very pretty retired man-
" ner, in a neutral town, about twenty miles
" from hence. Now, if you approve of it, it
" would be no bad fcheme for you, to go and
" pay her a vifit, till we fee how things go. I
" am fure fhe will be very well pleafed to fee
" you; and there you will be free from the in-
" conveniencies, and fafe from the dangers of
" a camp; and near enough for me to ftep to
" you as often as I can fpare a moment. I'll
" write a letter to *Will* about it directly; and
" as I know his finances are not in the beft
" fituation, I make no doubt but he'll be very
" glad of your ftaying there as long as you
" pleafe; for you fhall have money enough, to
" bear all the expence. I would not let you
" be

" be under obligation to any one. Well, what
" think you of my fcheme? Was it not a lucky
" thought? You and fhe were very intimate
" formerly, and will now be the moft proper
" and agreeable companions for each other."

It is impoffible to defcribe the different paffions which were painted in her face, while he
was making this propofal. She knew him too
well to take fuch a rational fcheme for a fudden thought; and concluded from thence, that
he was fatiated with her company, and had
formed a premeditated defign to get rid of her;
to facilitate which he had firft made a pretence
of his being ordered into action, and when that
did not take effect, forged this ftory of his wife's
coming; for, notwithstanding her diftrefs, fhe
had obferved the many inconfiftencies in what
he faid. However, her pride would not permit
her to difcover her fufpicions, as it would look
like ftriving to force herfelf longer upon him..

" When you are refolved, (anfwered fhe,
" with a moft expreffive look) I have nothing
" left but to obey. Give orders for my going,
" I fhall foon be ready. All places are indif-
" ferent to me, and all companions equally dif-
" agreeable. My own thoughts will afford me
" company enough. I leave you to yours."

" My deareft girl, (replied he, more pleafed
" at her compliance than affected at the man-
" ner of it) what I propofe is for the beft. I
" only ftudy your convenience and fatisfaction.
" If you can think of any other way, I am rea-
" dy to do it."

——" I have no power to think! I wifh I
" never could! But let me be gone. I have
" ftaid too long already. Let me not interfere
" with

" with your regard to decency and honour."
——Saying this, she directly huddled on her travelling habit, while he went to order his chaise to the door of his tent.

When he had done this, he returned to give her some necessary instructions for her journey, and palliate the offence he had given her, by caresses and professions of love and constancy. She heared him with the most contemptuous silence; and taking a purse of gold, which he gave her, with an air of indignation flung into the chaise the moment it arrived, without speaking a word, or making the least return to his fondness.

The spirit which she shewed on this occasion was evidently raised by resentment; and of course could not last long. Indeed she was scarce able to support it till she got into the chaise, where she melted into a flood of tears before she was out of sight. Her lover saw her distress; but the joy he felt at being freed from her company, prevented his feeling any concern at it. He shrugged up his shoulders in self-complacency; and, hugging himself on his deliverance, prepared to attend his commander at the appointed hour.

CHAP.

❀❀❀❀❀❀❀❀❀:❀❀❀❀❀❀❀❀❀

## CHAP. IV.

*War ! Horrid war ! They'll never want employ-*
*ment who think themselves well paid for their*
*pains with a mouthful of moon-shine. The great*
*channel of secret intelligence.*

THERE was something so deliberately
base in the whole conduct of this person,
that I left him with the highest contempt, and
returned to his commander, who was by this
time ready to wait upon the general to receive
his orders.

The moment he entered the tent, the general arose, and, dismissing every other person
present, received him with the highest respect.
" Well, my friend, (said he) I am now ready
" to communicate to you the plan which I have
" formed; but it will be proper that the per-
" son for whom you design the honour of the
" command, should be present."

" He is present, if your highness makes no
" objection to him. I know that all your plans
" are formed with judgment; and as your more
" than usual earnestness about this shews it to
" be of importance, shall be proud of having
" the execution of it entrusted to my care."

——" You, my friend ! I know not what
" to say; I cannot spare you from my side. I
" want your advice every moment. At the
" same time, I am unwilling to rob you of
" an opportunity of acquiring so much glory.
" Here is the intelligence I have received, and
2 " here

" here is the fcheme I laid down upon it. You
" will examine them, and alter any thing you
" don't approve, as circumftances may require.
" To you I give a difcretionary power, to act
" as you fee proper. Had I known you would
" have gone, I fhould not have drawn any par-
" ticular directions. Go; and fuccefs await
" you."

The other received this diftinguifhed mark
of confidence and favour with the higheft pleafure; and, taking leave of the general, haftened
away to join his troops, who were by this time
drawn out ready to march. As foon as he had
taken a view of them, he opened his inftructions; and looking them over, put himfelf at
the head of his men, with whom he marched all
night, through woods and moraffes deemed im-
paffible, and at day-break found himfelf juft before a quarter of the enemy, who, confiding
in the diftance and natural ftrength of their
fituation, had neglected to fortify themfelves, and expected nothing lefs than to be
ttacked.

The difficulties of the march had fatigued his
troops to fuch a degree, that it appeared next
to madnefs to let them attack an enemy greatly fuperior to them in number. But their ardour was fuch, that they defpifed every advantage, and demanded to be inftantly led on. The
proper improvement of that enthufiafm is generally decifive. The commander therefore indulged their impetuofity, confiding in their valour; and convinced that his fafety and fuccefs
equally depended upon furprize, if he failed of
which, it would be abfolutely impoffible for him
even to make a retreat in the condition they
were

were in, through such difficulties as they had struggled with in coming.

Scenes like this are impossible to be particularly described. Accustomed to conquer, they made their onset with a resolution that bore down all before them. In the confusion unavoidable on such occasions, their enemies fled at the first impulse, imagining they were attacked by the whole army, while the victors made an heavy slaughter of all who had no time to escape.

Had they stopped here, the advantage would have been important. But hurried on by their natural ardour, and flushed beside with success, they pursued the fugitives, who by this time had recovered from their first surprize, and formed upon an eminence, not very far from their late camp. The action now was really dreadful. The assailants were several times repulsed with severe loss, and owed their success at last to an effort of meer despair, being determined, to a man, to die rather than have their victory snatched thus out of their hands.

Their loss in this affair equalled that of their enemies, in the surprize of their entrenchments, and amounted to more than half their number; but they remained masters of the field, the honour of which they looked upon as a recompence for all.

On their return to the army the general met them, and embracing the leader, congratulated him on the glory of his victory; and *thanking* the men, in the orders of the day, sent them away happy; while he pleased himself with the success of his scheme, which gave him the appearance of doing something, flattered his em-

ployers

ployers with imaginary advantages, and raised his merit with them; at the same time, that in reality it served rather to protract than determine the war, by inspiring each party with a desire of revenging so equal a loss. However, it was deemed sufficient by him to be made the subject of congratulatory messages to the sovereign under whom he served, and all the powers confederate with him.

I was so sick of this mercenary method of making war, by which the miseries of that scourge of mankind were so highly aggravated, that I resolved to quit this army directly, and see whether that of the enemy, opposed to it, was conducted in a more rational manner.

I have said that my guide had given me power to transport myself, by a bare act of my will, wherever I pleased. Though this was necessarily a great advantage in many instances, there were yet some circumstances attending it, which made me chuse to decline making use of it, except upon extraordinary occasions. The instantaneous transition from one scene to another, distant and unconnected, was so unusual to me, that it left a chasm in my mind, and made me for some time at a loss to comprehend the things before me, for want of the introduction of entering gradually into them. This I had experienced more than once, when at any time my guide used to turn my eye suddenly and without some previous preparation, to any new scene in the review I made under his immediate direction. For this reason I resolved, when it was possible, to take the opportunity of accompanying some person, wherever I had a mind to go, whose business would serve as a clue, to introduce and di-

*rect*

rect me without perplexity or confusion; by which method I had also the advantage of observing several things worthy of notice, in the countries through which I passed, which would have escaped me if I only flew over them in the other way.

For such a guide and companion I was not long at a loss. The general that very evening held a council of war, the resolutions of which two of the members could not refrain from talking over that night, after supper. Not suspecting that they were overheard, they canvassed all that had passed very freely, and in the course of their conversation mentioned several matters of the greatest importance to be kept secret. This the valet de chambre of him in whose tent they were was not inattentive to. He was a native of the enemy's country, and retained by them to procure intelligence of every thing that happened in the army where he was. Accordingly he placed himself where he could distinctly hear all that was said; and pretending sleep, to avoid the danger of detection, listened to their discourse with the greatest attention.

As soon as they separated, and he had put his master to bed, he wrote an exact account of all that he had over-heard; and giving his letter to one of his associates, who passed for no more than a common purveyor to the camp, charged him to deliver it as directed, with the utmost expedition, as it was of the highest importance; and this experienced person I resolved to accompany.

CHAP.

## CHAP. V.

*The longest way about is often the nearest way home.*
*The pleasure of comparing notes creates friendship*
*in affliction.    A new species of knight-errantry.*

THE armies lay so near each other that my
guide might soon have performed his errand, could he have gone directly with safety.
Instead of that, to avoid every suspicion, he took
diametrically the contrary way, designing, when
he should be out of danger of being observed, to
make a turn, and go by a safer though more distant course.

I shall not attempt to describe the country
through which we travelled. Could the most ambitious power that ever waged a war view such
a scene with the dispassionate eye of reason but
for one moment, it would strike his heart with
horror, and make him desist from pursuits so destructive to his kind.

The first place we stopped at happened to be
the town to which the officer had sent his mistress, as I have said before, under a pretext of
her avoiding his wife.    I should have taken notice, that in the course of the action he had
often repented of not taking her advice, and
wished himself to be in safety with her; though
when it was over, his heart exulted so much in
the success, that for some time he could think
of nothing but war and glory.    Indeed his behaviour had been such as in a great measure re-

covered

covered the efteem of his leader; and with the reft of the army, who have a partiality for the indulgence of paffion, and are particularly fmitten with the more fhewy virtues, totally obliterated his reproach.

As we entered the town, I accidentally faw her at a window, and my fellow-traveller ftopping for refrefhment, I took that opportunity to fee how fhe liked her prefent fituation. When I joined her, fhe and her friend were going to take a walk in their garden.

There was fomething particularly ftriking in the appearance of the latter. Tho' fhe had never been a regular beauty, and now had loft a good deal of the bloom of youth, it was impoffible for man to behold her without defire; at the fame time, that the fire which flafhed from her eyes fhewed that fhe felt all the paffions fhe infpired. A fimilarity in their circumftances had very foon improved their former acquaintance into that degree of intimacy which is commonly called friendfhip. When they were feated in an arbour at the bottom of the garden, "I wonder, "madam, (faid the lady of the houfe) that you "have had no account from your friend, fince "this action. Public report fays it was very "warm; but as no particular mention is made "of him, it is certain he has come off fafe. Of- "ficers of his rank are never overlooked."

"Indeed, madam, (anfwered the other) I "know not what to attribute it to but the le- "vity that rules all his actions. I am out of "his fight, and confequently out of his mind. "But I have no right to complain. I deferve "it all, and more, for being fuch a dupe to "my own vanity and his bafe defigns, as to

"think

" think I could fix one whose soul is incon-
" stancy itself. My eyes are at length opened
" to my folly. I deserve to be slighted thus,
" and deserted in a strange place."

———" Have patience, dear madam! Do not
" seek for imaginary grievances. It is impof-
" fible he can defert you. No man can be fo
" infenfible as to slight such charms. The hur-
" ry of war is above our conception, and often
" prevents the performance of the duties deareft
" to the heart."

———" O my friend! you are too good to
" seek confolation for a wretch juft finking
" into defpair. But it is all in vain. What
" bufinefs had he with war? His fortune placed
" him above the common motive of neceffity;
" and he affured me that he was fick of the
" folly of ambition, and would retire to fome
" private place in Italy, where we fhould be un-
" known, and there dedicate his life to love
" and happinefs. But no fooner had he ob-
" tained his bafe ends than he changed his
" fcheme; and feigning I know not what rea-
" fons about laying down his commiffion with
" credit, and fuch idle ftuff, he led me hither,
" juft to fhew me about, and make the fhame
" of my being caft off the more notorious and
" mortifying, perhaps to enhance its merit,
" and prepare the way for a reconciliation with
" his wife, which his writing her that letter
" gives me fufficient ground to think he is not
" without thoughts of."

———" For fhame, dear madam! fummon
" up your refolution, and do not torture your-
" felf with fuch vain, fuch impoffible appre-
" henfions. I know your good fenfe, and would
" not

" not flatter you. A reconciliation with his
" wife is an abfurd thought. Not that I think
" it at all improbable, on her part. The foft
" nature of our fex can forgive any thing; but
" the difficulty lies in himfelf. After giving
" her fuch treatment, he can never forgive her,
" can never believe fhe is fincerely reconciled;
" and therefore will hate her for her hypocri-
" fy, and be always in fear of fome fecret re-
" venge. Or, even if fhe fhould convince him
" to the contrary, the contraft between her
" conduct and his, will be fo mortifying to him,
" and give her fuch a fuperiority in his own
" eyes, that he will never be able to bear it;
" and muft avoid her prefence, to preferve his
" own peace. This, my dear, is your fecuri-
" ty againft this worft misfortune poffible to
" happen to a woman. Shame, poverty, any
" thing, were preferable to being flighted for a
" wife."

——" What an infatuated creature was I to
" bring myfelf into this ftate, that my happi-
" nefs muft depend on fuch a bafe foundation?
" Happinefs, did I fay? It is mifery; the fe-
" vereft mifery. The conftant anxiety and
" fears, infeparable from fuch a ftate of uncer-
" tainty, are worfe than any actual misfortune.
" But I deferve it all. I am inexcufable in the
" eyes of the world, and odious in my own.
" But what will not the bafenefs of man and
" the folly of woman do?"

——" The bafe artifices of man to obtain
" his ends, and his fhamelefs perfidy after,
" fhould be a warning to our fex; but:
" *Nature is nature, let the wife fay what they*
" *will;*" and while woman has vanity and de-

" fires,

" fires, man will take advantage of the former,
" to flatter her into the gratification of the
" latter. You have this confolation, howe-
" ver, that your cafe is not fingular. I do not
" fay, example juftifies a wrong action; but
" ftill it certainly is a fatisfaction to think, that
" others have fallen into as great errors as our-
" felves; that we are not the worft of our kind.
" All the folly that you upbraid yourfelf for
" have I been guilty of, and with this fevere
" aggravation, that the perfon for whom I made
" fuch a facrifice was not in circumftances even
" to delude me with the romantic fchemes of
" happinefs, which helped to turn your head,
" but was forced by neceffity to apply himfelf
" to the horrid trade of war for fubfiftence; fo
" that the pain of his abfence, and the fear of
" lofing him, were heightened by the dreadful
" apprehenfion of being reduced to dependence
" on the friends, whofe refentment I had fo
" juftly provoked, if any thing fhould happen to
" him. Yet all this have time and reflection re-
" conciled me to, and taught me to fubmit with-
" out regret to a fate which I can't remedy.

" But let us drop this difagreeable and fruit-
" lefs fubject. My intercourfe with my native
" country is fo little, that I had not even heard
" of your affair till my friend fent me the plea-
" fing account of the honour defigned me by
" your company; and then without any parti-
" cular circumftances, which he either was un-
" acquainted with, or had not time to write.
" As I imagine there muft be fomething un-
" common and interefting in them, I fhall
" efteem it a favour, if you will indulge me
" with the relation; and to encourage that
" con-

" confidence, I will candidly inform you of
" every thing concerning myfelf, the account
" of which, I know, has been greatly and moſt
" cruelly mifreprefented ; and if you do not find
" much entertainment in it, you certainly will
" ample confolation, from a comparifon of my
" cafe with yours. Not that all my adven-
" tures have been barren of matter for the for-
" mer alfo, now that the danger and ridicule
" which attended them àt the time are over.

" You feem furprifed, my dear, at my men-
" tioning my adventures ; but ours is literally
" a life of adventure ; and the moment a wo-
" man takes the ſtep that we have done, ſhe
" as it were commences knight-errant, and fal-
" lies forth, if not to feek, at leaſt fubject to
" meet adventures wherever ſhe goes ; every
" man who thinks it worth his while affuming
" a right to make his attacks upon her in what
" manner he pleafes."

## CHAP. VI.

*Hiſtory of a remarkable Lady. The great benefit of
polite education, with the force of good example.
Common occurrences of various kinds, and their
natural confequences.*

"THERE is nothing more abfurdly ungenerous than the invectives levelled at
our fex indifcriminately, and without inquiring
into the nature of our faults, and making juſt
allowances for the caufes leading, or rather indeed impelling us to them.

C 5                    " The

" The youth of man is devoted to profitable inſtruction; but that of woman to initiation into the paths of ruin. While they are acquiring the general principles of knowledge, or learning ſome profeſſion for the exerciſe and advancement of their future lives, we are taught nothing but trifles uſeleſs in themſelves, and if not immediately criminal, yet leading indirectly to every crime, by turning the mind upon wrong purſuits, and weakning all its powers by an habit of idleneſs, impoſſible ever to be broken through; for idleneſs, my dear friend, is the bane of woman, let her attribute her failings to whatever other apparent cauſe ſhe will.

" The moſt important part of my ſtory may be compriſed in a few words. You are acquainted with my family, and the particular circumſtances of it, which made my ſituation more critically dangerous even than that of the generality of my ſex; a danger that was ſtill heightened by other circumſtances peculiar to myſelf, and which, far from being attended to in that light, and guarded againſt with proper care, were looked upon as advantages, and accordingly urged to their utmoſt force.

" Born in a rank that placed all the pleaſures of life within my reach, and bleſſed with a conſtitution equal to the enjoyment of them, I ſeemed marked out for the attacks of man; the luxuriance of my health kindling all the paſſions of nature, before reaſon could gather ſtrength to guide and keep them within proper bounds, and the liberties allowed by faſhion giving every opportunity for their gratification. Such an aptitude for pleaſure was alſo forwarded, where it ſhould have met with reſtraint.

" There

" There are some persons our relation to whom makes respectful mention of them a duty, be their conduct what it will. I shall therefore only say that, instead of instilling the principles of virtue by precept, and enforcing its practice by example, that person, whose example and precepts must have had the greatest weight with me, exerted them quite the contrary way, turning every thing serious into ridicule, and indulging every licentious passion in the most public manner. The consequence, with regard to me, may be easily concluded. Inclined by nature to pleasure, I willingly imitated the pattern set me as far as was in my power, and launched into every excess, as opportunity tempted; and if I paid greater regard to appearances, and conducted myself with more reserve, it was not from any restraint of principle; but because I saw that fashion did not authorise the same boundless liberty in youth, as it did in more advanced life.

" But this reserve soon began to be very uneasy to me, and the pleasures I enjoyed, to be confined within narrower limits than I liked. Ripened, as I have said, by the luxuriance of my constitution, I felt all the warmest passions of my sex before it was imagined that my tender youth was capable of such sensations, and was treated like a child long after I thought. myself a woman. The difficulties this laid me under were often very disagreeable. I made every explanation that was not a direct breach of decency, and gave hints, which would have been readily understood from any one of a more advanced age. But, to my severe mortification, all was attributed to meer imitation; and Miss.

was fignificantly faid to echoe her mama's words, when fhe would much rather have prac- tifed her actions.

"At length, however, I was relieved from this teazing fituation, by one of thofe accidents which determine the fate of human life. As I was fitting one evening at an affembly, fretting myfelf to death to fee feveral ladies, whom I looked upon as my inferiors in every thing but age, taken out before me, an officer, who read my thoughts and was refolved to have fome amufement with me, came up to the place where I fat, and entering into chat with a young lady who was with me, led her to afk him if he did not defign to dance; upon which, turning to me with an air of the moft refpectful politenefs, he anfwered that he would, if I would do him the favour to be his partner.

"Such a preference, though to one of my moft intimate acquaintances, for the manner in which fhe had afked the queftion was a plain of- fer to dance with him herfelf, was too pleafing to be flighted. I affented moft readily, and in the height of my fpirits at my triumph, gave fuch plain hints of the ftate of my inclinations, that he foon comprehended them; and being fomewhat warm with wine, made advances to me which I had long wifhed for, but never re- ceived before.

"The impreffion made upon us by a firft ap- plication is hard to be refifted. For my part, I was too much pleafed with it to make the at- tempt; and really feeling all that warmth he profeffed, met his wifhes more than half way. In fuch a life as I led, and to perfons fo difpo- fed, opportunity could not long be wanted;

5

but

but when my lover came in a cooler moment to reflect on the confequences of an intrigue with one of my age and rank, fhould it ever happen to be difcovered, prudence damped the ardour of his paffion, and prevented his carrying the conqueft he had made to the height of our mutual defires. But though he deferred it for the prefent, he did not abfolutely give up the defign, when circumftances fhould wear a more favourable afpect.

" In families like ours, every perfon who dreffed well and would play had ready admiffion. He availed himfelf of this, and, under the appearance of paying a compliment to my mother, took every opportunity of attending me to all places of pleafurable refort.

" The difference of our age, and particularly his being married, obviated every fufpicion of his intentions, as they fhould have opened my eyes to the infamy and folly of carrying on fuch a correfpondence. But I was incapable of confidering any thing befide the pleafure I felt in his company, which was evidently fo fincere that, beyond his defign, it affected him, and he began alfo to feel the paffion he had only profeffed before.

" Though he conducted himfelf with the utmoft circumfpection and addrefs, it was impoffible to keep up fuch an intercourfe long without the real motive of it being fufpected. The firft hint of this alarmed the pride of my relations, though the original caufe had not been thought worthy of their regard. They inftantly affailed me with expoftulations and reproaches, as they did my lover with menaces; but all in vain.

" There is nothing more injudicious than to

difcover

difcover a fufpicion of what it is not abfolutely
in our power to prevent. It takes off the reftraint of fhame, and raifes a falfe refentment
that urges the crime in revenge of the injurious
accufation. Inftead of working the effect my
friends defigned, this conduct only haftened the
confequence which they meaned to hinder.
Finding they could not themfelves break off
the intercourfe between us, though they knew
not certainly to what length it had been carried,
they had recourfe to fuperior authority, and
prevailed to have my lover fent on an expedition, from which it was more than probable
that he would never return; or at leaft if he
did, it muft be after fuch a length of time as they
doubted not would wean my affections from him,
and fix them on fome other more proper object.

"But all their fchemes were difappointed.
The expedition mifcarried, and he returned before they imagined he had even reached the place
of his deftination; and far from being cooled in
our mutual regards by abfence, they rather
gathered ftrength to break out with greater violence.

"For fome time, however, we obferved fo
much caution, as to fave appearances at leaft,
let fufpicions be what they would. But a garde-
ner furprifing us one evening in an arbour,
when we thought ourfelves fafe from obfervation, though the fellow was highly bribed to
fecrecy, we thought it imprudent to depend
upon him; my lover therefore threw up his
commiffion, and we immediately eloped together out of the reach of my friends refentment, who, we were well convinced, would
leave nothing undone to be revenged on the

man,

man who had thrown such a public scandal on. their family.

" I now thought my happiness compleat,, and, giving a loose to love, despised the cen-sure of the world, and looked no farther than the present moment. But a little time made a change in my sentiments, and I began to. languish for the other pleasures which I had. forfeited by the step I had taken.

" I would not by this intimate any uncom-mon alteration in my lover's behaviour; but the joy of novelty was worn off, desire was sa-tisfied, and reflection began to obtrude upon. us. Our situation necessarily precluded us from. society, at least any that could afford us satis-, faction, and confined us to each other; and when the tumult of passion began to subside, as. we dared not apply to reason for relief, time grew tedious, and we mutually sighed for va-riety, to give a relish even to pleasure. The. effect this had upon our tempers heightened our. unhappiness. Unable to look into ourselves for the real cause, each accused the other of in-. constancy and want of love; and these re-proaches, instead of removing the complaint,, were beginning to aggravate a coolness that. was unavoidable,. into determined dislike and aversion : for, my dear, let us in the warmth of youthful imagination flatter ourselves with. what notions we will of eternal constancy and. unalterable love, sense will soon be sated and languish for variety, if reason does not lend its. assistance to fill up the dull pause of passion. With us the consequence was obvious, as our connexion depended entirely upon ourselves. But before we had time to resolve absolutely

on a feparation, an event happened which removed the immediate caufe of our difguft, and
awoke all our former tendernefs.

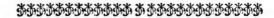

# CHAP. VII.

*Continued. An unufual effect of abfence. The lofs
of reputation fometimes inconvenient. Reflections
on a qualification which all pretend to, and few
poffefs; with a curious account of a man of confequence.*

" I HAVE obferved to you that my lover
had no fortune; all his hopes even depending on his military profeffion. The manner
in which he had come away with me cutting
off thefe for ever in his own country, neceffity
obliged him to feek employment among ftrang-
ers. This the tumult of my thoughts had
made me overlook, at the time when it was in
my power to have prevented the confequences
of it. But think what a ftate I muft have been
in when the hour of his departure came! I look
back to it with horror even now when ufe has
made his abfence familiar to me, and foftened
many of the inconveniences of it.

" Without the converfation of a friend, to
beguile the tedious melancholy hours, and blunt
the fting of grief; without the approbation of
my own mind, to fweeten thought and make
reflection a pleafure, I was left a ftranger in
a ftrange place; and, what was ftill worft of
all, every morfel I eat imbittered by the dread-

ful

ful confideration, that it was earned at the inftant hazard of the life deareft to me in the world; for the firft thought of our parting removed all that wearinefs which had been the caufe of our difguft, and the occafion of it doubly endeared us, by fhewing how much we had given up, how much more we hazarded for each other.

" Our parting exceeded the power of defcription. After the firft tranfports of my grief were over, I funk into a ftate of infenfibility, and grew abfolutely indifferent to myfelf and every thing about me, fixing my thoughts entirely on the days which were to bring me an account from him, and living only for their arrival.

" At length lenient time began to adminifter its never-failing relief; and youth and health united their powers to diffipate a gloom fo contrary to my natural difpofition; I gradually recovered my fpirits, and felt again a relifh for the pleafures of fociety. But thefe pleafures were very different from thofe which I had formerly delighted in. My mind had learned to think, and I had had time to view things in another light from that in which they had appeared before. My affections, it is true, were ftill the fame, invariably fixed upon my friend, and all the wifhes of my heart centered in him; how juftly though I did not dare to confider, holding every thing that concerned him too facred to be even enquired into.

" Thefe wifhes indeed were of a much more extenfive and exalted kind, than thofe which had given rife to our connexion. You may have obferved that I called him my *friend.* From this time, I looked upon him in that
light;

light; and if not entirely in that alone, the very uniting the idea of friendship with love was the higheſt improvement to the latter, and in a great meaſure purified it from every groſs allay.

" The effect this had upon my mind is ſcarce to be conceived. I was not incapable of thought; but I had never given myſelf time to think. The moment therefore that I began, I found a pleaſure in it which cannot be conceived; every hour brought me knowledge that made me both ſurpriſed at, and aſhamed of my former blindneſs and ignorance; I read in my own mind, though unhappily too late, all the wiſdom neceſſary for the conduct of life. I thus literaˈly became a new creature; and on my emerſion from the ſolitude in which I had buried myſelf ſince my friend's departure, ſought the company (and flatter myſelf that I was not unworthy of it) of the moſt valuable part of my ſex.

" But I ſoon had the mortification to find myſelf precluded from this pleaſing hope. Retired and unexceptionably as we had lived, the circumſtances of our elopement had ſome how been diſcovered; ſo that when I appeared in company, inſtead of meeting the reception I had fondly expected, my advances toward intimacy were repulſed by my own ſex, and I found myſelf expoſed to the familiarity and libertine addreſſes of the other, who always lay it down as a rule, that a woman who has broken thro' the laws of virtue with one man, has entirely thrown off all farther regard to them, and is a fair quarry for general purſuit.

" You may eaſily judge what a ſhock this was to me. I now began to feel the ineſtimable loſs of reputation, and returned to my

former

former retirement with an heart burſting with diſappointment, ſhame, and remorſe. But I was not ſuffered long to enjoy the peace I ſought even there. My new admirers purſued me, and in ſpite of all I could ſay perſiſted in their gallantry; and that often in a manner too groſs to have been offered to any but a profeſſed proſtitute.

" Had this happened ſome time ſooner, I ſhould have inſtantly written to my friend, to come to my *relief* from ſuch inſolent abuſe; but my thoughts had now taken a new turn, and I dreaded nothing more than its coming to his knowledge, for fear of any ill conſequences to himſelf from the warmth of his temper, which I knew would be provoked to the higheſt rage at ſuch an attempt. For this reaſon I reſolved to take no notice of it to him, but behave in ſuch a manner to my admirers as ſhould make them ridiculous even in their own eyes.

" Habits long confirmed are not eaſily broken through by the beſt reſolutions. I had a natural levity of temper; and the critical nature of my intercourſe with my friend before our elopement, laid me under a kind of neceſſity of practiſing coquetry in my general conduct, in hopes of covering my particular connection with him. I will therefore take ſhame to myſelf, and confeſs that in my preſent ſolitary condition, the proſpect of amuſement, in playing off their fooliſh addreſſes, had ſome weight with me in this deſign; never conſidering that ſuch a conduct was inconſiſtent with the principles in which I now prided myſelf, and muſt inevitably diſappoint my hopes of recovering the
eſteem

esteem of the prudent and virtuous of my own, and rational part of the other sex.

" I see you are affected with this melancholy detail; but my heart was so full, that I could not stop its overflowing. I shall now conclude with one of the many adventures which this new scheme of mine produced, the oddity of which will probably restore you to spirits.

" The persons who thought proper to do me the honour of declaring themselves my admirers were of every age and rank in the place. As they had discovered the nobility of my birth, they all thought it incumbent upon them to display their utmost politeness in the manner of making their addresses. Though every country has peculiar customs which constitute the rule of behaviour, true politeness is essentially the same every-where, and differs only in the external modes of expressing it. The mechanical part, as I may justly call it, which consists in cringes and compliments, may be easily learned; but the unembarrassed ease and proper freedom of address and deportment, which denominate the character at first sight, and that desire to give pleasure, which pleases in its very appearance, must have a foundation from nature, in a benevolent and generous disposition, and be confirmed by early education and long practice. The latter indeed may give an habit that shall deceive a superficial view; but where the former is wanting, the judicious observer will soon discover and despise the imposture.

" I had abundant experience of the justice of this remark in the behaviour of my new admirers. Had I had nothing more than meer common amusement in my thoughts, this would

**have**

have afforded me sufficient; but resentment at their impudence made me determined to push their folly to its utmost length, and then expose it to public ridicule.

" The few who really possessed that politeness which all aped, soon perceived, by the manner of my receiving their advances, that they were disagreeable to me, and accordingly desisted from giving me any farther trouble. But their aukward imitators in the externals of goodbreeding, forming their judgment of me from themselves, construed my complaisance into approbation, and thought I was pleased with what they said, because I did not directly fly into an outrage; but when I had taken time to look into their characters, and see which was fittest for my purpose to work upon, I gave the rest their dismission, in the manner most like to take effect.

" Among the selected few whom I permitted to flatter themselves with hopes of success was an old burgher, who had made an immense fortune by every iniquitous practice in the mysterious business of a *contractor*, for supplying the armies of the powers at war with provisions. Though he was sprung from the very dregs of mankind, and had passed his youth in the most sordid and servile employments, his heart was so puffed up by his riches, that he must on all occasions assume the man of birth and good breeding. This his own base disposition made it impossible for him to do in any thing beside their follies and vices, in all of which he made a most remarkable figure. He built fine houses, he bought pictures, he gamed; and, to compleat his character, he must now have a mistress of
*quality;*

*quality*; and I, forfooth, was the happy object he had pitched upon for this honour.

" I fhould have obferved, that as foon as he took it into his head to commence a man of figure, he had married a wife, whofe whole fortune confifted in the nobility of her family, being defcended in the ninth remove from a German baron, and none of her illuftrious anceftors having ftained their blood by any kind of induftry.

" Before he could obtain fuch an honour, he was obliged to hire an herald to deduce his ,pedigree, by the eafy means of changing only four letters in his name, from an equally illuftrious houfe; and to turn an only daughter by a former wife, whofe induftry had been greatly affiftant to his making his fortune, out of doors, without any provifion more than a bare fupport from abfolute want.

" The difpofition that could demand fuch terms was far from being foftened, when its tyranny was confirmed by marriage. She governed in the moft defpotic manner. He was obliged to quit bufinefs. His fortune was lavifhed upon her relations, who let him know they thought him honoured by their acceptance of it; and he was but a cypher in his own houfe, where every fervant quoted her command for difputing his authority, and told him directly that he was not qualified to give directions in fo genteel a family.

" In fuch a fituation it was not ftrange that he fhould feek for fatisfaction abroad; but even in this his defign was confiftent with the reft of his conduct, and very different from what might moft naturally be imagined. Infignificant as

he

he was at home, he gave himfelf the higheft
airs of politenefs and confequence among his
companions, where he was fafe from the terror
of his tyrant's power, to confirm his title, to
which character, as I have faid before, he
formed the project of paying his addreffes to
me, not from any particular paffion he had
for me.

\*\*\*\*\*\*\*\*\*\*\*\*\*\*\*\*\*\*\*\*\*\*\*\*\*\*\*\*\*\*\*\*\*\*\*\*

## C H A P.  VIII.

*Continued. A fhort way of making love. Bargains
beft made in few words; with an odd inflance of
old-fafhioned folly.*

" IT is impoffible to give any defcription of
this important perfon's courtfhip. His
politenefs, it is true, reached fo high as to ac-
coft me with as many bows and cringes as make
the aukward ceremonial of fome crowned heads,
and with an equally good grace. But here it all
ended; and when he came to fpeak to me, it
was in the fame phrafe and manner as he would
have bargained for a parcel of cheefe, or meal. -
" Madam, (faid he) underftanding as how
" your ladyfhip's favours are to be difpofed of,
" I come to treat about the purchafe. I like
" the appearance of your commodities, and do
" not doubt but they are in good order, and
" merchantable; and fhall therefore give you
" your own price. I am not one of your
" higgling chaps that make many words to a
" bargain. Ready money is my way; and the
" reft I leave to yourfelf."

"Though I had ſtudied my part very well, I was ſomewhat diſconcerted at ſuch an addreſs. Recovering myſelf however in a few minutes, I was rather diverted than offended at the oddity of it, and reſolved to drive the *bargain*, as he juſtly called it, in his own way. Accordingly I anſwered him with an affected confuſion, that I did not rightly underſtand what he meant.

"Madam, (replied he) my meaning is to— "to—to——. In ſhort madam, plain dealing "is beſt. My meaning is, to purchaſe ſome "certain favours from you, for which I am "willing to pay you the higheſt price of the "maket. I deſpiſe making fine ſpeeches; but "if you are inclined to deal, no one ſhall out- "bid me. I never think good wares too dear. "Come! Don't ſtand ſhilly ſhally! Say! Is "it a bargain, aye, or no?"

"It was impoſſible for me to pretend ignorance any longer; though I did not think proper to accept of his propoſals too readily, for fear it ſhould make him think ſlightly of my *ware*; at the ſame time that I ſaw it was neceſſary to keep up his hopes, by ſeeming to enter into treaty with him, as he was infenſible of that expectation and anxiety which to minds of more delicacy are the food of love.

"You men of conſequence (I anſwered) "have a peculiar way of doing every thing. "Your fortunes raiſe you above the formalities "neceſſary to be obſerved by other people. I "own I do not diſapprove of your propoſal; "but as it is a thing which I have never yet "thought about, I muſt take ſome time to "conſider what terms are proper for me to "make.

" make. In the mean while I fhall be glad to
" fee you as often as it is convenient for you to
" do me that honour."

" Odfo, madam, (returned he, overjoyed at
" his fuccefs) you are a fenfible woman, and
" fpeak like one that has been ufed to bufinefs.
" I like you the better for your franknefs. It is
" my own way. And when you have fixed
" your price, we fhall not differ. There fhall
" be no delay on my part. Ready money!
" Ready money is always my word."— " Saying this, my lover took his leave, and left me
not a little at a lofs how to manage with
him.

" As I was no ftranger to the circumftances
of his family, the firft thought that occurred
to me was, to reveal the whole to his wife, and
concert meafures with her for punifhing his infi-
delity and prefumption. But, upon reflection,
I enlarged my fcheme, and refolved to try if I
could not turn his ridiculous paffion to fome advantage for his deferted daughter, before I gave
him up to her chaftifement.

" Accordingly I went directly to a lady with
whom I knew fhe was acquainted, and enquiring, as if from common curiofity, into her circumftances and character, had the pleafure to
find her every way worthy of my regard and affiftance. I therefore fent for her very privately
that evening, as if to give her fome needle-
work to do for me, her father's allowance being fo fmall that fhe was obliged to have recourfe to induftry, to enable her to live with
any degree of comfort, though fhame made her
do it with as much privacy as poffible; and
giving my converfation that turn which I

D thought

thought moſt likely to win her confidence,
preſſed her to let me know her deſigns and proſpects for life, for making which enquiry I aſſured her I had other motives than meer curioſity.

"Moved by the manner in which I ſpoke,
ſhe burſt into a flood of tears; and, as ſoon as
ſhe was able to ſpeak, told me modeſtly, that
ſhe had no proſpects, and was incapable of
forming any deſigns; that indeed the height of
her wiſhes would be to be married to a young
man who had been bred to buſineſs under her father, but was turned off as well as herſelf on the
new-ordering of his family; that they had loved
each other from their infancy; but he having
no fortune to enter into trade with, his family,
which was very reputable, having been ruined
by the calamities of war; and her father aban-
doning her in the manner he did, they could
not think of tranſmitting their misfortunes to
their innocent poſterity by marrying; and therefore had vowed to each other to live ſingle, as
the only proof they could give of the ſincerity
of their mutual attachment.

"I was not proof to ſuch a ſtory. I embraced
her tenderly; and aſſuring her of my friendſhip, bade her hope for an happy change in her
fortune very ſpeedily. I then enquired how
much would be ſufficient to ſettle her huſband
in buſineſs with a proſpect of ſucceſs, and encourage them to marry? and on her anſwering,
that if they had about a thouſand crowns to add
to ſome little matter they had already made a
ſhift to lay up by their frugality, they would
venture, and truſt the event to the bleſſing of
providence on their honeſt induſtry. I told her,
                                             that

that if I was not difappointed much beyond my expectation, fhe fhould not long want a greater fum than that; but that all depended on her not taking the leaft notice of her having been with me, or even mentioning my name to any one living, till I fhould give her permiffion. This caution fhe promifed to obferve moft carefully, and then took her leave with a lighter heart than fhe had felt for fome time.

"My defign upon my *ready-money* lover was now urged by a better motive than either amufement or revenge, which had firft fet me upon it. The money, which I doubted not to extort from his abfurd paffion, I refolved to give to his daughter; and then to make ufe of the affiftance of his wife, to avoid performing my part of the bargain, and compleat my original fcheme, who, I was fenfible, would not only punifh him fufficiently for his vicious folly, but alfo expofe him to the higheft and moft public ridicule.

## CHAP. IX.

*-Continued. Many buyers raife the market. On ballancing avarice and vanity, the former kicks the beam.*

"ACCORDINGLY, when he came to pay me a vifit next morning, I gave him an opportunity of renewing his treaty, which he preffed fo warmly to be brought to a conclufion, that, after a little affected hefitation, I condefcended

defended to capitulate; and at length affented
to his propofal for the confideration of two thoufand crowns.

"At the mention of fuch a fum he looked
aghaft. "Two thoufand crowns! (faid he, as
"foon as he could fhut his mouth to articulate
"a word) Why, fure your ladyfhip can't be fe-
"rious! I never heard of fuch a thing in my
"life. Two thoufand crowns for a night's
"lodging! I have lodged a whole army for lefs
"before now. You furely can't be ferious, in
"making fuch a demand! A prince is not able
"to purchafe your favours at fuch a price."

"Then no prince fhall have them, Sir, (an-
"fwered I, putting on a look of offended dig-
"nity) and if you think my demand too high,
"you are welcome to go where you may be
"ferved cheaper. I know where I can have
"more from another perfon; but as you fpoke
"firft, I would not treat with any one elfe
"till I had concluded with you."

—— "More than two thoufand crowns!
"Death, madam, it is impoffible. Who is able
"to offer more than two thoufand crowns?"

—— "Really Sir, I do not think myfelf
"obliged to anfwer fuch a queftion. However,
"to let you fee that I am above impofing on
"you, What do you think of the *count?*"

"At that word his pride inftantly took fire.
He had been born a vaffal of the count's family, to efface the remembrance of which he now
took every opportunity of entering into competition, and infulting him with the oftentatious
difplay of his fuperior wealth. This I knew,
and therefore made ufe of his name, though
without any authority, as the fureft method of
working

working him up to my defign, being confident he would fcorn to be outdone in any thing, much more a matter fo effential to his character, by one whom he both hated and defpifed fo highly.

" The event fhewed I had judged right."

" The count, madam! (faid he, with an air of
" contempt) Why! What of him? Is not my
" money as good as his?"

—— " Yes, Sir, I believe it may; but you
" do not feem fo well inclined to part with it.
" I thought, after what you faid laft night, that
" we fhould not have a fecond word; but I find
" people can talk of their ready money, without
" opening their purfes."

" Madam! I'd have you to know, madam,
" that I fcorn fuch an imputation. It is well
" known that I never go back from my word,
" madam. When I fay it, I will do it. But
" really, don't you think you afk too much?
" Is there no prevailing on you to abate?"

—— " Sir, you faid yefterday, that you did
" not like to make many words; no more do I,
" Sir. On the ftrength of your offering ready
" money I fet the very loweft terms; and I
" wonder how you can think them much to a
" woman of my quality. In my country, I
" have known an orange-girl get more. But
" perhaps you would chufe fuch low-lived crea-
" tures; though I own I took you for a perfon
" of better fpirit, and above defcending to any
" thing unworthy of your rank; and I am for-
" ry to find that I am miftaken. It is true I
" had fome hints of the kind given me, and
" therefore did not give the count a pofitive de-
" nial; fo that I can eafily come to treat with

" him again. He knows what is due to a lady
" of diſtinction, and will not make words about
" ſuch a trifle. So, Sir, your humble ſer-
" vant."

" While I was making this notable and delicate ſpeech, which I could ſcarce ſuppreſs my
laughter to utter, he ſtood in the moſt whimſi-
cal ſituation, as if ballancing the account between avarice and vanity. At length the latter
prevailing, "Hold, madam, (ſaid he, catching
" me by the ſleeve, for fear I ſhould leave him)
" pray don't be in ſuch a violent hurry. I know
" how to behave to you as well as the count,
" and better too; and I'll ſee him damn'd be-
" fore he ſhall touch the hem of your gar-
" ment. I'll make him know that he ſhall not
" pretend to outbid me, for any thing I have a
" mind to! That I will! And ſo, madam, you
" ſhall have your price, without any draw-
" back; and in earneſt of the bargain, take this
" purſe of an hundred ducats. Only name the
" time and place; that's all. That's all; I won't
" ſtand for a receipt."

—— " Then, Sir, if you will pleaſe to come
" ſecretly, at ten to-morrow night, to my gar-
" den-door, I'll meet you there myſelf, and
" conduct you up."

—— " Very well; I'll be ſure to come. I am
" always punctual to a minute, in thoſe affairs;
" but muſt I bring the reſt of the money with
" me, or will you make me your banker, and
" draw it out as you want it?

—— " I ſhould, Sir, with all my heart; but
" it happens that I have occaſion for it to-mor-
" row-morning, and therefore muſt beg the fa-
" vour of you to bring it to me by nine o'clock."

—"How

—— " How, madam! Nine o'clock in the
" morning! I thought you faid ten at night."

—— " Yes, Sir, fo I did, to perform my part
" of the bargain. I only mean that you fhould
" bring the money fo early, as I have a preffing
" call for it in the fore-noon. I prefume you
" have no objection to obliging me fo far; and
" don't doubt my honour to keep my promife."

—— " N——N——No, madam! I—I—I
" can't fay as how I do doubt your ladyfhip's
" honour in the leaft, for the matter of that.
" But ftill, I—I—I—. Will not the evening
" do as well? I fhould be glad to oblige you,
" to be fure; but advancing money before we
" have even had a fample of the goods, is
" quite out of the way of bufinefs. It is what
" I never do."

—— " Then, Sir, here is your purfe again;
" and I am forry to have thrown away fo much
" time. I muft and will have the money to-
" morrow morning. I know the count will
" make no difficulty. Perfons of quality have
" confidence in each other."

—— " Madam, I have as much confidence
" as he, or any man; and as for *quality*, with
" the addition of my wife's arms, I have nine
" quarterings more than he. His rank indeed!
" And fo madam, I am ready to oblige your
" ladyfhip with all my heart, if it was ten times
" more. I only faid it was out of the courfe of
" bufinefs. I did not refufe you. No! No! I
" know better what is due to a perfon of rank,
" than to refufe fuch a trifle. We always have
" a regard for one another."

—— " Then Sir, I may depend upon you,
" at nine in the morning, without fail."

—" You

———" You may moft affuredly, madam; and
" fo take the earneft again."

" All things being thus fettled, I permitted
him the honour of a falute, as earneft of the
bargain on my fide, and fent him away quite
happy.

" I fuppofe his impatience for the arrival of
the next morning was not quite fo high as mine,
violent as his paffion was. However, he was
punctual to his time; and being immediately
admitted to my drefling-room, as foon as the
fervants withdrew, " Here, madam, (faid he,
" with an emotion that fhewed the ftruggle in
" his breaft at what he was doing) here is the
" money. You may tell it over. I have only
" deducted the hundred ducats I gave you in
" earneft, and the ufual difcount for advancing
" money before-hand; only five per cent, no
" more; and we never do it for lefs. Bufinefs
" will not afford it."

" Well, Sir, (anfwered I, fully fatisfied that I
" was fecure of fo much) I do not underftand
" thofe matters; but I leave it entirely to you.
" And to convince you that I am a perfon of
" honour, I will be as punctual to my appoint-
" ment as you have been to your's. At ten
" precifely, you fhall find me at the garden-
" door. But, for fear of being obferved, don't
" you think it would be better if you were to
" difguife yourfelf fome-way. A lady's repu-
" tation, you know, is a very tender thing;
" neither would it be fo proper, that a perfon
" of your dignity fhould be difcovered. It would
" leffen your importance in the eyes of the
" public." ,

———" Why, madam, to be fure, what your
" lady-

" ladyſhip ſays is very right ; and therefore,
" though I ſhall ſcarce know myſelf when I lay
" by my robes, I will ſtrive to do without them
" for once, and come diſguiſed in the dreſs of
" any private gentleman. I have heard that
" the greateſt pleaſure of an intrigue is in the
" ſtratagems and tricks that are practiſed to hide
" it. Hah ! hah ! hah ! And ſo I wiſh your
" ladyſhip a good morning. At ten ! Remem-
" ber at ten."

" My ſcheme having ſucceeded thus far, I
was impatient to communicate their good fortune to thoſe who were to reap the benefit of it.
I therefore wrote to his daughter, to come to
me that night about eleven o'clock, and bring
her lover with her. The great difficulty now
was how to open the affair to the wife, in ſuch
a manner, that ſhe ſhould be ready to be produced at a proper time, without danger of her
letting her wrath break out too ſoon, ſo as to
prevent the accompliſhment of my deſign.

" The only way I could think of was, to go
to the lady from whom I had the ſtory of the
family, and who, I had reaſon to believe, would
gladly give her aſſiſtance to promote any ſcheme
for puniſhing her huſband, and expoſing him to
ridicule. At the firſt mention of the affair, ſhe
entered moſt heartily into it ; and, to make ſure
of the lady, went directly and engaged her to
ſpend the evening with her ; not chuſing to let
her know a word of the matter till every thing
ſhould be ripe for execution, for fear of the violence of her temper.

　　　　CHAP.

❦❦❦❦❦❦❦❦❦ : ❦❦❦❦❦❦❦❦❦

## CHAP. X.

*Continued. Listeners seldom like what they hear. The danger of provoking high blood; with the great merit of peace-making in the modern way.*

" ALL things being thus prepared, the expected hour at length arrived when I attended to admit my gallant, who did not make me wait long. On my opening the garden-door, I was surprised to see the manner in which he had disguised himself. He had put on an old suit of cloaths all over dawb'd with lace, which had belonged half a century before to a relation of his wife's, whom the tradition of her family recorded to have been a general officer; and which she preserved with the most religious care, as an indisputable proof of her illustrious descent, supplying new lace or cloth occasionally, to repair the depredations of time.

" The absurdity of putting on for privacy a dress whose glaringness and singularity must attract the notice of every one who saw it, and would probably draw the mob after his heels, could not have escaped any one but himself; but his head was too intent upon making a figure in the eyes of his mistress, to mind any thing else; as I was far from being displeased at it, my motive for desiring him to disguise himself being only to expose him to stronger ridicule on detection, which I did not design he should escape.

" As

"As soon he entered the garden, his first care was to make me observe the brilliancy of his appearance, by telling me that according to my desire he had come in disguise, but could not possibly debase himself, or dishonour me so much as to put on any dress unworthy of his rank, or improper to appear in before me. I thanked him for my share of his compliment; and being apprehensive that he might be for taking some liberties which I did not like, if I made any delay there, led him directly up to my own chamber, where I left him in the dark, telling him I would return as soon as I saw my servants properly disposed of.

"I then went down into the parlour, where my confederate had just brought his wife, big with expectation of hearing something from me that nearly concerned her honour. Few words were requisite to introduce a subject which all were equally impatient for. I directly unfolded to her the injustice designed to her bed; (the affair of the money I thought proper not to mention for obvious reasons) and telling her, that having in vain tried every argument to get rid of his importunity, and convince him of the flagrancy of such a crime against a lady of her rank, I had at length pretended to comply with his desires, on purpose to give him up to her admonitions and authority, which I hoped might be more effectual to reclaim him; and therefore made an appointment with him, as if to gratify his vile desires, in consequence of which he was that very moment in my chamber, whither she was at liberty to go to him.

"It is impossible to describe the effect this story had on her. She stood for some moments

con-

convulfed with rage. At length recovering herfelf a little, fhe was for going directly and tramp-
ling the wretch under her feet; but her friend
interpofed, and infinuating, as we had concerted, that though what I faid might poffibly be
very true, it would yet be a fatisfaction to the
lady to be a witnefs to it herfelf; wherefore fhe
thought it would be the beft way, if I pleafed,
for me to return to him, and enter into fome
fuch diffuafive difcourfe as I had before ufed,
his anfwers to which would confirm what I had
faid, and be a teftimony againft him, that he
could not attempt to deny or evade. To this I
replied with an offended air, that I was not accuftomed to have what I faid doubted; however, on fuch an occafion as this I fhould wave
all punctilio, to give fatisfaction to one for
whom I had fo high a refpect as her ladyfhip;
and therefore was ready to do that, or any thing
elfe fhe fhould defire.

"Flattered by this compliment, fhe nodded
majeftically, and fuppreffing her wrath as well
as fhe could, let me know that fhe would attend me to the difgraceful fcene.

"My gallant was by this time beginning to
be impatient. On my opening the door (which
I left open for his wife, though I fhot the lock
to impofe upon him) he advanced to me, and
taking me by the hand afked why I had not
brought a light? "Deeds of darknefs (faid I,
"with a loud figh) fhould avoid the light. I
"do not believe I fhall ever bear to fee the
"light again after confenting to give you this
"meeting. But I hope you will reflect on the
"blacknefs of fuch a crime as this you have
"been fo long folliciting me to, and defift be-
"fore it is too late." —"Hey-

—— "Hey-day! What can be the meaning
" of all this? What fool's-play can you be at
" now? Come! Come! For fhame, ftand to
" your word. I cannot ftay long with you to-
" night. I muft be at home before my *Jeza-*
" *bel* of a wife, to pull off thefe cloaths. If
" fhe fhould fee them upon me, I fhould never
" hear the laft of it. I cannot ftay above an
" hour; and fo make hafte."

—— " I am amazed, Sir, that you can fpeak
" of a lady of your wife's rank in fo difrefpect-
" ful a manner! It gives me a very bad opinion
" of you. She merits better treatment; and
" after the honour fhe has done you in conde-
" fcending to be your wife, it is the higheft in-
" juftice and ingratitude in you to wrong her
" bed with any body elfe."

—— " Blood, madam, you are enough to
" make a man mad, to ftand trifling fo at fuch
" a time as this! As to what you fay about
" my wife's bed, it is all nonfenfe. No man
" can bear to bed with fuch an ugly, filthy
" brute; and for the honour fhe did me, I am
" fure I have paid dearly for it. I have raifed
" her great family from beggary. They had
" not a rag to cover their illuftrious nakednefs,
" till I took compaffion"——

" At thefe words, in burft his wife like a
tygrefs robbed of her whelps. " Villain! flave!
" bafe mechanic! (exclaimed fhe) You take
" compaffion on my family! You raife them
" from beggary! But I'll not ftoop to talk to
" you. I'll have fatisfaction! I will! The
" blood of your bafe heart fhall wafh away the
" affront. I'll fummon all my relations to-
" morrow-morning, and lay your villainy be-
" fore

" fore them. They'll vindicate the honour of
" our houfe; they'll do juftice to themfelves
" and me, in a manner that fhall ftrike terror
" into all fuch ungrateful wretches."

" While fhe poured out thefe threats, fhe
was fearching for him all round the room; but
he fortunately efcaped her by creeping under
the bed, the moment he heard her voice, where
he lay in a fituation that may eafily be conceived.
Not being able to find him, fhe roared out for
lights; but I thought it would be too fevere to
give him up, till her anger fhould be fomewhat
cooled, and therefore countermanded them;
and as fhe had by this time raved herfelf out of
breath, I took her by the hand, and leading
her to a chair, " Pray, madam, (faid I, in a
" foothing accent) fit down for a moment and
" ftrive to compofe yourfelf. I own, the pro-
" vocation you have received is very great, to
" have your bed flighted, and your perfon fpoke
" fo injurioufly of."—

" Mention not that! (anfwered fhe) men-
" tion not that! I defpife him too much to re-
" gard any thing he can fay of myfelf. But
" my family! The villain, to traduce my fa-
" mily, and talk of their being under obliga-
" tion to him! They who fuffered him to come
" into their pedigree, and quarter their arms!
" I will have revenge. I will have his heart's
" blood."

" The refentment you fhew, madam, (in-
" terpofed the other lady) is worthy of you,
" and proves the nobility of your blood. No
" perfon of family can bear fuch abufe. But
" ftill, madam, confider who it is that has of-
" fered it. A creature that is not worthy of
" the

" the refentment of your relations, and has not
" the fpirit to meet them to be killed fairly,
" and as a man of honour fhould kill him; and
" you would not have them turn affaffins and
" murder him, and fo let all his fortune go to
" his daughter, as you could not inherit it after
" fuch an action. For all thefe reafons I would
" recommend it to you to make up this ugly
" affair. What has paffed is known only to
" ourfelves, and need go no farther. Where-
" fore, if he will afk your pardon for what he
" intended to do, and actually faid to this la-
" dy, and will make over half his fortune to
" you, to fettle upon your own family, in cafe
" you fhould have no children yourfelf, I think
" your ladyfhip had better forgive him."

" The other heard her out with great patience; and then paufing for fome time, as if to
weigh matters, " Well, madam, (faid fhe, figh-
" ing) fince you advife it, I fubmit. For this
" offence I will accept of the fatisfaction you
" propofe; but let him take care how he repeats
" it."

" Matters being thus happily adjufted, I called for lights, and defired my gallant to make
his appearance, who having overheard all that
paffed, ventured to creep out of his hole, tho'
without daring to fpeak a word.

✳✳✳✳✳✳✳✳✳✳✳✳✳✳✳✳✳✳✳✳✳

## CHAP. XI.

*Concluded.  A relapse is often worse than the first*
*disorder.  By the help of good friends, the grey*
*mare proves the better horse.  The whole conclu-*
*ded with some interesting reflections, which prove*
*that people should look before they leap.*

" THE candles discovered a groupe of fi-
gures not easy to be described.  My unfortunate gallant,  all pale and trembling,  his
bushy wig turned awry,  and the powder of it
spread over his cloaths,  which were all tum-
bled and dropping wet from something he had
spilled in his creeping under the bed,  fixed his
haggard eyes upon his tender mate,  who no
sooner perceived the splendid relicks of her
kinsman's rank abused in such a manner,  than
forgetting her pacific resolution,  she relapsed into all her former fury.

" Audacious villain (exclaimed she,  her eyes
glaring with rage,  and her whole face distorted
with every diabolical passion) " to profane that
" sacred testimony of the honour of my family
" on such a wicked, base occasion!  Were you
" not afraid that the offended spirit of it's illu-
" strious owner would come and tear it from
" your vicious carcase ?  But he has left the task
" to me."

" Saying this,  she flew at the trembling
wretch with an impetuosity not to be prevented,
and, driving her fangs into his cheeks,  in an instant bathed his face in blood.  Cowards when
arouzed

arouzed are always moſt deſperate. Though
nothing could have made him face her fury deliberately, the moment he felt her claws in his
fleſh he forgot his fears, and giving an hideous
roar, returned her aſſault with equal violence,
faſtening one hand in her hair, and ſtriking her
on the face and breaſt with all his might with the
other.

" The combat now was really terrible, and
the victory for ſome time doubtful. But at
length with our aſſiſtance, who, when we
thought ſhe had ſuffered enough, under the appearance of parting them, overpowered him,
the amazon got the better, and kneeling on his
breaſt as he lay on the ground, vented her rage
upon him while ſhe was able to ſtrike a blow.
When ſhe could beat him no more, we made
a ſhift to ſeparate and raiſe them from the
ground, and having with ſome difficulty reſtored them both to their ſenſes, reſumed our mediation, in which we were ſo ſucceſsful, both
parties being ſufficiently ſick of the quarrel,
that a reconciliation was agreed to, which we
took care ſhould be on the moſt mortifying
terms to the old letcher.

" During all theſe tranſactions, my poor
gallant uſed frequently to look at me ſo ſignifi-
cantly, that I was afraid his wife would have
obſerved it, and extorted an explanation. But
it eſcaped her notice, and he thought proper
not to mention any thing of the matter; whether that he judged ſuch an inſtance of extravagance would only provoke her more; for,
laviſh as ſhe was of his money upon her relations, ſhe grudged him every penny he ſpent;
or concluded from my conduct, that I ſhould
deny

deny the charge, which in that cafe would only aggravate his fhame, as he had no proof of it.

"To confirm him in this opinion, which I gueffed to be the caufe of his filence when his lady and he were firft ready to depart, I muftered up all the affurance I could; and addreffing myfelf to her; "I hope, madam (faid I) "that if this odd affair fhould ever happen to "be known, you will bear witnefs to the pu- "rity and virtue of my conduct: And you, Sir, "I muft caution againft taking any liberties "with my character, with a view of extenuat- "ing your own crime, or laying any thing to "my charge which you cannot plainly prove, "as you regard your life; which, you are fen- "fible, would be made anfwerable for any in- "fult offered to me."

"To this fpeech fhe replied in the affirmative, while her hufband returned only one of his expreffive looks, and then they lovingly departed together.

"When my confederate and I had indulged our mirth for fome time, we went to my gallant's daughter, who, with her lover, was juft then come. On my entering the room where they were, the ftrongeft anxiety appeared in both their faces, though modefty prevented their giving it utterance. Not to keep them in pain, "You told me yefterday, madam, (faid I, tak- "ing her by the hand) that a thoufand crowns "would give you a profpect of happinefs, with "this deferving gentleman. I now have the "pleafure to inform you, that I have applied "to your father, with whom I have pleaded "fo fuccefsfully, that I have got you two "thoufand from him, which I have ready to "give

" give you, and hope heaven will bleſs it in your
" hands."

" What this happy pair felt on this occaſion,
may be eaſier conceived than deſcribed. They
fell together on their knees before I could poſſibly prevent them, and kiſſing my hands, bathed
them with tears of extaſy. My heart melted in
ſympathy with them. I raiſed them from the
ground, and embracing them both, led them,
unable to ſpeak, into the next room, where I
put the money into the lady's hands, who directly gave it to him. We then ſat down to
ſupper, during which, to relieve their ſpirits
that were ſinking under the preſſure of joy and
gratitude, I gave a looſe to the pleaſure my
heart was overflowing with, and entertained
them in the moſt obliging and familiar manner;
and when the ſervants retired gratified their curioſity, which I ſaw raiſed to a torture, with an
account of the whole affair, but in the light
moſt favourable to my old gallant, to avoid giving his daughter pain, who, notwithſtanding his
unnatural treatment of her, never mentioned
him but in terms of duty and reſpect.

· " Though the burgher and his lady had
promiſed, as really they ought for their own
·ſakes, to keep this curious affair ſecret, it ſoon
took wind. The lady, whoſe natural ſweetneſs
of temper was not much encreaſed by this af-
·fair, never ſaw the livid marks of her huſband's
proweſs upon her face, or thought of the profanation of her kinſman's cloaths, that ſhe did
not read him a comfortable lecture on his baſe-
neſs and debauchery before all companies; by
which means all ſhe knew of the matter became public. But this was not all. My gallant

lant had boasted among his intimates of his supplanting the count in my favour; and when he was so far recovered from the effects of his wife's resentment as to be able to shew his face, scrupled not to say that he had carried his success to the height of his wishes, though he never took courage to renew his applications to me, nor even, which I wondered at, to demand restitution of his money.

" This laid me under a necessity of telling the whole affair, in my own vindication, both his giving me the money and the use I had made of it, which gave the story another turn; those who were most unfavourable in their opinions of me before now changing their note, and extolling my justice and generosity to the skies. Nor was this the only advantage I received from it. The rest of my admirers, terrified by the burgher's fate, thought proper to draw off in time, and give up a pursuit that might be attended with danger; so that I was delivered from the persecution of their impertinence.

" By this time the campaign was ended, and my friend returned to me, who enjoyed the whole story with the highest pleasure; but as my gallant might some-way have it in his power to make my abode in that place disagreeable, for he was more vexed at the use I had applied his money to, than at his own losing it, before he took the field next season, he removed me hither where I have lived ever since, if not in the credit I could wish, yet without any new reproach, and where I want nothing so much as the approbation of my own mind to make me happy.

" You

"You may probably wonder why I do not feek this happiness, by breaking off my present connection with my friend, and returning to my family! But, alas, the things which we ought to do are not always in our power. I fee what is beft, but I follow that which is worft. My heart is now fo wedded to him, (if I may ufe the expreffion) that death only can part me from him; and though the pleafure I enjoy in his company is never without allay, even for the poor pittance of his time which it is in his power to fpend with me, from the reflection of its being criminal both in the commencement and continuation of it, I have not refolution, I cannot even fay I have a wifh to be feparated from him.

"Befide, whom fhould I return to? What happinefs could I expect at home? My family indeed have let me know that they would receive me; but how? Not to their efteem! That is impoffible. As a reprobate whom they have admitted out of charity, to give her an opportunity of repentance, and fave her from ruin in another life as well as this; as a reproach to them, which they would keep among themfelves to hide it from the world. Every look would upbraid me, every word infult my folly. At leaft confcioufnefs would take it in that fenfe, which were equally intolerable.

"I have thus, my dear friend, given you a view of my unhappy life, both to entertain you and eafe my own heart, by pouring out its griefs into your bofom. If you think me worthy of the like confidence, or that my advice can be of any advantage to you, I fhall give it with as much fincerity as I fhall receive yours with gratitude

titude upon all occafions; and I promife you the moſt inviolable fecrefy."

## CHAP. XII.

*One ſtory generally introduces another. The true
objeЄt of female attention to dreſs. Common conſequences of faſhionable intimacy, and female
friendſhip, with the ſecret of making a right uſe
of a ſhoeing-horn.*

THE other lady, who had liſtened to her
friend's ſtory with the ſtrongeſt attention,
was ſome time before ſhe made any anſwer.
At length, with a down-caſt look and heavy
figh, "I ſhould make a bad return, dear madam, (ſaid ſhe) for the good opinion you
have ſhewn of me, could I harbour any doubt
of you, or refuſe to comply with any thing
you deſire. My unhappy ſtory has few circumſtances; and O that the ſequel of it may
have fewer yet! Thoſe in which it differs
from your's are all to my diſadvantage. The
principles of virtue were inculcated in my
opening mind with the tendereſt care, and
enforced to my imitation by the moſt lively
example. I paſſed the moſt dangerous ſeaſon
of life, when ripening youth too often makes
paſſion an over-match for reaſon, without reproach; and at laſt ran head-long into ruin,
with my eyes open.

"You muſt wonder at a conduЄt ſo contrary
to every motive that ſhould influence a creature

3　　　　　　en-

endowed with the fainteſt glimmering of reaſon. But the cauſe of it may eaſily be traced.
Public fame had flattered me into an opinion of
my own beauty, and many examples juſtified
my ambition of riſing to the moſt exalted fortune on the merit of that alone. Yielding therefore to the impulſe of vanity, I thought of nothing but improving that advantage; and, under the appearance of ſtudying my own pleaſure, laid ſnares, with the moſt anxious and mercenary affiduity, for every man whom I thought
proper for my purpoſe : the wretched toil to
which the greateſt part of our ſex devote the
prime of life.

"I proceeded for ſome time on this plan,
when the gentleman with whom I am at preſent connected took it into his head to ſingle
me out for the object of his gallantry. Though
his being a married man cut off all hopes of
ſucceſs in my favourite ſcheme, there was ſomething ſo flattering to my vanity in being admired by a perſon of his rank, that I could not
reſiſt the pleaſure of it, eſpecially as I meant
nothing criminal, and this kind of gallantry
had the ſanction of faſhion.

"As the general intercourſe kept up among
people of diſtinction had been improved into
ſome degree of intimacy between this gentleman's wife and me, the affiduity with which he
paid attention to me upon all occaſions for
ſome time paſſed for the effect of familiarity and
friendſhip. But whether ſhe ſuſpected the
truth, and therefore thought proper to ſhew a
coolneſs to me, or that conſciouſneſs of deſerving it made me think ſo, I at length began
to fancy that ſhe ſlighted me ; and being confirmed

firmed in that opinion, by finding myfelf omitted in a general invitation of her acquaintances, I conceived the moft violent refentment againft her; to wreak which in the fevereft manner I affected to liften to her hufband's addreffes with pleafure, and gave reafon for fufpicions which were foreign to my heart, though at the fame time I was not infenfible that by fuch a conduct I ran the hazard of defeating my original defign; but this I vainly thought I could remedy when I pleafed, by breaking off all connection with him as foon as I had gratified my pique againft her.

" There is nothing more dangerous than liftening to the allurements of vice, though with the moft innocent intention. It is like playing on the brink of a precepice. By making the idea familiar, it takes off its terrors, and brings on a falfe fecurity that generally betrays into a fall.

" I expected that my admirer's wife would foon perceive this change in my conduct, and by breaking with me entirely give me an opportunity of triumphing over her in the moft mortifying manner, by fhewing the moft fovereign contempt for what made her fo unhappy. But inftead of this fhe continued to treat me with the fame if not greater intimacy than ever, and convinced me that the offence I had taken had been all groundlefs.

" Whether fhe did this to retort my fchemes, and make me look defpicable even in my own eyes, or in hopes of fhaming me into a proper fenfe of my behaviour by the contráft between it and hers, I cannot fay; but this I know that it had the former effect moft fully,

and

and would certainly have fucceeded in the latter alfo, had it not been for one of thofe accidents which, as you juftly obferved, fhew the infignificancy of human wifdom, and rule our lives.

"A gentleman of diftinguifhed rank and fortune, but who was far advanced in years, and in every refpect an object of averfion and contempt, unhappily took a liking to me. The advantages of fuch a match dazzled the eyes of all my friends, who exerted their utmoft influence to induce me to confent to it. But tho' it was the very object I had all along had in view, and exceeded the moft fanguine hope my vanity had ever formed, when it came to the teft, my heart rebelled, and I could not bring myfelf to barter happinefs for grandeur.

"Though I gave this anfwer in the moft determined manner, and fupported it with reafons impoffible to be refuted, my lover would not defift. On the contrary, he feemed determined to weary me out by his importunity, and, to fecond it, engaged the authority of my family, on the ftrength of which he always urged his odious fuit with the moft infulting confidence.

"The contraft between this conduct, and the refpectful infinuating addrefs of my former admirer was too ftriking. I began to hearken to him with more pleafure than ever; and, from a confirmed perfuafion that I could not be happy with the other, rafhly concluded that I muft be fo with him, as if the alternative was unavoidable.

"As my ancient fuitor had fettled his bargain with my friends, he looked upon me as secure, and therefore made no secret of the affair. The moment it came to my lover's ears, he expostulated with me upon it in the most passionate and tender terms ; and though I had yet formed no resolutions which made it necessary for me to account for my conduct to him, I held the other in such aversion, that in the weakness of my heart I could not conceal it ; nor my unhappiness and apprehensions from the authority and importunities of my friends.

" He was too well versed in the science of intrigue not to take immediate advantage of this. He condoled with me on the cruelty of such a persecution, enumerated the many instances in which it had been unhappily successful ; and heightened my dislike of the other into abhorrence, by several anecdotes of his character which I was before a stranger to. Nor did he stop here. As he was intimate with his rival, he instantly exerted all his art to urge him to press his suit with me more earnestly, imputing my refusal to coyness which wanted only to be wooed, and turning his bashfulness, as he called it, into ridicule.

" While he stimulated him in this manner, he made me believe that he used every argument which generosity and honour could suggest, to dissuade him from a pursuit that he saw was so disagreeable, but all in vain ; the other declaring, that, if I persisted much longer, he would have recourse to the authority of my friends, which they had promised to exert at a proper time, when resistance should be out of my power. This scheme was too successful. Urged on by him, my suitor pressed his addresses with redoubled warmth, and enforced them

with

with new offers, which engaged my friends still
more sanguinely in his behalf; and by that
means confirmed all my lover had said to me,
who aggravated my apprehensions of compul-
sion to such a height, fixing the very hour when
I was to be sacrificed to a particular day on
which I had been obliged to accept of an invitation to his country-seat, in company with
some of my nearest relations, that in the madness of affright I listened to the proposals he
made me, and consented to come away with
him, persuaded that, however blameable such a
step might be in other cases, self-preservation
justified it in me; so that I really ran away
from my suitor, rather than with my lover.

"The mystery of this management I was
not long unacquainted with. He was so proud
of the address he had shewn in it, that the moment he had me in his power, he could not
avoid boasting of it in the vanity of his heart.
This was the first thing that awoke me to reflection, though I have since had abundant reasons beside. The mortification of finding myself duped in such a manner, by one whose understanding I had ever held in too low esteem,
to have any apprehensions of the kind, with
the ridiculously vexatious circumstances which
attended my elopement, had such an effect upon me, that I wrote to my friends in the anguish of my soul, to beg I might be permitted
to return, and throw myself absolutely upon
their mercy in every respect but that of being
sacrificed to that odious old creature; but a
false pride prevented their complying with my
request. They concluded, though most in-
juriously, that my ruin was compleated, and

E 2                    rejected

rejected me with difdain, as a reproach to them.

"I then had no choice left, and was obliged to perfift from neceffity in the crime of folly, as, I am perfuaded, is the cafe of many of thofe who appear moft culpable. What will be the confequence I dare not even divine. This I am determined on : I will not be the fport of his caprice, carried about like an unneceffary part of his baggage, only for fhew, to gratify his vanity at the expence of my fhame. He fhall either quit his military life at the end of this campaign, and retire, according to his repeated promifes and oaths, to fome place where we fhall not be known; or I will quit him, and return home at every event. I am entitled to a fortune that will afford me a morfel of bread in fome country-village, where I may have leifure enough to repent of my folly; and even that is better than the life I lead now."

## C H A P. XIII.

*More military matters. Politics on one fide of the quefion.*

JUST as the lady had concluded her ftory, my fellow-traveller continued his journey. I therefore left the fair friends together, to compare the errors of their paft conduct, and confirm each other in their refolutions of amendment.

The

The suttler, having taken the circuit he intended, arrived at the camp to which he was going without any accident, and delivered his packet into the general's own hand, who running his eye over the contents, " This will do! " (said he) This will do! I have long waited " for an opportunity to-give them a decisive " stroke, and now I have get it; thanks to my " faithful and vigilant agents! Sure no other " people ever were so infatuated as to harbour " the subjects of their enemies thus in their very " bosom, in a time of open war! They do not " preconcert a motion that I have not notice " of. Indeed if it were not for the intelligence " which I receive in this manner, I should of-" ten be at a loss."

The purport of the intelligence which he had received was, -that the adverse army would be so considerably weakened, as the next day, by several detachments, that a general attack might be made almost with a certainty of success. Such an opportunity was not to be missed. He instantly set about making all the necessary preparations, and sent orders to another general, who commanded a separate body of forces, but subordinate to him, to second his design, by a vigorous attack at the same time on the side next him. The dispositions he made wore the most promising aspect; but, according to the usual uncertainty of military operations, his whole scheme miscarried. He met with so warm a reception from the enemy, who had an opportunity of opposing their whole force to him, the other general not attacking at the same time, that he was forced to retreat with precipitation and considerable loss, and leave

the

the other, who was juft then coming up, expofed to the victorious army, which might have
given him a total defeat, had not that been contrary to the general's fcheme of protracting the
war; who therefore, content with repulfing
one part of the enemy's forces, permitted the
other to retreat without a ftroke.

This difappointment inflamed the difcord
which already fubfifted between the two generals; the chief alledging, that he fhould have
fucceeded in his attempt, had his orders been
properly obeyed by the other, who retorted the
accufation, and faid he was abandoned on purpofe that he might be cut off, which muft have
been the confequence had not the enemy miftaken a retreat, for which he faw no neceffity,
for a ftratagem to draw him in between the two
corps, each of which was almoft equal to his
whole army.

The confequence of this difagreement is obvious. Each general had his own creatures
among the officers, who, openly efpoufing the
caufe of their patrons, began a kind of civil
war among themfelves, which threatened the
moft dangerous effects, had the enemy been intent upon taking the advantage of them.

On my proceeding to take a view of this army, I was fenfibly ftruck at the difference between it and that which I had feen before. In
the other, though a variety of interefts prevented the various corps of which it was compofed from holding that friendly intercourfe
with each other, that ought to fubfift between men engaged in the fame caufe, yet
ftill that jealoufy went no farther than an un-
fociable diftance, and never interfered with
duty.

duty. The men befide were well provided with the neceffary appointments of every kind, which preferved them in that health and vigor indifpenfably effential to fuccefs.

But here every thing wore a different afpect. Though all the fubjects of the fame fovereign, and therefore united in every view of intereft, the officers, as I have obferved, were divided into factions, and embroiled in conftant quarrels; and the private men fickly, half-ftarved, and half-naked; yet, under all thefe diftractions and diftreffes, the levity of temper which characterifes their nation difplayed itfelf in its greateft force; the officers forgetting their animofity the moment they had put up their fwords, and chatting together on matters of mirth and amufement with all the familiarity of friends, till fome accident revived their difputes; and the men dancing to divert hunger, and keep them warm, and all venting their refentment againft the authors of their feveral grievances in a fcurrilous fong or lampoon.

While I was making thefe obfervations the night after this mifcarriage, my attention was ftruck by a converfation which paffed between two officers on guard, who, having drawn off to fome diftance from their men, thought themfelves in no danger of being over-heard, and therefore opened their hearts without referve.

" I think, (faid one of them, whofe accent " fhewed him to be a foreigner) that confider- " ing all things, we got very well over this " affair. Had the enemy purfued his advan- " tage, I do not know what might have been " the confequence."

" That is very true, (anfwered the other)

E 4 " it

" it might have been somewhat disagreeable;
" but this will always be the case where court-
" favour is put in competition with merit, and
" rivals joined in command whose emulation
" is to supplant each other, though at the ruin
" of the public cause; and this is the very
" thing that has drawn this war out to such a
" tedious length. The general who began it
" gloriously was immediately removed, to make
" way for one whose sole aim was to make a
" fortune by every iniquitous and inhuman me-
" thod of ruining the unhappy countries which
" were the seat of the war, and defrauding the
" very army he commanded of their necessary
" appointments. When his avarice was sa-
" tiated, and the public clamour grown too
" loud, he was succeeded by another favourite,
" though of an opposite party, who was ho-
" nester, it is true, but had less military know-
" ledge, which brought a disgrace upon the
" glory of his country, not paralleled in its
" annals.

" To retrieve that, necessity pointed out the
" present general, on whose activity and va-
" lour great expectations were founded. Nor
" did he disappoint them. His entrance on
" the command was signalized by several suc-
" cessful and glorious exploits, which were to
" prepare the way for more important events;
" but before he had time to put his great de-
" signs in execution, the same prevailing in-
" fluence which had so unhappily removed the
" first general, and taken offence at the pre-
" sent also, found means to incumber him
" with his present colleague, and by that means
" stopped his progress, as you have seen this
                                    " day;

" day ; and where it yet may end, I tremble to·
" think."

" Faith, (replied the former) this is but an
" uncomfortable account, I own ; but I never·
" trouble my head with looking forward. My·
" bufinefs is to fight when I am in the field,
" and live as well as I can upon my pay when
" I am not ; and I mind nothing elfe. Not but I
" fhould like to know fomething of thefe matters·
" too ; but I can't tell how it is, I have a bad head
" for politics myfelf, and I never converfe with
" any one who is able and willing to inftruct
" me. If it be not too much trouble, I fhould
" be obliged to you for fome information. It
" will ferve to pafs away the time, as we have·
" nothing to do. Pray what was the caufe of
" this war that has coft us fo many fine ar-
" mies ? And what are we fent here for ? For·
" my part, I cannot comprehend it for my life !
" We are marched all this way, I know not
" for what ; and lofe our lives I know not
" how, dying like rotten fheep without any·
" credit to ourfelves, or advantage to our fove-·
" reign."

" You afk a queftion, my friend, (returned·
" the other) not eafy to be anfwered, nor fafe·
" to be difcuffed, were it poffible for us to be·
" overheard ; but as I think there is no dan-
" ger in that, I will ftrive to give you the beft·
" account I can of the matter.

" The Englifh and we, you know, are ne-
" ceffarily enemies, becaufe we obftruct each·
" other's views. If it was not for thofe head-
" ftrong Iflanders, we fhould long fince have·
" raifed the glory of our fovereign to the higheft·
" pitch, by the conqueft of all Europe ; as, on·

" the other hand, they would engrofs the com-
" merce of the whole world, and of courfe be-
" come mafters of all the wealth in it, did we
" not crofs their avaricious views by every pof-
" fible means. In negotiating, we always have
" the advantage of them; but when we come
" to war, I do not know how it is, but they
" fometimes are hard enough for us.

" As for the prefent war in particular, it
" took its rife folely from their prefumption and
" injuftice. Under pretence of our having
" forcibly poffeffed ourfelves of fome fpots of
" land which belonged to them in the bound-
" lefs deferts of America, they fell upon our de-
" fencelefs merchants without any previous de-
" claration of war, and took numbers of them
" in a cowardly pyratical manner.

" Provoked at this infolence, our monarch
" in his wrath fent one of his armies, and con-
" quered an important part of their dominions.
" Aftonifhed at this ftroke, they ftood looking
" at each other in the moft defpicable affright,
" while he proceeded glorioufly in his con-
" quefts in every part of the globe.

" Their terror was for fome time fo great,
" that they called in a parcel of their mercena-
" ry allies, to protect them from his vengeance,
" which they apprehended would purfue them,
" even in their own country; not giving them-
" felves time to confider, that there was a fea
" between them which it was impoffible for his
" troops to pafs.

" At length they were rouzed from this
" ftate of fear and ftupefaction into a kind of
" phrenzy, in which, by fome ftrange mifma-
" nagement in our affairs, they not only reco-
" vered

" vered almoſt all the conqueſts we had made
" from them, but alſo puſhed their ſucceſs
" to a length which a Frenchman can not
" think of without bluſhing.

" To ballance theſe advantages, and bring
" them to a proper way of thinking, we are
" ſent here, where our alliances and the num-
" ber of our forces encouraged us to hope,
" that we might make ſuch acquiſitions as on
" a treaty of peace ſhould be deemed equiva-
" lent to theirs, and exchanged for them. Hi-
" therto matters have not ſucceeded quite ſo
" well as we expected; but ſtill we have gain-
" ed one great point, in making them diſſipate
" that wealth, which is the foundation of their
" power, in a fruitleſs oppoſition to us; a fol-
" ly that will certainly reduce them to beggary,
" if they perſiſt in it much longer, which our
" monarch knows, and for that reaſon conti-
" nues to carry on the war, even under ſuch
" apparent diſadvantages.

## CHAP. XIV.

*A new ſcheme of carrying on a war. An ill-timed
doubt often diſconcerts a good ſtory. Anecdotes of
a loyal family. The hiſtory of Sir ARCHIBALD,
and ZELIDE princeſs of Armenia.*

" I AM very much obliged to you for this
" information, (replied the foreigner) I
" own I have never viewed things in this light
" before. I have indeed felt ſome of the bad

E 6                    " con-

" confequences of our want of fuccefs in the
" ftoppage of my pay; but I never dreamed of
" the advantages which might attend the profe-
" cution of an unfuccefsful war.

" But in the mean time, is there no danger
" that we may be out in our calculation, and
" ruined firft? By all appearances, the fi-
" nances of the enemy are in a much more
" flourifhing way than ours. They pay every
" body punctually, and even enlarge their
" expences every day, in pufhing their good
" fortune, and fupporting the conquefts they
" make."

" And fo much the worfe for them, (re-
" torted the Frenchman) their punctual pay-
" ments will foon leave them pennylefs. Our
" government acted more prudently. By re-
" fufing to pay their debts, they kept money in
" their hands to carry on their defigns, which
" the others will foon find themfelves unable
" to do.

" As to their enlarging their expence in fup-
" porting their conquefts, that is the very
" thing we defire. We let them conquer on-
" ly to draw them into more expence. You
" cannot think that our mighty monarch would
" have permitted their infolence to have gone
" unpunifhed fo long, if he had not fome great
" end in view. No! No! Their conquefts
" will be their ruin, take my word for it. As
" foon as they have exhaufted themfelves by
" conquering, they will be glad to give all up
" for a peace. It has ever been fo. It is but
" fending an able negotiator to treat with them,
" and the work is done; their heads are too
" heavy for politics. No! No! their mak-
" ing conquefts fignifies nothing.          " As

" As to what you fay of our being ruined
" firft, that is all a miftake. Our king can
" never be ruined while there is money, or mo-
" ney's worth, in his dominions. It is all his
" own. He need not ftoop to flatter his fub-
" jects to lend; he has power to take. They,
" it is true, may poffibly fuffer for a time? but
" what does that fignify where the glory of
" their fovereign is concerned? No true
" Frenchman ever thinks of that. He leaves
" fuch felfifh confiderations to Englifh mer-
" chants and mechanics. He is above them.

" I fay, *for a time*; becaufe our refources
" are all within ourfelves. Let us be never fo.
" exhaufted by war, a few years of peace never
" fail to reftore us; and we have the pleafure
" to reflect, that the attention paid to our in-
" terefts then always makes amends for what
" we fuffered before; whereas our enemies.
" think of no fuch thing. The moment they
" get a peace, which their eagernefs for it fel-
" dom lets them have patience to wait for on
" good terms, they fall to wrangling among
" themfelves, and never trouble their heads
" about the good of the public, till they have
" occafion to call for affiftance again; fo that
" their affairs are always better managed in
" war than in peace, even in refpect to the
" matters moft foreign to war.

" The reafon of this is, that their gover-
" nors not having any direct property in the
" goods of their fubjects, they think it not
" worth their while to take any care about
" them; whereas with us, all being in our
" fovereign's power, he looks upon them as
" his own, and ftudies their improvement ac-
                                    " cordingly.

" cordingly. Of this there might innumera-
" ble inftances be given in all the articles of
" commerce, the ballance of which we con-
" ftantly continue to bring into our favour, in
" peace, by fome means or other, in lefs time
" than they wreft it from us in war."

" All this may be very true, for ought I
" know, (faid the foreigner) but one thing I
" am convinced of, which is, that however
" conducive this power may be to the monarch's
" glory, it were better for his fubjects that he
" fhould be without it. I have experienced
" both cafes, and therefore am the better able
" to judge."

" If fo, (anfwered the Frenchman with fome
" tartnefs) I wonder why your countrymen
" chufe to come and fix themfelves among us!
" Few people leave a place they like for one
" they do not."

" Very true, (replied the foreigner gravely)
" they feldom do. But there may be circum-
" ftances to influence fuch a choice. I have
" heard this glanced at more than once; and
" in fuch a manner, that I had difficulty to
" refrain from taking notice of it. I am not
" captious in my temper; but ftill I cannot bear
" infinuations injurious to my country. For
" this reafon, as I efteem you, and confequent-
" ly defire your good opinion, give me leave
" to relate a few of the particulars of my own
" cafe, which, I imagine, will make you view
" the matter in a different light, from what
" you feem to have done hitherto; and convince
" you of the injuftice of fuch reflections for the
" future; nor fhall I trefpafs on your patience
" long.

" You'

" You are not a ftranger to the revolutions
" which have happened in the Britifh govern-
" ment. I will not enter into a difcuffion of
" the power which the people of England have
" on many occafions exercifed over their fove-
" reigns. That part of the Britifh dominions
" in which I was born has ever been remark-
" able for the contrary principles; our un-
" fhaken loyalty having always been proof to
" temptation, and even to tyranny.

" In this antient monarchy my anceftors en-
" joyed diftinguifhed honours, before the fa-
" milies of many of the prefent fovereigns of
" Europe had emerged from barbarifm and ob-
" fcurity. Our poffeffions were extenfive ; and
" if nature had denied the enervating delicacies
" of luxury, Heaven made ample amends by
" the number and virtue of our vaffals, whofe
" valour, guided by the loyalty of their lords,
" often fupported their fovereign's throne in
" the dire conflicts of ambition, the ftruggles
" which the untamed fons of favage liberty
" made againft law and rule.

" The virtuous actions of our anceftors are
" handed down for imitation; nor is the facred
" record difcontinued, till a feries of unworthy
" deeds makes the degenerate pofterity blufh
" at the upbraiding comparifon. Doubt not
" therefore the tale which I am going to re-
" late; nor think it to be the fiction of vanity
" or imagination. The reverend fire has ftill
" delivered it invariably to his attentive fons;
" nor has a fyllable been altered in the courfe
" of fo many generations.

" Our fame was not unknown in foreign
lands. Wherever the fhrill trumpet called the

warriors forth to arms, our banners waved the foremoſt in the field; and trophies, won by feats of hardieſt prowefs, graced our ſocial halls.

"We had proceeded in this honourable path for many ages, when holy Lewis, glowing with pious zeal, undertook to deliver the ſacred repoſitories of the bleſſed ſaints, the places hallowed by the footſteps of our Lord, from the profanation of infidels. Fired at the news of ſuch a glorious deſign, the heir of our illuſtrious houſe led forth the choſen youths of all our hills, to fight the battles of the faith. The name of their chief prepared a welcome for them, and juſtified the choice which Lewis made of youthful Archibald, to lead the van in all his armies, after he had dub'd him his own knight.

"The unhappy event of this great deſign is too well known. I ſhall therefore confine myſelf to what immediately concerns this my moſt honoured progenitor. During the ſtruggles which Lewis made with the malevolence of fortune, the actions of ſir Archibald made him the terror of the hoſts of the infidels; at the ſame time that his exemplary virtues were a reproach to the looſer manners of his fellow-ſoldiers. In an excurſion which he made one day, in queſt of intelligence, fate directed his ſteps to the banks of a rivulet in the neighbourhood of the Saracen camp, the beauty of which tempted him to trace its courſe along the woody vale.

"He had not proceeded far, when the ſound of female voices ſtruck his ear. The ſongs with which they filled the winding valley, declared the innocence and happineſs of their hearts. He liſ—

tened

tened for a while; and then, as he was a truly
chaste and courteous knight, was turning about
to retire, for fear of intruding on their privacy,
when a shriek of affright told him his assistance
was necessary to them. He hesitated not a moment; but, rushing forward, saw that a troop of
the marauders who swarmed around the camp of
Lewis, and dishonoured the christian name with
their atrocious crimes, had surprised a band of
helpless females, and having dispersed their
feeble guard of eunuchs, were carrying them
forcibly away. He knew their danger in the
hands of such worse than brutal ruffians; and
proclaiming his own name in a voice that
shook the hills, ran forward to their rescue.

"Awed at the well-known name, they
seemed to pause; but their leader seeing that sir
Archibald was alone and on foot, for when he
first heard the voices he had left his horse with
his men, that he might not disturb them as he
advanced to listen more distinctly, waved his
hand to his associates to follow, and clapping
spurs to his horse's sides was out of sight in a
moment. But all did not escape so easily; the
well-aimed javelin of sir Archibald pierced the
hindermost as he had turned himself for flight,
and brought him life-less to the ground. The
active knight instantly seized the steed of the
fallen caitif, and vaulting nimbly on him rode
after the ravishers, whom he soon over-took,
the struggles of the females impeding their
flight, and their cries directing his pursuit.
The villains at first taking him for their companion avoided him not, nor stood on their defence; but the deaths of the two first of their
number, who fell within the reach of his
sword,

fword, convinced them of their error, and that it was impoffible for them to fly from him.

"Cuftom had inured them to danger, and defpair now made them valiant. Their number alfo againft his fingle arm gave them a profpect of fuccefs. They let go the women therefore, and forming themfelves into a troop bore all together upon him. But he difdained to wait for their affault; and rufhing furioufly into the midft of them, for fome time maintained the unequal combat, and ballanced their numbers by his valour. Five of their bodies now lay breathlefs round him, when his horfe, pierced to the heart with a fpear, fell to the ground fo fuddenly, that all his agility and ftrength were not fufficient to difengage him from him. In this fituation he expected nothing lefs than inftant death, when all at once the affailants turned their backs, and fought their fafety in flight.

"Surprifed at this, fir Archibald looked round, and faw his faithful men galloping up toward him. They had heard his voice when he firft called to the ruffians, and imagining that he wanted their affiftance advanced with fpeed by the fide of the rivulet, till they found the wretch whom he had pierced with his javelin; alarmed at the fight of whom they doubled their hafte, and happily came up time enough to fave their lord.

"The firft care of fir Archibald was to fearch for the women, whom it was difficult to find, their fright having made them hide themfelves the moment they had been let go by the ruffians. At length, however, the diligence of his men difcovered them all but one,

th

the lofs of whom the reft deplored in the moft paffionate terms. Sir Archibald concluding that fhe muft have been carried off by fome of the ravifhers, while the reft ftopped to attack him, was at a lofs what to do. It was in vain to think of overtaking them without fome guide to direct his purfuit, and whom to get he knew not.

" In this perplexity he bethought himfelf of trying whether fome intelligence might not be gained among thofe who had fallen by his fword, if they all were not as yet quite dead. He was not difappointed. From one of them he learned their place of rendezvous; and that their leader had borne away his prey, as fir Arcibald had conjectured. The generous knight was alarmed at her danger, and, ordering two of his men to conduct the difconfolate damfels back to the Saracen camp, fet off himfelf with the reft in fearch of her.

" The place to which he was directed was a cave in the darkeft recefs of a wood, at a confiderable diftance from him. The day was now far fpent, and the way fo difficult to be found, that it was night before they reached the cavern. Sir Archibald waited not to demand entrance, but drawing his fword rufhed boldly in. Heaven feemed to have delayed him to the moment that fhould make his coming moft critical. Inflamed with brutal paffion, the mifcreant, when he could not perfuade the damfel to compliance, had refolved to gratify his bafe defires by force. Her cries reached the ear of fir Archibald as he entered the cave, and directed him to her refcue; which he effected juft as her ftrength was exhaufted in the ftruggle, and
fhe

she lay a defenceless prey to the spoiler. With one stroke he severed the wretch's head from his body; when, raising the astonished maiden from the ground, he strove to restore her spirits by the most tender and encouraging assurances of safety and protection.

"At first she threw her eyes wildly round the dreary cave, and, filled with the horror of the scenes she had just gone through, could scarcely believe her senses that she was delivered. At length recovering power to speak, " What " man, or rather what angel art thou" (said she in the Saracen tongue, fixing her eyes upon him as he stood without his helmet, which he had pulled off when he had first raised her from the ground) " whom Heaven has thus miracu- " lously sent to save me from ruin? The be- " nefit is so great, that I had rather think the " latter, as the obligation is too much to owe " to man."

" Lady, (answered he in the same language, " which he had learned in the war) I am a " man! a sinful man, who knows it is his du- " ty to succour virtue in distress."

" A man! (replied she earnestly) Say then " of what lineage and country art thou come, " that I may study the most acceptable reward " for thy courtesy and valour!"

" Thou seest before thee, (returned he) lady, " a Christian knight, whose faith makes virtue " a duty, and looks not for reward."

" A Christian! Gracious Heaven! (exclaim- " ed the lady, as recovering herself after a long " pause) Pardon courteous stranger the ravings " of a distracted brain! No reward can return " the obligation I am under to you, and yet I
" must

" muft fue for more; I muft intreat you to
" conduct me directly to the Saracen camp,
" and reftore me to my diftreffed parent, who
" now laments the lofs of his only child."

" Talk not of rewards, moft beauteous lady,
" (faid the knight, gazing in rapture on her)
" the pleafure of doing you a fervice is it's own
" reward. All I require is to know your name;
" and O! tell me, I conjure you, (continued
" he, falling on his knees before her) if it be
" poffible for a foldier of no ignoble birth or
" fame, to make the offer of his honeft heart
" acceptable to you."

" Brave knight, (anfwered fhe) an heart
" like thine is worthy of the moft exalted maid's
" acceptance; but there are infuperable obfta-
" cles to thy defire. As for my name, it would
" avail you naught to know it. Let me adjure
" you therefore by that virtue which your foul
" reveres, to defift from any farther enquiries
" about me; and conveying me to the camp
" of your enemies, there to leave me to my
" fate."

" Thy will, O beauteous arbitrefs of my
" deftiny, (replied he) is a law to thy devoted
" fervant. I obey thee; but firft permit me
" to pour out the fulnefs of my foul."— Then
taking her fair hand as he kneeled before her,
and holding it between his, "Accept my ho-
" mage, fovereign lady of my heart! (faid he)
" and receive me from this hour for thy true
" and conftant knight; and by this facred
" pledge I fwear, (touching her hand devout-
" ly with his lips) no other dame fhall ever
" raife a wifh in my breaft contrary to the faith
" I here plight unto thee."——

" And

" And in return I promise thee, most valiant
" and right gentle knight, (said she) that the
" remembrance of thy courtesy shall never be
" erazed from my grateful heart ; nor any other
" man supplant thee in that regard which it is
" lawful for a virgin to feel for her deliverer."

" Comforted by this kind promise, sir Archibald took her by the hand, and, leading her
to the mouth of the cavern, mounted her behind him on his able steed, and bore her without accident to the Saracen camp.

" As soon as they came to the most advanced
guard she dismounted, and pulling a costly
jewel from her breast, " Wear this (said she
" tenderly) in remembrance of one who will
" never forget her generous deliverer."

" I accept, dearest lady, (answered he bend-
" ing his knee to the earth) a gift made pre-
" cious by thy hand, and promise to wear it as
" a badge of thy authority over my heart ; as
" thou, if I have found favour in thy sight,
" wilt also condescend to take this ring from
" thy servant. My honoured mother bestowed it
" with her dying benediction, and enjoined me
" never to give it till I could truly give my heart
" along with it."—-She kindly took the pledge
of his love, and put it on her hand directly ;
then, biding him adieu, advanced alone to the
guard, who instantly conducted her where she
commanded them.

" Sir Archibald stood for some time, unable
to stir ; his eyes followed her as far as he could
see through the shades of night, and he listened
to her steps till the sounds insensibly died away
from his ear. Awaking at length as from a trance,
" Unhappy Archibald (said he, striking his
" hand

" hand upon his grief-fwollen breaft) to what
" misfortunes has thy wayward fate referved
" thee? Never till this day did my heart feel
" the power of beauty. I laughed at love, and
" called his bondage folly; but amply has the
" tyrant now avenged his caufe, and pierced
" me with his fharpeft, moft invenomed lance.
" Ye maids of Caledonia, who oft have wept
" your flighted charms, and called the heart of
" Archibald infenfible, now triumph in his
" fall. He loves without a ray of hope to pro-
" mife him fuccefs."

" Thus did he confume the remaining part of
the night in fruitlefs lamentation, till his followers at the approach of morning reminded
him, that it was neceflary for him to return to
the chriftian camp.

" From this hour his heart was a ftranger to
happinefs. Did he know even who the object
of his wifhes was, he might at leaft have pleafed
himfelf with forming imaginary fchemes for obtaining her love; but her command, which he
moft religioufly obferved, precluded him from
making any enquiries about her, as his men's ignorance of the Saracen language had alfo prevented their learning any thing from the damfels whom they had conducted to the camp.

✳✳✳✳✳✳✳✳✳✳✳✳✳✳✳✳✳✳✳✳✳✳✳✳✳✳✳✳✳✳✳✳✳✳

## CHAP. XV.

*The History of* SIR ARCHIBALD, *and* ZELIDE
*princefs of* Armenia, *continued.*

"BUT though his private peace was thus
poifoned, it flackened not his attention
to the duties of war. On the contrary, the
troubles of his mind making him weary of life,
he eagerly fought every occafion of lofing it
with honour. In the laft unfortunate action
between Lewis and the Saracens, Sir Archibald, at the head of his bonny lads, charged the
infidels with fuch impetuofity, that he broke into the main body of their army; and had he
been followed with equal fpirit by the other
fquadrons under his command, might poffibly
have altered the fate of that unhappy day. But
envy, which always follows fuperior merit, had
inflamed the hearts of certain French lords, who
thought themfelves eclipfed by his fame, to fuch
a degree againft him, that when they faw him
break like a torrent into the battle of the enemy, inftead of following his fteps with emula-
tive virtue, they bafely drew back, and gave
the infidels an opportunity of furrounding him,
and his few brave men.

" Thrice did he penetrate fo far through
their numbers, as to feize the imperial ftandard;
but the multitude, whom dread of fuch a difgrace made throw themfelves defperately between him and it, as often bore him back. At
length

length, collecting all his force for one laſt effort, he burſt in irreſiſtibly among them, and
ſeizing it with one hand had raiſed the other to
ſmite the chief, whoſe vigorous gripe with-held
it from him, when a ſtone, hurled by a daſtard
ſlave who dared not approach within the reach
of his ſword, felled him to the ground. The
baſe herd inſtantly ruſhed in, and were ready to
wreak their cowardly revenge upon his defence-
leſs body, when the chief, who reſpected valour,
though in an enemy, and judged by the rich-
neſs of his armour that he muſt be ſome perſon
of note, whoſe ranſom would well reward his
humanity, interpoſed; and, diſcovering that he
ſtill breathed, ordered him to be removed to his
own tent, and there taken proper care of. With
ſir Archibald fell the ſpirit of the chriſtian army, and left the infidels an eaſy and compleat
victory.

"He had not been long in the tent of the
chief, when, by the aſſiſtance of thoſe into
whoſe care he had been given, he began to recover his ſenſes. Opening his eyes he looked
around in ſilent aſtoniſhment for ſome time;
then turning to the attendants who were buſied
about him, he aſked them courteouſly where he
was, and to whom indebted for ſuch friendly
treatment; but they laid their hands upon their
mouths, to let him know that they muſt not
converſe with him. This increaſed his perplexity. The tent, and the habit of thoſe who
adminiſtered ſuch kind aſſiſtance to him, ſhewed him that he was in the hands of the enemy;
but that very aſſiſtance, ſo contrary to their
uſual practice, heightened his aſtoniſhment ſtill
more and more.

"The

" The next morning he found himself so well recovered, that he desired permission to wait upon his benefactor to return him thanks, and learn what ransom he demanded, which he doubted not but Lewis would readily pay. The chief received him courteously, and informing him of the total defeat of the christian army, gave him to understand that his hopes of liberty were at an end.

" The effect which this account had on him was easily perceived. The manly fortitude that sat upon his brow before gave place to listless dejection. " Thy will be done, O God!" (exclaimed he with a loud sigh) then fixed his eyes upon the ground.

" The chief, who imagined that his grief arose from the thought of his captivity, encouraged him with assurances that he should not receive unworthy treatment. But sir Archibald soon shewed him that his distress arose from a more exalted motive. " Think not, " most courteous and noble lord" (said he, raising his eyes slowly from the ground and fixing them on the chief, with a look that shewed a soul overburthened but not broken by woe) " think " not that my grief is for myself. Liberty is " the jewel of every virtuous soul; without it " the sentiments of honour, generosity, and cou- " rage, are a torture. But still I mourn from " a more extensive cause. I mourn the mis- " fortunes of my royal master, the princely and " pious Lewis. I mourn the defeat of the ar- " mies of the Lord. I am but a worm, an " atom in the creation, unworthy of a thought " in such a scene of ruin."

. " The chief was struck with such greatness
of

of soul, and, repeating his kind confolation, demanded who fir Archibald was, and what rank he held in the army of Lewis. But the high-minded knight had formed the refolution of concealing his name and quality, to hide the difgrace which he thought his captivity would reflect upon his noble houfe and country. " No! (faid he to himfelf) never fhall it be " faid that fir Archibald is a flave! that a no- " ble *Scot* was forced to bend the knee to bar- " barous infidels. Let me perifh unknown, " and let my reproach die with me."——Then, as if recollecting himfelf, " I am no more than " a private knight, O noble lord, (anfwered " he) whom a defire of fame brought to this " fatal war. I was not born in the ligiance of " royal Lewis, nor bore any high rank in his " armies. I led a few brave youths, the fol- " lowers of my way-ward fortune, to the field, " who all, as I fuppofe, have fallen with ho- " nour; and O! that I had fhared their glo- " rious fate; but I was unworthy, and am re- " ferved for flavery."

" There is a fympathy between noble fouls, which foon unites them. The chief, who be- fore admired the valour, now loved the virtue of his captive. He directly received him into his intimacy, and was fo ftruck with the charms of his converfation, that he opened to him all the fecrets of his foul. As they fat together one day, beguiling the heat of the noon-tide hours, in pleafing difcourfe, the chief paufed for fome time as if loft in thought; then ftarting in a kind of tranfport, " It fhall be fo; (faid he) " 'tis Heaven infpires the thought."——Then addreffing himfelf to fir Archibald, " *Selim*,

F 2 " (that

" (that was the name he had given him) thou
" must go and plead the cause of thy friend.
" That eloquence which can charm the fiercest
" passions of the soul to peace, can surely kindle
" the more gentle ones of pity and desire. I
" love, most warmly love ; but the object of
" my wishes is insensible to my pain, nor will
" listen to my intreaties. Go then and soften
" her heart, paint my passion in proper co-
" lours, and teach her to make a just return
" to it. Attempt not to disswade me from the
" thought. It is Heaven that inspires ; and I
" will pursue it."

" Sir Archibald, who knew by sad experience
that love is an over-match for reason, answered,
that, far from contradicting his will, he was
ready to obey him in any thing he should command ; and only desired to know how his weak
endeavours were to be applied. The chief embracing him tenderly, " I will inform you of
" every thing, (said he) and will not doubt of
" your success. You must know that, about
" three moons since, the guard of one of the
" advanced posts brought to my tent a damsel
" most richly attired, who they said had come
" to them just before the morning-watch, and
" required to be conducted to the commander
" of the night. The moment she entered and
" cast her eyes upon me, "Achmet, (said she,
" with an air of dignity that awed my soul)
" lead me to the pavilion of thy master. I am
" Zelide, his daughter, who was this day sur-
" prized by the enemy, as I walked along the
" banks of the rivulet ; and have now recover-
" ed my liberty in a manner not necessary to
" be told.

" I

" I was so dazzled at the sight of her beauty,
" for she had no veil on, that I was some time
" before I had power to make her any answer.
" At length, prostrating myself at her feet,
" Forgive, O beauteous princess, (said I) the
" ignorance of thy slaves, who have not paid
" the respect due to thy sublime state."——
" Rise, (answered she) and lead me to my fa-
" ther; I forgive every thing."——

" Encouraged by this condescension, I ven-
" tured to rise, and taking her hand, which she
" graciously held to me, conducted her to the
" pavilion of the Armenian monarch. The joy
" that her return raised can no more be descri-
" bed than the situation of my heart. All was
" tumult, extacy, and madness.

" As soon as I had delivered her into her fa-
" ther's hands, I prepared to retire, when cal-
" ling to me, " Stay Achmet, (said the inrap-
" tured monarch) and receive the reward of thy
" service. I have sworn to give Zelide to the
" man who should rescue her out of the hands
" of the ravishers, and restore her to me. Her
" maidens have told me what noble spirit you
" exerted for her. Here Zelide, take an huf-
" band who has deserved you."

" I prostrated myself at his feet in transport,
" and embraced his knees, unable to express
" the joy of my full heart; when the princess
" replied to her father, " The merits of Ach-
" met are sufficiently great, without assuming
" those of another. I owe my liberty to an
" unknown hand."

" It is impossible to express what I felt at
" hearing her say this. The manner in which
" she spoke convinced me that her heart was

F 3                              " not

" not inclined in my favour; and I knew the
" fondnefs of her father too well, to think that
" he would put any conftraint upon her incli-
" nations. However, I yielded to the impulfe
" of my paffion, and throwing myfelf at her
" feet, " Revoke not, O beauteous princefs,
" (faid I) the gracious words of my lord; nor
" reject an heart that is devoted to thee."—

" Defift, Achmet, (faid the monarch ftern-
" ly) my hafty vow is faved; and the hand of
" Zelide to be obtained only on the terms pro-
" pofed before."—Awed at thefe words, I re-
" tired in dejection equal to the height of my
" late fhort-lived hopes; and from that day has
" my heart been a prey to defpair.

" The affiftance which I now require from
" you is this: In pious gratitude to Heaven,
" for her efcape from bondage, Zelide has ob-
" tained permiffion from her father to relieve
" the captives of the war. For this purpofe
" they are ordered to repair to a certain place
" before her pavilion, where fhe fees them
" through the filken curtains of her tent, and
" frequently converfes with fuch as have any
" thing particular in their appearance to ex-
" cite her curiofity. Thither you fhall go;
" and I promife myfelf that you will plead my
" caufe with fuccefs, if it fo happens that fhe
" enters into converfation with you."

" Had the chief attended to the effect which
his ftory had upon fir Archibald, he would not
have been fo ready to fend him as his advocate.
Every circumftance convinced him that the
princefs was the object of his own love, whom
he had defpaired of difcovering, and filled him
with emotions which he could not fupprefs.

Re-

Recovering himfelf, however, time enough to efcape the obfervation of Achmet, whofe mind was too intent upon his own ftory to give much heed to any thing elfe. "It is my duty, "(faid he) to obey thy commands; and diffi- "dent though I am of the abilities which your "partiality beftows upon me, I am yet ready "to undertake any thing which you think can "conduce to your happinefs."

"Achmet again embraced him, and inform- ing him at what time and where he fhould wait upon Zelide next morning, left him, while he went himfelf to attend his fovereign, in the courfe of his duty.

"No fooner was fir Archibald alone than he began to reflect on the commiffion which he had undertaken, and the diftreffing fituation he was in. In the firft emotions of his high fpirit he blamed himfelf for not having avowed his paffion, and afferted his prior claim; but a con- fideration of his unhappy ftate immediately checked this rafh thought, and the defire of meeting the dear object of his love at any rate determined him to go, and truft the event to fate. "What fhall I do? (faid he) Shall I "plead for the love of Achmet and deftroy my "own hopes? Or fhall I betray his confidence, "and fpeak only for myfelf?" Then paufing a while, "I will do neither; (he continued) "if nature forbids the former, honour equally "oppofes the latter. Never fhall it be faid "that fir Archibald broke faith with man. I "will reprefent his love with fidelity; I will "declare my own with honeft truth, and leave "the decifion to herfelf."——Pleafed with this determination, his heart grew lighter; and the thought of meeting Zelide filled him with joy, to which he had been long a stranger.

## CHAP. XVI.

*Continuation of the history of* Sir ARCHIBALD *and* ZELIDE, *princess of* Armenia.

"HAVING received his last instructions from Achmet, sir Archibald went at the appointed hour next morning to the royal pavilion. Though he was habited in the humble weeds of a slave, there was something in his appearance that spoke his noble birth, and prejudiced every heart in his favour. His stature was above the common size of men, his limbs turned in the exactest symmetry of strength and beauty. His auburn locks flowed in ringlets to the middle of his back, and his dark-blue eyes sparkled with sensibility and manly spirit; while a gloom of melancholy, suited to his present station, softened their fire, and threw a pallid veil over the ruddy bloom which youth had painted on his cheeks.

"He had not stood long, with his eyes fixed on the ground, and his heart throbbing with the most anxious emotions, when an eunuch came to distribute the relief which the princess sent to the captives, ordering such of them as she had pointed out to him to advance to the side of her tent, that she might enquire into the nature of their particular distresses.

"The

" The ftate of fir Archibald's heart, when
the eunuch paffed him by unnoticed, may be
eafily conceived. All his high hopes funk at
once. " She knows me not! (faid he to him-
" felf) or fhe fcorns to know me! Miftaken
" Achmet! to think that I could have any in-
" fluence upon her."

" He continued thefe melancholy reflections
while the princefs was examining fome of the
other captives, and was departing with them,
when the eunuch beckoned to him to advance
to the tent. His emotions now were ftronger
than he could bear. He fcarce had power to
obey the fummons. As foon as he approached
the curtain, " Chriftian, (faid a voice from be-
" hind it) how long haft thou been a captive,
" and to whom?"

" Moft gracious princefs, (anfwered he trem-
" bling and in agitation, that almoft deprived
" him of utterance) for fo I am inftructed to
" addrefs you, I loft my liberty in the late bat-
" tle that proved fo fatal to the unhappy Lewis;
" and my poor fervices belong to the illuftrious
" Achmet."

" To Achmet! (replied fhe) Great honour
" muft he have acquired by the conqueft; and
" fhould he treat fuch a captive as thou appeareft
" to be with uncommon courtefy!"

" The honour of Achmet (returned he) wants
" not fo mean an addition. Thy flave was the
" captive of an hoft. As for my treatment, it
" is that of a man. An heart that is foftened
" with love, like Achmet's, cannot want the
" gentleft virtues of humanity."

" Thou fpeakeft of that paffion (faid the
" princefs) with a voice of fympathy. I fup-

" pofe

" pose thy own heart is not free from it, and
" that the loss of thy liberty is imbittered by
" that of a wife, or mistress in thy native land."

" Thy slave is not married, most gracious
" princess, (answered he) nor had my heart
" felt the power of love before I saw these fatal
" plains."

" Then it should seem (continued she) that
" some of our beauties have subdued you to him.
" How long have you born his yoke, and who
" has bent your stubborn neck to it?

" The captivity of my heart, O sovereign la-
" dy, (answered he) is scarce three moons old;
" but the particular severity of it has made that
" time an age. To cut off every hope, the very
" name of the person whose chains I wear is
" hidden from me in impenetrable darkness."

" That's hard, indeed; (said she) but true
" fortitude is above despair. Perhaps you may
" find her yet. Come just at the close of eve-
" ning to this place, and you will meet a per-
" son who will inform you of strange things;
" but mention not a word of this to Achmet.
" Adieu! Be discreet, be resolute, and be hap-
" py."

" The surprize with which this conversation
struck sir Archibald was so great, that he more
than once questioned himself whether he must
not be only an illusive dream. Satisfied, however, at length, that it was real, he retired to
his own quarter, among the attendants of Achmet, till his emotions should subside, and he
could recollect himself sufficiently to appear before him without danger of discovering what
had happened. He threw himself in a corner
of the tent, and covering himself with a carpet

2                                    that

that he might not be difturbed, lay motionlefs
and loft in thought. He had not lain long when
two of the domeftic flaves of Achmet, natives
of Greece, came into the tent, and not perceiving that any perfon was prefent, entered into a
converfation upon murdering their lord, and
flying into their own country with the booty
which they fhould be able to plunder in the
confufion caufed by his death. After confidering upon feveral methods, they at length agree-
ed to poifon him in a bowl of fherbet, which
one of them, who was his cup-bearer, undertook
to give him that very evening, while the other
fhould pack up all his gold and rich jewels
which were in his care, ready for them to carry
off. Having thus concerted the fcheme, they
immediately went to prepare for the execution
of it.

" The firft mention of this horrid defign
awoke all the attention of fir Archibald. He
liftened to their difcourfe, without giving them
any alarm; and as foon as they departed gave
thanks to Heaven for directing him to that
place fo opportunely, to fave the life of his
preferver, and fo return the obligation he owed
him; arifing, therefore, he went to the tent of
Achmet, who entered juft at the fame time.

" The moment the chief caft his eyes upon
fir Archibald he called him to him, and waving
his hand to his attendants to withdraw, " Se-
" lim, (faid he, his eyes gliftening with rap-
" ture) congratulate your happy lord. My
" gracious fovereign has this day bleffed my
" hopes with a promife of the hand of Zelide;
" and, as if Heaven meant to endear you ftill
" farther to me, has made the refcuing of the

" royal.

" royal ſtandard from your hand the glorious
" cauſe of giving me the preference to all my
" competitors. Have you been with the prin-
" ceſs? Have you mentioned my love to her?
" The only delay to my happineſs now is, to
" obtain her conſent. O bleſs me therefore by
" ſaying that ſhe liſtens to my love."

" I have mentioned it to her, (anſwered ſir
" Archibald, who had need for all his preſence
" of mind on ſuch a trying occaſion) in the
" moſt affecting manner; but it is too ſoon to
" expect the ſatisfaction you deſire. Much
" time and many words are requiſite to warm
" a virgin's heart."

" For this you ſhall have ample opportunity,
" (replied Achmet) to-morrow I will ſend you
" with a preſent to her; and every morning it
" ſhall be your pleaſing taſk to carry her the
" tribute of my love."

" The confidence with which Achmet ſaid
this was a pain to the honeſt heart of ſir Archibald, as he knew he muſt neceſſarily diſappoint
it. To change therefore to a topic more pleaſing to him, " You ſaved my life, (ſaid he) and
" now Heaven ſhews its approbation of that
" generous action, by making me the means of
" ſaving yours."—— " He then informed him
of the conſpiracy he had juſt diſcovered in ſo
providential a manner, and gave him advice
how to detect it in the very moment of execution, to make the puniſhment of the wretches
more ſignal.

" The ſoul of Achmet was ſtruck with terror at this account. The near hopes of happineſs which poſſeſſed him at this time armed
every thing that might defeat them with double
terrors.

terrors. He embraced fir Archibald in a tranfport, and refigned himfelf entirely to his direction, his own mind being in too great agitation to attend to any thing.

"As the time for executing their flagitious
defign was juft arrived, Achmet went to take
his evening's repaft, and feating himfelf on the
carpet, without any appearance of fufpicion,
called for fome cooling beverage, to flack his
thirft. The cup-bearer, who had every thing
prepared, prefented him the bowl, when fir
Archibald, who watched his looks, and plainly
perceived the anxiety of guilt in his face, made
a fignal agreed upon to Achmet, and then went
into the inner tent, where he found the other
loading himfelf with the gold and jewels of his
lord. Dragging him forth, therefore, with this
indifputable evidence of his guilt upon him, as
foon as he came into the prefence of Achmet,
he feized the cup-bearer alfo, who ftood panting with impatience to fee his lord drink the
fatal mixture, which he yet held untafted in his
hand.

"The accomplices no fooner faw each other
apprehended in this manner, than they funk
into the defpondency of confcious guilt, and
waited, pale and trembling, for the fate which
hung over them. "Mifcreants, (faid Achmet,
"rifing from his feat in a rage) what could
'prompt you to this wickednefs? Speak! De-
'clare this moment at whofe inftigation you
"made the bafe attempt; or torture fhall
"wring the fecret from your burfting hearts."

"The wretches were unable to make any
reply, when fir Archibald interfering, "Migh-
"ty Lord, (faid he) the nature of their crime
"fhews

" ſhews it was all their own; and points out
" the puniſhment proper for them. Let them
" drink the poiſon they had prepared for you,
" and periſh by their own device. Baſe as they
" are, remember they are men; nor tempt them
" to aggravate the guilt with which their mi-
" ſerable ſouls are loaded by accuſing the in-
" nocent."

" Be it ſo, (anſwered the chief) their fate
" is in your hands."

" Sir Archibald upon this took the bowl, and
dividing the horrid contents, gave it to the
trembling wretches, whoſe lives, torn from them
by the moſt dreadful torments, ſoon paid the
price of their guilt. Achmet then, embracing
his deliverer once more, retired to try if he
could calm the agitations of his ſoul by reſt."

## C H A P. XVII.

*The hiſtory of Sir* ARCHIBALD *and* ZELIDE,
*princeſs of* Armenia, *concluded.*

" THE time when the princeſs had ordered the attendance of ſir Archibald was
now arrived; he therefore haſted to the appointed place, where he had not waited long
when an eunuch coming up and beckoning to
him ſaid, " Be diſcreet, be reſolute, and be
" happy."

" Sir Archibald, who well remembered theſe
words, followed him, without heſitation or reply, into the royal pavilion, where he was led
through

through several sumptuous tents, one within another, till his guide, stopping and making a signal to him to wait there, left him. He waited not long, when a female covered with a veil entered, and seating herself on a sofa, "Christian, (said she, in a low voice, and beckoning to him to come near her) "the damsel whom you re-
"scued from the ravisher in the cave, desires
"you should know that she retains a grateful
"sense of your courtesy and virtue."

"Gentle lady, (said he, in a voice of rapture)
"accept the warmest thanks of your servant for
"this benign condescension; and O! compleat
"the favour, by telling her, that her devoted
"slave lives only in the hope of seeing her
"again, and pouring out the fullness of his
"heart before her."

"Her heart (answered she) perhaps is not less
"full than yours; but before she can comply
"with what you desire, it is proper she should
"know who you are, and what your rank was
"in your native land."

"My rank, (replied he, with a sigh) most
"courteous lady, was noble, scarcely inferior
"to royalty; the honour of my ancient house
"unstained."

"Say then, (returned she) if she whom you
"profess to love should stoop from royalty it-
"self to listen to your suit, what you would do
"to merit such a favour? Would you forego
"your country, renounce the worship of your
"ancestors, and happy in the recompence of her
"love, and of the state to which she would raise
"you, swear you never would think of either?"

"Sir Archibald was struck with such horror at this proposal, that it was some time before

he was able to make any reply. At length, as if awaking from a dream, "Support me, Hea-
"ven! (exclaimed he with a figh that feemed
"to burft his heart) Support me! and pro-
"portion the trials of your creature to his
"ftrength!"——

"Then turning to the female, "There is
"nothing, lady, (faid he) within the power of
"man to do, or fuffer, which I fhould not at-
"tempt with joy for fuch an ineftimable re-
"compence; nothing which did not clafh with
"honour or virtue. But what you propofe
"would overturn both; and fhould I be
"tempted to comply, I were unworthy of a
"reward fo bafely earned."

"Is this your anfwer? (replied fhe with an
"accen of indignation) Can you pretend to
"feel the power of love, and yet to flight its
"object for the idle fictions of fuperftitious
"priefts? Can you mention honour, and pre-
"fer fubjection to royalty? Think better; nor
"blaft your ripening hopes with fuch a mean
"ungrateful choice. Search your heart well,
"your fate depends upon the word you fpeak;
"for, never more will you be afked the quef-
"tion."

"Burft then, O wretched heart! (fighed he)
"and put a period to your torture. To live
"without my love is impoffible; and Heaven
"itfelf forbids the terms on which alone I can
"obtain her. Tell her, kind lady, that, dear-
"ly as my heart adores her beauties, a prin-
"ciple higher even than love, and ftronger than
"ambition, places an infuperable bar between
"us. But O, fay at the fame time, that the
"word which thus gives up my hopes, gives up
"my

" my hated life also. I muſt not have her, and
" I cannot live without her."

" Virtuous Chriſtian, (ſaid ſhe, lifting up
" her veil, and diſcovering her beauties to his
" raviſhed ſight) thou proveſt thyſelf worthy of
" the beſt bleſſings of Heaven by this thy no-
" ble attachment to its laws. Behold the object
" of thy love, who glories in an equal flame: yet
" had thy heart wavered in the cauſe of virtue,
" I ſhould have diſdained the diſhonourable ſa-
" crifice, and quitted thee for ever. Reſtrain
" your raptures, and hear me for a moment.
" You know not yet whom your virtues have
" ſubdued, or what you muſt attempt to obtain
" her. I am Zelide, the only daughter of the
" monarch of Armenia. My anceſtors long
" gloried in the name of Chriſtians; but un-
" able to reſiſt the barbarous Saracens, accord-
" ing to the policy of the world, they renounced
" their faith, to preſerve their power.

" My father, miſtakenly attached to the re-
" ligion of Mahomet, in which he was thus
" bred, led his forces againſt the invaſion of
" Lewis; and, to excite the ardor of his gene-
" rals, declared, that he would beſtow me the
" heireſs of his throne, in marriage upon him
" who ſhould deſerve beſt in the war. The emu-
" lation which this raiſed was often fatally ex-
" perienced by their enemies; but ſtill their
" merits were ſo equal, that none could claim
" his promiſe until the laſt battle, when Ach-
" met's recovering the royal ſtandard from the
" enemy unhappily decided in his favour. Too
" ſoon I learned the unwelcome news; but ſtill
" by my intreaties prevailed upon my father to
" ſuſpend or at leaſt conceal his determination,
" till

" till this fatal day, when all his generals fol-
" liciting him together to put an end to their
" importunities, he declared his choice. What
" canft thou do to avert this misfortune? Canft
" thou by any means accomplifh our efcape to
" thy native land? Gold and jewels in abun-
" dance I can bring, to procure the means for
" our journey, and make our retirement happy.
" To thy honour I am bold to truft myfelf, nor
" afpire to a more exalted ftate than to be thy
" wife; for though I nave been obliged to
" profefs the religion of Mahomet, in my heart
" I am a Chriftian. My mother, who was a
" native of Circaffia, believed and inftructed
" me in that holy faith; to preferve which I
" promifed her, in her laft moments, to give
" up every thought of worldly grandeur. My
" foul is grieved to difobey, and leave my fa-
" ther; but a fuperior duty calls me."

" O beauteous princefs, (faid fir Archibald,
" proftrating himfelf at her feet) how fhall the
" labours of my life make a return for this hap-
" pinefs, this honour?"

" Reftrain your raptures, (replied the prin-
" cefs) our time is too precious for them
" now. Three days refpite only have I been
" able to obtain from my father; before they
" are expired we muft efcape from hence, or I
" am for ever loft. I leave the manner of
" our flight to you. In this cafket is fome
" gold. More, with the richeft of my jewels,
" will I bring with me to-morrow night, as
" foon as darknefs fhall favour our defign, to
" the hermit's cell on the fide of the hill, weft-
" ward of the camp. There let me meet thee
" with all the neceffary means for our flight.
" One

" One only companion shall I bring with me.
" Adieu."—Saying this, the princess departed,
and the eunuch entered and conducted sir Archibald back through the royal pavilion to the
place where he had first met him, who immediately returned to the quarters of Achmet.

" He laid himself down, as if to rest; but
spent the remainder of the night in forming
schemes for his intended flight; but the difficulties which attended all he could devise drove
him almost to despair. At length he resolved
upon one that appeared least liable to disappointment. As soon as Achmet arose he went
to him, and accosting him with an air of perplexity and distress, " I come (said he) a sup-
" pliant to thy compassion, O generous and
" princely Achmet. If ever thy servant has
" found favour in thy sight, listen to the
" request of my heart. I was troubled on my
" bed this night, and my soul was terrified by
" visions. The object of my love, whose
" image is never absent from my mind, ap-
" peared before me in agonies of grief. " Fly
" (said she) to my rescue! My father, deaf to
" my intreaties, and regardless of my distress,
" prepares to give my hand to another. O fly
" and save me! Save us both from ruin and de-
" spair."——I awoke in dismay, and in the an-
" guish of my soul am come to thee. Permit
" me, assist me to go to my native land;
" and, on the faith of a true knight, I will send
" you the ransom which you shall require."

" I require not a ransom for the liberty of
" my preserver, (answered Achmet) and wil-
" lingly consent to your return as soon as my
" nuptials with the princess shall have confirm-

" ed

" ed my happineſs. You muſt not leave me till
" you have ſeen and ſhared in my joy."

" O name not happineſs or joy (replied ſir
" Archibald) before a wretch ſinking in deſpair ;
" the ſight of my miſery would damp your joys.
" By all your fondeſt hopes I conjure you there-
" fore, not to delay me a moment. Let me
" be gone this very night ; for ſomething warns
" my ſoul never to cloſe my eyes, till I have
" ſet out on this important journey."

" Far be it from me (ſaid Achmet, moved at
" the poignancy of his diſtreſs) to oppoſe the
" intimations of thy better genius. Go in
" peace; and may thy journey be ſucceſsful. If
" aught in my power can contribute to it, de-
" mand my help with freedom."

" O·generous prince, (anſwered the knight)
" thy goodneſs overwhelms my ſoul, and
" makes my parting from thee, even on ſo
" dear an occaſion, painful. If thou wilt give
" the impreſſion of thy ſignet, I will ſet out
" with two, the poor remains of all my faithful
" followers, whom I this day have found among
" the captives, as ſent by thee on ſome impor-
" tant buſineſs ; and truſt the conduct of my
" ſteps to Heaven."——To this propoſal Achmet not only agreed, but alſo gave him ſome
gold, to make proviſion for his journey, and
then diſmiſſed him with a tender embrace.

" Sir Archibald ſpent the reſt of the day in
procuring ſwift and able horſes, with every
other convenience requiſite for his journey; and
at the appointed hour repaired to the hermit's
cell, where the princeſs ſoon after arrived, diſguiſed in the habit of a man, and attended by
one of her moſt favourite maidens in the ſame
dreſs. The illuſtrious fugitives ſet out directly,

paffing all the guards by virtue of the fignet of Achmet,·and made fuch expedition, travelling through private and unfrequented ways, that by the dawn of morning they thought themfelves fafe from danger of purfuit. As foon as it was light, they ftopped by the fide of a ftream that ran through a thick wood, where they refrefhed themfelves, and their horfes, and refted till the clofe of the day, fir Archibald watching while his princefs flept.

" In this manner they continued their journey under the immediate protection of Heaven, till they arrived at Conftantinople, chufing the road leaft liable to fufpicion, to baffle purfuit; there they directly embarked on board a French fhip, which landed them at Marfeilles, from whence they journeyed by land to Rochelle, and there hired a fhip that carried them fafe to Scotland.

" The joy raifed by the arrival of fir Archibald was not confined to his father's houfe. The whole kingdom, which had fhared in his glory, fhared in it. His aged father,· who feemed to have lived only to refign his honours to his worthy heir, was unable to fupport the emotions of his rapture, and expired in his embraces, after having beftowed his benediction on his fon, and the fair partner of his efcape, to whom earl Archibald was joined in the holy bonds of wedlock, as foon as he had performed the laft duties to the honoured remains of his father ; for her delicacy had not fuffered her to think of marriage, till fhe was arrived at the end of her travels.

" Prudence and modefty fuggefted it to this illuftrious pair to conceal the countefs's high

5

descent, that they might avoid the vain parade of ceremony, and enjoy their lives in retirement, in which earl Archibald's high sense of honour, in concealing his name and country, when a captive, secured them from discovery.

" The only cloud that seemed to over-cast their joy, arose from the pious concern of the countess to hear some account of her father. To procure this, the earl sent one of his faithful men, who had accompanied him in his escape, who undertook not only to gain his lady tidings of him, but also, by some means or other, to lighten his sorrow, by letting him know that she was happy. He set out in the dress of a pilgrim, and performed his journey with success, bringing her word, that, struck with her flight, which he looked upon as a punishment from heaven for his professing the religion of Mahomet, against the admonitions of his conscience, which was secretly inclined to the christian faith, he had resigned his crown to Achmet, and devoted the remainder of his days to Heaven, in a monastry.

" This account compleated the happiness of the countess, who blessed the wise dispensations of providence, which had thus made her the cause of her father's conversion. The earl designed never to have quitted his sweet retirement; but the stronger attachment of loyalty once more called him forth into the busy world. His sovereign dying suddenly, and leaving an infant heir, several of the nobles, stirred up by impious ambition, strove to get the royal infant into their hands that they might murder him, and so usurp his throne; but the vigilance of

his

his mother prevented their defigns, and conveyed him fecretly into France.

" Arouzed by the diftrefs of his fovereign and his country, which was now a prey to all the miferies of anarchy, earl Archibald arofe, and by his valour and prudent conduct foon reftored peace. The people, in gratitude for this fervice, with one voice offered him the crown; but he refufed it with noble difdain, and obliging them to fwear allegiance to their rightful prince, recalled and placed him on the throne of his anceftors.

## CHAP. XVIII.

*Anecdotes of a loyal family concluded. Several inftances of uncommon loyalty rewarded in the common manner, with fome reflections interefting to thofe whom they may concern.*

" THE defcendants of earl Archibald followed his fteps in the paths of honour and virtue. In the days of the unfortunate MARY, whofe fufferings ended not even with her life, her fame being ftill maligned to extenuate the injuftice of her fate, the noble earl, head of our houfe, ftood firm in the caufe of injured majefty, facrificing the greater part of his ample poffeffions, to fupport his royal miftrefs.

" When JAMES fucceeded to the rights which had proved fo fatal to his mother, thofe fervices were all forgotten, and his favours lavifhed vished on a set of upstart hungry parasites : but not discouraged by this ingratitude, when his ill-fated son wanted the assistance of his loyal subjects, in the impious contest between the ENGLISH and their sovereign, which cost him his sacred life, again our house stood forth, a noble pattern of unshaken loyalty, and were the greatest sufferers in his cause.

"At the restoration of the monarchy, they met the same reward as they had before from the grand-sire of CHARLES; nor reaped any other benefit from that happy event, than the gratification of the loyalty, which was the ruling principle of their lives.

"Gold is purified by fiery trials. This only made their virtues shine with brighter lustre. They shewed the same attachment to the son as they had to his father; and disdaining to submit to power which they looked upon as unnaturally usurped, followed misguided JAMES, when he abandoned his throne, into a foreign land, exerting their loyalty in service to his person, till Heaven should point out a propitious moment for accomplishing their hopes of recovering for him at least the ancient crown of his ancestors; a crown which they wore with distinguished glory, till Heaven in its wrath joined another to it, greater indeed in wealth and power, but not of greater honour.

"Since that fatal period our glory has shone with diminished splendor; and we have been looked down upon as dependants, by those who dreaded us before as rivals; and at length, to compleat the ruin of our wretched country, some of her degenerate sons, seduced by bribery and vain hopes of power, sealed their own
                                        infamy,

infamy, and her difgrace, by formally renoun-
cing every fhadow of royalty, and giving up
the very ftyle and title of a kingdom which had
flourifhed, for a long fucceffion of ages, before that to which they bafely thus betrayed its
rights had even gained a name.

"The venal and inconftant Englifh, a
mingled race, made up of every people under
heaven, and thofe whom their example had debauched, may practife and applaud fuch corruption; but Scotland's true-born honeft fons
will ever watch occafion to fhake off the fhameful yoke, and reftore the honour of their country by reftoring to its throne a race of kings
defcended from themfelves.

"Educated in thefe principles, though under the power which I abhorred, it was natural for me to feize the firft opportunity of drawing my fword in the caufe of my rightful fovereign. I joined in the attempt made by his
fon, and was a fharer in his unparalleled fufferings.

"I had been too active in his intereft to
efcape unnoticed. This precluded every
thought of living in my own country, even if I
could ftoop to diffemble my principles, and fubmit to the prevailing powers. The honour of my
anceftors was now the only inheritance which
I derived from them. In the difficulties therefore which fuch a fituation was fubject to, my
natural recourfe was to the profeffion of arms,
the only profeffion which would not be a difgrace to my blood, unftained from endlefs ages
by the mean arts of induftry: and whom
fhould I offer my fword but to the prince

to whom my royal mafter had himfelf fled in
his diftrefs; and who, I flatter myfelf, has had
no reafon to repent of the afylum he afforded
me; for though my actions have not been yet
rewarded by fortune, my name is not unknown
to fame?

"This honeft reprefentation will to every
candid mind remove the prejudices fo injurioufly entertained againft me, and all in my unhappy circumftances. We come not as preferring another country to our own, or ftriving
to fupplant the natives in the favours of fortune. Neceffity, irrefiftible neceffity, urges our
reluctant fteps; and we are received and rewarded accordingly, not with the refpect of
welcome guefts, the liberality and honours due
to merit. The coldnefs of charity frowns upon our approach, and all our fervices are
thought to be overpaid by a bare fubfiftence.
Indeed, fuch are the fentiments which this un-
deferved treatment infpires, that, did not the
fhort-fighted policy of our native country bar
our return by injunctions infignificant to them,
and impoffible to be complied with by us, the
ardour of our loyalty would be damped, and
many of us gladly go home and live in peace;
by which means, if we did not actually become
their beft fubjects, we fhould at leaft rid them
of their moft dangerous enemies."

The appearance of the morning here put an
end to his difcourfe, which his companion
heard without interruption, though with vifi-
ble indifference, and affented to in the politeft
manner. When they were relieved they retired to their refpective tents with equal expedition, though on different occafions; the
former

former to replenish his snuff-box, which he had emptied in the earnestness of his conversation, and the other to wash his neck-cloth and ruffles, and powder his hair, that he might make a proper appearance when he waited upon his general.

✳✳✳✳✳✳✳✳✳✳✳✳✳✳✳✳✳✳✳✳✳

## C H A P.  XIX.

*The difference between fighting battles in the field, and in the cabinet. The happiness of having good friends, with further instances of military equity.*

AS the late miscarriage had made a considerable alteration in the situation of affairs, it was necessary to send notice of it to all the parties engaged in the same cause, that they might regulate their measures accordingly. Nothing could draw a stronger picture of human vanity, than the terms in which this account was given. Instead of owning with candour that they had been severely repulsed, and in danger of an absolute defeat, they only said, " that the enemy having escaped by accident " from an attack by which they designed to " have gained a decisive victory, they had " thought proper to make some alterations in " the plan of their operations for the rest of the " campaign."

But this vain evasion was instantly seen through; the steps they were obliged to take, in consequence of a disappointment which they affected to treat so lightly, shewed that it was a

G 2                    matter

matter of the most serious nature, and had effectually broke through all their measures for that campaign, on the success of which they had built such sanguine hopes, and exerted their utmost efforts to promote it.

As there was nothing more to be seen here, I took the opportunity of accompanying a courier who was sent on this occasion to another of the armies, confederate in the same cause, the general of which had acquired such reputation by his conduct, that I expected to find the art of war reduced by him to a regular science, and carried on in a manner worthy of a rational being: how well my expectations were answered, the event will shew.

I found him in his tent, reading over some orders which he had just received from his court. When he had finished them, "What " trouble have I (said he to himself) to keep " these people from ruining themselves ? A wo- " man has the vapours, and therefore I must fight " a battle to raise her spirits with the news of " a victory. A minister wants to display his " talents, and I must take a town, that he " may draw up the articles of capitulation; " and yet the least miscarriage in the execution " of their orders, however ill-timed or absurd, " will be laid entirely to my charge. This " is the happiness of serving under people who " know nothing of the matter; who direct the " operations of a campaign in their closets, " draw up armies upon paper, make marches, " and form sieges with their fingers in the " wine spilled on the table; and fight battles, " and beat their enemies as they get drunk. " But I am not to be moved by their humours.
" I

" I have preferved them hitherto in fpight of
" themfelves, by adhering fteadily to my own
" op'nion; and I will continue to do. fo, or
" refign the command, and leave them to
" their fate."——— Saying this, he gave orders to double all the fortifications of his camp,
and then returned a fummary anfwer to the minifter, that the fituation of affairs at that time
made it impoffible for him to obey his directions.

Such cautious conduct in an army, whofe
ftrength feemed almoft to make all caution unneceffary, appeared very extraordinary; but a
little obfervation explained the reafon of it. In
the mean time other occurrences, new to me,
and ftrange in fpeculation, though common in
the military practice, attracted my attention.

As the general went to take a view of his
entrenchments, that he might fee where it was
moft proper to add to their ftrength, according
to his own fyftem, he was met by a deputa-
tion from the inhabitants of the country, on a
moft interefting occafion. Though he was determined not to take the leaft notice of any
thing they could fay, he thought proper to give
them an hearing, to fave appearances.

The perfon who fpoke to him, in the name of
the reft, addreffing him with an air of refpect,
mixed with indignation, " I am fent to your
" excellency (faid he) by the few remaining
" inhabitants of this wretched country, to im-
" plore your commiferation of their diftreffed
" ftate. The misfortunes, impoffible to be
" avoided in the feat of a war, have long fince
" confumed their ftrength, and exhaufted all
" their regular refources. The contributions

de-

" demanded by your excellency yesterday, ex-
" ceed their utmost power. The indispensible
" means of subsistence is all that is left them;
" to take the smallest portion from which must
" make life a curse, and aggravate their mise-
" ries to despair. Your sovereign and our's
" are confederates in this war, the cause of
" which was originally your's; and so must
" the advantage be in the end. We expect
" nothing. Why then must the weight of it
" be laid entirely upon us? If you come for
" our protection, Why do you not drive our
" enemies away? If that is not to be done,
" Why not march into their territories, and
" remove to them a burthen which we can no
" longer bear? It were better for us to sup-
" port but one army, even though that were
" of enemies, than two. The number of our
" very friends has eaten us up. We throw
" ourselves therefore upon your excellency's
" justice and compassion, and beg an allevia-
" tion of distresses, which we are unable to
" sustain. Represent our case in its proper co-
" lours to your sovereign; and, in the mean
" time, suspend the execution of orders which
" overwhelm us with despair."

The general heard this pathetic speech without the least emotion; and as soon as it was
concluded, " I am sorry for your sufferings;
" (answered he coldly) but the redress of them
" lies not in my power. You must apply to
" the ministry. If they supply me with other
" means to support the war, I shall be glad;
" till then I must make use of those in my
" hands."——Then turning directly to an officer who stood near him, he ordered the contributions

tributions to be levied, without favour or delay.

The unsuccessful advocates had scarce departed when an express arrived from one of his advanced posts, to inform him that the enemy had laid all that side of the country in flames, and were just then making some motions which appeared as if they intended to attack him in his entrenchments. His officers heard this account with the highest indignation; and, confiding in their numbers, expressed their eagerness to prevent such an insult, by marching out directly to meet them.

But the general disregarded their ardour, and firmly resolved to pursue his own system; " The enemy should know me too well, (said " he) to imagine that I can be taken with " such a bait! When there is nothing more " to burn, the flames will go out of them- " selves. All their braving shall not make me " quit the advantage of my situation. The " event of battles is uncertain, and often " proves contrary to the best founded expec- " tation. Beside, their affairs and ours are in " a very different state. A victory might ac- " complish all their designs, which are disap- " pointed as effectually by delay as by a defeat; " it is therefore right in them to risk every " thing. But the contrary is our case; we " might lose every thing by a defeat; and do " gain as much by delay, as we could by vic- " tory; so that to put any thing to the hazard " were madness. As to the disgrace to our " honour, in being braved thus, that is nothing. " Success alone is honour in war. I am sor- " ry, it is true, for the ruin of the country;

G 4 " but

" but I have other bufinefs here befide prefer-
" ving that, and which I muft firft attend to ;
" and I fhall think myfelf happy if I can ac-
" complifh it at fo eafy a rate as the ruin of a
" country that does not belong to us."——
Saying this, he continued his ride, abfolutely
unmoved at the fight of the flames which arofe
from all the villages in that particular part of
the country from whence he had drawn his fubfiftence, while there was any remaining for
him.

There was fomething fo deliberately cruel in
protracting the miferies of the innocent in this
manner, in order to wear out an enemy whom
he was evidently afraid to face in the field, that
however confonant it might be to the principles of military equity, and however juft his
maxim, that " Succefs alone is honour in
" war," I turned away from the fight with abhorrence.

✻✻✻✻✻✻✻✻✻✻✻✻✻✻✻✻✻✻✻✻✻

## CHAP. XX.

*War! War in procinct! The comforts of Great-
nefs. A night-fcene, with a continuation of it,
neither of the moft agreeable nature.*

THOUGH my heart was by this time fick
of war, curiofity ftill had force to make
me take a view of the army oppofed to this
the character of whofe commander promifed
fome variety, and more active fcenes at leaft,
if not more rational and humane than thofe I
had

ıad hitherto feen. "It is not poffible (thought
" I ) that the military fcience, which has been
" fo highly extolled by men of the greateft ge-
" nius in every age and country, and made the
" feal of fame, the indifputed title to every ad-
" vantage of this world, fhould be fuch a con-
" fufed medley of blunders and butchery, car-
" ried on headlong, without regard to the moft
" indifpenfible principles of juftice or humani-
" ty, or attention to any rational or determin-
" ed point, befide avarice, or a favage paffion
" for revenge. The generals who make fo
" grand a figure in the writings of poets, and
" hiftorians, could not have been like thefe;
" nor the battles, by which they acquired their
" immortal glory, fuch fruitlefs random fcenes
" of blind, and worfe than brutal carnage! I
" have been often cautioned againft forming
" my judgment too haftily."

Having confirmed myfelf in my refolution by
thefe reflections, I was fo defirous to put it in
execution, that I would not even ftay to travel
with any other perfon, as I had done before;
but availing myfelf of the powers with which
the fpirit had endowed me, I *wifhed* myfelf
directly into the enemy's camp.

The firft things that ftruck me here were
the eagernefs and affiduity of every individual,
fo different from the liftlefs ftupidity and care-
lefsnefs which had given me fuch difguft in the
other armies. The foldiers feemed by their
looks to underftand the motives of the war in
which they were engaged, and to think themfelves interefted in the event. Such a fight
gave me pleafure. " This (thought I) is fome-
" thing worth beholding! Thefe act like men;

" by

" by exerting that reason which diftinguifhes
" them from brutes; and that caufe muft be
" juft which fo many approve of, and fupport
" with their lives."

As I was making thefe reflections, the commander (whom I found to be their fovereign)
paffed me, and by his affability and encouraging addrefs added wings to the diligence with
which they all ftrove to execute his commands.
I joined him directly, ftudious to obferve every look and action of fo extraordinary a perfon.

. He was that morning making a general review of his army, which was drawn out for
that purpofe. Though every thing was ftrict-
ly regular, and bore the moft martial appearance, I remarked that the monarch frequently
fighed as he darted his experienced eye along
the ranks. He feemed to look for fomething
which he could not find, and melted almoft
into tears at the tender youth of the greater part
of his troops.

But if the private men appeared young and
unexperienced, the officers of every degree
wore the oppofite characters in their counte-
nances. Birth, riches, or favour, evidently
had no place in their promotion. They rofe
by merit alone, and the foldier who 'eferved
command was fure of obtaining it. This was
the moft effectual provifion which human prudence could make to enfure fuccefs; nor did
the event difappoint it. If the inferiority of
his numbers hindered his obtaining decifive
victories, the excellent difcipline of his forces
fo far ballanced that advantage, that h's enemies
could not prevail againft him.

When

When he had finished the business of the morning, he retired to his tent, and throwing himself, with a fatigued look and discontented air, into a chair, " When will this horrid " work be at an end ? (said he) When shall " my wearied heart have rest ? O ambition, " thou madness of misguided man ! Thou " source of the worst evils which afflict his " wretched race ! To thee are sacrificed all " the tendernesses of humanity, all the most " sacred principles of social and moral virtue. " And for what ? To pursue an unessential " phantom, to grasp at a bubble that melts at " the touch, and illudes the empty hand ! For " such is the glory of this world, however " highly blazoned by prejudice and vanity ; the " echo of a sound that has passed by, the sha- " dow of a cloud that floats in the air."

He was interrupted in these reflections by the arrival of a courier, with dispatches from one of his ministers. The moment he ran his eye over them, that gloom of lassitude and discontent which overcast his brow vanished, his eye flashed with resentment and martial ardour, and his whole frame seemed to be on fire. He gave orders for all his generals to attend him directly, and then walking a turn or two about his tent, " No! (said he) it is not " come to that yet. Never will I submit to " such ignominious terms, while I have one " subject able to draw a sword. Never will I " tarnish the glory of so many victories by the " least concession. Is my fate to depend on " the caprice of a woman ? Are my domini- " ons to be parcelled out by dreaming states- " men ? Sooner shall the ravages of war con-

" sume

" fume them all, than I will yield to such dif-
" honour. I'll fight it out to the laft man, fet
" fire to the laft town with my own hand, and
" perifh in the flames, before my foul fhall
" bend to their defires, or comply with such
" difgraceful conditions."

The entrance of his officers broke off his meditations. He paufed a moment, to moderate
the emotions of his foul, and then addreffing
himfelf to them, " My friends, (faid he) our
" enemies infult us. They make propofals too
" haughty and fevere to be received even' from
" victors. But we will bring them to a more
" moderate way of thinking. I am refolved to
" make one effort, to put an end to this de-
" ftructive war. We will this night attack
" the enemy in fuch a quarter. Our wary ad-
" verfary will not run the hazard of fuccour-
" ing his colleague in the dark, for fear an at-
" tempt fhould be made upon his own camp
" in the mean while; fo that, for this time, the
" advantage of numbers will not be againft us.
" In other refpects, I know the difficulty of
" the undertaking; but difficulties never dif-
" courage a brave mind from great attempts.
" I am fick of the horrors of war, and will
" fee no more of them. We will either con-
" quer or die."

His generals heard thefe words with a melancholy, fierce delight. They all wifhed to
fee an end put to the calamities which laid their
country wafte; if that could not be accomplifhed, death appeared a defirable releafe from
the horrors with which they were furrounded.
As foon as they left their fovereign's prefence,
therefore, they embraced each other, as men
who

who expected not to meet again, and then went to prepare every thing for putting his commands in execution.

As for the monarch, the approach of such a scene seemed a relief to his mind, by diverting his attention from the reflections which tortured him before. Unentangled in the tender connexions of nature, which, as it were, multiply a man into many selfs for the safety of each dear particular of whom, his anxiety is greater than for his own, he looked forward to the dreadful hour unmoved; and, despising any danger which threatened himself, was not disturbed with sympathetic apprehensions for others.

At length the moment, loaded with the fate of so many thousands, arrived. The horrors of such a fight are beyond description; my soul still sickens at the thought. I have said that the attack was to be made in the night. Nature, as if to hide the madness of mankind, wrapped the guilty scene in tenfold darkness. This was favourable to the assailants. Inspired with the resolution of their sovereign, they knew that their road to victory was right forwards, and rushed on with an impetuosity impossible to be resisted; while their opponents, attacked on every side, knew not where to direct their force. But neither did they know whither to retreat. If distraction therefore made their efforts less effectual, despair supported their resolution. They fought at random, and destroyed their friends as well as their enemies: but still they fought with valour, heightened by despair. At length their entrenchments were all forced, and they were

driven,

driven, themselves scarce knew whither. The darkness, which before was against them, proved now their security. Pursuit was impossible. The advantage also had already cost the victors so dear, that they were cautious, as the least miscarriage might reverse the success.

The heart of man must be seared against every feeling of humanity, to support such a sight as the morning-light disclosed. The victorious monarch, animated with all his martial enthusiasm, was unable to bear it. He led his men, harrassed as they were, in pursuit of the enemy, though he expected not to overtake them; but then it removed him from this horrid scene.

As soon as his spirits had cooled a little from the ardour, or rather madness, necessary to support them through their late exertion, he sought to relieve nature by rest. But the labours of his mind were far from being at an end. Sleep had no sooner overpowered his weary senses, than his imagination was at work, and placed him in the midst of the tumults and confusion from which he was but just delivered. He gave aloud the several words of command, and fought over again the whole battle of the night before, with as much eagerness and anxiety as if he was actually engaged, till at length the hurry of his spirits and agitation of his whole frame awoke him, little refreshed by such broken slumbers. Such a life could not afford pleasure in the contemplation. I was just turning from him, surfeited with *heroism* and *greatness*, when an affair that shewed his character in a new light attracted my attention.

CHAP

✿✿✿✿✿✿✿✿✿✿✿ ✿✿✿✿✿✿✿✿✿

## CHAP. XXI.

*An approved medicine for a sick mind. A curious*
*conversation between two great persons, with a*
*compendious method of acquiring fame.*

WHEN he arose from his thorny pillow,
he went to a trunk, and taking out a
book, " Learning (said he, sighing) has been
" called the medicine of the mind. Let me
" try if I can find it so. No mind ever wanted
" a medicine to heal its sickness, more than
" mine does at this moment."—Then reading
a page or two, " Aye, (continued he) these
" are fine schemes, if they could but be
" brought to bear. Any of them would en-
" sure the wished-for, envied epithet of *great*,
" without the fatigue of this horrid trade of
" war; though I much fear this too will dif-
" appoint me as that did, and that in the end
" I shall find I have consumed my life in build-
" ing castles in the air."

He then paused a moment, in a discontented
mood, and, throwing by the book, took up a
written paper, on which he had scarce cast his
eye when he seemed to have found the remedy
he wanted. A smile of self-complacency softened his brow, his eyes sparkled with pleasure,
and his heart throbbed with conscious pride, as
he read it over most emphatically to himself.
" Why did I not fix my hopes of fame, my
" claim to immortality, on these? (said he,
4                              " swelling

" fwelling into tenfold confequence as he
" fpoke) the mufes would not have difdained
" my addreffes; they would have crowned me
" with that glory which I fought for in vain in
" philofophy, and fear I purfue with no better
" profpect of fuccefs in war. But foft! Is not
" this the day on which that favourite of the
" mufes, *Crambo*, promifed to come and fhew
" me his laft work? Who knows but I may
" effect the fum of all my defigns by his affift-
" ance? Every other bufinefs muft give place
" to this. I would not mifs the pleafure of
" converfing with him, or run the hazard of
" any other's feeing his works before me, for
" many reafons."——— Saying this, he called
one of his attendants, and, fending fome general directions to his officers, gave orders that no
one fhould be admitted to him that morning
but a particular perfon, whom he defcribed.

He had not waited long, when the expected vifitor arrived, difguifed in fuch a manner
as muft effectually conceal him. The monarch received him with the greateft familiarity, and pointing to a chair near himfelf, "Sit
" down, my friend, (faid he) diftinction is un-
" neceffary among the mufes fons. You won-
" der, I doubt not, at my defiring you to
" come in that difguife; but the reafon was
" this : In my fituation every motion is ex-
" pofed to notice. When I have a mind,
" therefore, to fteal an hour from care, I am
" obliged to ufe fome artifice of this kind, to
" conceal my defign. I am now thought to
" be engaged on the moft weighty affairs;
" and your drefs, with the myfterious manner
" of your introduction, favours the deceit, and

" makes

" makes you pass for some secret emissary who
" has brought me intelligence. Were it known
" that I enjoy one hour of social converse,
" like another man, it would take off from my
" importance, and weaken that implicit respect
" which the nature of my affairs makes indis-
" pensible.  This is the blessing of pre-emi-
" nence : painful pre-eminence, eminent in
" woe.

" But let us quit so disagreeable a subject.
" Have you brought me the piece you men-
" tioned in your letter ?  I long to see it ; and
" hope you have not taken the least notice of
" it to any other person living.  Alexander
" was not more jealous of his tutor's publish-
" ing his knowledge for the instruction of the
" world, than I am of your communicating
" your works, even by the bare mention of their
" names, before I have had the first perusal of
" them.  Like him, I would engross the sole
" enjoyment."

" Your majesty does me the highest honour
" by this jealousy ; (answered the other) but I
" am afraid the object will be found unworthy,
" However, such as it is, I lay it at your
" feet."

——" But has no living person seen, nor
" even heard of it ?"

——" None, I can most truely assure your
" majesty.  I obeyed your commands with the
" greatest care.  Here it is.  The subject, I
" own, is trifling ; but I hope the execution
" will not displease you.  It is a short confu-
" tation of all the prejudices which have so
" long enslaved the human mind, under the
" title of religion.  I have proved, in an alle-
" gorical

" gorical hiſtory, by familiar inſtances taken
" from real or at leaſt poſſible life, which is
" the ſame thing, that chance governs the
" world, and every occurrence in it ; and that
" to attribute them to any other cauſe, ſuch as
" infinite power, wiſdom, goodneſs, and ſuch
" like, is moſt abſurd, as they are plainly con-
" trary to the effects of ſuch a cauſe ; and to
" give a greater force to my reaſoning, I have
" all along affected to treat theſe very notions,
" which I controvert, with the moſt ſolemn
" reſpect."

" Juſt as I have written with the greateſt
" acerbity againſt maxims (interrupted the
" king) which I practiſe every hour of my
" life."———Then running his eye haſtily over
the firſt page, which chance had opened to
him, " This is the thing (continued he, in a
" rapture) which has been ever wanted to clear
" the eyes of man, and enlighten his mind
" with the radiance of real knowledge. The
" voice of reaſon here utters the ſacred words
" of truth, adorned with all the beauties of
" imagination. How exactly have you hit
" upon my ſentiments! how forcibly expreſſed
" them ! My actions muſt have long proved
" to all who are capable of lifting up the veil
" which neceſſity obliges man to wear, that
" this is my opinion. You muſt leave the
" manuſcript with me, that I may peruſe it at
" my better leiſure ; and remember, I have
" your promiſe, that you will not mention a
" word of it to any mortal. I have reaſons for
" this injunction, which may not be diſagreea-
" ble to you."

———" Nothing that your majeſty commands
" can

" can be difagreeable to me; nor need you
" doubt my fervice. Here is another little
" thing, a mock-heroic poem, in which the
" folly of all the philofophy, and the falfe pre-
" tenfions to knowledge, which have impofed
" upon the world for fo many generations, are
" properly difplayed. It is fomething of the
" fame nature with the other, the defign of
" which it compleats, by fhewing that there
" is nothing certain in this life; and, there-
" fore, that true wifdom confifts in doing that
" which is moft agreeable to ourfelves, with-
" out regard to any contrary opinions, how-
" ever hallowed to foolifh veneration by the
" ruft and cobwebs of antiquity."

———" My fyftem ftill. Yes! let me have it.
" My head is ftunned with the noife of war,
" and wants the harmony of your numbers to
" compofe it. This is poetry. This is the
" genuine effufion of a mind infpired. Such
" writing difdains the critic's rage, and even
" rifes above the wreck of time. What ele-
" gance! What fire! How bold, and yet how
" clear."

———" Your majefty's approbation is the
" higheft object of my ambition. It is fame.
" Though till that fanction is made public, I
" doubt not but I fhall have an outcry raifed
" againft me, particularly on account of the
" firft work, for bringing ridicule to aid my
" arguments, againft opinions fo long confe-
" crated, by ignorance, to blind refpect. But
" it was impoffible to reftrain the fallies of wit
" on fubjects which lay fo open to its lafh."

———" Moft

——" Most certainly; nor are they in the
" least reprehensible.  A poignant jest often
" shames a man out of an opinion which no
" argument could make him give up.  You
" tell me with the assurance of sacred truth,
" that no man living knows any thing of ei-
" ther of these works.  In return for your
" complying with my desire in that, I will
" now intrust you with the darling secret of my
," soul.  No man must ever know any thing
" of them.  I mean, as your's.  Shall I tell
" you all ?  You are sensible of the ardour with
" which I pant for fame.  Though chance has
" thrown me into the more turbulent scenes of
" life, my heart languishes for the happiness of
" retirement, for the glory that is acquired of
" the calmer works of learned ease : nor were
" my first essays to obtain it so unsuccessful as
" to discourage the pursuit, did the indispen-
," sible duties of my station permit it.

" Can you then, my friend, indulge this
" ruling passion of my soul so far, as to give up
" these children of your brain to my adop-
" tion, and let me produce them to the world
" as my own, without danger of paternal
" fondness's breaking out, and claiming them ?
" I know it is a delicate and difficult request ;
" but I will amply recompense your com-
" pliance, and then you will soon be able to
" produce more.  The spring from whence
" these flowed is not exhausted.

" Beside, I claim a kind of right to them.
" They are the very sentiments of my soul,
" which I designed to have published as soon
" as I could spare time to dispose them into
" proper order.  In this you have prevented
                                    " me;

" me; may I not say rather, saved me the trou-
" ble, and now present my own anticipated
" offspring to me, with the advantage of being
" educated by your hand. The matter is
" literally mine, as much as it is your's : the
" form indeed is all your own. What do
" you say? Are you willing to gratify my de-
" sire?"

———" Every command of your majesty's is
" entitled to immediate obedience; I most
" willingly consign them into your hands, to
" dispose of as you please, either to publish or
" absolutely suppress them for ever. Could I
" have thought of their having such a glorious
" fate, I should have laboured to make them
" more worthy of it."

———" They are very well. It is the sub-
" ject that particularly strikes me. If I find
" any thing amiss in the manner of treating
" it, I will myself correct it. Here! take this
" order to my treasurer: You see it is expresly
" said to be for *secret* service."

" Your majesty's munificence (answered the
" lucky author, who was so astonished at the
" greatness of the sum, that it was some time
" before he had power to speak) overwhelms
" me with confusion. This is too much; too
" much for me to take!"

———" But not for me to give (replied the
" monarch, smiling). Let me see you again be-
" fore you go away. I must now give some
" orders, which are this moment come into
" my head; but I shall be at leisure by the
" time you return from the treasurer."

The author bowed with the most profound
respect, and departed in evident happiness of
heart.                    6            When

When he was gone, the king, looking at his new purchafe with the higheſt delight, "At length (faid he) I have accompliſhed my "defign. Theſe will extend my fame through "the whole circle of the human powers. I "ſhine already as a legiſlator and hiſtorian; "theſe add the characters of a poet, and a "divine. Singularity is the firſt ſtep to emi- "nence. A *great* man ſhould do nothing in "the common way. Now that I have un- "hinged the religion of the world, as foon as "I am at leiſure I will deviſe a new one of my "own, and erect it on the ruins of the old. "This is all I want to confirm my being the "*greateſt* man of this, or any age."

When he had pleaſed himſelf with theſe re- flections for ſome time, he reſumed his wonted thoughtful look, and went to meet his mini- ſters, who, ſtruck with his appearance, liſten- ed to his words with a kind of religious vene- ration, prepared to obey whatever he ſhould command, without preſuming to difcufs it even in their own minds, as if he had been a being of a ſuperior nature.

Having diſpatched theſe affairs, he retired to meet the happy author, who had received the money, and was returned according to his orders. "Well, (faid the king) I hope you "don't regret the exchange you have made. "I have nothing more to ſay to you at this "time, but to defire that I may hear conſtant- "ly from you. Much as I am involved in "other affairs, I ſhall always find time to "correfpond with you; and obſerve, that I "infiſt on your laying aſide all formality, and "writing your thoughts as freely as they riſe "in

" in your mind; as I, and all lovers of phi-
" losophic truth do."

" Your majesty (answered the other) heaps
" new honours on me, by every new com-
" mand. I will obey you with the utmost
" punctuality, and think myself happy if my
" poor works can merit the approbation of so
" consummate a judge."——The scene now
grew so fulsome, each flattering the other in
the grossest manner, that I was glad when it
was ended.

This contemptible instance of vanity sullied
the lustre of the monarch's other qualities,
and made me so sick of ambition in every
shape, that I could bear the sight of him no
longer. I therefore took my leave of heroism
and *greatness*, of which my heart was sick, and
departed along with the author, in whom I
saw something that raised my curiosity to be
better acquainted with him.

## CHAP. XIII.

*A remarkable instance of poetic gratitude and*
*justice, with some anecdotes of a celebrated*
*genius.*

THE moment he left the monarch's presence, he made all possible haste to get
out of his reach also, for fear of his changing
his mind, and resuming his most profuse present. When his heart was freed from this fear,
on his entering the territories of a neutral
power,

power, he ſtopped, to recover his fatigue, and
conſider how he ſhould diſpoſe of his new fortune in the moſt proper manner. After a variety of ſchemes, he at laſt reſolved to fix his
abode in the territories of a certain free but
poor ſtate, where he ſhould be at liberty to
purſue his own inclinations without interruption, and gain reſpect by the magnificence which
he was now able to diſplay.

This firſt point being ſettled, his thoughts
naturally recurred to the means by which he
had acquired his fortune. Amply as the monarch had paid him for the honour of fathering
his works, his vanity took the alarm at the
fame he ſhould loſe, and envy determined him
to break faith with his benefactor, and betray
his weakneſs by publiſhing the works in his
own name, as ſoon as ever the king ſhould declare them to be his; for he would not do it
ſooner to prevent him, that the detection might
heighten the diſgrace, the thoughts of his being
under obligation, to which he meant to make
ſo baſe a return, inflaming his heart with the
moſt malignant hatred. " I will expoſe him
" to the contempt of mankind, (ſaid he) for his
" meanneſs and vanity. He never ſhall have
" the honour of my works. When he has
" plumed himſelf in the merit of them for a
" while, I'll ſtrip the gawdy daw of his ſtolen
" feathers, and point him out to univerſal ri-
" dicule. He make alterations too! and cor-
" rect my errors! Let him, let him expoſe
" himſelf! The coarſe patches will betray the
" bungling hand that puts them on, and ſerve
" for a convenient foil to the reſt. If he de-
" ſires fame, let him earn it, and not ſtrive
" thus

" thus to steal it from another. He never shall
" have the honour of my works. Had he not
" been a fool, he might have foreseen this, and
" in the plenitude of his tyranny have put it
" out of my power to defeat his design, by
" taking away my life ; but I am now beyond
" his reach, and shall take care to keep my-
" self so."——— Then melting into rapture, at
the thought of his wealth, " I will live (con-
" tinued he) like a prince among those repub-
" licans, whose parsimony will be a foil to
" my munificence. Every thing about me,
" every thing I do shall have an air of gran-
" deur; I'll build a theatre at my own house,
" where I will have my works represented ac-
" cording to my own taste, to my chosen
" friends."

The deliberate baseness of this resolution, so
contradictory to the proper use of the powers
which produced the occasion of it, tempted me
to look back to the principal occurrences in the
life of so extraordinary a person. He was born
in a neighbouring country, where genius is
encouraged by approbation, and starves in the
midst of flattery. Abilities, such as his, soon
distinguished themselves. He became the favourite of the publick, and heard nothing but
his own praises. But his reign was not long.
He thought with a freedom and spirit which
gave jealousy to a government established on
the principles of despotism, and was obliged to
fly his native land, to avoid falling a sacrifice
to his fame.

The country in which he took refuge was
in every respect the reverse of that he left. Approbation was given sparingly, and never soon;

**H**                              but

but the more fubftantial reward of prefent profit feldom difappointed merit; and rational liberty gave genius its full fcope. Here he firft
tafted the fweets of independency, and formed
fchemes for eftablifhing himfelf in the poffeffion of that ineftimable bleffing. But his eagernefs difappointed him, by betraying him into
fome actions which obliged him to quit that
country as precipitately as he had his own, to
avoid a more ignominious fate.

After fome time fpent in difcontented rambling, this prince, whom his fame had reached,
not only gave him an afylum in his dominions,
but alfo heaped his favours on him fo lavifhly,
that he refumed his hopes of independency,
which this laft affair enabled him to accomplifh
in a manner he had never even raifed wifhes
to. The return he meditated, and did afterwards partly make (for when he confidered
more cooly, he dropt that part of his fcheme
of letting the king publifh them firft, for fear his
credit fhould overbalance his own, and make
himfelf appear the plagiary, and therefore
printed them directly in his own name; a perfidy which the difcontented monarch did not dare
to impeach, and could not punifh) was agreeable to the natural tendency of his difpofition,
and of a piece with his behaviour to the people whofe beneficence had afforded him relief,
and firft raifed his hopes, whom he calum-
niated with the moft malignant virulence, as
foon as he was out of the reach of their offended laws.

The abilities which enabled him to triumph
over fo many difficulties as his folly drew him
into, were certainly very great, though vanity
much

much leſſened their merit. An affectation of ſingularity, of ſhewing himſelf wiſer than all the reſt of the world, making him diſpute the truth of, and treat with contempt theſe principles which had ever been held in the higheſt reſpect, and eſtabliſhed as the rules of moral action, the foundations of religious faith.

Impious and abſurd as ſuch vanity was, it found applauſe and imitation from the kindred vanity of the greater part of mankind; and the intereſt they had in ſupplanting an authority that contradicted their practice, and made it criminal in the eyes of others, and dangerous in their own.

To this cauſe chiefly he was indebted for the rapidity of his riſe to fame; for literary merit, however great, is obliged to ſtand the teſt of time before it meets general approbation, where ſome lucky circumſtance does not concur thus to favour it.

Shocked at ſuch a proſtitution, I left him to purſue his own machinations; and, having abundantly ſatisfied my curioſity with military matters, reſolved to change the ſcene of my obſervations, and go to the courts of the powers engaged in war, in hopes that, for the credit of human nature, I might find the meaſures of their civil government deduced from more rational principles than thoſe which appeared to influence the conduct of their armies.

## END OF THE FIRST BOOK.

THE

# THE
# REVERIE;
## OR, A
## Flight to the Paradife of Fools.
# BOOK II.

**********************************

## CHAP. I.

*A council fcene. The mildnefs of female govern-
ment ; with a remarkable inflance of the happy effect of reproof upon great minds.*

THE firft court which I thought proper to
take a view of was that of the power moft
immediately engaged in the war againft
the prince whofe camp I had juft left. Accordingly I *wifhed* myfelf thither directly, to
avoid the pain of travelling through the fcenes
of defolation and mifery exhibited by all the
countries around.

On my arrival I found the fovereign feated
in council, in the midft of his minifters.
There appeared in his looks a phlegm, which

in different countries is taken to denote the different qualities of wifdom and ftupidity; and which here feemed to have extended its foporifick influence over all prefent, who fat with their eyes fixed upon the table, as if waiting in fufpenfion of thought for fomething to fet their faculties at work.

They had continued in this ftate for fome time, when a female entered and placed herfelf at the right hand of the fovereign. Her features were ftrong, and mafculine; fhe was dreffed in the robes of independent royalty, and the haughtinefs of her looks and deportment fhewed that fhe efteemed herfelf fuperior to all the princes of the world.

The moment fhe entered, the whole council affumed a new appearance. The fovereign looked abafhed, and the minifters, rouz d from their former ferenity, waited for her words with fear and trembling. " I ordered your " attendance, (faid fhe, looking fiercely round, " the fire of her foul flafhing from her eyes as " fhe fpoke) to let you know what I will have " done in the prefent conjuncture. I will no " longer bear to be braved thus by my vaffals, " who by the weaknefs of fome of my prede- " ceffors have acquired this unnatural power " of rebelling againft their fovereign. They " fhall be declared public enemies to the gene- " ral ftate, and the reft of the feudatories oblig- " ed to join their forces, according to the or- " dinances of thofe who gave them the power " they now poffefs, to reduce them to their proper " ftate of obedience. When thefe have done " that, the troops of my own dominions fhall " humble them alfo. I will no longer be op-

H 3 " pofed

" poſed by ſuch ingrateful ſlaves; for ſuch they
" were, and ſuch they ſhall be again. And
" you, ſir, (addreſſing herſelf to the ſovereign)
" muſt enforce this ſentence with your autho-
" rity. The rank to which you have been
" raiſed by your alliance with me, enables
" you to do any thing, if you had but proper
" ſpirit.

" Madam, (anſwered the ſovereign) I—I—
" I can do nothing. You have taken all the
" power into your own hands, and left nothing
" for me to do."

" Yes, (replied ſhe, with a look of the
" higheſt contempt) you can drink away your
" ſenſes; and that is all you mind. Had I
" been bleſſed with an huſband of ſpirit equal
" to my own, we ſhould have ſubdued the
" world. All mankind would have been my
" ſlaves. But now the work is all my own;
" you only contribute an empty name."——
Then turning to her ſecretary, " Let this de-
" cree be notified to all the other vaſſals with-
" out loſs of time, that they may prepare to
" obey it."

" May it pleaſe your moſt auguſt majeſty,
" (ſaid the ſecretary, making an obeiſance as
" low as adoration) is this ſentence intended
" only againſt the principal power with whom
" you are at war? Or are all his friends, thoſe
" I mean who have not directly declared againſt
" you, to be included?"

" All, all; (anſwered ſhe) their preſump-
" tion is equal, and ſo ſhall be their puniſh-
" ment. Thoſe who even heſitate to obey my
" commands I hold to be my enemies, and
" will treat them as ſuch."

" Your

"Your moſt ſacred majeſty's commands (re-
"plied the ſecretary) ſhould be a law, to all
"the world. Here is a memorial which I have
"this day received from the miniſter of his
"principal ally. It relates immediately to the
"purpoſe of this your majeſty's moſt magna-
"nimous and juſt reſolution, their conſcious
"dread of which anticipates your tremendous
"declaration."

"Let it be read; (ſaid ſhe, impatiently) I
"will hear what it contains, though all the
"world ſhall not make me alter my reſolu-
"tion."

"Far be it from your ſervant to ſuppoſe
"any ſuch thing; (anſwered the ſecretary)
"the will of ſo mighty a princeſs ſhould be as
"immutable as fate. Shall I read the whole,
"or only give a ſummary of the contents? It
"is very long; and not always conceived with
"that reſpect due to your ſublimity, from the
"other ſovereigns of the earth."

"The ſubſtance of it (replied ſhe haughti-
"ly) will be as much as I ſhall hear; and
"more than I ſhall pay regard to."

"Hem! ahem! In the firſt place, (ſaid he,
"clearing his voice, and caſting his eye upon
"the paper in his hand) the memorialiſt pre-
"ſumes to throw the blame of the preſent war
"entirely upon your majeſty; accuſing you of
"a deſign to overturn the juſt rights and li-
"berties of thoſe whom he calls the ſovereign
"princes and independent members of the
"ſtate; and in conſequence of this accuſation
"juſtifies the oppoſition made by your enemy,
"and the aſſiſtance contributed by others to
"the ſupport of a cauſe common to them all.

H 4                                    "He

"He presumes likewise to deny and protest
"against your irresistible majesty's undoubted
"right of employing the authority of his most
"serene majesty, your royal consort, in a dis-
"pute which interferes not with his state, but
"belongs entirely to your own hereditary do-
"minions, audaciously and directly insisting,
"that, instead of aiding your majesty's designs,
"he ought to oppose his whole force to defeat
"them, agreeably to the true intent of the
"high trust reposed in him when he was raised
"to his present exalted station. In quality
"then of sovereign of other dominions, he
"takes the liberty to upbraid your incompar-
"able majesty with ingratitude, asserting, that,
"without mentioning the many obligations
"conferred upon your royal ancestors, your
"majesty has yourself been supported on your
"throne by his assistance, against the efforts
"of those very enemies of your august house,
"whom you have now most unnaturally join-
"ed with against him, your only firm and ef-
"fectual ally; and, lastly, he has the assur-
"ance to declare, that he will now employ the
"same power in defence of what he calls his
"own rights, and those of his allies; with
"which he most insolently adds, that he fears
"not to humble that ingrateful——"

While the secretary was making this recital,
every feature of his mistress's face was disto_ted
with the different passions of pride, rage, and
revenge; but these last words hurried her beyond all patience. "Villain! (said she, snatch-
"ing the memorial from his trembling hand,
"and throwing it in his face) How darest thou
"repeat such insolence before me? Obligations
"to

" to him! he only did his duty; and was over-
" paid by my acceptance of it. My house,
" the first on earth, has a right to every thing
" in the power of inferior princes, to contri-
" bute to its exaltation; nor shall any petty,
" limited, sovereign presume to call my com-
" mands in question, or censure my making
" alliances with whom I please. Whatever I
" will is right; and this I will support against
" all their opposition, while I have a subject
" able to draw a sword."

The vehemence with which she spoke these
words awoke her royal consort, who was so
affected by the rebuke she had given him just
before, that he fell asleep. Starting therefore,
" Hah! What! What opposition? (said he,
" staring about, and repeating her last word)
" What opposition?"

" Peace, idiot! sot! (answered his gentle
" mate) the only opposition I regard, is that,
" of your indolence and stupidity."——Then,
turning again to the secretary, " Draw up the
" decree (continued she) directly, and enforce
" it with every expression of contempt for the
" writer of this insolent memorial. I'll shew
" him what regard I pay to his upbraidings;
" and that I hold the services he values himself,
" so highly upon, to be all cancelled from the,
" moment he dared to disobey my sovereign,
" will in any instance."——

Saying this, she arose; and, dismissing the
council with a motion of her hand, retired,
her royal consort not venturing to speak a
word.

## C H A P. II.

*A ready salve for a sore conscience, with a proper reward for piety. An unexpected disappointment shews greatness of soul in a striking light. A day concluded consistently.*

FROM council her majesty went into her own apartment, where she met her confessor, who was waiting for her. "I sent for you, "father, (said she) to unburthen my consci- "ence, which cannot bear the weight of any "thing that even looks like a crime. The "event of this war not immediately answering "my expectations, I have consented to a pro- "posal made to me, of having my enemy taken "off by poison : I have also given orders to "one of my generals, to march into the terri- "tories of those states who refused to join with "me in the war, and to burn and destroy all "before him, putting man, woman, and child, "to the sword, to revenge the disrespectful "manner in which they refused to comply with "my demands, and strike a terror into others "for the future. Now, as I conclude that "both these orders have been put in execu- "tion this morning, I sent for you to receive "absolution."

"The piety of your most sacred majesty "(answered the ecclesiastic) is highly com- "mendable, and deserves the indulgence of the "holy church in the most unlimited degree..
"Such

" Such things, to be sure, are in general crimi-
" nal; but particular circumstances may change
" their nature. The urgency of your majesty's
" affairs requires dispatch, and your honour
" must be vindicated. These considerations
" are in themselves of weight to authorize what
" else ought to be avoided. But there is ano-
" ther reason still stronger, and which makes
" the actions that hurt the tenderness of your
" conscience meritorious, instead of reprehen-
" sible. Your enemy is an heretic, and there-
" fore out of the protection of all laws human
" and divine; and those who refused to assist
" you against him, though not formally here-
" tics themselves as yet, discover by that re-
" fusal a kind of tendency that way, and
" should be prevented by wholesome chastise-
" ment; the first duty of all true sons of the
" church being to extirpate heresy."

Having quieted her majesty's conscience by
this pious distinction, he proceeded to the ceremony of giving her absolution, which he performed with a solemnity and parade equally
impious and ridiculous on such an occasion.

When this important affair was finished,
addressing his penitent with a look of joy, " I
" have the happiness ( said he ) to congratulate
" your majesty on the highest honour which
" can be obtained in this world. Our most
" holy father, in token of his approbation of
" your zeal for the glory of the church, has
" thought proper to grant you an addition to
" your titles, which gives you the pre-emi-
" nence over all the potentates on earth; and
" has blessed me with the office of imposing it
" in his name, whenever your majesty pleases

" to.

" to appoint a time for the glorious ceremonies
" which his wisdom has instituted for that pur-
" pose."

" I have a just sense of his holiness's favour,
" (answered she) and shall be glad to receive
" it in the proper manner as soon as possible,
" as my whole soul is implicitly devoted to
" the ceremonies of our divine religion."

" To-morrow then (said he) will I perform the
" sacred office of this second baptism, and give
" you a title that shall be expressive of the regard
" you so nobly shew at this time for the ad-
" vancement of the faith; for which purpose I
" will go directly and give orders for adorning
" the great church with all the precious and
" costly images, and relics of the saints and
" angels, who will look down with pleasure
" to behold your majesty raised to a degree of
" honour superior even to their own. You
" will please to command all the great officers
" of your court to attend, that nothing may
" be wanting to make the ceremony truly
" grand."

While her majesty was preparing for this
great affair, my curiosity prompted me to see
how her royal consort disposed of his time.
As soon as the council was broken up, in
which he made the important figure that
has been related, he hastened to his own particular apartments, where, throwing off the
mockery of royalty with which he was encum-
bered, he sat down with some of his most intimate favourites, to drown the cares of state
in wine.

The conversation was suited to the occasion. " For my part (said the sovereign, filling
" his rummer) I cannot conceive what plea-
" sure

" sure those people find in politics, and wars,
" and such like turbulent perplexing matters.
" I never think of the former, that they do not
" make my head ake; though the truth is, her
" majesty, for the most part, saves me that
" trouble. And then, for fighting! I bless
" my stars I am no hero; nor, while I have a
" bottle of such wine as this before me, envy
" any of them their laurels."

" It would be happy for the world, (said
" one of the company, while the sovereign
" quaffed off his bumper) if all princes
" were of your majesty's way of thinking.
" The pleasures of life might then be enjoyed
" in peace and satisfaction."——This turned
the discourse naturally on those pleasures, which
they all talked over with the greatest keenness,
till it was time to go to the opera, where his
majesty seldom failed to spend the evening.

His royal consort, elated at the thought of
the mighty things which had been done for her
that morning, and of the sacred honour she
was to receive next day, went thither also, to
indulge the happiness of her heart; but happening in the course of the entertainment to
observe that her husband looked with more than
common earnestness at one of the female performers, she gave orders to one of her officers
to remove her that very night out of her dominions, without permitting her husband to
see her, not bearing that any other should interfere with her in the only advantage she
reaped from her marriage.

The ceremony of the next day exceeded all
description. Every instance of pomp, both secular and religious, which superstition and vanity

6

nity

nity could fuggeft, was difplayed to make the
farce complete, without any regard to the danger
of offending the Deity by fuch an hypocritical
proftitution of rites appropriated to his fervice,
and many of them appointed by himfelf.

But the joy of her moft pious majefty was
foon damped. She had flattered herfelf, that
the fcheme for poifoning her enemy was laid fo
well, and committed to fuch trufty hands as to
be fafe from difappointment or detection. On
this her confeffor built fo ftrongly that he refolved to promife fome fignal and fpeedy inftance of fuccefs, as a divine ratification of her
new title. Accordingly, in the oration with
which he concluded the ceremony, he worked
himfelf up into the appearance of prophetic
enthufiafm, and ventured even to point out the
death of her enemy, as if by immediate infpi-
ration, defcribing his agonies in a rhetorical
flourifh, and attributing his fate to the hand of
Heaven, as a punifhment for his rebellion
againft his fovereign.

The effect which this had upon the multitude is not to be expreffed. Prepared by their
natural fuperftition to believe every thing their
priefts pleafed to tell them, they looked for the
inftant accomplifhment of this prediction with
fuch ftrong faith, that, had the expected news
arrived at that time, they would have received
it implicitly as a miracle ; and moft probably
have fallen down and worfhipped their fovereign, in whofe favour it would have appeared
to have been wrought.

But, unluckily for the poor prophet, juft as
he had finifhed his declamation, an account was
received that the attempt upon the king's life

had

had mifcarried, and her moft pious majefty's privity to it been detected in the plaineft manner, fo as to reflect an indelible difgrace upon her in the eyes of the world; and that her army, which was to have ravaged the territories of his friends, had been repulfed with great lofs, and by a body of fuch inferior force as to look like the immediate interpofition of Providence. The confequence of this may be eafily conceived. The preacher was afhamed to fhew his face: the glorious title was turned into ridicule; and her majefty was overwhelmed with vexation at her difappointment.

As foon as fhe had recovered herfelf a little, fhe fummoned her council again on this important occafion. After long deliberation, it was at laft concluded to give up a confiderable part of the territories of fome of her moft faithful friends, to one of the powers confederate with her in the war, to induce it to exert all its force to opprefs an enemy from whom they met fuch unexpected refiftance; for, fo ftrong was the hatred of her foul againft him, that fhe would ruin herfelf rather than he fhould efcape ruin. As to the charge of being concerned in the infamous and horrid fcheme of poifoning him, fhe affected to treat it with contempt, as a groundlefs flander, to which fhe difdained to make any anfwer.

But the fanguine hopes fhe built upon this abfurd expedient, which brought into her neighbourhood a rival infinitely more dangerous than the one whom fhe wanted to deftroy, were foon overthrown. Her expreffes were fcarce difpatched, when fhe received an account of the death of her ally, upon whofe
affiftance

affistance she depended; and from whose suc-
ceffor she had juft reason to apprehend even
worfe than the difappointment of her hopes, as
his avowed attachment to her enemy had engaged her in intrigues againft his life alfo,
which he had difcovered, and would now moft
probably fhew his refentment of, by turning
his forces againft her.

This event difconcerted all her fchemes,
and fhewed her that the ruin of her enemy,
which fhe had purfued with fuch inveteracy,
and flattered herfelf with the thought of being
fo near, was now removed farther off than
ever, if not abfolutely out of her power to accomplifh. However, the blind implacability
of her foul was not to be convinced. She refolved to double all her efforts; fhe ordered
every fubject in her dominions to take arms;
and laftly propofed to the profeffed enemies of
her faith, to fhare with her the conqueft which
they fhould affift her to make in a war, alledged to have been undertaken on a religious motive, facrificing every obligation, human and
divine, to an impotent defire of revenge; and
thus concluded a day hallowed in the annals
of her reign, by the reception of her facred
title.

Such fcenes were too fhocking to be dwelt
on. I refolved to leave that court directly;
and took the opportunity of travelling with a
courier whom her facred majefty fent to one of
her allies, that I might take a view of that
part of his dominions in which he refided at
that time, and learn fomething of the manners of the people with whom I was yet unacquainted.

CHAP.

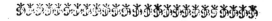

## CHAP. III.

*More happy effects of greatness; with a new way of punishing disobedience, and making the most of power.*

THE courier had scarce entered the territories of the prince to whom he was sent, when he was seized by a band of free-booters, who, without any regard to his character, dragged him away to their chief. It was late when he fell into their hands; and as they had prowled to a considerable distance from home, they concluded to stop at their own place of habitation till morning.

Nothing could equal the brutal behaviour of these savages, but their worse than brutal insolence, and the misery in which they lived. They threw their captive into the corner of a hovel, in which the leader of the gang dwelt, among their swine and cows; the best place in the hut, if any could be called by that title, being reserved for their horses, who fared in every respect better than their masters; and then, devouring a mess of food which any human creatures, not immediately impelled by famine, would have turned from with loathing, lay down to sleep upon an heap of straw, all mixed together, without any regard to decency or difference of sex, where they snored till next morning; when they arose as soon as it was light, and licking up what their dogs had

left

left of their over-night's fare, hurried their captive away to their lord.

When they arrived at his caftle they met him
going to his ftables, and, falling on their knees
in the wet and mire with which the whole
place was plentifully covered, informed him
of their fuccefs. The courier, without waiting
for his lordfhip's making them any reply, addreffed him boldly, and, telling what he was,
complained heavily of the outrage he had fuffered, and demanded to be fet immediately at
liberty, to purfue his journey, as he was charged
with difpatches of the utmoft importance to his
fovereign. The air of freedom with which he
fpoke offended the pride of the mighty lord;
but his dignity was ftruck at by this laft word
in a manner that he did not think proper to
bear, for he would not have his vaffals even
fufpect that he paid obedience to any power
upon earth. "Take hence that flave, (faid
"he, without deigning to look at him) and
"throw him into the dungeon. I'll chaftife
"him for his infolence. My fovereign! A
"*nobleman* owns no fovereign." Then turning
to his people, who ftill continued kneeling,
"What more have you brought me? (faid he)
"I fent you word that I was going to at-
"tend the great convention of the ftates, and
"wanted money."

To this terrible fpeech the principal of the
gang anfwered, that they had no money themfelves, nor were able to get any, though they
had fcoured the whole country in fearch of it.
"Villains! dogs! (exclaimed his lord, flying
"at the poor trembling wretch, and beating
"him unmercifully with his horfe-whip) Tell
"me

" me not that you have no money. You muſt
" find it for me, or I'll ſell yourſelves, your
" wives and children, for ſlaves. Be gone ;
" and either bring me money to-morrow morn-
" ing, or every female in your families. I'll
" make you know that I will be obeyed."

The wretches went away without daring to
expoſtulate, while their potent lord ſtrutted off,
ſwollen with the thought of having ſo many of
his fellow-creatures ſubject to his pleaſure.

As ſoon as he entered his caſtle, he ordered
the courier to be brought before him again, and
having reprimanded him ſeverely for behaving
with ſuch inſolence to a perſon of his importance, diſmiſſed him, now that his own vaſſals,
into whom he meant to ſtrike a terror, were
departed. Every thing about him was in character. His caſtle, which his own people
thought one of the grandeſt palaces in the
world, was a mean, incommodious, but indif-
ferently ſtrong place ; the furniture, ſome of it
rich, but old, aukward, and ill-ſuited, and
moſt of the leſſer conveniences of life utterly
wanting ; and here was this petty tyrant ſerved
with a parade and oſtentation, which were a
ſevere though juſt ridicule upon the pomp and
vanity of ſtate.

There was ſomething ſo new to me in this
ſcene, that I reſolved to purſue it farther. I
therefore quitted the courier for the company
of this *nobleman*, with whom I ſaw I ſhould
have an opportunity of travelling to the court,
when he ſhould go to the convention of the
ſtates, in equipping his horſes, for which grand
occaſion he ſpent the reſt of the day ; for on
them was all his pride diſplayed.

The

The next morning produced a scene that was a disgrace to the human name. His wretched vassals, in obedience to his dread commands, came with all their mothers, sisters, wives, and daughters, for he had made no exception of age or infirmity, driven before them like a herd of cattle to the market. They also brought all their worldly substance, consisting of the wretched utensils of their houses, their implements of husbandry, and their cattle, to give in the place of their women, if their lord would be graciously pleased to accept of the exchange, and let them starve together.

The cries of the females, and the distress painted in the faces of the men, for they did not dare to complain, are not to be expressed; but neither made any impression on their lord, whose noble heart was above the vulgar weaknesses of humanity. "So! (said he sternly) then " you have dared to disobey my commands, and " not brought me the money?"

" Mighty lord! (answered an ecclesiastic, " who had ventured to come as their interces- " sor) they have obeyed your commands as far " as was in their power, and brought all their " women; but money it was impossible for " them to bring. The armies, which have " marched so often through the country of " late, have plundered them of every thing " which they might sell to raise money for your " use; nor do travellers venture to carry any " thing valuable with them in such dangerous " times; so that they cannot obtain any that " way neither. Have compassion therefore on " their distress, and tear not from them their " families, the only comfort which they enjoy " in

" in life. They have brought all their poor
" subftance."——

While the prieft was making this pathetic
addrefs, the lord was viewing his property, and
bargaining for them with fome Jewifh flave-
merchants, whom he had fummoned on the
occafion, and who are always ready to purchafe
fuch unhappy creatures, to fell again to the
Turks. " It is in vain for you to fpeak (faid
" he, when he had concluded his bargain)
" whatever I command fhall be done; and
" fince they have neglected to provide money,
" their women fhall go. This will teach them
" to be more diligent another time. They
" mind nothing now but dallying with their
" wives; but they'll do better when they are
" gone."——Saying this, he made a fignal to
the Jews, who drew out the number they had
bought, and, paying down their price, drove
them away, without the leaft regard to their
cries and diftrefs at this violation of all the
tendereft ties of nature.

The horror I felt at this abominable tyranny is not to be exprefled; nor the gratitude
with which I offered up my thanks to Heaven,
for the ineftimable happinefs of living in a country where I was fecure from fuch outrages
againft the common rights of mankind. " Too
" happy Britons! (faid I to myfelf, in the over-
" flowing of my heart) did you but know your
" own happinefs! You live under the protec-
" tion of laws enacted by yourfelves; under the
" government of a prince who exerts his power
" only in acts of benevolence and virtue!"

CHAP.

## CHAP. IV.

*Account of an uncommon kind of council; with its natural conclusion.*

WHEN this important affair was finished, the nobleman set out for the convention of the states, with a numerous and grand retinue. The country through which he travelled bore every-where the same appearance with his own territories; the vassals in the most abject slavery and wretchedness, and their tyrants in slovenly profusion, and aukward splendor.

The convention to which the *nobles* were all at this time going, was one of the most glaring instances of human absurdity. It was held in a large plain, where all these petty tyrants met on horse-back, armed, and at the head of their vassals, under the specious pretext of deliberating on the public welfare; but how likely they were to promote it is sufficiently obvious : for if the voice of reason is seldom heard with respect in the best regulated assemblies, and among the most civilized people, where every precaution which human prudence can suggest is taken, to prevent the animosity inseparable from difference of sentiment, from breaking out into acts of violence, what must be expected from a number of men like these, bred up in lawless insolence and outrage, and gathering together without a rule to direct, or power to controul them, prepared to support their own opinions by force

when

when arguments fhould fail, let them never be fo extravagant and unjuft; what, I fay, muft be expected from fuch a meeting but tumult, confufion, and flaughter?

This confequence was fo well known to their fovereigns, that, although they could not abrogate a cuftom hallowed by its antiquity, whofe fanction too often makes abfurdity venerable, and which owed its rife to the moft barbarous ignorance, they never would confent to fo dangerous and ineffectual an expedient, except in times of public calamity, when their licentious fubjects extorted fuch a conceffion from them; for the right of convening them was entirely in the fovereign, from whom the fupreme power in its utmoft latitude was tranfferred to the collective body of the nobles the moment they met, and for the time of their continuing together; which, however, was always limited to one day, to obviate their abufing their truft.

They affembled accordingly at fun-rife, and feparating from their attendants, who ftood around them at fome little diftance, waited for the arrival of their fovereign, to explain to them in form the caufe of his fummoning them to meet. The time of their waiting was fpent in forming cabals, fomenting their mutual difcontents, and ftimulating each other to fedition, by aggravating every exertion of the royal authority into a breach of their priviledges, and an encroachment on the liberty of the public; in behalf of which they declaimed with as much vehemence as if they were refolved to banifh tyranny from the face of the earth, and reftore all mankind to their original equality.

At length the sovereign appeared in a magnificence almost exceeding imagination; but his looks shewed that grandeur often gilds unhappiness. Advancing into the midst of the assembly, he opened the convention with a most affecting speech, in which he set forth the public distresses in the most lively and pathetic colours; and desired their assistance to remedy them, with as much condescension as was consistent with the dignity of his rank.

But it was far from their intention to comply with any thing he should require: they scarce gave him liberty to finish his speech, when, throwing off all respect and restraint, an hundred mouths opened upon him at once, accusing him of being the cause of all the public calamities, by the weak and pernicious measures of his government; and upbraiding him with tyranny, and a design of overturning the liberties of his subjects, which he had sworn to maintain.

The sovereign, unable to prevent, and, unwilling to hear such indignities, thought proper to retire, and leave them, to pursue their deliberations among themselves, from which he had never expected any advantage, though their clamours had obliged him to call them together. The event was what reason must easily foresee. All was tumult, riot, and confusion. Every one spoke at once; and though in the main they all intended the same thing, which was to dethrone their sovereign, that they might act their ravages with impunity, till another could be elected; their ungoverned heat and impatience defeated their design, and made them fall into the snares of some who

were

were his friends, who defignedly raifed a quarrel in which all took part; and in their madnefs fell to fighting, they kney knew not for what, nor cared with whom, without a poffibility of their being calmed to conclude upon any thing. Their attendants, whom they brought to awe their fovereign, thinking it their duty to affift their lords, joined in the fray, which foon became more horrible than any pitched battle, every one murdering his neighbour without diftinction of friend or foe. Night at length feparated the furvivors, who, without ever enquiring what had been the caufe of the quarrel, returned to their refpective homes, enflamed with the moft virulent animofity againft each other, which they wreaked with a fury that aggravated the public calamities a thoufand-fold.

The confequence of this conftant end of thofe meetings, and which only could induce the fovereign to fubmit to the hard expedient of permitting them, was, that it generally delivered him from a great part of his enemies, and diverting the rage of the reft from him for a time, left him at liberty to purfue his own meafures, with whatever friends he had been able to attach to him; for all their power ended with the day, they having no right to meet again without a new fummons, which fuch an event gave him juft reafon to refufe, could they even be reconciled among themfelves to require it.

From this horrid fcene I went to court, with one of thofe who had firft began the quarrel; and having flipped out of the danger, as foon as he had fet them together by the ears, haftened, as foon as all was over, to give an account

count of the event to the minifter. The pleafure with which the latter received the fhocking detail was painful to humanity to behold.
He made it be repeated to him over and over,
that he might not lofe the minuteft circumftance, and then went with the pleafing news
to his mafter,

The moment he came into his prefence, "I
"congratulate your majefty (faid he, with an
"air of exultation) on the event of the con-
"vention. It has concluded properly in a
"general broil, in which the greateft part of
"your enemies have met the fate they de-
"ferved."

High as the triumph of the minifter was, he
could not communicate his joy to his mafter.
"It is a melancholy cafe (anfwered the king,
"with a deep-drawn figh) that a fovereign, who
"ought to be the father of his people, and ftu-
"dy only their happinefs, fhould have reafon
"to hear fuch an horrid account with plea-
"fure."

"I have often told your majefty, (replied
"the minifter) that this injudicious tendernefs
"was the ruin of your affairs. Had you let
"your enemy be taken off in the manner I
"propofed before the war broke out, you
"would have avoided all the misfortunes
"which you have experienced fince. There
"is no being any thing by halves. A *great*
"man is above the reftraints which bind the
"prejudices of weaker people."

"Would to Heaven (returned the king)
"that I had never afpired to that wretced cha-
"racter. All the true happinefs of life was in my
"poffeffion, and I was bleffed with a tafte to
"enjoy

" enjoy it; but I unhappily miftook the part
" nature had defigned me, and afpiring at what
" I could not be, fell from that which I
" was."

" Why will your majefty (interrupted the
" minifter, with an accent of the moft engag-
" ing tendernefs and fubmiffive expoftulation)
" torture yourfelf with thefe vain reflections?
" Every thing you have done was with the
" beft and greateft defigns; and if fortune has
" hitherto frowned upon your attempts, the
" fault lies not in you; nor fhould you be dif-
" couraged by the difappointment. Perfever-
" ance conquers the greateft difficulties; and
" one lucky event may yet put you in poflef-
" fion of all your hopes. At any rate, it is
" beneath you to retreat now. It would argue a
" dejection more difgraceful than a thoufand
" defeats. Refume your fpirits therefore, and
" hope for the beft. You have many refources
" yet, before it can be neceffary for you to
" fubmit to the difhonour of receiving peace
" from your infulting foe; a foe whofe affairs
" have been often in a much more defperate
" fituation than your's, till his refolution re-
" trieved them."

" My dear baron! (anfwered the king,
" fomewhat encouraged by this fpeech) I leave
" every thing to you. I know your attach-
" ment to my intereft; I know your abilities,
" and confide in them. Do you what you
" think beft; and may Heaven grant you fuc-
" cefs."

CHAP.

❁❁❁❁❁❁❁❁❁ ❁❁❁❁❁❁❁❁❁❁

## CHAP. V.

*Myſtery of favouritiſm. A remarkable inſtance of the art of making the moſt of a misfortune.*

THERE was ſomething in the abſolute aſcendancy which this miniſter evidently poſſeſſed over his ſovereign, ſo contradictory to the natural reaſon, and ſpirited ſenſibility, which marked the looks of the latter, that my curioſity led me to take a view of both their characters, that I might ſee by what means it had been obtained.

The prince was deſcending faſt into the vale of years. He looked dejected, and melancholy had thrown over his whole appearance a veil of liſtleſsneſs and diffidence, whoſe gloom obſcured the luſtre of his virtues.

Born to the ſovereignty of dominions on which nature had beſtowed her bleſſings with a bounteous hand, the firſt cares of his life had been exerted to improve them by every aſſiſtance of induſtry and art. The ſucceſs exceeded his moſt ſanguine hopes; encouraged by his ſmiles genius raiſed its head in his court, and every finer art flouriſhed in the ſunſhine of his favour.

So fair a morning promiſed the brighteſt day ; but ambition ſoon overcaſt its radiance, and he forfeited thoſe ſolid advantages, to graſp at this crown, more dazzling than his own to a ſuperficial view, but far leſs rich in every real good,

good, without being warned by the fate of his father, who had ship-wrecked his happiness on the same rock.

Adorned with every virtue that dignifies humanity, he seemed designed by Heaven to make his people happy; but the excess even of these virtues produced the contrary effect. He had contracted an intimacy in his earliest youth, when the tender mind receives the strongest impressions, with his present minister, who was placed in an honourable employment about his person by the king his father.

The superiority which a few years advance gives in the beginning of life, generally imprints a respect difficult to be got over ever after. This person was blessed with every qualification which nature could bestow, to improve the advantages of his situation; nor wanted address and care to exert them in their utmost force. He soon attached the infant fondness of his young master by every pleasing art, and, as his reason began, to expand itself, attracted the respect of that also, by displaying his own superiority in the most striking though delicate light.

The talents and disposition of the prince were such as, in the general sense of the world, denominated him rather *good* than *great*; whereas those of his favourite, on the contrary, were all of the other kind, and calculated to make a noise and figure in the highest scenes of life.

In a good mind friendship often arises from the same cause which would have produced envy in one of a different cast. The prince admired the qualities which he was conscious he wanted himself; and as they were never osten-

tatiously

tatioufly fhewn in oppofition to him, foon conceived the ftrongeft efteem for their owner, and refolved to reap the benefit of them, by attaching him to his intereft. The other, who foon faw the fuccefs of his hopes, omitted nothing that could poffibly improve the influence he had acquired. He ftudied every turn of his temper, and read his inclinations as foon as they arofe; fo that he was able to anticipate his very wifhes.

But the principal thing that eftablifhed his afcendancy beyond a poffibility of being fupplanted, was the perfonal attachment, which he fhewed upon every occafion for his mafter, whofe pleafure appeared to be the only object of his attention and regard; and to which he was ready to facrifice the ftrongeft ties of nature. Of this he had had the good fortune to give an early inftance of fuch a nature, as made reafon and paffion equally join to confirm his empire over the prince's heart.

He had fallen in love with a moft beautiful and accomplifhed young lady, heirefs to one of the richeft nobles of the kingdom, and was fo happy as to have his paffion not only returned by her, but alfo approved of by her father.

In the overflowing of his heart, on this joyful occafion, he defcribed his intended bride in fuch rapturous terms to the prince, that he raifed his curiofity to fee her, when her charms made fuch an impreffion upon his heart, naturally fufceptible of every warm fenfation, that he could not refrain from gazing at her with an earneftnefs too plain to be mifunderftood, though refpect reftrained them from feeming to take notice of it. Inattentive to the confequence

quence of fuch an indulgence, the prince repeated his vifits fo frequently, that the lovers
took the alarm, and fhe feigned ficknefs, to
waive an honour which began to give them
pain.

The manner in which he informed the prince
of her illnefs opened his eyes to the nature of
it. He took the hint in a proper light; and, as
he had never had any particular defign in vifit-
ing her, found no difficulty in refolving to go
no more. But it was eafier to form than keep
fuch a refolution. Her beauty had taken
too ftrong poffeffion of his heart to be fo eafily expelled, and he was actually in love, without having fufpected any fuch thing.

As refpect had made the favourite conceal
his fears, fo delicacy kept the prince in filence
alfo. He refolved to fubdue his paffion, however difficult the attempt ; nor would feem to
underftand a fufpicion that implied a doubt of
his generofity. But his behaviour foon betrayed the conflict in his breaft. He grew melancholy, fought retirement, and particularly
avoided the company of his favourite, whofe
happinefs, though he would not obftruct, he
could not think of, without pain.

The other immediately perceived the criti-
calnefs of his fituation, and was in the higheft
diftrefs how to act between love and ambition ; for he too plainly faw that one muft be
facrificed, to fecure the other. While he was
in this fufpence, an unexpected event decided
the difficulty.

The king, whofe age had not cooled his paffion, happened one day to fpeak warmly in
praife of the young lady's beauty; her lover,
who

who was prefent, was fufficiently acquainted
with his temper, to fee the confequence of this.
He knew that he had been all his life a profeffed votary of love, and had never ftopped at any
thing, however unjuftifiable. to gratify his defires. Convinced, therefore, that he muft inevitably lofe his miftrefs, his ready genius fug-
géfted it to him to difpofe of her in fuch a
manner as fhould turn the lofs to his advantage. He inftantly waited upon the prince,
and throwing himfelf at his feet, with an air of
the moft paffionate and refpectful tendernefs,
" What (faid he) is the caufe of this gloom
" which hangs upon my prince's brow ? What
" uneafinefs preys upon his heart, which he
" conceals from his faithful and devoted fervant ?
" Say, I conjure you, is there any remedy in my
" power to procure ? If my life, if any thing
" dearer than my life can give you but a mo-
" ment's pleafure, fpeak, and you fhall fee that
" I hold nothing in competition with it."

The prince was fo ftruck with this unexpected addrefs, that he had no power to make
any anfwer ; but his filence fufficiently expreffed what the other wanted. " It is fo, (conti-
" nued he, embracing his knees in a well-feig-
" ned rapture) my anxious heart divined aright ;
" the charms of *Louifa* have attracted your re-
" gard. Take her ; and may you both be hap-
" py. I refign her to a worthier lover. Let
" what will be my fate, my happinefs fhall ne-
" ver interfere with yours."

It is impoffible to exprefs what the prince
felt at fuch an exalted inftance of regard. He
raifed him from the ground, and embracing
him tenderly, " No, my dear baron ! (faid he,
" as

" as soon as he could speak) I cannot, will
" not put your attachment to such a severe
" trial. The very offer you have made is a
" pain to me to hear; and I were the most un-
" generous of men, should I take advantage of
" it."

These words, but a few hours before, would
have made the baron happy; but circumstances
were altered now, and he was resolved to complete the obligation, by appearing to bestow
what he could not keep. He therefore repeated
his offer so strongly, that he at length subdued
all the prince's scruples, and brought him to a
compliance which his heart panted for.

## CHAP. VI.

*Continued. A mirrour for the female mind. Fear
and resentment triumphant over love and virtue.*

BUT this was much the easiest part of his
undertaking. The prince's inclinations
assisted his arguments, but his mistress's were
on the opposite side. She really loved him,
and had beside so high a sense of honour and
virtue, that it seemed in vain to attempt per-
suading her to take a step so contrary to her
principles, and so destructive to her passion.
But he was not to be discouraged by difficulties. He had conquered his own love, and his
opinion of female constancy was not so high as
to make him despair of the same success with
her; though he judged that some address might

be neceſſary to ſave appearances. He went to her, therefore, directly, when he left the prince, and putting on an air of the deepeſt diſtreſs, on her inquiring tenderly what ailed him, burſt into a flood of tears, and turned from her; the regret which he really felt at the thought of loſing her aſſiſting his deſign.

Struck with ſuch ſtrange behaviour, ſhe eagerly aſked him what could be the matter? when, looking wiſhfully in her face for ſome moments, "O Louiſa! (ſaid he) muſt I loſe " you? Why have I not power to ſupport my " right againſt the lawleſs invaſions of tyranny?"

"Good Heaven! (exclaimed ſhe, terrified " and amazed) What can you mean? What " tyrant invades your right? Or, who ſhould " take me from you?"

" And have you not heard of it then? (ſaid " he) Has not the mandate yet arrived, that is " to tear you for ever from my arms? Give " orders to be denied to every one, even to the " king. Let them ſay you are ſick, confined " to your bed; or any thing, to prevent your " being ſeen. I muſt leave you now; but I " will return, privately, in half an hour, when " it will be dark, and unfold the whole of our " misfortunes to you."——Saying this, he left her abruptly, with all the appearance of diſtraction and deſpair.

The aſtoniſhment and terror with which this ſtruck the lady, may be eaſily conceived. She inſtantly gave the orders he deſired, and withdrew to her chamber, where ſhe waited for his return, with the moſt anxious impatience. At length he came; and, being admitted with every alarming circumſtance of caution

tion and fear, after some most passionate exclamations at the severity of his fate, he acquainted her of the king's having unhappily taken a liking to her ; the consequence of which was, that he would certainly enjoy her either by persuasion or force.

The character of the king made such a story too probable, especially as a woman wants but little proof of the power of her beauty. She seemed astonished at the news, and expressed the strongest concern ; but vanity glistened through her grief, and the many and particular questions which she asked betrayed a levity at least, which lessened her in her lover's eyes.

As soon as she had recovered herself, however, from the first emotions of her surprize, she asked if there was no way of escaping such a misfortune? and even proposed an immediate marriage, to prevent it ; but he replied, that such a rash expedient would only provoke the king's resentment to his ruin, without being any protection to her, as he had shewed on many occasions, that he made light even of that sacred tie, when it interfered with his pleasures.

When he had let her dwell upon her fears for some time, which he still heightened by new circumstances of danger, from the capricious and cruel temper of the king, whose fatal effects, the objects he was one moment fondest of often felt the next, the least violent of which was to be immured for life in a convent, he at length answered to her repeated intreaties of devising some way for her to escape such a misfortune, that he knew but

of.

of one which would prevent the king's defigns; but at the fame time would be equally deſtructive to his own hopes.

" O name it! (ſaid ſhe eagerly, terrified to
" death at the thought of a convent) Name any
" thing that will ſave me from him; and Hea-
" ven will inſpire us with ſome means for ac-
" quiring evey thing elſe afterwards."

" The prince (anſwered he with a ſigh) the
" prince alone can ſave you from him."

" Why do you heſitate then to apply to him?
" (interrupted ſhe eagerly) his friendſhip, his
" goodneſs will do any thing."

" Say rather his love; (replied he) for that
" alone can do it."

—— " His love! I underſtand you not."

—— " Nothing but the love of the ſon can
" ſave you from that of the father. You muſt
" inſtantly reſolve, therefore, which you will
" accept of. The king waſtes no time in
" courtſhip. He will apply directly to your
" father, and tempt his ambition with ſome
" gilded bait; or, if that ſhould not prevail,
" what ſubject can reſiſt a monarch's power?
" The miniſters of his pleaſures may be this
" moment at the gate."

—— " Direct me Heaven! Is there no other
" way, no other method of avoiding this dread-
" ful alternative? Beſide, the prince— he has
" never declared. What ſhall I; can I do?
" No! I will die firſt. Let us this inſtant fly
" this hated place. It were better to live in a
" deſert, than under ſubjection to ſuch tyran-
" ny."

—— " O my Louiſa! it were happineſs to
" live any where with you; but, alas! whither
" could

" could we fly to efcape his power? We fhould
" only heap tenfold ruin on our heads by fuch
" an attempt. No! fince I cannot be bleffed
" with you myfelf, let me confult your happi-
" nefs. The prince loves you, paffionately
" loves you. His eyes, his whole behaviour
" has long fince declared it. He is generous,
" tender, and conftant; and with him I fhall
" at leaft have the confolation of feeing you
" happy: confider the difference between being
" dragged away by violence to the loathfome
" bed of an old imperious tyrant, the beft re-
" leafe to be expected from which is to be
" locked up for ever in a convent; and yield-
" ing to a young and amiable prince, whofe
" heart doats on you."—— Then feeing that
her refolution began to waver, " I will go
" (continued he) this inftant, and refign my
" pretenfions to him; and make him believe
" that I facrifice to his favour what is the ef-
" fect of irrefiftible neceffity; for he knows
" not of his father's intentions. Do you, O
" Louifa! imitate my example, and, appearing
" ignorant of our misfortune, yield as if from
" inclination. It will enhance the favour,
" and eftablifh his love on the folid bafis of
" efteem. I'll go this inftant and fend him
" to you. A moment's paufe for thought
" would lead me into madnefs and defpair,
" Take care to be denied by every-one but
" him."

The fituation in which he left her is hard
to be defcribed. Her love for the baron, her
principles of honour and virtue, all refifted the
complying wi h the prince; but, on the oppofite hand, there was no other way of efcaping

from

from his father; and the baron's making the proposal raised a resentment that almost ballanced her passion for him; for she would have had him meet ruin rather than think of parting with her.

In this distress, she formed a thousand different resolutions; but was still unresolved till the arrival of the prince decided the conflict; when the reluctance with which she yielded confirmed him in the opinion of her love for the baron, and consequently of the greatness of the sacrifice he had made to him, to prevent the lessening the merit of which, by a discovery of the motive, the latter took care to make the prince's amour immediately public; which prevented the king's taking any farther notice of her.

This affair, which in the beginning threatened to ruin the baron in the prince's favour, by this prudent management secured it to him for ever. He thought it impossible that a man, who had made such a sacrifice to him, should not be as faithful to his interest in every instance; and the king, his father, soon after dying, he resigned the reins of government absolutely into his hands.

CHAP.

CHAP. VII.

*Mystery of favouritism concluded. The necessary effects of ridicule. Ministerial use of unlimited power; with the natural consequence of ill-placed confidence.*

THE first use which the new minister made of his power was, to traverse the measures, and remove all the ministers of the late king. To reconcile his master to a step so contrary to the natural mildness and benevolence of his temper, he had long taken every occasion to decry the understanding of the late king, and turn all his ways into ridicule. Every man has peculiarities which will not bear to be shewn separately, and in an unfavourable light. Not considering that he was guilty of many, equally inconsistent, and reprehensible, the young king had insensibly accustomed himself to find fault with, and deride the oddities and foibles of his father, which his favourite was never weary of displaying in the must ludicrous light.

The sting of ridicule is always poisoned. Though the wound it marks is at first so slight as even to be over-looked, the deadly venom soon spreads through the whole body, and infects the most distant parts. From laughing at the late king's foibles, the transition was easy to hold his most serious measures in contempt. He that was a fool in one thing, could not be wise in any; nor were the servants, who

could

could proftitute themfelves fo far as to minifter to his folly, worthy of truft from a wifer
mafter.

The court immediately affumed a new appearance. Every office of honour and profit was
filled with the minifter's creatures; while the
king, who faw only with his favourite's eyes,
looked fo coldly on all who difdained to enter
themfelves into that ignominious lift, that they
forebore coming into his prefence, where they
were fure of being infulted by thofe whom but
a little before they would have fcorned even to
fpeak to; and left him invironed with a mercenary band, joined by their common intereft
in a confederacy, to keep honour, truth, and
juftice at a diftance from the throne.

In the mean time, the minifter was not at a
lofs how to maintain the influence he had acquired. He flattered the king's tafte for pleafure and magnificence, and diverted his attention from every thing that looked like bufinefs;
embarraffing with innumerable difficulties every
motion which he did not immediately fuggeft
himfelf; while he contrived fo, as that all his
own fchemes met the readieft fuccefs.

The importance which this management gave
him, with a prince naturally indolent and vo-
luptuous, is obvious. Sure to be gratified in
every thing he liked, he thought himfelf happy
in having one upon whom he could fo entirely
depend, to eafe him of the cares and fatigues
of government. Not that his minifter prefumed
to obtrude his opinions directly, or feem to
dictate to his mafter; on the contrary, he infinuated his fentiments with fuch delicacy and
addrefs, that the king miftook them for his
own,

own, and imagined he governed the man who directed his very thoughts.

But this happiness was far from being solid. The affections of the nobles, who were the real ornaments and support of the throne, were alienated from their sovereign, by a partiality equally injudicious and disgraceful; and the people, who saw the taxes under which they groaned, and which were more than they were able to bear, lavished upon an insolent favourite and his greedy followers, swelled with discontent and indignation, which threatened to burst in a storm that should shake the throne; while the minister, as if he was impatient for his fate, lived in a magnificence that exceeded even that of his sovereign, and was an insult to their misery.

Nor did he stop here. Scorning to have the effects of his power confined within his master's dominions, he madly involved himself in the intrigues of the neighbouring princes, and entered unprepared into a war in which he had no concern. The consequence was what reason might have foreseen. His sovereign was driven from his capital, his country was laid waste, his cities plundered; his palaces, on which he had expended so much care and cost, spoiled of all their magnificence and riches, and his subjects compelled to serve in the armies of his enemies; and, to compleat his misfortunes, his reception from those to whom he fled for refuge, cold and insolent to such a degree as gave him too just reason to apprehend their proceeding to actual rebellion, and tearing the crown from his head. Yet amid all this ruin, though evidently the consequence of

*bis*

his favourite's counsels, the latter still preserved his ascendency by the same flattery which first acquired it, and made him persist in his wild schemes, chusing that he should plunge into the gulph to the brink of which he had brought him, rather than enter into measures of accommodation, in the course of which his eyes might be opened, and his indignation raised to deliver himself from such a state of slavery, and take the reins of government out of such unworthy hands.

"Unhappy is the people (said I to myself, "shocked at so gross an infatuation) whose "king is governed by a favourite! Unhappy "is the king who lets another stand between "him and his people; who sees not with his "own eyes, nor is able to redress their griev- "ances, and reward their merits from his own "experience; but, besieged by a set of syco- "phants whose aim is to deceive him, is kept "in a state of darkness and delusion, till he is "awoke from his dream of happiness by the "stroke of ruin."

I was diverted from these reflections by the entrance of the minister to his sovereign. "I "congratulate your majesty (said he, with an "air of exultation) on the most fortunate event "that could have happened. The king of "*Spain* has at length declared for our allies. "The wealth and power of that mighty king- "dom will overwhelm those haughty Islanders, "and oblige them to withhold the assistance "whch has hitherto supported the enemy; so "that you are now delivered from the dif- "graceful necessity of accepting terms from "him."

"Is

" Is it poffible ( anfwered the king ) that he
" can have been prevailed upon to break a
" neutrality which has been fo advantageous,
" to him ? Who has been able to make him
" take fuch a ftep ? Or what motives can have
" urged him to intrude himfelf, as I may fay,
" into a war in which he may lofe much, and
" can gain nothing ?"

" The motives, replied the minifter, which
" fhould influence every fovereign. A gene-
" rous indignation to fee the different branches
" of his own family oppreffed ; and a prudent
" care to ftop the progrefs of their enemies in
" time, before their power fhould become fo
" great as to be dangerous to all their neigh-
" bours. All will go now as we wifh. Your
" majefty's enemies will be humbled in the
" duft ; and you will return to your capital in
" triumph, ftrengthened by your victorious al-
" lies, to fubdue this rebellious kingdom alfo,
" and make it hereditary in your family. Will
" your majefty honour me with your prefence
" this evening, at an entertainment which I
" defign on this happy occafion. I have fome-
" thing to fhew you that will give you plea-
" fure. The painter and ftatuary whom I fent
" to Italy are returned, and have brought fome
" of the moft curious and valuable remains of
" antiquity in their feveral arts. There is one
" in particular moft remarkably fine. It is a
" ftatue of *good fortune*, dedicated by *Marius* on
" his laft triumphant return to Rome, from
" whence he had been driven by his enemies,
" I was juft looking at it when this account
" from Spain arrived, and own that I was af-
" fected with fo ftriking a circumftance." .

" I

" I wish it may prove an happy omen ; (an-
" swered the king, somewhat elated at the news,
" and still more pleased with the account of the
" arrival of the painter and statuary ) but we must
" hope the best. What is it o'clock ? I'll go
" directly. I have a mind to see your new
" acquisition, and ask those people some ques-
" tions about *Herculaneum.*"

Such an infatuation was too gross. I could
bear it no longer ; but turned away, sick at
heart, from the mortifying sight.

## C H A P. VIII.

*The scene changed. A national character. Ano-*
*ther great man. Curious account of an inn,*
*with an entertainment of political puffs.*

THE motives which the minister had alledged for the king of Spain's entering
into the war, wore such an appearance of plau-
sibility, that I resolved to visit his court, that I
might see if all his measures were conducted
with equal prudence and spirit.

I had seen enough of the country in which
I was, to satisfy my curiosity ; nor did I desire
to travel again through the scenes of military
glory, exhibited by those around it. I therefore *wished* myself directly into Spain, but at
more distance from the court, that I might
have an opportunity of observing the manners
of the people, which, I apprehended, seldom
appear in their genuine colours there.

The

The firſt thing that ſtruck me, on my arrival, was the poverty in which the middle and lower ranks of the people lived. The real wants of nature are very few; but the conveniencies which human ingenuity has diſcovered to make life more agreeable, (I ſpeak not of the vitiated cravings of luxury) and which cuſtom has made almoſt indiſpenſible, comprehend a wider circle. Of theſe they were in a manner as utterly deſtitute, as if they were incapable of the arts which could procure them.

The compaſſion, which ſuch a ſtate of wretchedneſs muſt naturally raiſe, was ſoon turned into contempt, when it appeared to proceed wholly from themſelves. The face of the country ſhewed that nature had moſt amply done her part to make the inhabitants happy; but every aſſiſtance of their own was wanting: and after a long and profound peace, the defects of idleneſs equalled the ravages of war in other countries. The lands were uncultivated, the cities in ruins, and the people wretched. Yet, amid all this, a pride peculiar to themſelves appeared in every word and action, that made their miſery ridiculous; but then at the ſame time it alſo enabled them to bear it, by diverting their attention from their diſtreſſes to their imaginary importance. They looked upon themſelves as ſuperior to the reſt of mankind; and in conſequence of this opinion ſubmitted without repining to the ſevereſt wants, rather than debaſe their dignity by the exerciſe of any induſtry or art.

While

While I was making thefe remarks, I happened to take notice of two men, from whofe converfation I learned that they were going to court. They were Frenchmen, and by their equipage and drefs appeared to be perfons of diftinction; but I directly faw through their difguife, that they were ecclefiaftics of the order of the Jefuits, who concealed their character for a fpecial purpofe. My opinion of thofe religious made me attach myfelf to them without hefitation, as the beft guides I could poffibly have.

When I joined them, they were entering the yard of an inn to which they had been directed as the beft in the town. At the door of it fat a man who appeared to be in the vigour of life, healthy, ftrong, and formed for any kind of exercife or labour. Though the day was uncommonly hot, he was wrapped clofe in his cloak, with one leg thrown carelefsly over the other knee, and his elbow refted on a heap of ftones, which feemed to have been piled up as a buttrefs, to fupport the wall of the houfe, while he lolled back, loft in the contemplation of his own confequence.

As the travellers advanced to the door, one of their fervants called aloud. The Don, without deigning to move a limb, or difcompofe the gravity of a fingle feature, having eyed him for fome time, vouchfafed to afk him what he wanted. "We want (anfwered the elder "of the two gentlemen) fome body to take "our horfes, and fhew us into the houfe."

"Yonder is the ftable (replied the Spaniard, "pointing to an hovel half of which was tum-
"bled

" bled down and the reſt ready to follow,) you
" may put your horſes there, and by that time
" the people of the houſe may be at leiſure to
" come to you."

" At leiſure! (returned the gentleman im-
" patiently) is not this an inn?" Then calling
" again, an old woman half naked came out,
" and going to take his horſe; " What, woman,
" (continued he, vexed at being kept broiling
" ſo long in the heat) is there no other ſervant
" beſide you? Where is the maſter of the
" houſe?"

"Here I am (anſwered the Don, riſing de-
" liberately and adjuſting his whiſkers) what
" is your buſineſs with me? I ſuppoſe you do
" not expect that I ſhould wait upon you?"

" By no means, ſir, (ſaid the other, who
" did not deſire any altercation with ſuch an
" adverſary;) I only want to have ſome of
" your ſervants called."

" It is very well; (anſwered the Hoſt) the
" woman will put your horſes in the ſtable; and
" you may follow me into the houſe."

The travellers, who directly ſaw into their
hoſt's character, thought proper to accept his
polite invitation; and attended him into a room,
the furniture of which conſiſted of two or three
broken ſtools and an old table; but the very
wretchedneſs of it proved at this time a convenience; the cracks in the walls drawing an
air on every ſide, that was the beſt refreſhment
they ſeemed likely to find in ſuch a place.

When they were ſeated, the gentlemen
turned to their hoſt, who had not waited for an
invitation to ſit down with them, and aſked
him what they could have for dinner. " Sir,

5                                    " anſwered

" (answered the other) the house is plentifully
" provided with every thing, as my wife will
" inform you when she comes; I mind not
" these matters." Then stroaking down his
whiskers, with great solemnity, " Pray, gen-
" tlemen (continued he) what news is there? I
" hear the wrath of the king is kindled against
" the English; and that he is determined to
" extirpate their whole nation: It is a glori-
" ous resolution, and worthy of his power and
" magnanimity. I only wonder, why he has
" suffered them upon the earth so long."

As he said this, the mistress of the house
entered; and after the customary cant of being
exhausted by an extraordinary run of company
of late, confessed that all her house afforded
was some bacon and eggs. " For, (said she)
" this unlucky war has ruined us all. We
" used to have fish fit to entertain an Abbot,
" and flour that made bread white enough for
" the king's table; but now we have nothing
" at all. They pretend indeed to comfort us,
" with leave from the pope to eat flesh; but
" they do not tell us where we shall get
" it. I wish those who advised his majesty
" to this war, may be the first who perish in
" it."

" Silence, woman, and mind your own af-
" fairs! (interrupted the husband, with a tone
" of authority) how should you know any
" thing of peace or war? Leave those mat-
" ters to us, who understand them."

His wife obeyed the sovereign mandate without reply, and retired; when he, swelling with
double importance from such a triumph,
" When we have subdued these English (continued

tinued he, addressing himself to his guests) "we
" shall be better supplied with those things,
" and many others than ever. They will be
" obliged to bring them to us as tribute, not
" for sale ; and to perform for us all the servile
" offices of trade, which it would be a disho-
" nour to a Spaniard to defile his hands with.
" Our slaves in America work better than
" when they had their liberty. Beside, they
" are heretics ; and it is a sin, as well as a dis-
" grace, to be at peace with such. Our cu-
" rate preached us an excellent sermon to this
" effect, last Sunday; when, among other
" things, he told us, that all the catholic
" powers had at length agreed to join and root
" them out. It is a glorious and a pious
" undertaking. Since the holy wars there has
" been nothing like it."

As their sumptuous fare required not much
time for preparation, the entrance of it interrupted this magnanimous politician here, at
which he seemed not better pleased than the
travellers were with their entertainment.

While they were refreshing themselves as
well as they could, I took the opportunity of
going to see the town, the inhabitants of which
I found most exactly characterized by the inn-
keeper and his wife ; all those who applied to
any kind of industry repining, like her, at the
war ; and the drones of society, who starve in
idleness, vapouring with him of conquest and
glory.

CHAP.

## CHAP. IX.

*Wheels within wheels. Certain great transactions deduced from unsuspected causes; with the advantage of having two strings to a bow.*

AS soon as the heat of the day was abated, the travellers continued their journey, when the elder addressing himself to his companion, "You seemed surprised (said he) at "the odd composition of our host; but a little "acquaintance with these people will make it "familiar to you. Pride and poverty are the "characteristics of this nation, not only in his "low sphere, but also in the very policy and "government of it, in which they maintain a "struggle that makes them justly held in con- "tempt by the rest of the world."

"If that is the case, (answered the other) I "am the less surprised at their entering thus "madly into a war, for which they appear to "be so ill-provided; though, I own, the cau- "tion with which they avoided it so long gave "me a better opinion of them; and I should "be glad to know what motives induced them "to alter a conduct which they seemed to un- "derstand the advantages of so well."

: "The measures by which most of the na- "tions in the world are governed (replied the "former) are so inconsistent not only with rea- "son and justice, but even with themselves, "each day producing a new system contradic- "tory to the last, that you must not expect a "satis-

" fatisfactory account of them. As an inftance
" of this, the motives of the Spaniards for en-
" tering into this war are hidden, even from
" the perfons who think they are the authors
" of it; and who, unknown to themfelves,
" are ferving a caufe which they had rather
" ruin.

" It may be neceffary to explain this to you.
" The jealoufy which the power of our order
" has for fome time raifed in the very courts
" whofe favour principally exalted it to that
" power, has at length burft upon us in a
" ftorm, not to be refifted in Portugal, and
" threatened not much lefs in France. To
" avert this misfortune required the utmoft ad-
" drefs. Our influence in Spain, though ra-
" ther in decline, is ftill confiderable. This
" we obliquely propofed to the French mini-
" ftry, to exert in their behalf, to bring the
" Spaniards to affift them in a war under which
" they were ready to fink, on condition of their
" protecting us from any farther difturbance in
" France; which they accordingly have pro-
" mifed.

" The lure, which we held up to the Spa-
" niards, to draw them into a meafure fo con-
" trary to their intereft, was the crown of Por-
" tugal. We know, by experience, that it
" was not poffible to make the court of Lifbon
" break with the Englifh. We therefore firft
" inflamed the ambition of the Spanifh mini-
" ftry, by blazoning their king's claim to the
" Portuguefe throne in the ftrongeft colours;
" and perfuading them that this was the pro-
" per opportunity for afferting it, when the
" hearts of the people were alienated from their

" fo-

" sovereign by the disasters of his reign, and
" the English so taken up with the wars in
" which they were already engaged, that they
" could afford him no protection, though he
" was so bigotted to their alliance, that he
" would certainly give a colourable pretence
" for attacking him, by refusing to enter into
" the confederacy against them. Our scheme
" was successful. The Spaniards, without
" considering farther, broke with the English,
" and we obtained the protection, for a time
" at least, which we desired in France.

" But this was not our only motive for urg-
" ing this court to take these measures. The
" wound we have received from Portugal is
" not to be forgiven, nor to be healed but by
" the ruin of that monarchy. If the Spaniards
" should be able to establish the claim which
" we have spirited them up to assert, our re-
" venge will be amply gratified ; though could
" we even foresee the contrary, that would make
" no alteration in our measures. The war it-
" self, be the event what it will, must in some
" degree wreak our vengeance, and be of far-
" ther service to us, by diverting to other ob-
" jects an attention that boded unfavourably
" to our hopes.

" Weighty as these reasons were, we had
" others still of greater importance, which we
" pursued with a policy so deep as to defy de-
" tection. You know that the great object of
" our attention has long been to establish an
" independency in some part of the world.
" A thorough knowledge of the present cir-
" cumstances of Europe convinced us, that we
" must not think of such a thing there. We
" there-

" therefore naturally turned our eyes to Ame-
" rica, where the weakness of the possessing
" powers was a temptation as strong as the
" riches and fertility of their possessions. By
" both these the dominions of Portugal were
" from the beginning marked out for our at-
" tempt; to give success to which we have,
" for near half a century, been labouring to
" make that crown break with England. In
" that case, we should have immediately join-
" ed with the latter, and, by giving them a
" share of the spoil, gained the assistance of
" their naval force, to execute our designs.
" But the Portuguese were too wary, and for
" once understood their own interests too well
" to go so far, though we absolutely led them,
" in many instances, to act in such a manner
" to the English, as would have drawn the
" resentment of a people less prudent upon
" them.

" Being disappointed in this our first scheme,
" all that remained for us to do was, to make
" the like attempt upon the Spaniards, against
" whom we intended to turn the same wea-
" pons at a proper time; and doubt not but,
" by the help of the English, we shall be able
" to accomplish our design of erecting an em-
" pire in some part of their American domi-
" nions, while they are pursuing the chimeri-
" cal claim we have set them upon here, and
" wreaking our revenge upon Portugal. As
" to the equity of these measures, that never
" comes into question till after the event. If
" they are successful, no one will deny it; if
" not, they will be condemned, though dic-
" tated by the voice of Heaven. Thus you see

K 3                    " that

" that, at any rate, the war muſt anſwer ſome
" of our purpoſes, at the ſame time that we
" do not appear to be in the leaſt concerned
" in it."

" I am much obliged to you for this ac-
" count, (ſaid the younger) which ſufficiently
" explains the motives of your engaging ſo
" warmly in matters apparently ſo little inte-
" reſting to you. I ſhould be glad alſo to know
" by what arguments you can have perſuaded
" the court of Spain into meaſures evidently ſo
" contrary to their intereſt. The voice of the
" people, who ſeldom judge wrong, is loud
" againſt the war."

" Gold, my friend! (anſwered the other)
" Gold, the great perſuaſive of the world, was
" the argument we made uſe of. This was
" the weight which ſet the main ſpring of the
" machine in motion. The ſpecious pretexts
" indeed that covered it were prudence and ho-
" nour, which a proper application to their
" natural vanity made the croud receive with-
" out examination; not to omit religious pre-
" judice, that abſolute tyrant of weak minds.

" We perſuaded them, that it was a dero-
" gation from their honour to ſee a prince, ſo
" nearly allied to their mighty monarch as the
" king of France, diſtreſſed in ſuch a manner;
" that his conquerors, if not ſtopped in time,
" would fall upon them next; and that it was
" ſerving the cauſe of God, to attack heretics.
" By theſe various arguments we have gained
" our great point of making them break with
" the Engliſh; but our trouble ended not there.
" It will require equal addreſs, and infinitely
" more pains, to keep up their ſpirits, and pre-
                                             " vent.

" vent their quitting it as poorly, as they un-
" dertook it rashly. This is the occasion of
" my coming here at this time; and as the
" bright abilities you are known to possess, and
" the strong attachment you have to our cause,
" have made the whole order expect the greatest
" things from you, I chose you for my com-
" panion and associate, and have given you
" this general view of the present state of affairs
" here, to direct your own observations in the
" course of our most delicate and difficult ne-
" gociations, and enable you to act in case any
" thing should happen to me."

This account, which I have here thrown
together, was the substance of several different conversations, during their journey to
Madrid.

## C H A P.  X.

*More great matters. Home truths. A character
out of nature; with a new definition of the laws
of war; and a certain method of reducing a nation to obedience.*

THE morning after they arrived, the elder went to wait upon the first minister.
The silence and solemnity which reigned
through the whole court struck me with respect.
" Certainly, (thought I) the Jesuit must have
" misrepresented these people. Instead of the
" hurry, noise, and giddy bustle, so offensive
" in other courts, every thing here bears that
" ap-

K 4

" appearance of ferioufnefs, which is the fha-
" dow of wifdom."

The firſt fight of the miniſter confirmed me
in this opinion. He was dreſſed in black
cloaths, whoſe hue added a gloom of additional gravity to his whole appearance. By his
looks and motions, his foul feemed to be
wrapped in the moſt intenfe thought. His
eyes were fixed; his features all ſtrained to the
ſtrongeſt attention, and his ſteps ſlow and
ſtately.

When the ceremonials of addreſs were performed with proper punctuality, and the attendants difmiffed, the Jefuit entered directly upon bufinefs. "I am come (faid he) accord-
" ing to your excellency's defire, to fettle every
" thing that may have been omitted, and con-
" clude the treaty; for which purpofe I have
" brought the proper powers from his majeſty
" my maſter; who has alfo honoured me with
" the pleafing office of delivering to you fome
" particular tokens of his efteem."

" I am obliged to his majeſty; (anfwered the
" Don, with an air of more than miniſterial im-
" portance) he does me juſtice in believing
" that my inclinations are to ferve him; tho'
" what I have undertaken is really moſt diffi-
" cult, if not dangerous. We have declared war
" as you defired; but how we are to carry it
" on is hard to fay. Our magazines are empty,
" our troops not half compleat, and even thefe
" undifciplined and badly provided; and our
" marine, far from being in a condition to
" cope with that of the enemy; fo that really
" I am almoſt afraid to look forward to the
" confequences."

" Your

" Your excellency will pardon me for saying
" (replied the Jefuit) that your apprehenfions
" are too ready; you have money, and that
" will foon procure every neceffary of war.
" The wealth of our enemies alone overpowers
" us; but with the addition of yours we fhall
" be as much too powerful for them. You
" will have the honour of ferving us in fo cri-
" tical a conjuncture; nor is there any danger
" in the attempt. They are tired of the war,
" and want a pretence for making peace, as
" much as we want a peace itfelf. The in-
" conftancy of their temper, never long plea-
" fed with any thing, is furfeited with fuc-
" ceffes. To take the advantage of this humour,
" our emiffaries have fet their minifters toge-
" ther by the ears in fuch a manner, that they
" think of nothing but fupplanting each other;
" to effect which they would willingly facrifice
" every intereft of their country.

" Of this I can give you an inftance, that
" will remove every doubt. Their king having
" lately thought proper to change his miniftry,
" thofe who were turned out, from a fpirit of
" refentment, move heaven and hell to blacken
" the characters and decry the abilities of their
" fucceffors; and, as difgrace with the prince
" is the fure means of favour with the people,
" exert their popularity with the utmoft licen-
" tious boldnefs to make them diftrufted, and
" defeat their meafures, chufing to undo all
" their own work, and lofe every advantage
" gained by the war, rather than their rivals
" fhould have the honour of bringing it to an
" happy conclufion; while the latter, with
" equal judgment, think it neceffary for them

" to.

" to retort the abuse, and act directly contrary
" to the-system of the others, as it were in
" justification of their removal; as if a king
" were the only master who had not a right to
" change his servants when he pleased; and
" thus, while this altercation goes on, the
" business of the nation stands still.

" Advantageous as this is to us, it is not the
" only good effect we promise ourselves from
" these disputes. The old ministry, who pur-
" sued the war so obstinately while they had
" the management of it themselves, will, by
" this indiscriminate opposition to all the mea-
" sures of the new, force them into a peace on
" any terms, to preserve their power; for how-
" ever finely it may found in speculation, a
" minister who will sacrifice his own ambition
" to the interest of his country, and resign his
" power to his rival rather than have the bu-
" siness suffer by a competition for it, is a cha-
" racter if not absolutely out of nature, yet so
" rarely to be found, that there is no necessity
" to guard against it; so that both parties
" equally serve our interest, by their animosity
" against each other.

" From this plain state of the matter, you
" may see that you run no hazard in joining
" with us, as a peace must necessarily and
" speedily be the consequence of the measures
" we have taken; and whatever expence you
" may be at, will be amply paid by the con-
" quest of Portugal, which you will never
" have such another opportunity of annexing
" to the crown of Spain, if you miss this:
" besides that so close a connection between
" your court and ours, will henceforward
                                    " en-

" enable them to give law to the reft of
" Europe, and yours in particular, at a proper
" opportunity to recover the many parts of
" your dominions which have been torn from
" them, in the former divifion of our in-
" terefts."

" According to your reafoning then (faid
" the Spaniard) there is no neceffity for our
" making any extraordinary efforts but in
" Portugal, which I am very glad of, as we
" were never fo unprepared."

" No! (anfwered the Jefuit) nothing ex-
" traordinary; or that can be attended with
" inconvenience is neceffary. But ftill, fome-
" thing muft be done, if only to fave appear-
" ances. Your laying fiege to Gibraltar——"

" Gibraltar! (interrupted the minifter) that
" is impoffible! abfolutely impoffible! We are
" as well able to befiege the whole ifland of
" Britain, as Gibraltar. We have no provi-
" fions made which could give the leaft hope
" of fuccefs to fuch an attempt."

" Your excellency is too precipitate; (an-
" fwered the jefuit.) Succefs! If by fuccefs you
" mean taking it, I never thought of any fuch
" thing. No! All we propofe is to raife a
" ferment in England, and give their miniftry
" an excufe for making a peace. We are fuf-
" ficiently fenfible that it cannot be taken."

" But if we fhould make this feint, (replied
" the minifter) do you really think the Englifh
" will ever fuffer us to conquer Portugal?
" They are bound, by intereft as well as ho-
" nour, to defend it."

" I grant they are, (returned the jefuit) but
" that fignifies nothing. Set but their mini-

K 6 " ftry

" ftry to wrangling among themfelves, and
" you may bring them into any thing.
" Their defertion of the Catalans, on a fimi-
" lar occafion, is an inftance of what the
" Portuguefe may expect by depending on
" them."

" Why, indeed, that is an encouragement,
" (faid the other) and therefore we will do all
" we can to be ready to take the advantage of
" it."

" I am glad to find that affairs go on fo well
" in Portugal, (faid the jefuit) the people, as
" I travelled through the kingdom, are full of
" fpirits at the good news; and every one eager
" to have a fhare in the conqueft."

" Yes! (anfwered the minifter) if they could
" get it by vapouring at home. As to the
" good news, it is neceffary to propagate fuch,
" to amufe the populace; but, in reality, our
" troops advance but very flowly, and meet
" difficulties every day, which we did not fore-
" fee. If the affiftance promifed us by your
" court does not arrive before the Englifh join
" the enemy——"

" Affiftance! (interrupted the jefuit) Never
" let it be faid that the mighty monarch of
" Spain wanted affiftance to over-run the lit-
" tle kingdom of Portugal. It would be an
" indelible difgrace to your honour to accept,
" affiftance. As to the Englifh, I have told
" you already how they will be taken off; and
" then you will have the Portuguefe entirely at
" your mercy. But has your excellency con-
" fidered of the advice I took the liberty to
" hint to you, of extirpating the prefent race
" of inhabitants by every feverity authorized
" by

" by the laws of war; that is, by every method
" which the conquerors pleafe to make ufe of.
" Their hatred to your nation is fuch, that it
" is impoffible ever to reduce them to a proper
" degree of fubjection and loyalty. Above all
" things, there fhould not be one of the race
" of the prefent king or even of the nobility
" left, as experience fhews that they will
" watch every opportunity to revolt, and
" affert an independency, in the fame man-
" ner as this family gained the crown by re-
" bellion."

" What you fay ( anfwered the minifter )
" agrees entirely with my own opinion. I had
" refolved upon this from the firft moment I
" thought upon the war. I am juft now going
" to attend the king, and, as matters of fuch
" confequence cannot be conducted with too
" much caution, will obtain an order exprefs-
" ly to that purpofe, under his own hand, to
" the general of his forces, to vindicate me
" from the odium of fuch an unpopular mea-
" fure. His natural turn is to cruelty, fo that
" he will moft gladly take the hint. In the
" mean time, you may affure his majefty of
" France of every fervice in my power, to
" humble his haughty enemy, and procure him
" the peace he defires."

Satisfied with the fuccefs of his negociation,
the jefuit then withdrew, and the minifter compofed his countenance into proper gravity, to
appear in public.

The natural pride and oftentation of the
Spaniards at firft made me fomething furprifed
at the freedom and candour with which the
minifter confeffed the weaknefs and wants of
the

the Spanish government: but a moment's reflection explained his conduct, and shewed that
he acted with the strictest consistency of character. He had suffered himself to be gained
by bribery, to serve the interests of France, and
therefore could not pretend to assume a consequence; or make a vain parade of power which
he could not exert, to the very agent who had
corrupted him, and was beside as well informed
as himself.

## C H A P. XI.

*A peep behind the curtain. Royal amusements;
heroic principles and valour; with an approved
shield against certain terrible dangers.*

WHEN the minister had gone through the
ceremonies of his levee with proper dignity, he went to his master. The king appeared to be in the prime of life, hale, strong,
and active. He was seated at a table with a
parcel of shuttle-cocks before him, and mending a racket with as much earnestness as a
school-boy of seven years old.

The moment he raised his eyes from his
work, and saw his minister, " Come (said he,
" starting up, and stripping himself to his shirt)
" I have been waiting for you some time. I'll
" try if I cannot beat you more shamefully to-
" day than I did yesterday."

The minister, who knew his cue, forgot all
his gravity in an instant, and following the
                                                    royal

royal example set him, threw off his cloaths
also, and, taking up a racket, prepared for the
attack, which he seemed to maintain with as
much eagerness and delight as his master, till
he saw him begin to be tired, when, feigning
himself unable to strike another stroke, he dropped the racket out of his hand, and sat down
puffing and blowing on the floor, while the
king, to shew his superior abilities, and insult
his antagonist, gave half a dozen strokes more
by himself.

As soon as they had recovered their breath,
and put on their cloaths, " May it please your
" majesty, (said the minister, resuming his so-
" lemnity) I have just received an account
" from Portugal. Your invincible arms bear
" all before them, and will soon reduce the
" whole kingdom. They have already taken
" a considerable village, and burned two farm-
" houses."

" Have they so? (interrupted his sacred ma-
" jesty) that's well done. Send them orders
" to burn all before them. I wish I was with
" them. I love such sport in my heart. I'd
" soon make their king rue his refusing my
" friendship. But how soon will they take
" Lisbon? I long to go there, and see how it
" looks after the earthquake, whether it is
" any thing like Herculaneum."

" Your majesty's army is advancing toward
" it, (answered the minister) but the roads
" are bad, and the country-people oppose
" them, so that they are obliged to march
" with great circumspection."

" Why do not they shoot them? (replied
" the monarch) If I was there, not one of
them

" them fhould efcape. I'd kill them all my-
" felf, as I'll fhew you juft now. The enemy
" is drawn up ready for battle, and I only
" waited for you to fee me attack them."

Then going into another apartment that
looked into a clofe court, and leading his minifter to the window, "There they are, (con-
" tinued he, laughing with delight, as he point-
" ed to a number of cats which were immured
" in the court;) there is the army of the enemy.
" The red ones are Englifh, the reft are Por-
" tuguefe. Go, reach me thofe guns yonder.
" I'll attack them directly. It will be a glo-
" rious furprize. While I fhoot with one gun
" you fhall load the other, fo that we'll keep
" up a conftant fire."

With thefe words he began the attack,
fhouting in triumph at every fhot, "There
" falls an Englifhman. There a Portuguefe!
" Now I charge them on the right; now on
" the left; now in the front; now in the rear.
" I'll fhew them that I am a general. See
" how they run! helter, fkelter, pell mell."

His heroic majefty carried on his attack in
this manner with fuch eagernefs, and continued it fo long that his minifter was more tired
of loading for him, than he had been of his
match at fhuttle-cock; at length, obferving
that one of the wounded cats fcreamed in an
uncommon manner, "A truce! A truce!
" (faid he) your majefty fhould flacken your
" fire. The enemies acknowledge your vic-
" tory, and fend a trumpet to defire leave to
" bury their dead. According to the laws of
" war, that is never refufed: befide, if you kill
" them all to-day, what will you do for an ar-
" my

" my to attack another time? There is not
" one cat left in all Madrid; your majefty's
" wars have confumed the whole fpecies."

" Well then, (faid the victorious monarch,
" who was by this time fufficiently fatigued
" himfelf) I will grant them a truce; and do
" you take care that there is a fupply of pro-
" vifions fent them. Their magazines I ima-
" gine are nearly exhaufted; I fcorn to ftarve
" my enemies. Hah! hah! hah! Don't you
" think now that I could kill all thofe Portu-
" guefe? Egad I'll go and head my army my-
" felf, as I did once before, and not let one
" of them efcape."

The fmoak of the monarch's artillery, and
the fcreaming of the wounded cats making the
field of battle not a very agreeable place to ftay
in, the king and his minifter returned to the
clofet. As foon as the latter had once more
compofed his features, " May it pleafe your
" majefty, (faid he) by the accounts from your
" invincible army in Portugal I find, that it is
" in vain to think of reducing that people to
" fubjection and obedience. Thofe who fub-
" mit one day rebel again the next; fo that
" there is no end of giving them quarter. Be-
" fide, the Englifh are expected every day to
" land to their affiftance, and then their num-
" bers may prove troublefome. I am therefore
" come to know what orders you will pleafe
" to fend to your generals, to direct their con-
" duct."

" Orders! (anfwered his moft facred ma-
" jefty) to put them all to the fword; that is
" the fureft way to make them obedient. As
" for the Englifh, we muft take care what we
do

" do with them: they are all hereticks, and
" magicians, and deal with the devil. I re-
" member very well how they frightened me
" once before, till I got the pope to blefs my
" night-cap; and then I defied them and their
" witchcraft too. They could do me no harm
" while I had that on. I am forry that it is
" worn out, or I would go and have a ftroke
" at them myfelf; but I could never bear to
" be one minute without it, while there hung
" a rag of it together. However, I'll fend to
" him for another; and, at the fame time, it
" would not be amifs to fend enough for the
" whole army, and his holinefs might blefs
" them all together; and when the fol-
" diers have got them, they'll be a match
" for the heretic Englifh, and the devil to
" help them."

" What your majefty fays is extremely right,
" (replied the minifter) and it would be very
" improper for you to hazard your facred life,
" before you have gotten fuch an infallible de-
" fence to guard it. In the mean time though,
" will your majefty pleafe to fend orders to
" your generals, for putting the country un-
" der military execution? They will have
" double weight, when under your own
" hand."

" Aye! (returned the gracious monarch)
" Give me pen and ink, and I will write to
" them this inftant, to burn and deftroy all
" before them, and put man, woman, and
" child to the fword, without mercy or dif-
" tinction. Or, ftay! It will do as well after
" the puppet-fhew; I am in hafte now: and,
" do you hear! Order public rejoicings to be
" made,

" made; and fend to the bifhops, to fing *te*
" *Deum* for what we have already done."

It was fome time before I could recover myfelf from the aftonifhment and horror with
which this fcene ftruck me. " Juft Heaven!
" (thought I) are thefe thy fubftitutes on earth?
" Can the vices of man have funk him fo en-
" tirely below thy care, that he fhould be given
" up thus to the moft defpicable deftruction?
" be made the play-thing of a fool, and flaugh-
" tered for his meer amufement? I can bear
" the fight no longer."

Saying this, I flung out of the court, in honeft indignation, and *wifhed* myfelf directly into France, in hopes of being relieved by the
contraft between the manners of that diffipated,
gay people, and thofe where I was. " If I
" muft be among fools, (faid I) let them be
" merry ones. Let not the affectation of wif-
" dom make folly more difgufting."

## CHAP. XII.

*Scene changed. Pleafant inftance of the power of*
*example. Grand attendance at a lady's toilet.*
*Secrets of favouritifm.*

THE effect which I felt from this change
is fcarce to be conceived. The fmile of
pleafure and complacency that foftened every
face I faw, foon difpelled the gloom which I
had contracted in the late folemn fcene, and
infected me alfo to fuch a degree, that my features

tures began infensibly to relax into a grin, and I could hardly keep my feet from capering as I went along with the croud, whom I found going to pay their court to the king's miftrefs.

They all ftopped in the antichamber to her apartments, where they waited with the moft complaifant patience for the return of the favoured few who were admitted into her prefence, to learn from them the modes of thought and action which fhe pleafed to prefcribe for the day.

Curious to fee a perfon who was able thus to rule the happinefs of fo many, I entered the dreffing-room, where I found her at her toilet, attended in a manner that exceeded my imagination, accuftomed as I was to uncommon fcenes. At her feet kneeled a bifhop, in all his facred robes, buckling her fhoes. The bafon in which fhe wafhed her hands was held by a peer of the firft rank. A counfellor of the parliament painted her cheeks. A farmer of the revenues fet her jewels in order. A general powdered her hair. An admiral tied her ribbons; and, to entertain her, a cardinal read a loofe lampoon.

When this important work was finifhed fhe arofe, and, rewarding her happy fervants with a gracious nod, retired with the cardinal into another room, to talk upon bufinefs. As foon as they were alone, " Your ladyfhip, I think, " (faid the cardinal, laughing) has been " grandly waited on this morning. Pray, have " you the fame attendence every day?"

" If I would receive it, (anfwered fhe) I " might have ten times more. There is no-" thing fo fulfome that thofe fycophants will

" not

" not fay; nothing is fo fervile that they will
" not do. I know the bafenefs of their fouls,
" and therefore trample them thus under my
" feet, to anticipate the infults which I am
" fenfible they would heap upon me on any
" reverfe of fortune. As they worfhip the fun-
" fhine of court-favour, it is but juft to let
" them toil in the heat of it for a while."

" But how did your ladyfhip gather fuch a
" groupe? (interrupted the cardinal, who feem-
" ed not much to like fome part of what fhe
" faid, and therefore was defirous to put a ftop
" to reflections fo general) Almoft every pro-
" feffion in the ftate had a reprefentative at
" your toilet."

" Yes, (replied fhe) and I defign to fet moft
" of thefe reprefentatives at the head of their
" profeffions too, which was the occafion of
" my defiring to fee you this morning."

" But does your ladyfhip know (faid the
" cardinal) whether they are qualified to fill
" thofe places? Many of them require parti-
" cular judgment and experience."

" Qualified! (interrupted her ladyfhip, with
" a contemptuous fmile) Yes; I have taken
" care to be fatisfied, that they all have the
" qualifications I want; and as for any other,
" they are anfwerable themfelves; fo let them
" take care of that. I am to give them all
" their definitive anfwers this morning; fo if
" you will go into that clofet, you may over-
" hear what paffes, and will be a judge of
" their qualifications."

The cardinal obeyed; and her ladyfhip ringing for one of her attendants, ordered him to
let

let the general know she was at leisure to speak
with him.

As soon as he entered, "Well sir, (said her
" ladyship, cutting short all compliments, and
" entering directly upon business) I have spoken
" to the minister about you, and am sorry to
" find there are so many objections made, that
" it will be necessary for me to exert my ut-
" most interest to serve you. However, as I
" have undertaken it, I will not be foiled."

" I am under infinite obligation to your la-
" dyship, (answered the general) and shall en-
" deavour to make a return."———

" Sir, (interrupted she) the return I expect
" is a punctual performance of your proposal;
" which was, to give me two thirds of all
" (exclusive of your pay) that you can possibly
" make by this commission, as well what you
" can subtract from the superfluous appoint-
" ments of your own army, as the plunder and
" spoil of the enemies. You remember, sir,
" that this was your own proposal."

" I do, Madam, (answered he) and shall
" faithfully perform it, though really the ap-
" pointments of the army at present are so very
" short, and even these so badly supplied, that
" I fear what may be saved from them will not
" answer your expectation, though I will do
" what I can; in an enemy's country soldiers
" may shift for themselves. But whatever this
" falls short shall be made up in the other ar-
" ticle. The enemies have have had a long
" opportunity to enrich themselves, which will
" turn out well to your account now. I'll
" strip them to the skin for you. It is good

6                                          " po-

" policy to ruin an enemy's country which we
" do not defign to keep poffeffion of; as it dif-
" ables them from making head again for a
" confiderable length of time. I hope alfo to
" conduct the military operations of the cam-
" paign in fuch a manner, that your ladyfhip
" fhall not be afhamed of having recommend-
" ed me to the command."

" As to that, fir, (replied fhe) it is no affair
" of mine. You are to take care of that up-
" on your own account; and I wifh you may,
" if it were only to difappoint the prefages of
" thofe who oppofed your promotion; fome of
" whom went fo far as to fay, that you were
" deftitute of every qualification neceffary for
" fo important a charge."—— Saying this, fhe
turned from him, leaving him to enjoy the pleafure of meditating on her laft words.

The departure of the general made way for
the entrance of the admiral, who was fummoned next, and whom her ladyfhip addreffed
with as little ceremony as fhe had fhewn to
the former.

" You have been recommended to me, fir,
" (faid fhe) by one of my women to whom, I
" underftand, you have the honour of being
" related, as a proper perfon to be entrufted
" with the command of a fleet, to cruize upon
" the enemy; and, on her vouching your me-
" rit, I have got you preferred before feveral
" officers of known ability."

" I am eternally devoted to your ladyfhip,
" (anfwered he, elated at his fuccefs) and hope
" I fhall be fo happy as not to difappoint your
" expectations in any refpect."

" I

" I hope not, (replied fhe) and, as I con-
" fide in the character given me of you, have
" not yet exprefsly ftipulated any conditions;
" but you muft not imagine upon that account
" that I do not expect any. You know the
" nature of the command which you are to go
" upon. It is to attack the enemy's trade,
" and plunder their fettlements in thofe places
" where you expect to meet the leaft refiftance.
" Now, fir, in executing fuch a commiffion
" you muft certainly make many valuable cap-
" tures; three fourths of the clear produce of
" which I fhall expect, for procuring you the
" command; the reft you may divide among
" yourfelves. If you approve of this, your
" commiffion fhall be made out directly."

" I am too fenfible of your ladyfhip's favour,
" (returned he) to diflike any thing you pro-
" pofe. As for myfelf, I have nothing in view
" but honour; and that, at leaft, I fhall have
" an opportunity to acquire."

" Honour, fir! (interrupted fhe haftily)
" How do you mean? If it is by fighting with
" the fleets of the enemy, you quite miftake
" the matter. Inftead of that, you muft ufe
" all poffible care to avoid them, and not run
" the hazard of difappointing the defign upon
" which you are fent, and lofing the fleet en-
" trufted to you in attempting to acquire ho-
" nour. Acquire profit, and leave honour to
" the enemy."

" Yes!—— But pleafe your ladyfhip, (an-
" fwered the feaman, who did not fo well re-
" lifh the latter part of his inftructions) How
" fhall I anfwer that to the king? I fhall be
" broke with infamy."

5

" Never

"Never fear, (replied she:) do you take "care to make a profitable cruize, and I will "protect you from all danger of that kind; "and perhaps make interest also to have you "sent out again with a greater force, when "you shall not be under a necessity of ob- "serving such caution." Encouraged by this, the admiral promised to obey her orders, and went away with an high heart.

The admiral was succeeded by the farmer-general, who, advancing to her ladyship with a confident air, " I have taken the liberty (said "he) to bring your ladyship a suit of jewels, "which I hope you will like. I should not "presume to offer them, if they were not fit "for the first sovereign in Europe to wear."

" You are always very obliging; (answered "her ladyship, casting her eye carelessly upon "the jewels as she took them) they are indeed "pretty enough."

" Your ladyship does not see half their beau- "ty; (replied the farmer) if you will please to "look a little closer, you will have a better "notion of their value."

" I beg your pardon, sir, (returned she, tak- "ing notice of the paper they were wrapped in, "which was a bill of exchange for a great "sum of money) I like them extremely. They "certainly are very fine; and I must say that "you have the politest method of presenting "any thing of any man I know. I have "wanted to see you for some time, to let you "know that your proposal is accepted of."

" I am much obliged to your ladyship (an- "swered he) and shall strive to merit your fa- "vour on all occasions; though really I am

" not quite free from apprehenfions of meeting
" with fuch difficulties in this affair, as may
" make it much lefs advantageous than is ima-
" gined.   The people are fo exhaufted by the
" multitude of their taxes, that they declare
" themfelves unable to pay any more,  and in
" their defpair exprefs a difcontent little fhort
" of rebellion ;  fo that I believe we fhall be
" under a neceffity of calling for affiftance from
" the army to levy any thing."

" And you fhall have it, (replied her lady-
" fhip) whenever you require it.   That is a
" proof of their being exhaufted, indeed !  If
" they are in want, let the men all lift in the
" army, that is the  proper place for them ;
" and then the women and children will have
" enough.   Don't you fhew the leaft tender-
" nefs to one of them.  It only encourages the
" reft.   Their complaints are all feigned.   If
" they were in fuch diftrefs as they pretend,
" their fpirits would hardly be fo high.

" I fhall punctually obferve  your ladyfhip's
" directions, (returned he) and depend on your
" protection, if any thing fhould happen.

The counfellor of the parliament fucceeded
the farmer-general, to whom her ladyfhip addreffed herfelf with as little ceremony as the
others.  " Sir, (faid fhe) I have confidered of
" what you faid to me, and fear the fcheme
" is impracticable.  Your people feem too
" refractory to be influenced by fuch me-
" thods."

" Madam, (anfwered he) I muft beg leave
" to fay,  your ladyfhip's apprehenfions are
" groundlefs.   I know the temper of every
" man among them,  and what will prevail
                                        " on

" on each. If you pleafe to make the experi-
" ment, I will anfwer for the event."

" Well, fir, (replied fhe) then it fhall be fo,
" and you fhall have the place on the terms
" propofed; though, if your fcheme fucceeds
" readily, 1 fhall expect a farther confidera-
" tion, as it will then be much more valu-
" able."

" Your ladyfhip (returned he) may depend
" on my obedience to any thing you require."

" That's true, (added her ladyfhip, calling
" him back juft as he was going out of the
" room) there is one thing which I had like
" to have forgot mentioning, though indeed it
" was plainly implied in what we faid. It is
" likely that the jefuits will offer large fums of
" money, to avert the ftorm that threatens
" them. That, you know, I am to fhare in,
" equally with the other perquifites of your
" place."

" Why—really—(faid he) if your ladyfhip
" infifts upon it——; though, as it is but a
" contingency, it is difficult to bring it with-
" in any rule."

" Sir, (anfwered fhe warmly) I do and will
" infift upon it; and think it odd for you to
" make any difficulty."

" No, Madam! by no means! (replied he)
" I make no difficulty at all; but till your la-
" dyfhip had declared your pleafure, it was
" impoffible for me to forefee it. Is there any
" thing elfe?"

" No, (returned her ladyfhip) not that I
" recollect now. If I fhould think of any
" thing farther, I will let you know."

The

The next who was admitted to an audience was the nobleman who had held the bafon to her ladyſhip, as ſhe waſhed her hands. " I " am ſorry, my lord duke, ſaid ſhe, (as ſoon as " he had paid his compliments) that I have " been obliged to make you wait ſo long ; but " buſineſs, my lord———"

" Your ladyſhip (anſwered his grace, with " the utmoſt complaiſance) need be under no " concern. I am no ſtranger myſelf to the " urgency of ſtate-affairs."

" Well, my lord, (ſaid ſhe) at length I have the " honour to congratulate your grace on your " ſon's ſucceſs. His majeſty made many diffi- " culties at firſt ; but they all vaniſhed when " I told him of the match between the mar- " quis and my couſin. He ſaid, he could re- " fuſe nothing to any one who was to be allied " to me."

" My ſon is in duty obliged to his majeſty, " (replied his grace) and I have a juſt ſenſe of " your ladyſhip's favour."

" I am glad, my lord, (continued ſhe) that " your good ſenſe and prudence have enabled " you to conquer that abſurd pride of family, " which makes fools of ſo many. Though " your ſon's intended wife is the daughter of " a mechanic, ſhe is my kinſwoman; and, if I " live, I'll make the proudeſt peer of France " glad to marry into my family. The king is " the fountain of nobility, and what he can " beſtow they ſhall not want."

" Your ladyſhip's own merit (anſwered he " cooly) makes it an honour to any family to " be allied to you. I will ſend my ſon to re-
" turn

" turn his thanks to your ladyſhip, and re-
" ceive your farther commands."

The biſhop was now the only one who remained; but her ladyſhip had already had too
much buſineſs that morning, and therefore ſent
him word, that ſhe could not ſee him till ſome
other time.

## CHAP. XIII.

*Make hay while the ſun ſhines. All go to the
market, where they can have moſt for their
money. A converſation concluded in character.*

THESE important matters being thus
diſpatched, the cardinal came out of his
cloſet, and ſmiling at her ladyſhip, " It is a
" pity (ſaid he) that your ladyſhip cannot pub-
" licly aſſume the office of prime miniſter, you
" do buſineſs in ſuch a maſterly manner."

" Why, (anſwered ſhe, laughing) I have no
" notion of making many words, when I have
" reſolved upon a thing; nor of uſing the
" agency of others in what I can do better
" myſelf. They always make ſuch bungling
" work, that I have no patience with them.
" Plain-dealing prevents miſtakes. Beſide, they
" cannot get ſuch good terms as I do. People
" chaffer and higgle with them, who do not in
" the leaſt object to what I require. As to
" the breach of decency, I deſpiſe it. I ſtudy

L 3 " my

" my own conveniency, not other people's opi-
" nions."

" Your ladyſhip judges very rightly; (re-
" plied he) great minds are above the rules
" which direct the conduct of their infe-
" riors."

" Well! (reſumed her ladyſhip) Do not
" you think now that all theſe perſons are pro-
" perly qualified for my purpoſe? I hold my
" power by a very precarious tenure, and there-
" fore think it prudence to make the moſt of
" it while it laſts. What is the intereſt or
" honour of the kingdom to me? I know that
" with the king's favour I gained the hatred of
" every other perſon in the kingdom, and that
" on the loſs of that I ſhould feel all the weight
" of the latter; to avoid which I'll take care
" to provide what ſhall make my retreat elſe-
" where comfortable, for I will never ſtay a
" moment after I become ſubject to their in-
" ſults; and for that very reaſon I ſend my mo-
" ney before me as faſt as I can."

" Then your ladyſhip (replied the cardinal)
" is reſolved on going to England!"

" Moſt certainly; (ſaid ſhe) What other
" place could I expect the ſame ſafety or ſatis-
" faction in? A perſon that has but money
" enough to give into the extravagancies of the
" mode will never want an agreeable reception
" there. As to the difficulty you made about
" going with me, there is nothing in it. There
" will no more objection be made to your cha-
" racter than to mine. As ſoon as the novel-
" ty is worn off, we ſhall paſs as unnoticed as
" we can wiſh, and meet as much reſpect as
" we can pay for. The pope himſelf, ſo-
" lemnly

" lemnly as he is abjured, would find a wel-
" come in England for his money; fo that you
" need not be fo delicate and timorous. It is
" but laying afide your red hat, and you need
" apprehend nothing."

" Your ladyfhip (anfwered the cardinal, who
" did not much like the manner in which fhe
" fpoke thefe laft words) cannot think that I
" fhould make any difficulty of following you
" to the remoteft part of the world. The hap-
" pinefs I enjoy in your favour exceeds every
" other confideration. As to thofe people who
" have been with you this morning, is it your
" pleafure that I fhould mention them to the
" king; or will your ladyfhip rather do it your-
" felf? Thofe I mean whom the importance of
" the employments which you defign them for
" makes it neceffary to obferve fuch caution
" about. There will be great murmuring at
" their promotion among the nobility, who
" have applied for thofe commands."

" Let them murmur on; (replied fhe haugh-
" tily) I defpife every thing in their power to
" fay or do! I'll humble their pride, by fhew-
" ing them how little I regard them. I made
" the duke wait fo long to-day, to let him fee
" that his fon's marrying my relation gave him·
" no confequence with me. As to this affair,·
" I'll fpeak to the king myfelf, for form-fake;
" but you may order their feveral commiffions
" to be got ready in the mean time."

" Really, (returned the cardinal) I think,
" you gave his grace fufficient reafon, even·
" after he was admitted, to fee that you
" held him not in very high refpect. But how

" came

" came you not to fee the bifhop? Had he
" any particular bufinefs?"

" Bufinefs! (faid her ladyfhip, after a loud
" laugh) Yes; and that no lefs than a cardi-
" nal's hat, I affure you. Becaufe I got you
" one for garte-ing my ftockings, he founds
" his pretenfions on buckling my fhoes. Hah!
" hah! hah! It is true he offers fair. He un-
" dertakes to be either for or againft the Je-
" fuits, for or againft the *conftitution*; in fhort,
" any thing, or every thing I pleafe, now, or
" at any other time."

" Pious prelate! (added the cardinal, after
" he had joined in the laugh) He has a moft
" convenient confcience, and cannot fail to
" rife in the church. I prefume you have not
" rejected fo ample offers."

" I am not refolved about him yet; (re-
" plied fhe) I muft try his patience here firft
" for a while. When I have broken him fuf-
" ficiently by attendance, I'll then confider
" whether it is proper to gratify his ambition,
" or give him a refufal."

Their political conference was broken off
here, by one of a fofter nature. The cardinal
was too gallant not to dedicate fome part of his
private audience to love, and her ladyfhip too
tender to refufe his addreffes. After fome time
fpent in dalliance, the cardinal recollected that
the king was by that time returned from hunt-
ing, and accordingly haftened away to wait
upon him; while her ladyfhip prepared to receive the vifit which his majefty never failed
to pay her every day.

C H A P.

✿✿✿✿✿✿✿✿✿✦:✦✿✿✿✿✿✿✿✿✿

## CHAP. XIV.

*A curious, though not an uncommon picture. Play*
*a trout properly, and you'll catch it. The faf-*
*cination of eafe.*

IT was not very long before the king arrived.
From the nature of their connection I expected that their meeting would be attended
with the warmeft expreffions of paffion; but
there appeared no traces of any fuch thing between them. The king entered her apartment
with a liftlefs, indifferent air, as if he knew
not what elfe to do with himfelf; and, lolling
into a chair, fcarce returned any anfwer to her
enquiries after his health; which fhe alfo expreffed with the coolnefs of compliment and
words of courfe.

When he had fat, or rather dozed thus for
fome time, in a kind of fufpenfion of thought,
he feemed as it were to awake, and turning to
his miftrefs, gave her an account of his morning's fport, as particularly as if fhe underftood
it as well as himfelf; while fhe liftened to him
with the greateft attention and appearance of
pleafure, afking him every now and then fuch
queftions as fhould lead him to repeat thofe
paffages in which fhe faw he took the moft
delight.

When his fpirits were fomewhat raifed in
this manner, and the lady thought him in a
proper humour for her purpofe, fhe artfully

L 5 turned

turned the conversation upon bufinefs. "I "hope (faid fhe, as if carelefly and only from "common curiofity) that your majefty has re-"ceived agreeable accounts from your armies "this morning. I hear there are expreffes ar-"rived."

"Aye! (anfwered he) fo the cardinal in-"formed me; but I fuppofe they have brought "nothing material, as he faid no more."

"I cannot help thinking it very ftrange, "(continued fhe) that fuch powerful armies as "your majefty fends into the field do not bear "down all before them. Your enemies are "no way able to oppofe them with equal force. "I fhould fear that there muft be a fault fome-"where."—— Then obferving that he feemed to liften to her with fome attention, "Is your "majefty certain (continued fhe) that the ge-"nerals to whom you intruft the conduct of "your armies are equal to the charge, or at "leaft that they do not protract the war, for "the fake of continuing in their commands? "Some thing or other muft be the reafon of "it."

"Why, yes! (replied the king) I have of-"ten thought fo myfelf; and therefore I be-"lieve I'll even make a peace, and fo have "done with them all."

"A peace! (exclaimed fhe fuddenly, equal-"ly furprifed and alarmed at the word) I did "not know that your majefty had any thoughts "of peace; to be fure, it is moft defireable— "on proper terms."

"I can't fay (returned he) that I fhould "have any thought of the kind in the prefent "fituation of affairs, if fo many mifcarriages "did

" did not in a manner force me to it. It is
" very difagreeable to be difappointed in all my
" great defigns, and that after fo vaft an ex-
" pence of blood and treafure."

" Difappointed! (returned her ladyfhip, who
" now took her cue) Your majefty can never
" be difappointed in any defign, till you are
" pleafed to drop it. Inferior princes, who
" want power to execute their will, may be
" difappointed; but not a monarch, whofe
" word is a law to millions."—— Then raifing her voice, and affuming an air of indignation, " A peace! No! (continued fhe) Your
" majefty will never think of a peace, till your
" enemies are brought to beg it on their knees.
" It were beneath the dignity of your crown,
" and a leffening of your own honour. As for
" the trifling fucceffes, which have dejected
" fome of your own fubjects as much as they
" have elevated the infolence of your enemies,
" one campaign, properly conducted, will ef-
" fectually reverfe them. Shall it be faid that
" the mighty kingdom of France, governed by
" a prince equally the delight of his people, and
" the terror of his foes, was obliged to receive
" the law from a few mechanic iflanders?"

" But what can be done to prevent it? (faid
" he, rouzed from his lethargy by the fpirited
" manner in which fhe fpoke) They tell me,
" that my revenues are quite exhaufted, and
" my fubjects crying out for peace."

" Who tells your majefty fo? (anfwered fhe)
" A daftardly, flothful fet, who, regardlefs of
" your glory, think of nothing but enjoying
" in luxurious eafe the fortunes they have
" amaffed by every iniquitous means. The reve-

" nues -

" nues of a king of France can never be ex-
" hausted, while his subjects have a penny left.
" All the wealth in your kingdom is yours.
" You are not obliged to beg from your peo-
" ple, as the king of England does. As to
" their seditious cries for peace, if your majes-
" ty was to pay attention to them, you would
" never carry on a war; and for their wants,
" they are all feigned. Look around your
" court, look at those very people (traitors I
" had almost called them) who tell you such
" stories, and see whether any thing like want
" appears about them. Perhaps they mean
" that the populace is dissatisfied, because they
" cannot live in such luxury as they do them-
" selves. If they really do want, why do not
" their compassionate advocates assist them out
" of their abundance, without applying to your
" majesty? Are you only to suffer for the wants
" of the people? Must your glory, your ho-
" nour be given up, to save the superfluous
" wealth of your nobles? The very thought is
" treason; and no loyal subject would harbour
" it himself, much less presume to suggest it
" to your majesty. Every one who mentions
" peace till your enemies are humbled, and all
" your great designs accomplished, is a traitor
" to your interest and glory."

" But if I continue the war, (said the king)
" how can I be sure of better success than I
" have met hitherto?"

" Change the persons who have the conduct
" of the war, (answered her ladyship, who had
" now drawn him to the point she wanted) and
" never doubt of the success. You have hi-
" therto employed the nobility, who look up-

5.                                    " on

" on the command of fleets and armies as their
" birth-right, and confequently take no pains
" to acquire that military knowledge which
" alone gives a juft title to command, and
" promifes fuccefs; but upon any misfortunes,
" though evidently occafioned by their own er-
" rors, grow weary of the war, and advife
" peace. I would remove them all, and em-
" ploy only thofe who have given inftances of
" merit equal to fuch a truft; and who, having
" no dependance but upon your majefty's fa-
" vour, fhall omit nothing poffible to obtain
" it; nor, when their own ambition is fatis-
" fied, infolently prefume to advife your ma-
" jefty to facrifice your glory to their eafe."

" But where (replied he) fhall I find fuch
" perfons? I know of none."

" There are enough, (returned fhe) if you
" majefty pleafes to make ufe of their fervice.
" I myfelf could at this very time name both a
" general and an admiral, for whofe fuccefs I
" would be fecurity to your majefty: and as to
" your revenues being exhaufted, and your
" parliament uneafy, I have juft now been
" talking with a counfellor who undertakes to
" make the latter as implicitely fubmiffive to
" your will as you can defire: as I alfo know
" a farmer, who will make no excufes of the
" people's incapacity to pay your majefty's
" taxes. All the difficulties which thofe peace-
" makers talk fo much of are owing folely to
" their own mifmanagement; and they are
" unfaithful fervants, who make fo many ob-
" ftacles to obeying your commands. When
" the proud lazy nobles fee that you can be
" better ferved without them, their infolence
" will

" will be humbled, and they will ſtrive to me-
" rit the employments which now they in a
" manner demand as their due."

" Well! (ſaid the king, who was now
" worked up to the proper pitch) Be it ſo
" then! Let thoſe people whom you ſpeak of
" be employed. I am reſolved I will hear no
" more of peace, till I have accompliſhed my
" deſigns. I will not ſubmit my will to their's,
" nor poſtpone my glory to ſuch mean conſi-
" derations."—— Then, riſing from his chair
in a heat, he expreſſed ſeveral ſentiments of
magnanimity and heroiſm, as he walked about
the room, till, cooling from his paſſion, he
ſunk into his former ſerenity, and, returning
to his chair, took a nap, to dream of conqueſts
and glory, and compoſe his ſpirits for his dinner; while his miſtreſs diſpatched a billet to
the cardinal, to let him know that ſhe had ſettled every thing, and he might give their ſeveral commiſſions to the perſons ſhe had appointed in the morning.

" By what deſpicable agents (ſaid I to my-
" ſelf, turning away in diſguſt) does Heaven
" work the moſt dreadful events! How weak
" is the thread by which a mighty people are
" guided! At length I ſee the myſtery of fa-
" vouritiſm. To leave the mind abſolutely at
" eaſe, watch its ruling paſſions, and, without
" ſeeming to have any thing elſe in view, art-
" fully ſuggeſt the objects of one's own de-
" ſigns, as the means of their gratification.
" My ſoul is ſick of vice and folly. I'll ſeek
" relief in that happy land where a free peo-
" ple is governed by a king who is himſelf
" free, before ſuch manifold abuſes of the bleſ-
" ſings

" fings of Heaven, as have for fome time en-
" groffed my attention, make me hate my own
" nature, and abjure the name of man."——
Saying this, I *wifhed* myfelf directly into England.

* * * * * * * * * * * * * * * * * * * * *

## CHAP. XV.

*The fcene changed. A pleafing profpect fuddenly
over-caft. An eafy way to get rid of a wrangler, with a comfortable plaifter for a broken head.
He that throws dirt always fouls his fingers.*

ON my arrival in England, I found myfelf
near the feat of a nobleman of the firft
rank, in that part of the ifland which lay next
to France, not having thought of any particular place when I *wifhed* myfelf from thence.

The largenefs of the houfe, and the flourifhing condition of the extenfive demefne around
it, fhewed the wealth of the owner, as the
fmile of content on the faces of his tenants
proved his generofity and juftice. Induftry
procured plenty, and liberty fweetened at the
fame time that it fecured enjoyment.

Struck with the contraft between this, and
the fcenes I had lately feen, I fhared fympathe-
tically in the general joy; and in the honeft
pride of my heart refolved to pleafe myfelf with
taking a more particular view of the man whofe
virtues diffufed fuch happinefs around him. But
what was my furprize and difappointment, to
find the profpect overcaft where I expected to
have feen it brighteft! In his own family, and
where

where his more immediate prefence fhould have operated with the greateft force, ambition had banifhed harmony, and poifoned every breaft with animofity and rancour.

The flames of this diffention, which had long been fmothered, burft out with the moft ridiculous violence, juft at the time I entered. Though fuch a domeftic fcene as this was a defcent from thofe *great* ones which I had lately been engaged in obferving; yet, as it difplayed the inconfiftency of the human heart in a new light, I thought it merited my attention.

The occafion of the breach was this: One of the lord's agents, who, by the activity and fanguinefs of his temper, had in a manner engroffed the whole management of his mafter's affairs, had taken it in his head to go to law with one of the principal gentlemen in the neighbourhood, from an apprehenfion that he intended to take the part of a coufin of his, with whom his lordfhip had had a long fuit for encroaching upon his fide of the common.

The agent had conducted this fuit with equal judgment and fuccefs, and at a very great expence, for it was not his difpofition to ftarve any caufe he took in hand, foiled his adverfary in all his attempts, and not only recovered from him the places he had unjuftly poffeffed himfelf of, but alfo obtained feveral decrees for cofts, by which he turned him out of fo many other parts of his eftate, that he had not left him a penny to fee an attorney to carry on the fuit any longer, though his proud and litigious temper would not permit him to give it up.

Matters

Matters were in this situation, when the agent proposed filing a bill directly against the cousin, who (he said he had received undoubted intelligence) had entered into a private agreement with the other to supply him with money to go on with his law-suit, and assist him also with his interest to recover his losses. This was a direct breach of a former agreement between him and his lordship, by which he had obliged himself not to meddle in the dispute at all; the agent was for falling upon him without any ceremony, alledging, that it was much better to be plaintiff than defendant in any suit; as must certainly be their case if they were not before-hand with the other, who was at that very time preparing to attack them, as appeared by several late instances of his behaviour.

To this proposal his lordship did not think proper to give a determinate answer, till he should consult with the rest of his tenants and servants; as, by their leases, they were all bound to defray the expences of any suits which were for the general good of the estate. But when the agent acquainted them with his design, though he supported it with very strong reasons, and which in the sequel proved to be well founded, they were all of a different opinion, and said, it would be very imprudent to entangle themselves in a new dispute before they were out of the old, especially as they were already at a greater expence than they could well bear.

The agent, whose temper was too warm to brook opposition, without any respect to his master's presence, flew into a violent passion, and

and called them a parcel of poor-spirited trim-ming fellows, who would lose a pound to save a penny. They were not behind-hand with him in abuse, but said, that he was a hot-headed beggarly upstart, who, having no for-tune of his own to lose, cared not what ex-pence or danger he drew others into.

The lord thought it but just, in such a case as this, to follow the opinion of the majority, and therefore rejected the agent's proposal. But he did not give it up on that account; but resolved to try another method, by which he did not doubt of carrying his point. The great success with which he had managed his master's business, ever since he had been em-ployed, had made him such a favourite with the tenants, and given him beside so great a consequence in his own eyes, that he thought his lordship could not do without him, and would therefore submit to any thing rather than part with him. Full of this opinion, he went to him next morning, and giving him up his keys, in a kind of pet, told him, he was sorry he could not serve his lordship any lon-ger, as he thought proper to prefer other peo-ple's advice to his.

His lordship, as if he had been prepared for the thing, received the keys very calm-ly, and telling him he was also sorry to lose so good an agent, dismissed him most po-litely, with thanks for his past services.

This was a stroke the other was not pre-pared for. He stood thunder-struck for some moments; then, bursting into a flood of tears, kissed his lordship's hand passionately, and, declaring himself overcome by such goodness,

said,

faid, he was ready to fpend the laft hour of his life in the fervice of fo kind a mafter. The confequence of this he thought would have been, that his lordfhip would directly return him his keys, and re-inftate him in his employment, for he was far enough from defigning to refign it; but he found himfelf difappointed in this alfo. The lord, much as he valued him for his abilities and honefty, both of which were unqueftionable, had for fome time felt the warmth of his temper, not without uneafinefs, and was glad of fo fair an opportunity of getting rid of a fervant who had fhewed on many occafion, as well as this, that he meant to be mafter; not doubting but he had others in his family capable of managing his affairs with equal fidelity and judgment.

The fituation of the late agent on this occafion may be eafily conceived. He retired to his own houfe, and throwing himfelf on his bed, gave his mind up to the moft mortifying reflections. But what he felt from his own thoughts was nothing to the vexation he received from others. Such an affair could not in the nature of things be long kept a fecret. The moment it came to the ears of his relations, and dependants, that he had loft his employment, they all flocked about him, croaking like fo many ravens about a carrion; fome of them afking impertinent queftions, others giving abfurd advice; this upbraiding him with his rafhnefs, that accufing his mafter of ingratitude; and all lamenting the difappointment of the hopes they had built on his favour, till their noife and nonfenfe quite turned the poor man's head; the confequence of which was
tha

that in his delirium he wrote a letter to the clark of the parish, which he was to read at the veſtry, giving as a reaſon for his throwing up his employment, that his lordſhip truly would no longer ſubmit to be guided by him; and therefore he did not think it proper to ſerve him any longer.

This effectually clinched the affair. If his maſter had even been inclined to over-look what had paſſed, and take him into his ſervice again, the folly and inſolence of this letter put it out of his power; as it would have been plainly acknowledging, that he reſigned himſelf abſolutely to his guidance.

The late agent's enemies did not fail to exaggerate this unaccountable conduct in the moſt malicious manner; but his lord viewed it in another light, and juſtly imputing it to madneſs, not only took no notice of it, but alſo, to comfort him in his diſtreſs, generouſly gave him an annuity ſufficient to ſupport him in the rank of a gentleman, expreſsly as a reward for his paſt ſervices; and wrote a letter with his own hand to his wife, who was an high-ſpirited dame, and came from a good family, in which he ſoothed her vanity, by paying her the compliment of calling her a lady.

Though this act of bounty proceeded meerly from the generoſity of his lordſhip's heart, the enemies of the late agent gave it a very different turn. The ſucceſs which the latter had had in his buſineſs, and his ſanguine profeſſions of regard for the intereſt of the tenants, had won him their confidence and favour to ſuch a degree, that they immediately looked upon his giving up his employment as a ſign

that

that there were fome fchemes to their difadvantage in meditation, which he would not
join in; and, confequently, that their interefts
would be betrayed, and the law-fuit which he
had conducted with fo much credit, and
brought almoft to an happy conclufion, at
fo great an expence, patched up in a paultry
try manner, and all the money loft.

To leffen him, therefore, in the opinion of
the populace, was confidered as the moft effectual method to ftop their clamors, and difable
him from making mifchief between them and
his lordfhip's fervants. For this purpofe, to
make the news of his having got the annuity
foon enough and fufficiently known, the town-
crier proclaimed it at the market-crofs; and it
was immediately infinuated, with the greateft
induftry, that it was the price of his boafted
regard to the tenants; that he had fold his influence over them, and engaged to make them
approve any meafures his lordfhip pleafed,
however contrary to their intereft and honour.

But though this ruined his confequence, it
was far from having all the effect that was expected. The tenants feemed refolved to think
that their intereft was to be facrificed, becaufe
the perfon who fucceeded to the management
of his lordfhip's bufinefs was not immediately
of their own chufing; and therefore, inftead
of minding their work, and going to plough
and cart, as they ought to do, they fpent their
time tippling in ale-houfes, and railing at the
new agent, even before he had time to do any
thing that fhould fhew whether he was capable
of the bufinefs or not; and for fear this humour
fhould cool, fome mifchief-making folks hired
a pack

a pack of ballad-singers, to go about the streets singing black-guard songs of the agent and all his friends; who, to return the compliment, got as scurrilous a crew as the others, who threw dirt and called foul names as fast as they, for their lives : so that the whole village was in an uproar, and any stranger, who should have heard both sides, must have concluded, that there was not a man in the parish who was not a beggarly, lousy, lying, pick-pocket, vagabond, cheat, and scoundrel.

# C H A P. XVI.

*A receipt for popularity. Turn a cast-horse to graze on a common. The old steward acts the second part to the agent's farce. An hint by the bye.*

THE lord, whose own good-nature made him wish to live in harmony with all the world, was greatly vexed at such scandalous wrangling thus under his nose; not that he knew it all either : the new agent, who from a long acquaintance had a particular influence over him, let him hear no more of it than he thought proper, contriving to keep every one from him who should say a word which he did not dictate ; so that his lordship was made to believe, that all the disturbance and abuse came from the other side, and was levelled at him, as well as his servants.

Though

Though all the servants were glad of the late agent's disgrace, in hopes of sharing some part of that power which he had engrossed so entirely to himself, that they were no more than meer cyphers in the family, the one who rejoiced most openly, was the old steward.

He had been many years a faithful servant, to the best of his knowledge and abilities, to his lordship's family; and though he was never thought to be so clear-headed or resolute in the management of affairs as the late agent, yet he was very useful in some things. He had made a considerable party among the tenants, for this lord's father, when he came first to the estate, to which he was apprehensive of having his title disputed, by the generous manner in which he gave his beef and beer among them, for he was very well to-pass in the world, and never failed to treat the mob with a bonfire and a barrel of stingo every now-and-then; by which meens he also won their hearts so, that he had always a party among the parishioners, to choose what officers he bade them, so that he was able to carry any point he pleased at the vestry, which, to do him justice, was ever what his lordship directed.

By this extravagant way of living, it is true, he had gone behind-hand a good deal, but he never stopt for that, he had still something left; and the stewardship, which he had had so long that he looked upon it as his own, brought him in a good penny beside, that enabled him very well to live on at his old rate.

The imperious manner in which the late agent behaved, had made the steward long wish to be rid of him; but he did not know

how

how to bring it about; and, especially at this time, he would not even attempt it, for fear of giving any hinderance to his lord's affairs, which the other managed so well: but when he saw it thus done to his hand he could not contain his joy, but ran up and down to every servant in the house, from the butler to the scullion, poking his nose in their faces, and shaking hands with them on their happy deliverance. Coming among the rest to the new agent, and addressing him in the same manner, " My good friend, (returned the latter dryly) " take care. Do not run mad with joy to- " day, nor with grief to-morrow."

The steward's heart was too full to take notice of this speech now, but he understood it when it was too late. I have observed that the new agent was in particular favour with his lord. Though getting rid of that over-bearing wrangler was a great point gained, it was far from being all that he had in view. The stewardship was the thing he had fixed his heart upon. It was the first place in rank in the service, and, by the command of the cash, gave a power of every thing to one who had spirit to exert it; which he was resolved to do to the utmost extent, and not be encroached upon and brow-beaten by any under-servant, as the other had been.

But, though he was sure of getting the place from his lord when it should be vacant, the long services of the old steward, and the interest which his hospitality had acquired him among the tenants, from the wealthiest of whom he had always found means to borrow any money his lord wanted, till the rents came in, in, made him think it neceffary to proceed with addrefs, in getting him turned off. For this reafon he paid him uncommon compliments, and let him go on juft as he pleafed, in expectation of his doing fomething, now that he was freed from reftraint, that might give a colour for removing him; but, whether by chance or defign, he difappointed his fchemes, and proceeded fo regularly that he could take no hold of him.

This obliged him to change his meafures. Accordingly he gave orders to the receivers under the fteward, (fome of whom, tho' brought in by him, and under the greateft obligations to his bounty, bafely betrayed him, the moment they faw him totter in his place) to perplex the bufinefs of his office as much as poffible, and even difpute his orders, which, it was not doubted, would put him off his guard, and make him give the advantage that was fought for againft him, by doing fomething irregular, in his refentment.

This fcheme had the defired effect, though not precifely in the manner that was expected. The fteward, ignorant of the fnare laid for him, in the ufual courfe of his bufinefs gave one of the attorneys, concerned in carrying on the law-fuit, an order upon the receivers, for a fum of money to clear off his bill of cofts. The receivers, as they had been directed, made a difficulty of paying it without an exprefs order from his lordfhip. This was a direct attack upon the fteward's authority. He ran inftantly to the lord, and fputtering out his ftory as well as his paffion would permit him, demanded that thofe infolent fellows fhould be

difcharged directly, or he could not do his bufinefs any longer.

The lord, who by the bye was prepared for
this fecond part of the agent's farce, anfwered
him carelefsly, that he was forry to lofe fo old
a fervant; and, turning about, walked away,
humming a tune. The fteward, who had lived
in a kind of familiarity with the late lord, could
not bear fuch a flight; he left the room directly, and ran about the whole houfe, telling
every one he met how ill his lordfhip had ufed
him.

But he foon found that he had more caufe of
complaint than he knew of; for the very next
morning his letter of attorney was fuperfeded,
and the ftewardfhip given to the new agent,
who thus got the whole bufinefs into his own
hands, having put a creature of his own into
the agency, who dared not to difobey his orders in any thing.

It is not eafy to defcribe the old fteward's
aftonifhment at fuch an unexpected ftroke.
However, he preferved the dignity of his character much better than the late agent had
done; for when he waited upon his lordfhip,
to give him up his keys, &c. he made no mean
attempts to recover his favour and keep his
place; and when the lord, in the goodnefs of
his heart, offered him an annuity alfo, being
unwilling that he fhould want in his old days,
he refufed it with difdain, declaring it fhould
never be faid, " that old *True-penny*, who had
" fpent fo many pounds in good beef and ftrong
" beer, in his lordfhip's fervice, was glad to
" take up with a paultry annuity at laft."

Such

Such a return for his labour and expence
should have been sufficient to open his eyes to
the folly he had been so long guilty of, and
have taught him to live frugally and quietly the
remainder of his days; but the habit had taken
too fast hold on him to be ever shaken off.
The moment he went home to his own house,
he gathered all his old pot-companions and
trencher-friends about him, and fell to carous-
ing as usual, flattering himself with a foolish
hope, that they would stand so firmly by him
at the next vestry, that his lord should not be
able to have his business done, and therefore
must be glad to give him his place again.

While he squandered away the remains of
his substance in this idle manner, and his new
friend the late agent (for society in disgrace had
united them) sat brooding over his resentment,
and meditating schemes of revenge, the new
steward was far from enjoying his triumph in
happiness. The fall of his predecessor, who
had so long thought himself as firmly fixed as
man could be, was a warning to him; and
though he took all possible care to secure himself, by filling every place in the family, down
to the very stable-boy, with his dependants,
and letting no body, as I have observed before, come near his lord, who he was not satisfied was absolutely in his interest, yet his
fears every moment formed new dangers to
torment him; and he could not see his lord
smile upon the most devoted friend he had in
the world, without feeling a jealousy of having
his own arts played upon himself, and being
supplanted in his turn as he had supplanted the
others.

How-

However groundlefs thefe fears were at firft, they foon threatened to realize the dangers which were only of their own creation. That opennefs and gayety of temper, which firft gained him his lordfhip's favour, gave place to gloomy filence and referve; and the univerfal benevolence and philanthropy which gave irrefiftible charms to his converfation, and commanded the efteem of every good mind, were foured into jealous envy, and fufpicion, that fickened at the mention of a virtuous action.

## CHAP. XVII.

*An holiday, and a jolly day. A fumptuous feaft, and a raree-fhew.*

SO many fucceffive inftances of folly, which could thus poifon a profufion of happinefs, and turn it into mifery, filled me with the moft melancholy reflections; but I was foon diverted from them, by fomething of a lefs ferious nature.

The conftable of the village in which the lord's houfe ftood, in conformity to old cuftoms, made a feaft at this time for his lordfhip and his whole family, to which he fent them a folemn invitation by the parifh-officers. Such a fcene promifed fome amufement at leaft. I therefore returned with the officers who had come upon this important errand, defirous to fee the whole procefs of fo extraordinary an affair.

As

As the feaſt was to be given at the joint expence of the village, the principal inhabitants
had aſſembled at the conſtable's houſe, and
were ſitting over a pot of beer, waiting for
the return of thoſe who had been ſent with the
invitation ; though the whole was a thing of
courſe, their anxiety was ſo great that not one
of them could ſpeak a word till their arrival :
the moment they entered the room, all the reſt
laid down their pipes, adjuſted their perriwigs,
and wriggling their chairs nearer to the table,
liſtened to the account with open mouths, and
looks of the profoundeſt ſagacity.

"Well, gentlemen, (ſaid the conſtable, who
" ſat in an arm-chair to ſhew his authority)
" ſince his lordſhip has condeſcended to accept
" of our invitation, we ſhould take care that
" every thing is prepared in the beſt manner
" for his reception. There will be many
" things wanted to make a proper appearance
" on ſuch an occaſion, and no one would ſtop
" at a trifling expence, eſpecially as the money
" will be laid out among ourſelves."

This ſpeech opened every mouth in the
room at once. "We ſhall all want new
" cloaths," cried the taylor.

——"New ſhoes,"—ſaid the ſhoe-maker.

——"New ſtockings,"—ſaid the hoſier.

——"New wigs,"—ſaid the barber.

——"Our horſes muſt be ſhoed,"—ſaid the
farrier.

——"Our houſes repaired,"—ſaid the brick-
layer.

——"Our chimneys ſwept,"—ſaid the chim-
ney-ſweeper.

M 3                    ——"Our

——" Our vaults emptied,"—said the night-
man.

——" We muſt have a ſermon,"—ſaid the
curate.

——" A ſpeech,"—ſaid the veſtry-clerk.

——" A vomit, in caſe of repletion,"—ſaid
the doctor.

——" A clyſter,"—ſaid the apothecary.

——" A coffin,"——ſaid the undertaker. In
ſhort, every perſon preſent aſſerted the want of
ſomething in his own way, to make the entertainment compleat; and the leſs neceſſary
it was, the louder they roared.

When they had all bawled themſelves hoarſe,
and the conſtable, by repeated thumps with his
fiſt upon the table, obtained leave to ſpeak,
" Silence, gentlemen, (ſaid he) we ſhall never
" do any thing at this rate. You are all for
" providing other things before we have fixed
" upon the victuals. Let us ſettle about them
" firſt."

This word raiſed a tumult, ten times greater
than the former; every one in the room roaring
out at once for ſome particular diſh, either that
it was his trade to provide, or which he was
fond of himſelf.

The butcher bawled out, Beef.——

The poulterer, fowls.——

The fiſhmonger, fiſh.——

—" A turtle,"—ſaid an alderman.

—" A ragou,"—ſqueaked a Frenchman.

—" Pickled herrings,"—belched Mynheer.

—" Potatoes,"—cried an Iriſhman.

—" An haggis,"—ſaid a Scot.

—" Leek-pottage,"—ſputtered Taffy. In a
                                         word,

word, they all raised their voices with such vehemence, not one attending to what another said, that, since the building of Babel, there was not such a scene of confusion.

At length, the contest grew so high that they were just ready to fall together by the ears, when the constable, who sat all the while fretting his guts to fiddle-strings at this interruption of his speech, which he looked upon as an insult to his authority, put a stop to the whole tumult, by an accident. "Fire and fury! " (exclaimed he, raising his voice as loud as " ever he was able) Are you all mad?"

The word *fire*, which was all they attended to, filled them with affright. They thought the house was on fire, and repeating the cry with equal vehemence, they overturned the table, spilled the beer, and tumbling over one another, made the best of their way out.

As soon as they were undeceived, they returned into the room, and having recovered themselves a little by the help of a fresh supply from the ale-house, the constable, composing himself into proper dignity, resumed his speech: " I say, gentlemen, (said he) that, if we go on " in this manner, it is impossible for us to con- " duct this affair with due decorum. We had " better chuse out a set of us who understand " these matters, to agree upon what is proper; " and because there will be a great many things " wanted beside victuals and drink, that no " business should be overlooked, it will be right " to have one of every trade chosen, and then " there can be no mistakes."

This motion was universally approved, and accordingly they proceeded directly to make the

M 4　　　　choice;

choice; but in this they were very near falling
into as great confusion as before, every one
being ambitious of the honour. At length,
however, and with difficulty, it was settled;
and then the selected few withdrew to the next
ale-house, to consult undisturbed upon the affair.

When they were seated and had smoaked a
whiff or two, to settle their heads, the constable, who by his office was one of the number,
opened their deliberations." "Gentlemen,
" (said he, puffing out a pillar of smoak) I be-
" lieve I may say, without vanity, that there is
" no one in this company who understands
" these matters better than I do : I keep a good
" house myself, an hot joint every day, and
" roast and boiled, both, on sundays; beside,
" my wife, it is well known, was bred up in a
" gentleman's family, and there learned a pro-
" per notion of doing things genteely. It is my
" opinion, therefore, that you leave the *whole*
" to me, and I will prevail upon her to give
" me advice."

" With your leave, Mr. constable, (answer-
" ed a person who sat opposite to him, and
" heard him out with great impatience) though
" it be your luck to be in office this year, there
" are others in the parish who keep as good
" houses as you; and I believe my dame also
" has as good an opportunity of knowing these
" matters as another : I serve two or three
" gentlemen who keep French cooks, and she
" never goes to their houses with goods, that
" she does not learn some new piece of cook-
" ery from them; for she is a well-spoken bo-
" dy, and always asked to sit down among the
" up-

" upper servants; and then she is so fond of
" practising what she thus picks up, that I
" hardly ever know the name of what I eat;
" but she tells me they are quite the mode, and
" so I submit; though, in truth, I cannot say
" but I should often prefer a cut of honest old
" England; in my opinion, there is nothing
" beats a roast sir-loin."

This eloquent speech was followed by one
as eloquent from every one present, declaring
his own ability for this important affair, and
putting in his claim to it. At length, when
all saw that not one would give up his pretensions to another, they came to an agreement,
that each should draw a bill of fare according
to his taste and judgment, out of which they
imagined they should certainly be able to make
a proper choice.

Accordingly, they all went to work; and the
streams which flowed from every mouth, while
they were writing, proved with what candour
they set down the things they liked best, and
how glad they should be to eat them.

The bills of fare, produced upon this occasion, shewed that the English were not dege-
nerated, in their stomachs at least, from their
mighty ancestors. Buttocks upon buttocks,
and sirloins without number.—Legs of pork,
and saddles of mutton.——Fillets of veal and
flitches of bacon.——Hams by the dozen, and
fowls by the groce.——Flocks of geese, and
droves of turkies.—— In short, the quantities
of meat, when the bills were all read over together, turned the stomach of every one present, and made them readily accept the proposal of the man of the house, who undertook to

M 5                    furnish

furnish out a magnificent feaſt, if they would leave the whole to him. This great point being thus happily ſettled, they ſettled their ſtomachs alſo with a glaſs of right coniac, and then retired to their reſpective homes, to give their wives an account of theſe important tranſactions.

The fuſs which was raiſed among the females upon this occaſion, is not to be deſcribed. All their finery was immediately drawn forth, and examined ; and then ſuch conſultations, and diſputes with one goſſip or another; ſuch a clatter with mantua-makers, and milleners, putting lappets to this, and flounces to that, altering and turning, to ſet all things in order for making a proper appearance before my lord and my lady, that every houſe in the whole village was a ſcene of litter and diſtraction, from that till the day of the feaſt ; many a poor tradeſman ſacrificing more than a year's profit of his buſineſs to his wife's vanity. Not that the huſbands entirely neglected to adorn themſelves either; but as their wives care was chiefly about their tails, theirs was confined to their heads, upon which every one heaped a bundle of grey hairs, as an emblem of his wiſdom and experience, more huge than ever grew upon the oldeſt goat on *Gilead*; he that peeped out of the largeſt fleece thinking he cut the moſt reſpectable figure.

As for the feaſt, the ale-houſe man was not a moment at a loſs in providing it. He had formerly been ſcullion in a gentleman's kitchin, ſo that he was not utterly unacquainted himſelf with the naſty ways of toſſing up nice diſhes : and now, with the help of an old

*French*

*French woman* who fold *Bef-à-la-mode* in a cellar, a *German* who made *Bologna* fauffages, and a *Jew* who travelled about the country with *ginger-bread* and *cheefe-cakes*, he made up a fufficient number of *things* with hard names, to fatisfy the vanity of the entertainers, and poifon all their guefts, had they been fools enough to tafte them; banifhing the wholefome victuals of the country to the tables of the fervants, as coarfe and unfafhionable; and giving nothing in the way that God made, or nature required it for nourifhment and health.

Nor were the decorations lefs elegant and grand than the feaft. As every trade in the parifh had a reprefentative in the fet, to whom the management of matters was committed, it may be thought that they had a proper underftanding among themfelves, and did not neglect any article, however unneceffary and even abfurd, which could poffibly be foifted in to fwell their refpective bills.

## CHAP. XVIII.

" *Impreffes quaint caparifons, and fteeds;*
" *Bafes, and tinfel trappings; gorgeous knights,*
" *Then marfhalld feaft*
" *Serv'd up in hall, with fewers and fenefchals.*

AT length the much wifhed-for day arrived. Words are too weak to convey an idea of the noife, hurry, and confufion, which reigned through the whole village; it feemed as if chaos was come again. The ſtreets, the lanes, the tops of the houſes were filled with gaping crouds, who left their houſes, at the firſt dawn of the morning, to ſecure the moſt convenient places where they might ſtand faſting all day, to ſee others go to a feaſt, in the afternoon. Nor were the happy few, who were admitted to the envied honour of ſeeing them eat, more provident. The thought of ſuch a ſight took away their appetites ; and beſides, they could not ſpare a moment from the important work of dreſſing, to take the leaſt refreſhment.

Tired of ſuch complicated folly, I turned to his lordſhip's houſe, to ſee in what light he, and his attendants, looked upon this grand affair. My former knowledge of his natural good ſenſe made me judge that he was above being infected with ſuch abſurdities. I was not deceived. He looked with pity upon the extravagance and folly of his tenants, at the ſame time that he received every teſtimony of their attachment with pleaſure. But his ſervants were far enough from being ſo cool. The paſſion for ſeeing, and being ſeen, raged as violently in them as in the villagers themſelves, and produced effects to the full as ridiculous.

When it was time for his lordſhip to go to this grand feaſt, he was ſummoned by a proceſſion, from the village, who came to wait upon him. The extravagancies ſhewn upon this occaſion exceed deſcription ; *devices without deſign, antics and emblems, deſtitute of meaning, humour, or ingenuity,* led the van; *aſſes in fur'd-gowns, and lambs in baſte-board armour,* marched lovingly together. *Fools, from the hand of nature,* drop'd their their broad ſneers,

and

and grin'd as favages; in a word, every guife, that folly could put on, without even attempting to mimick reafon, made up the motley cavalcade, and kept the croud agape.

When they had expofed themfelves in this manner through the whole village, they ufhered their guefts into the place appointed for their entertainment, where they were marfhalled according to their different ranks. I went with the croud, and took my ftation in the place from whence I could moft conveniently fee all that paffed.

The numbers of every age, fex, and rank, which I faw around me, prefented fuch a complicated fcene, that notwithftanding the extraordinary powers confered upon me by my guide, my eyes were dazzled, my head grew giddy, and I was unable to view it with that diftinnefs which alone could give me pleafure. I hung down my head, difappointed and abafhed, and fwelling with an hopelefs figh, "O that "I had my kind guide here now (faid I) to de- "liver me from this confufion and diftrefs, by "directing my attention to the objects moft "worthy of it, and enabling me to over-look "every thing elfe, as he did before."

I had fcarce uttered thefe words, when raifing my eyes, I faw, to my inexpreffible joy, my guide ftanding before me. "I heard your "wifh (faid he, fmiling at my furprize) and am "come to gratify it. I fee your fenfes fink "under the preffure of fuch a multitude, and "variety of objects."——Saying this he touched my eyes once more with his wand, when inftantly the mifts which fwam before them were

dif-

difpelled, and I beheld all things with the greateft clearnefs and accuracy.

When I had indulged my curiofity for fome time in gazing idly round me, "The fcene "before you (faid my guide) is a juft reprefen- "tation of the world in which you are. This "truly may be called, *The Paradife of Fools.* "You have feen with what eagernefs and pains "thefe people prepared themfelves for this great "occafion; with what anxiety they panted for "the arrival of this moment; and you now "fee to what a wife end! In fuch purfuits is "the life of man, in general, confumed. He "looks forward to fome particular object, "paints it in the colours moft pleafing to his "imagination; and then, full of the idea, "flights the enjoyment of every thing elfe, and "fixes his happinefs on the attainment of this ; "but when he has fucceeded, when that for "which he fo long fighed, fo eagerly laboured, "is at length in his poffeffion, his wifhes are as "unfatisfied as ever, and he finds it is no more "than *gaping at a feaft, which others are eating.*

"The perfons who compofe this croud are "principally the inhabitants of the village, and "the fervants and attendants of the lord and "his lady. The different purfuits of thefe two "claffes of people ufed formerly to create as "great a difference in their manners, and ap- "pearance; but of late the cafe is quite alter- "ed; the bounds, which were wont to fepa- "rate them are for the moft part broken down, "and they intrude into each other's provinces "without diftinction; his lordfhip's fervants, "and the gentlemen of their neighbourhood "practifing every mean craft to get money,

"for

" for which they were accustomed to despise
" and ridicule the villagers; as these, in their
" turn, affect all the follies and vices of the
" fashion, and with an aukward profusion run
" into the expences and extravagancies which
" used to mark the character of the others.
" Hence you see tradesmen keep hounds and
" running horses, and their wives go as fine
" as ladies; while gentlemen turn stock-job-
" bers, and compound their debts to cheat their
" creditors: and this is the reason of that odd
" contrast, that contradiction of character in
" every face you meet.

" Just as these general reflections are, they
" will be still more convincing when confirmed
" by particular instances. Observe that over-
" grown heap of mortality who sweats beneath
" the load of her lace and jewels. From the
" splendour of her appearance, you might rea-
" sonably conclude that she was a person of the
" first rank; but examine her nearer, and you
" will see that the meanness of her looks sul-
" lies the lustre of her diamonds, and her over--
" acted airs of gentility shew that she is not in
" her natural sphere.

" She was the daughter of a country farmer,
" who tho' he had several good farms of his
" own, was so bad a manager that he never
" could keep a penny in his pocket. To pre-
" vent his posterity's feeling the same incon-
" veniencies, he married his daughter to that
" person, who sits neither asleep nor awake in
" yonder corner, a shop-keeper in the village,
" that she might be able to go to the till, and
" take out money, whenever she pleased. For
" some time they had good business, and went

" on

" on very well, till he unluckily got in with
" fome of his lordſhip's people, whom he muſt
" immediately imitate in all their ways, drink-
" ing and carouſing at every public houſe in
" the pariſh; while his wife, not to be leſs
" genteel than he, ſcraped an acquaintance
" ſome how at a puppit-ſhew with one of her
" ladyſhip's maids, from whom ſhe learned all
" thoſe fantaſtic airs, and became ſo fine a
" gentlewoman, that ſhe would ſcarce vouch-
" ſafe to take the leaſt notice of the green-
" grocer's or haberdaſher's wife, at the next
" door, or indeed any of her old neighbours
" in the village, with whom ſhe had been in-
" timate before.. The conſequence of this was,
" that while ſhe was learning faſhions, among
" her ladyſhip's maids, and he tippling at the
" tavern with my lord's men, or perhaps treat-
" ing them at his own houſe, his ſhop was
" neglected, and his buſineſs left at ſixes and
" ſevens.

" But their folly is ſtill aggravated by this
" circumſtance, that the perſons, for the ſake
" of whoſe company they do all this, laugh
" at them the whole time, and would not fail
" to turn their very ruin into ridicule. Of this
" they both have had inſtances enough to open
" the eyes of any who were reſolved not to
" ſee. One or two of theſe may not be unen-
" tertaining.

" As the wife's education had been entirely
" in the country, her father took pleaſure in
" ſeeing her practiſe all the rural ſports he had
" formerly excelled in himſelf; by which
" means ſhe could ſoon cudgel, vault, and play
" at cricket as well as any of the ruſtic ſwains
                                        " around

" around her. Of these polite accomplishments
" she could not forbear boasting, in the pride
" of her heart to her new acquaintance; who,
" to humour her vanity, and expose her folly,
" not only seemed to approve of them, but al-
" so mischievously encouraged her to display
" her dexterity at them in public company,
" while, under a sneer of seeming applause, she
" joined in the general laugh against her.

" There is nothing that betrays a weak head,
" into more or grosser absurdities, than imita-
" tion. The great emulation among the fe-
" male sex at present is, who shall gather the
" greatest number of persons, no matter whe-
" ther of their acquaintance or not, or how in-
" famous in life or character, provided they
" dress well, and will game, at those nocturnal
" meetings, called with emphatical propriety,
" *Routs*.

" As this woman's new acquaintance was
" particularly famous for the multitudes that
" always assembled on these occasions, she too
" must have her *Routs*, to shew her politeness
" and importance. An affair of such conse-
" quence required much deliberation. Whom
" to invite, and where to put them, were the two
" material questions. The way to the parlour
" was through the shop; that therefore would
" not do by any means; and the room up-
" stairs, which for fashion-sake was called the
" dining-room, was so little, that three females
" in full dress could not move in it together.

" After much consultation, a lucky thought
" at length removed both the difficulties. As
" the route was desired out of pure respect to
" her new acquaintance, she judged that it
" would

" would not be proper to invite any person to
" it, who was not not a fit companion for her.
" This reduced the number to the constable's
" wife, and two or three more, and even these
" were desired to come without their hoops,
" that they might not incommode her, a com-
" pliment, that it was thought could not fail to
" please her.    These difficulties being thus
" happily got over, the lady was applied to, to
" fix her own time, and cards of invitation
" sent accordingly to the rest of the intended
" company.

" But an unlucky accident had like to have
" spoiled all, in the very critical minute.
" When the dining-room was swept out clean,
" and lighted up in readiness, the mistress of
" the route went down, and sat in the par-
" lour to be at hand to receive her principal
" guest, before whose arrival she did not
" think it proper that the rest should go up
" stairs.    While she waited thus, with heart
" pit a pat, for the rap at the door, the appren-
" tice, who had put on his sunday-cloaths to
" officiate as a servant out of livery on the oc-
" casion, happened to peep into the dining-
" room, and not seeing a great chair at the
" upper end of it, as he had observed in the
" club-room at the alehouse where he used
" some times to go for his master, he conclud-
" ed it was forgot in the hurry.    He resolved
" therefore to correct such an over-sight, with-
" out saying any thing of the matter, that the
" surprize might enhance his merit with his
" mistress : accordingly he would not go down
" for his master's smoaking-chair, that stood
" by the kitchen fire, but opening the bed-
                                        " chamber

" chamber to look for one there, he unluckily
" cast his eye on the night-chair, by his mif-
" tref's's bed-fide, and never confidering what
" it was, brought it out, pan and all as it ftood,
" and placed it in ftate at the upper end of the
" dining-room.

" He had fcarce finifhed this notable piece of
" management, when a thundering at the door
" proclaimed the lady's arrival, to the whole
" neighbourhood. The new-made groom of
" the chambers inftantly flew to his poft, happy
" in the thought of what he had done, and held
" open the door, while his miftrefs fhewed her
" guefts up ftairs.

" The lady, who of courfe led the way, no
" fooner entered the room, than fhe was ftruck
" with the fight of the uncouth piece of furni-
" ture. Her delicacy inftantly took the alarm,
" fhe puckered her noftrils up to her eyes, and
" turning away, exclaimed in a voice of difguft,
" *Lard!* where am I got to."

" The miftrefs of the *route*, who brought
" up the rear, and had not yet come into the
" room to fee the horrid fight, nor heard dif-
" tinctly what the lady faid, imagined fhe was
" taken fuddenly ill, and ran up to her to
" know what was the matter. *Lard!* woman!
" (fnuffled her ladyfhip through her handker-
" chief, which fhe held to her nofe) where
" have you brought me? What is that?

" It is impoffible to exprefs the aftonifh-
" ment and confufion of the other, when fhe
" faw the unfortunate chair. Ruined and un-
" done! (exclaimed fhe, as fhe fainted away
" on the floor, where fhe lay for fome time
" before fhe could be brought to herfelf.)

" If

"In the mean while one of the compa-
"ny, perceiving the cause of all this con-
"fusion, ordered it to be taken away, and
"assuring her ladyship, that it must have
"been brought there by some mistake, as she
"herself had been in the room but a few mi-
"nutes before, when she could vouch that
"there was no such thing to be seen, her la-
"dyship was pacified; and, when the mistress
"of the house at length recovered, conde-
"scended to comfort her, and even staid four
"minutes longer than she had designed (for
"she had many visits to make that afternoon,
"and could not possibly sit down to cards) to
"shew that she was not offended; though, not-
"withstanding all her good-nature, she told
"the whole affair, with several ingenious il-
"lustrations of her own in every company she
"went into that night; which was the real
"motive of her being in such haste to go away.

"But this ridiculous end of an affair, that
"cost the person before us so much anxie-
"ty, was not sufficient to make her see her
"folly. She goes on still in the same strain
"of aukward imitation, sacrificing every solid
"happiness of life to the absurd vanity of striv-
"ing to appear in a character for which nature
"never designed her."

CHAP.

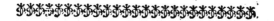

## CHAP. XIX.

*In what the great are easiest to be imitated. This humble ambition more dangerous, if less ridiculous, in man than in woman. Another interview with a couple of old acquaintances.*

"NOR is her husband more fortunate in" his attempts of the same kind. Behold "him yonder, dozing off his last night's de-" bauch. The virtues of the great are gene-" rally above the ambition of their inferiors; "but their follies and vices are of easy imi-" tation. By these they descend to the level "of the lowest part of the human species, who, "proud to resemble them in any thing, take "every opportunity of aping their example. "Hence those unnatural inconsistencies, which "offend reason in every view of life. Servant-" maids in silk gowns, and countesses drink-" ing gin. Tradesmen keeping whores, and "lords riding races.

"The bloated features and bursting blood-" shot eyes of this person shew how eagerly he "imitates his betters in the most beastly vice "that can disgrace a rational being; but his "ambition stops not here. Resolved to be "upon an equal footing with the freeholders "of the manor, he has made interest to be put "upon the jury of the court-leet, that he may "have an opportunity of displaying his abili-" ties and consequence.

"In

" In fpeculation, it muft appear advantageous
" to have the trades-people admitted thus to
" fhare in the government of the manor, as
" they fhould naturally be fuppofed to under-
" ftand their own myfteries beft, and for that
" reafon be moft capable of making fuch regu-
" lations as fhould promote trade, as well as
" for their own intereft, moft careful to prevent
" the land-holders from burdening it with
" unjuft or injudicious impofitions.

" But experience has proved the vanity of
" fuch expectations. No fooner can a tradef-
" man get upon the jury, than inftead of tak-
" ing care of the intereft of his trade in gene-
" ral, he immediately enters into a combi-
" nation with the lord's fervants ; and, for the
" fake of bringing their cuftom to his own
" fhop, affifts them to carry every by-law they
" propofe to ferve any prefent purpofe, how-
" ever ruinous in its confequences to the very
" trade in which he earns his bread. Thus,
" for inftance, a fhoemaker, for the fake of
" fupplying fhoes for his lordfhip's labourers,
" fhall confent to lay a tax upon leather, that
" muft ruin his craft in the end : and if they
" betray their own trades in this manner, what
" will they fcruple to do to others !

" It is true, they take care to pay them-
" felves well for this proftitution ; the badnefs
" of the goods they fupply giving them fuch
" an exorbitant profit in their contracts, that
" they expect foon to be, and too often re-
" ally are, raifed above the neceffity of at-
" tending to their bufinefs, at the fame time
" that the poor labourers, who are obliged to
" take thefe goods as part of their wages, fuf-

" fer

" fer hardſhips, ſhocking to humanity, from
" this double diſhoneſty.

" But juſtice obliges me to acquit the per-
" ſon who gave occaſion for theſe reflections
" from all ſuch deſigns. Vanity was the ſole
" motive for his getting upon the jury, and in
" the gratification of that conſiſt his only plea-
" ſure and employment ; though this vanity
" is in its effect no leſs prejudicial, than the
" venality of the others ; for, as the ambition
" of his ſhallow heart is to be upon good
" terms with his lordſhip's ſervants, he never
" refuſes any thing they require : ſo that the
" only difference between his conduct and
" that of the others is, that he does thoſe dirty
" jobs for nothing which they do for hire.

" In contraſt to theſe inſtances of vi-
" cious and abſurd vanity, behold in yon tall
" meagre-looking perſon, and his wife, who ſits
" behind him in the croud, inſtances of mean-
" neſs, equally vicious and out of character.

" The place in which he ſtands ſhews the
" rank he holds among his lordſhip's ſervants,
" to which he has been raiſed, not for any
" perſonal merit in himſelf, or liking of his
" maſter, but ſolely on account of the influ-
" ence which his wealth gives him among the
" tenants ; be being poſſeſſed of the greateſt
" property in the whole manor.

" It has been ſaid that Heaven ſhews its
" diſregard for riches, by the unworthy ob-
" jects on whom they are generally beſtowed.
" The remark is rather witty than juſt ; but,
" perhaps, there never could a ſtronger in-
" ſtance be alledged in ſupport of it than this
" perſon. Though his wealth exceeds not
" only

5

" only the wants of nature and reason, but
" also almost the very wishes of avarice itself,
" his soul still yearns for more, with as much
" greediness as a wretch perishing of famine
" can for a morsel of bread. The whole bu-
" siness of his days, his dreams by night, are
" how to encrease his boundless store, to do
" which there is not a mean or iniquitous art
" invented by the perverted ingenuity of the
" human mind, when sharpened and made
" desperate by want, which he will not prac-
" tise.

" Versed in the whole black mystery of gam-
" ing, how often has he drawn in unexperi-
" enced youth to ruin? How often have the
" rewards earned by the merits of illustrious
" ancestors, the fruits of the industry of ages,
" melted in the magic of his art, and sunk in-
" to his possession?

" Nor is he content with this exertion of
" his skill, which, infamous as it really is,
" custom, that can efface the distinctions of
" nature, has sanctified it with the name of
" *polite*. For those whose fears may fortunately
" prevent their encountering him at his fa-
" vourite weapons, cards and dice, he spreads
" the inexplicable snares of usury, keeping a
" public office for lending money to all who
" can give him security on every contingency
" of life, the chances of which he has calcu-
" lated with such accuracy, that his expecta-
" tions of gain are seldom disappointed. And
" this is the source of his influence, there be-
" ing few of the tenants of the manor, and
" more especially of his lordship's servants,
" who are not in his debt. As for the place
" he

" he holds in his lord's service, he sought it
" only for the lucrative emoluments which at-
" tend it. Stranger to every praise-worthy
" ambition, he sets honour at nought, and
" grasps even at power, only as it brings him
" profit.

## CHAP. XX.

*He that plays at* BOWLS *must meet* RUBS. *The
biter* DRUB'D. *An old fox caught nap-
ping. A penny saved is a penny got. Splendid œconomy; with the unfortunate candle-ad-
venture. A mortifying instance of the force of
vanity.*

" IN the occurrences of such a life, it is
" not possible for all his art, consummate
" as it is, to save him from some rubs. An
" instance in each character of a gamester
" and an usurer, will gratify honest indigna-
" tion.

" Exerting his talents in the noble science
" of *betting*, some time ago, at a cricket-
" match, a butcher, whom he had taken in,
" (for the first rule of gaming is, that it le-
" vels all distinctions; a porter, who can
" pull out a full purse, being equal to a
" lord) was so provoked at being *bit*, that he
" resolved to take satisfaction with his hands,
" for the mistake of his head, and paid him with
" a hearty *drubbing*.

" Such

" Such an affair naturally made a noise;
" but the sufferer had the address not only to
" evade the scandal, but even to turn it to
" his own advantage with his lord, making
" him believe that he had met with such an
" insult on account of his known attach-
" ment to his interest, the butcher being an
" avowed partizan of a certain gentleman's,
" who was at that time going to law with his
" lordship for the best part of his estate.

" But he did not come off so much to his
" own satisfaction in an affair that happened
" to him, some time after, in his other capacity
" of an usurer. A gentleman took up at his
" office a sum of money, payable at the death
" of an uncle to whom he was heir; for which
" he mortgaged the reversion of his uncle's
" estate : as he did not rightly understand *the*
" *calculations*, he agreed to pay an exorbitant
" premium; but, his uncle dying very soon,
" when the usurer went to demand his debt,
" the gentleman expostulated with him on the
" unreasonableness of the terms which he had
" inadvertently submitted to, and offered him
" the sum he had borrowed, with an handsome
" gratuity, beside the interest allowed by the
" law. But the other, unmoved by any thing
" he could say, insisted positively on his whole
" demand, and threatened to seize upon the
" estate mortgaged to him, if it was not paid
" directly.

" Incensed at such iniquitous extortion, the
" gentleman had immediate recourse to a learn-
" ed practitioner of the law, to try if he could
" not have redress; who, on perusing the deeds
" which had been executed between them,
" found

" found that, by an overfight of all parties,
" the mortgage affected only a very fmall part
" of his eftate, which was not worth half the
" fum lent, much lefs what was demanded; a
" particular fubdenomination only, which had
" always been diftinctly known from the reft,
" being named in the deeds.

" Though the gentleman was above taking
" any difhoneft advantage in fuch a cafe as
" this, he thought it juftifiable to fight the de-
" vil at his own weapons, and defend himfelf
" by any means he could; accordingly he fent
" the ufurer word, that, if he would not ac-
" cept of his debt, with the bare legal intereft,
" he might take poffeffion of the eftate mort-
" gaged to him, as foon as he pleafed; but,
" at the fame time, let him know what that
" eftate was.

" Surprized at fuch a meffage, the ufurer in-
" ftantly fent for his lawyers, who, upon con-
" fultation, informed him, that the affair was
" too true, and the miftake now irremediable;
" and, therefore, he muft only ftrive to make
" the beft he could of it. When he had vent-
" ed his rage on his agents and lawyer, and
" curfed himfelf for confiding in them, he was
" not afhamed to go in perfon to the gentle-
" man, to try if he could not prevail upon
" him, at leaft to give him the gratuity he had
" offered at firft. But his arguments were
" now as ineffectual as the gentleman's had
" been before; and, for once, he was obliged
" to take only his juft debt, where he had
" thought himfelf fecure of finking the whole
" eftate.

" While

" While he labours with this affiduity to
" heap up wealth by every iniquitous means,
" his wife is equally diligent in her province,
" practifing every fpecies of parfimony, how-
" ever fcandalous and unjuft, to cut off her
" tradefmen's bills, and fhorten the moft ne-
" ceffary expences of life by faving from the
" very bellies of her fervants; for, however
" her fortune may feem to raife her above at-
" tention to fuch minute œconomy, there is
" nothing by which money can poffibly be got
" that fhe thinks beneath her. An affair that
" happened not long fince, will fhew this in
" the ftrongeft light.

" It has been remarked, that the moft oppo-
" fite and apparently irreconcileable paffions
" often fpring from the fame caufe, and in-
" habit the fame breaft. The profufion that,
" in a particular manner, marks the character
" of the prefent age, is blended with an ava-
" rice fo ftrong, as to feem capable of coun-
" teracting all it's effects. An inconteftible
" inftance of this is the mean practice which
" prevails among thofe whofe elevated rank
" makes them lead the mode, of permitting
" their fervants to receive hire from their
" guefts. Upon this practice fome of fupe-
" rior œconomy have improved fo far as to
" lay a tax upon it, and bargain with their
" footmen to defray a great part of the ex-
" pence of their entertainments out of thefe
" fcandalous perquifites.

" But even this did not fatisfy this lady.
" Her rank, as well as her eager paffion for
" play, laid her under a kind of neceffity of
" making a fplendid appearance, and invit-

" ing

" ing as much company as she could to her
" gaming parties. I have observed that the
" expence of these entertainments was borne
" by the servants. But still there was one
" thing which she had set her heart upon,
" though custom had not *yet* given her a
" right to it; this was the pieces of candles
" that remained after the company retired
" from her *routes*, which she thought would
" serve in her family on ordinary occasions,
" and save the expence of buying; but how
" to get them was the difficulty, as the foot-
" men who found the lights, retained them
" as their due.

" At length, one night, when the compa-
" ny by some accident broke up much sooner
" than ordinary, so that the candles were not
" half burnt out, she was not able to resist
" the temptation, but resolved to have them
" some way or other. Accordingly, as soon
" as the hurry was over, and the servants, as
" she thought, all gone to sleep, she stole
" out of her bed, and went down stairs, naked
" to her shift as she was, with a design to
" steal them; which she imagined she might
" easily do, as the servants, impatient to get
" to rest after their fatigue, used only to blow
" them out, and to leave them in the candle-
" sticks, till they went to clean up the rooms
" next morning.

" It happened unluckily that one of the
" footmen suspected some of his fellows had
" found a way of opening the box, in which
" their alms-money (for, literally, they stood
" like beggars to receive it) was kept, till it
" was divided, and resolved to be upon the

" watch

" watch this night, to try if he could difcover
" the thief.

" He had not waited long, when he heard
" his miftrefs treading foftly through the
" apartments; and imagining that fhe was the
" perfon he watched for, (for there was no
" light to let him fee who it was) he ftood
" ftill till fhe came to him, and then, fpread-
" ing his arms in her way, caught her, load-
" ed as fhe was with the pieces of candles,
" with which fhe had filled the fore-part of
" her fhift; for fhe had, in her hafte, for-
" got to bring any thing to carry them off
" in.

" It is eafy to conceive her furprize and
" confufion at fuch an encounter; nor was
" the fellow's much lefs. But the difcovery
" of her fituation foon reftored him to his
" fenfes, and inftantly fuggefted the method
" of his revenge. "And fo, my dear, (faid
" he) you want wax-candles! But I'll make
" you pay for your pilfering." Saying which
" he prepared to gratify a paffion more na-
" tural at leaft, if not more delicate, than
" that which had brought her into fuch a
" fcrape.

" The lady, who could not be at a lofs
" to know what he defigned, was in the
" higheft diftrefs. Her *virtue* inftantly took
" the alarm at fuch an attempt; but how to
" avoid it was the difficulty. If fhe fpoke
" to refufe him, fhe knew her voice would
" betray her, and fhe fhould be expofed for
" ever, at the fame time that the fear of lofing
" her booty prevented her letting go her hold
" to ftruggle with him, and ftrive to repel

" force

" force by force. It is not eafy to fay what
" refolution fhe would have taken in fuch an
" embarrafiment; or, indeed, whether fhe
" would have taken any before it was too
" late, had not a very fingular circumftance
" moft unexpectedly proved the fafeguard of
" her honour.

" The fellow had fcarce taken her in his
" arms, when the perfumes, which fteamed
" from every part of her, gave fuch offence
" to his noftrils, accuftomed to no ftinks but
" thofe of nature, that, his ftomach inftantly
" turning, he difcharged its contents full in
" her face, before he had time to let her go;
" and then, damning her for a ftinking brim-
" ftone, fpurned her from him with abhor-
" rence. As foon as fhe had wiped her face
" with her fleeve, and recovered her breath,
" fhe picked up fome of the candles which fhe
" had dropped, and retired, the manner of her
" deliverance a good deal leffening the plea-
" fure of it; though it was fome fatisfaction
" to her, however, to think that fhe had
" preferved her booty, and efcaped undifco-
" vered.

" But, in the latter, fhe foon had the mor-
" tification to find herfelf deceived. The fel-
" low told the whole ftory, with fome obvious
" additions, to all the fervants next morning
" at breakfaft, when her waiting-woman,
" (from whom fhe could not poffibly conceal
" fome part of it, as fhe was obliged to have
" recourfe to her affiftance to get herfelf clean-
" ed; though at the fame time fhe gave her
" the ftricteft charge not to mention a fyl-
" lable of the matter, laying it upon her huf-

N 4                                              " band,

" band, who, she said, had drank a little too
" freely the night before) her woman, I say,
" out of a principle of conscience, and that
" none of her innocent fellow-servants should
" be under such a scandalous aspersion, be-
" trayed the whole secret to them all, from
" whom, through the channel of intelligence
" of their fraternity, it soon spread over the
" whole village.

" The feast, you see, is finished, at which
" you must have observed that the hospitable
" entertainers and their guests seemed to have
" exchanged characters; the former, willing
" to have something for their money, eating
" as voraciously as if they were half starved,
" and never expected to meet so good a meal
" again; while the latter have been wholly taken
" up in looking about them, and making good-
" natured remarks on every thing they have
" seen. But, soft! a curious scene yonder
" demands your attention for a moment, after
" which we will return to the lady's husband
" again, who will supply more matter for your
" observation."

Just as my guide said this, I heard an uproar at the door of the house, and, turning
about to see what was the occasion of it, was
witness to a scene sufficiently ridiculous to
have put vanity itself out of countenance.

As his lordship's late agent, who had been invited by the villagers to their feast, was going
away, a parcel of attorneys clerks and bai-
liffs, who had been employed by him while he
conducted the law-suit, gathered about him,
and insisted on carrying him in triumph to
his own house on their shoulders.

The

The zeal of the poor fellows on this occafion was natural. The agent had given them conftant employment, in which, to do them juftice, they had earned their wages very well, and on his lofing his place they apprehended the fuit would be made up fome how, and they fhould want work; they therefore took this method of teftifying their grateful regard for him, which they imagined might alfo convey an advantageous opinion of them to his fucceffor; but the affected modefty with which he faintly repelled their attempts, while the vanity of his heart gliftened through the thin difguife, fhewed in the moft mortifying light the inability of man's boafted reafon to refift the impulfe of the moft contemptible paffions. The fight was too painful; I turned away, vexed and difgufted, while he went off intoxicated with their empty fhouts and applaufe.

The tumult and confufion at the breaking up of the company are not to be defcribed. " You fee (faid my guide) the conclufion of " an affair that raifed fuch expectation. The " life of man has not unaptly been compared " to a feaft, from whence fome depart empty, " others fatiated; and all unfatisfied and dif- " appointed, and as impatient to get away as " they were eager to come. We will leave " the entertainers to congratulate themfelves " on their elegant tafte and judicious conduct " in this important matter, to fpread the fame " of which they have refolved to hire the " common crier, to proclaim the bill of fare " of their fumptuous entertainment at the " market-crofs, and follow that perfon who,

" as

" as I told you, will foon do fomething that
" fhall compleat his character."

## CHAP. XXI.

*Interefting hints, which fet fome matters much can-*
*vaffed in a new light.*

AS foon as his lordfhip was returned home
from the feaft, his fervants met together
to confult upon the conduct proper for them
to obferve in the prefent critical conjuncture.
" While thefe people are making the unmean-
" ing preambles (faid my guide) with which
" the moft urgent bufinefs muft be ufhered in,
" I'll give you a few leading hints, to enable
" you to enter the readier into the fpirit of the
" fcene opening before you.
" You muft have obferved that the bubble
" of the day, the fubject that engroffes the
" thoughts of all the inhabitants of the ma-
" nor, is the law-fuit in which they are
" at prefent engaged. About this they are di-
" vided into two parties, directly oppofite to
" each other in their opinions; one for profe-
" cuting it with the utmoft vigour, without
" confidering what confequences may attend
" fuch a conduct, or fetting any limits to
" their expectations; the other, for compound-
" ing the difpute almoft at any rate, to fave
" the expence of carrying it on. At the head
" of the latter is the perfon whom we have
" followed hither; as the former flatter them-
" felves

" felves that they have the late agent on their
" fide, becaufe he had conducted it with
" judgment and fpirit, while he was in his
" office.

" It is hard to fay which of thefe parties
" acts on the moft irrational principles. The
" One, from a mean and abfurd motive of
" parfimony, would betray the honour of their
" lord, and the intereft of the manor; the
" other, compofed principally of the various
" retainers of the law, and tradefmen who
" make an advantage of fupplying them with
" goods, on the lord's account, from motives
" equally felfifh, though difguifed under the
" pompous pretext of public fpirit, and a paf-
" fion for glory, which never fail to take
" with the mob, are for pufhing on their fuc-
" ceffes againft the dictates of reafon and juf-
" tice, magnifying every advantage that has
" been gained as of the moft effential im-
" portance, and not only grafping at more,
" but alfo infifting on keeping all they have
" gotten; while the former with equal fincerity
" decry them as infignificant, and not worth
" the trouble and expence of acquiring, much
" lefs of retaining, and therefore are for giv-
" ving up them all indifcriminately.

" In the fame manner do they differ about
" the conduct to be obferved with fome of
" their neighbours, who have taken part with
" them in the difpute; thefe are for dropping
" them directly, and leaving them to fhift for
" themfelves as well as they can, without re-
" gard to any promifes which may have been
" made them to the contrary, or to their be-
" ing drawn into the fcrape, merely becaufe

" of

" of their being some way connected with this
" manor; as the others are for supporting
" them, right or wrong, without ever confi-
" dering whether they are able to bear such an
" expence, or not.

" It is obvious that the right course lies in
" the middle between these opinions, could
" their directors divest themselves of preju-
" dice, to discern and find resolution to pur-
" sue it. As the suit was entered into at first
" not wantonly, or from a litigious disposi-
" tion, but to assert a legal right, and recover
" losses unjustly suffered, it would be both
" dishonourable and weak to drop it before
" those ends are obtained; and if in the course
" of the contest some acquisitions have been
" made, which were not originally even claim-
" ed, the voice of reason directs to retain as
" many of them as shall indemnify for the ex-
" pences of the law-suit, and disable the ag-
" gressors from attempting the like injustice
" for the future; as, on the other hand, when
" that right is incontestibly established, and
" not only those losses recovered, but also a
" sufficient indemnification for the past, and
" security against the future obtained, to grasp
" at more inverts the nature of the contest,
" and makes those the aggressors who before
" had justice on their side.

" The same middle rule holds equally good
" in respect to their associates in the suit; such
" of them as have been involved in it merely
" on account of their connection with the ma-
" nor, should most certainly be protected;
" that is, if it can be done without ruining
" their protectors; farther than which nothing

5                                    " can

" can oblige a community to go. Where that
" cannot be, self-preservation cancels every
" tie; and prudence commands to yield to a
" necessity that cannot be resisted, till an hap-
" pier hour shall offer for redressing their
" grievances, and making them amends for
" their losses; and for those who may have
" entered into the dispute, to serve particular
" purposes of their own, or for the sake of
" hire, it is abusing honour to say that it is
" any way concerned to keep up a connection
" with them, one moment longer than it is
" convenient. All that is necessary to be done
" is, not to break with them without giving
" them timely notice to provide for their own
" safety.

" Of this the steward is not insensible; but,
" though he is secure of his lord's concurrence
" in whatever he thinks proper to do, there
" are difficulties in his way, which make him
" at a loss how to proceed, and imbitter the
" enjoyment of his envied power. The par-
" ty which is for continuing the suit is against
" him of course, from the circumstance of his
" coming into the management of affairs in
" the place of their favourite, the late agent;
" (as for the old steward, though some of
" them perhaps have not yet forgot the good
" cheer he used to give them, as they have no
" opinion of his capacity for business, they
" give themselves no great concern about his
" dismission) and even the more rational of
" those who wish to see the dispute termin-
" ated, in an amicable and just manner, are
" afraid he will be in such haste to make it
" up, in hopes of securing himself in his place,
" that

" that he will not take sufficient care of their
" interests, nor make the most of the advan-
" tages gained by his predecessor, for fear any
" part of the merit should redound to him.

" Opposed thus by one party, and distrusted
" by the other, he stands in the utmost em-
" barrassment, unable to follow the dictates
" of his own judgment, and obliged to adopt
" the measures of those who alone will join
" with him. These are they who are for
" *compounding* matters at any rate, at the
" head of whom is this person, who, as his
" great property makes a large portion of the
" expence of the suit fall to his share, has
" ever been averse to carrying it on, *weeping*
" over the successes which have attended it, as
" he imagined they would raise the expecta-
" tions of the tenants still higher, and con-
" sequently make the composition he wanted
" to bring about more difficult.

" I have drawn this short sketch, to assist
" your judgment in a matter which preju-
" dice and party represent in such different
" colours. To some, perhaps, the concerns
" of a private manor may not seem worth so
" much trouble; but the heart of man, and
" the motives of his actions, which are the ob-
" jects of your observation, are often as clear-
" ly shewn in such trifles as in matters of the
" greatest moment. " But soft! the grand de-
" bate begins."

CHAP.

✿✿✿✿✿✿✿✿✿✿ ✿✿✿✿✿✿✿✿✿✿

## C H A P. XXII.

*Difputes will arife, where every man is for him-
felf. A fure method of removing fcruples, and
reconciling oppofite opinions. The character of
the GRAND COMPOUNDER finifhed. The
conclufion.*

COMPLIMENTS being mutually paid, and
judgment paffed upon the feaft, and the
drefs and characters of the entertainers and
their various guefts, the company at length
feated themfelves round a table, and the fteward proceeded to bufinefs.

"I have defired this meeting, gentlemen,
" (faid he) that I may have your advice how
" to act in the affair of this law-fuit in which
" we are entangled. Whether it is to be car-
" ried on, or made up? and how we are to
" accomplifh which ever we refolve upon? It
" is a matter of confequence, and requires the
" moft deliberate care and attention."

" Whether the law-fuit is to be carried on,
" or made up, fir! (anfwered the *grand com-
" pounder*) cannot admit of a moment's doubt
" with any one who confiders the diftreffed
" fituation to which we are reduced by it.
" All our ready money is gone, and our farms
" mortgaged fo deeply that no one will lend us
" any more. How then fhould we carry it
" on, if we were fo inclined? Or, how far are
" we to go, even if we were able? When firft
" we

**3**

" we begun it, we were told that a term or
" two would certainly bring our adverfary to
" reafon. But we have gone on, term after
" term, I don't know how long, at an ex-
" pence that no other people upon earth would
" be fuch fools as to undertake ; and ftill are as
" far from a conclufion as the moment we fet
" out. As for the mighty advantages, which
" the lawyers and their party make fuch a noife
" about, what have they done but filled our
" wife heads with notions of new demands,
" which our adverfary will never comply with;
" and we fhould not have dreamed of making,
" had it not been for them : So that, the more
" advantages as they are called we gain, the
" farther we are from the conclufion we wifh
" for. The lawyers, indeed, have gained
" advantages. They receive their fees from
" us, and extort cofts from the adverfary alfo;
" which, in our great wifdom, we have given
" up to them, as an encouragement to be ho-
" neft, inftead of reimburfing ourfelves with
" them as we ought ; and therefore they are in
" the right to fpin out the fuit as long as they
" can. But I hope their reign is at an end ; and
" that we have feen our folly too plainly, to
" be dupes to them any longer. My opinion,
" therefore, Mr. Steward is, that we compound
" the matter directly. We muft take care of
" ourfelves. *Any* compofition in our cafe is
" better than *none*."

" It is to be hoped (replied one who fat at
" the other fide of the table, and by his green
" bag full of papers, appeared to be their clerk
" in court) that Mr. Steward will have more
" regard to his own character (a confideration
" that

" that appears to have loſt all weight with the
" gentleman who ſpoke laſt; as well as to his
" lordſhip's honour and the intereſt of the ma-
" nor, than to be influenced by ſuch ſordid, baſe
" advice. It has been owing to ſuch ſcandalous
" complaints of our inability to carry on the
" ſuit, that it has continued ſo long, they only
" having encouraged our adverſary to perſiſt,
" not from any hope of getting the better of us
" fairly, but of wearing out our reſolution;
" and if this is not directly betraying his lord-
" ſhip, the conſequence is juſt as bad."

So home a charge put the *compounder* out of
all patience. He ſtarted up, ſputtering and
foaming like a madman, for his paſſion had
deprived him of the power of utterance, and,
tearing open his waiſtcoat, was going to demand inſtant ſatisfaction from his accuſer.
But a gentleman who ſat at the upper end of
the table interpoſed, and catching hold of his
hand, " For heaven's ſake, Sir, (ſaid he) how
" can you take notice of what he ſays? The
" gentleman perhaps thinks that he will have
" no more buſineſs, if the ſuit ſhould be made
" up, and therefore ſays any thing to ſupport
" it. But you have a fortune of your own,
" and do not depend upon the precarious in-
" come of a place."

" Whatever I depend on, (returned the
" clerk eagerly) I do not proſtitute my honour
" and abilities, and make myſelf the hackney
" tool of every party that is uppermoſt, to
" keep that place, changing like a weather-
" cock with every guſt of wind, and counter-
" acting one day the meaſures of the laſt, as
" I happen to be ordered."

Such

Such reflections were too general. Every mouth was instantly opened to reply, when the steward commanding silence, with a tone and air of authority, " I was in hopes, gen-
" tlemen (said he) that you would have thought
" proper to deliberate coolly on the matter I
" proposed to you; but, instead of that, you
" have fallen out among yourselves, and that
" about nothing at all. You may all be af-
" sured, that whatever measures I take, no
" gentleman here shall be a sufferer. You,
" Mr. Clerk need not be so warm! If the
" suit is made up, there are other places as pro-
" fitable as the one you have at present. I
" design to make you first clerk in my own
" office, which I hope will remove all your
" scruples; and on the other hand, if it can-
" not be made up quite so readily as you, Sir,
" (addressing himself to the *grand compounder*)
" may wish, there are ways of making up to
" you, not only what you may suffer by the
" delay, but also a good part of what you have
" been out of pocket already: so that you had
" no occasion for being so much alarmed at
" what the gentleman said, nor stripping to
" fight with him, like a porter. Such wrang-
" ling is most unbecoming gentlemen."

This speech healed all animosities, and restored the general harmony in a moment.
The clerk bowed with a smile of the most
chearful acquiescence; and the *grand compounder*,
unable to conceal his joy, blubbered out, between laughing and crying, " I am sorry, Sir,
" that I should misbehave myself before you;
" but it was impossible to bear such an asper-
" sion unmoved. I am sure I have shewn my

" at-

" attachment to his lordſhip's honour and in-
" tereſt in many different inſtances, in the
" ſeveral capacities I have ſerved him in.
" When I was *cockſwain of his barge*, I
" obliged his watermen to wear a particular
" livery, at their own expence, and regulated
" their rank; and t'other day again, when I
" was ſteward of the manor on the other ſide
" of the river, I drove away that *ſmuggler* and
" his gang who put them all into ſuch a pa-
" nick, by the great preparations which I
" made to attack them; and even in this very
" affair of the law-ſuit, I have been at greater
" expence than any man in the whole manor;
" and it is very hard if a man may not even
" ſpeak who parts with ſo much money for
" nothing. I am ſure it has gone to my heart
" many a time, when I have given away the
" rent of a whole farm at once! After all this,
" I ſay, it is too much to be accuſed of be-
" traying his intereſt and honour. But, as I
" can depend upon your word, I ſhall think
" no more of it."

When the *grand compounder* had thus unbur-
dened his heart, the ſteward once more reſumed the ſubject of their meeting. " As for
" this law-ſuit, gentlemen, (ſaid he) I own I
" am heartily tired of it, as I preſume every
" man in his ſenſes is; and am determined to
" make it up as ſoon as I can, that is, without
" prejudice to his lordſhip's honour and the
" real intereſt of the manor, which, however
" ſome people may pretend to diſtinguiſh be-
" tween them, are eſſentially one and the ſame
" thing. But how to bring this about is the
" difficulty. The mob is intoxicated with
" our

" our succeffes to fuch a degree, that they
" would be ready to drag any man through
" the kennel who fhould only mention ftop-
" ping, though they do not even know what
" they would be at, in going on. In thefe cir-
" cumftances, I think it will be the beft way
" to let our adverfary privately know, that
" we are not averfe to an accommodation;
" and that if he will fend one of his people
" here with fuch a propofal, to give a colour
" to the affair, one of us will go to him, with
" full power to fettle all matters in difpute
" between us. In the mean while we muft
" let the lawyers go on, at leaft till the end of
" the term, to keep the mob in good humour;
" and when the affair is finifhed, we muft con-
" trive to throw fome new bubble or other up
" in the air, for them to gaze at, which may
" divert their attention from every thing elfe.
" This, gentlemen, is my opinion: I only am
" at a lofs for a proper perfon to fend. It
" muft be one of fome confequence, to give
" weight to what he fays, and who does not
" regard the abufe and infults of the mob, of
" which he will probably be the chief object,
" in the firft fallies of their refentment, before
" there can be any thing done to appeafe them."

" I am the man! (faid the *grand compounder*,
" ftarting up in a tranfport) I am the man!
" I have given proof, that I defy the refent-
" ment of the moft defperate mob; and no
" perfon's word will have more weight with
" our adverfary than mine. I am intimately
" acquainted with moft of his principal fer-
" vants, with whom I have all along kept up
" a friendly intercourfe; which has made him

" think

" think that I am well inclined to his interest;
" so that he will have proper regard to every
" thing I propose. Let me but go; and I will
" undertake to settle every thing."

" With all my heart, Sir, (answered the
" steward) you shall go, since you desire it.
" But take care that your eagerness is not seen
" through, and taken advantage of. I'll draw
" up your instructions without delay, and give
" you a sum of money to bear your charges,
" that shall make you easy; for I know you are
" not extravagant in your expences."

" And do, pray Sir, (added the *grand com-*
" *pounder*) add some little matter on my wife's
" account. I know she will be for going too.
" It will not be thrown away : she has an ex-
" cellent knack at fishing out secrets, and will
" be a great assistance to me."

" Well Sir, (returned the steward) we shall
" not differ about that. But, gentlemen, there
" is one thing more, which I must observe to
" you. As you all approve of this step, I
" shall expect that when the accommodation is
" concluded, you will all sign it as well as I ;
" for light as some people make of the resent-
" ment of a mob, I do not chuse to stand
" single before it neither."

Matters being thus settled, the company
broke up; and the *grand compounder*, in the
fullness of his joy, muttering to himself as he
passed me, " Aye ! aye ! let me alone to com-
" pound matters ! I shall not stand upon terms.
" *Any* composition is better than *none* !" I was
so provoked at his premeditated baseness, that,
forgetting the positive injunction of my guide,
I could not forbear crying out aloud, " Vil-
' lain !

" lain ! take that !" and at the fame time gave him a kick on the pofteriors with all my might.

But I foon had reafon to repent of my rafhnefs. The whole fcene inftantly vanifhed ! I awoke from my *Reverie*; and found myfelf fitting in the fame chair, where I had forgot myfelf a few hours before, with the additional vexation of having broken my fhin againft the frame of the table by my inconfiderate kick.

# ERRATA.

Vol. I. Page 11. line 7. *Dele*, with my mother.
———————line 8. *For* (her fortune) *read*,
his wife's fortune) &c.